Love Notes

and

Line Drives

Famous in a Small Town

Book 3

M.L. Pennock

Copyright © 2026 M.L. Pennock
Cover design by Elizabeth Aud
Cover photo by Cheryl Holt

All rights reserved. No part of this book may be reproduced or transmitted in any form or by any means, electronic or mechanical, including photocopying, recording, or by any information storage and retrieval system without the written permission of the author, except where permitted by law.

This book is a work of fiction. Any similarities to real people, living or dead, is purely coincidental. All characters and events in this work are figments of the author's overactive imagination.

Also by M.L. Pennock

To Have series

To Have — Brian and Stella's story
To Hold (To Have #2) — Stephanie and Max's story
To Cherish (To Have #3) — Tommy and Jacelyn's story
Letters from Emily (To Have #4)

Famous in a Small Town series

Foster to Family (Book 1) — Delilah and Fisher's story
The Bakery on Main (Book 2) — Maggie and Maverick's story
Love Notes and Line Drives (Book 3) — Alex and Wren's story

Standalones

The Perfect Plan

Coming soon ...

For What It's Worth (Famous in a Small Town, Book 4)

Dedication

For the ones who play with fire

Table of Contents

Prologue: Wren 1
Chapter 1: Alexander 5
Chapter 2: Harper 7
Chapter 3: Alexander 11
Chapter 4: Harper 19
Chapter 5: Alexander 27
Chapter 6: Wren 33
Chapter 7: Alexander 43
Chapter 8: Wren 47
Chapter 9: Alexander 57
Chapter 10: Wren 65
Chapter 11: Alexander 73
Chapter 12: Wren 79
Chapter 13: Alexander 85
Chapter 14: Wren 89
Chapter 15: Alexander 93
Chapter 16: Wren 99
Chapter 17: Alexander 109
Chapter 18: Wren 117
Chapter 19: Alexander 123
Chapter 20: Wren 131
Chapter 21: Alexander 139
Chapter 22: Wren 149
Chapter 23: Alexander 163
Chapter 24: Wren 169

Chapter 25: Alexander 183

Chapter 26: Wren 189

Chapter 27: Alexander 197

Chapter 28: Wren 203

Chapter 29: Alexander 211

Chapter 30: Wren 225

Chapter 31: Alexander 233

Chapter 32: Wren 239

Chapter 33: Alexander 249

Chapter 34: Wren 257

Chapter 35: Alexander 265

Chapter 36: Wren 275

Epilogue: Wren 285

Acknowledgments 289

About the Author 291

Prologue

Wren

"I know it's already November, Tash, but these interviews come when they come. I'll take whatever I can get at this point. Most of the jobs don't start until next year. I'm not worried about it," I say while grabbing socks out of my top dresser drawer. "I probably won't even get offered any of the jobs I'm interviewing for. I'm not good enough to head coach at a Division I school."

"Wren, you're delusional."

Leave it to my roommate to call me out when I talk down about myself. She's been doing it for years, but I still don't believe her most of the time.

"I'm not delusional. I'm honest. I've been an assistant coach my entire career and I've loved every minute with these girls, but I don't think a Division I college here is going to pick me up. So, we'll see what these other schools have to say. Maybe I'll luck out and get a slot at a good Division III and I can really focus on the team instead of optics. I just want to help people grow."

That's one of the reasons I'm looking for new opportunities. Regardless of how much I love the team I played for and now coach for, there's something missing. I want to do community outreach and have the team volunteer and feel like a family not just a group. I'm hoping to find that.

I want to teach them that there's more to life than the 43 feet between the pitcher's circle and home plate.

Another reason? My boyfriend of two years keeps telling me to chase my dreams.

Throwing long pants in my suitcase, I make a mental note to pull my big coat out of the storage bin in my closet. Tasha sits in the chair next to my bed and watches as I check things off my list, but doesn't say anything. She's eerily quiet.

"But ... New York?" she says softly. "It's on the other side of the country."

I knew she was going to have trouble with that part of it. Tasha and I have been together since our own undergraduate days. Not "together," but teammates. We've gone through college for sports medicine together and went from sharing a dorm room to sharing an apartment when we graduated and started med school.

Yeah. Med school.

No, I'm not a doctor. Tasha is, though. I pivoted after starting and went back for physical therapy. Would I like to be a doctor? Maybe. But I have the background in sports medicine and the physical therapy license, and continuing for the extra letters after my name just wasn't something I wanted to do. So, unlike my teammate who is finishing up her fellowship, I got a job doing physical therapy for the sports department of our alma mater and then hired on as the assistant softball coach.

That's what I really wanted to do anyway. I love playing ball and if sticking around to do that meant having to get an extra degree and working with the team in any capacity ... it was worth it.

I'll always believe it's worth the work I've put in.

"I know it's not California, but you can always come visit," I say. "Have you ever seen snow?"

"Not on purpose," she says. "What's on the agenda? Buffalo, Rochester, Syracuse? Are there any other decent colleges out there?"

I bite my tongue. She doesn't want me to leave, but I can't stay.

"There are plenty of decent colleges," I say, laughing gently. "There are some good state schools, too. I have an interview set up at Brockport and a few others. It's going to be a busy week."

The part I don't say is the in-person interview at Brockport is a formality. They've already offered me the job. I haven't accepted yet. I want to see what the other three schools are like before making my decision. The difference is, the openings at the bigger schools are for assistant coaches. Brockport is as well, but my conversations with the head coach tell me there's more involved that just being her second in command. There's more responsibility. There are other things drawing me to the small Western New York town, too, but that's not something I've shared with anyone.

I haven't told Tasha or even my cousin, Veronica, about the information I've been holding onto about my dad. Maybe I don't want them to look at me differently, but deep down I know it's because even after all this time I'm still coming to terms with it.

Sighing and pushing herself up out of the chair, Tasha walks toward the door. Stopping to look at me, a sad smile slips free and I know how hard this is for her. We've done pretty much everything together since our freshman year of college.

"You're going to be amazing, no matter where you end up. Whoever snags you, is going to be one lucky school," she says, then steps out of the room.

"I sure do hope you're right, Tash," I say quietly to myself as I add another pair of socks to my bag. "I just want to be happy for once."

M.L. Pennock

Chapter 1

Alexander

NOVEMBER

"Yeah, I'll be there for sure," I say into the receiver. "Uh, I'm not sure if I'll have a date yet. Sorry. I know ... yeah, I know they're doing a seating chart. I guess I'll have them label it as 'guest.' I asked Maggie a while ago and she definitely can't come. ... I know you want to meet her. I'm hoping she'll come with me."

She. My roommate. The woman sharing a house with me. The sister-in-law of the girl I dated a couple times before we realized we were absolutely not made for one another.

Harper.

"Look, man, between the two of them I'm ready to jump off a cliff," my cousin, Danny, says. "Jayden's been up my ass about this because he doesn't want you to be the only single one there."

That's how they're referring to me these days? The only single one? Fantastic. I love that for me.

"Tell your brother to calm down. It's just a chair at a table. There are more than six months before the wedding, so I'll figure it out before then," I say. I don't even know why they sent out invitations already. The wedding isn't for another eight months. "I'll send the response card back before the RSVP date and Penelope can take a deep breath knowing I'm responsible, unlike her soon-to-be brother-in-law."

"You better," Danny says. "Then again, if you don't find someone and you come stag we can find a stripper to stand in."

"Gross," I say.

I have nothing against strippers or sex workers. Everyone is out here trying to make ends meet. If I absolutely need a date and a stripper is the only person available to hang out and eat overpriced hors d'oeuvres with, then so be it. I just really want Harper to come with me. She's fun.

"Whatever, nerd. Those girls are working just as hard as you are. I'll talk to you later," he says.

Before I can tell him I agree with him and say goodbye, he hangs up. I sit with my thoughts, which is stupid because I just keep thinking about her. About the non-commitment we made to one another after that first night. I never should have agreed to no strings.

Not while we're living together.

This isn't happiness.

It's a recipe for disaster.

Chapter 2

Harper

My chest is heaving and I have ... regrets. I have so many regrets.

He crawls up my body, trailing his tongue along the valley between my breasts until my back arches and he pulls a moan from me. The head of his cock finds the slick crease between my legs and as he clamps his teeth down on my right nipple, he pushes his hips forward.

Regrets.

But I don't want him to stop. Ever.

My hands find his hair and tug, not very gently, because sometimes I want it rough. He's so good at knowing what I want and how to deliver, and as soon as he feels the yank of my fingers in his mussed-up hair his pelvis pounds into mine.

"You want it hard?" he asks.

"So hard. Fuck me," I say, pulling my knees up so he can go deeper.

"God, I love your pussy," he whimpers, thrusting again.

This was a very bad idea. I'm going to destroy our lives if we keep this up.

The sensations begin to grow stronger. I know he's close to finishing, and I'm getting there. He'll wait as long as he can to make sure I finish first.

My brain won't shut off. It isn't until that first slow wave takes control that I mute it and let my body just ... feel. With each slow thrust, it builds more, and when Alex finds that magical rhythm and reaches between us to strum my clit like the strings of one of his guitars, I explode. Stars invade my sight and all that's left is feeling. So many sensations all at once and as much as I want him to stop, I want him to never stop.

"Please," I beg, hoping he doesn't hold out on me much longer. "Please, finish with me."

He slides his hand from my clit up to my neck and carefully wraps his hand around my throat. It's the hottest thing a man has ever done to me and he does it almost every time. Never malicious, and always makes me yearn for him that much more. I had no idea how good a little consensual, gentle choking could feel after a hard day of being a verbal punching bag.

I love my job, but it's hard.

"Harder," I say.

When he grabs behind my knee with his free hand and lifts my hip so he can angle himself just so ...

"Oh my god," I say, slamming my eyes shut. "Again."

He moans. With each stroke he gets louder and I love every second of it as the noise brings me closer to the edge of climax. The sweat pools between my breasts and as he thrusts again, Alex releases my throat and dips his head to kiss my neck. Holding both my hips where he wants them with his weight, wrapping his arms beneath my head for leverage, he knows exactly when to take all the control and pump his pelvis fast, fast, slow, and repeat.

I grab his biceps, digging my nails into the muscular flesh as wave after wave reaches me, until his low groan turns to a primal need and he finishes. But he doesn't just stop. He's not a lover like I've had before. Alex continues to slide his cock in and out of my swollen pussy until he coaxes another small orgasm from me.

When he's finally done with me, he kisses my lips, my cheek, my neck, and slowly works his way down my body as he pulls out ... leaving me feeling full and empty at the same time.

He crawls off his bed to go to the bathroom, throw the condom away, and clean himself up as I curl up beneath his blanket and hope I have the energy to leave this room before he comes back. But I'm never quick enough.

"Here," he says, climbing under the covers with me, holding a bottle of water in the space between.

"You didn't have to—"

"I know. But I'm not an asshole," he says. Leaning down, he kisses me once again on the cheek, "Maybe someday you'll see."

I laugh, because I know he's not and I do see it. All the time.

"Don't make this difficult. We agreed," I say, a gentle reminder of the promise we made to one another a few months ago.

The attraction was slow and subtle. We both needed a place to call home and sharing a house just seemed like the best option. The opportunity just kind of fell in our laps — Alex's first, really, because he's good friends with my sister-in-law, but he was generous enough to let me rent it as well. Essentially, we rent the house together from Maggie and split the cost. That was our normal when we both moved in back in May.

But it's November now, and for the last several weeks at least one of us catches the other needing to relieve some stress. Sometimes a few times a week.

And last night was Thanksgiving at my brother's house where he and Maggie and their friend Lilah were caught in the throes of a conversation about ... us.

"They think there's something more happening," Alex says, as if he's reading my mind. "There could be more."

"There can't."

"I still don't understand why not," he says, laughing as he leans back against his pillows and slides his arm behind his head.

"I don't have a good answer for you. I just don't think I'm in a good enough place to go from fucking my roommate to being in an actual committed relationship with him," I say, sticking my tongue out at him for good measure. "Things at work are just ... a lot lately. I like when you help me burn off calories and relieve my stress. How's work for you?"

He snickers, then lifts the bottle of water from my hand and takes a generous sip.

"It's music, so I don't think it's nearly as demanding as social work, but it has its moments," he says. "My classes at Eastman are way more taxing, but this semester is almost over."

"Are you excited? You're going to be a music doctor someday," I say, and watch as his ears turn bright red. I sigh, and say, "I think it's amazing."

Rolling over to face me, Alex says, "Stay with me tonight."

For a split second I think about how good it would feel, wrapped up in him all night long like the very first night. But, then my brain catches up.

"I don't think that would be a good idea," I whisper in the dim lamp light.

"I think it would be a phenomenal idea," he whispers back.

"This isn't supposed to be like that, Alex. This is no-strings. We promised."

"Promises are meant to be broken," he says, stroking his finger down the edge of my cheek.

"Not this one," I say, taking a deep breath before leaning in to kiss his lips once more. "Not this time."

Chapter 3

Alexander

It's been months and we keep playing these games. She doesn't want this to go further, though, so I'm respecting that and keeping my emotions out of it the best I can. We go about our days as if everything is normal. We move through the house like a well-oiled machine, chores and meals and existing together every morning and evening.

Then at night, she comes alive and I find myself ravaging her until we are both soaked with sweat. She brings out a part of me I never knew existed. She has to be strong and on her game all day long, and then when we're at home, alone, she's perfectly submissive and wants nothing more than for me to control all of her. To take it away and make it so she doesn't have to think about everything.

"What are we even doing?"

"Having fun. I thought that's what we agreed on," Harper says. "This was supposed to be fun."

Sitting at a restaurant, waiting for our drinks to arrive, I made the snap decision to jump right into the difficult questions. It doesn't matter how much I enjoy pinning her to my mattress, the living room floor, or the kitchen table ... it's time we have a real conversation about what we're doing.

"But what about more? Come to Jayden's wedding with me. See what we can be outside the bedroom."

"No." She laughs. "It's not that I don't want more, but, Alex, we promised we weren't going to get attached. Me going to your cousin's wedding with you would be getting attached. I show up with you and next thing you know someone is going to insist I try to catch the bouquet and you catch the garter and ... that's not what we agreed to. We agreed to some good, stress reducing, fucking and that's it. I want a hand necklace from you, not a commitment."

The waitress arrives with my beer and her pineapple bourbon lemonade, and when I look up to thank her, the poor girl looks shellshocked.

"She didn't ..." I trail off. There's no getting her to think what Harper said isn't what Harper said. I swallow hard and push my glasses up further on the bridge of my nose. "Thank you. We're going to need a few minutes to finish looking at the menu."

"Take your time, Romeo," she says before turning and walking away with a smirk on her face.

Harper snickers as I drop my head into my hands.

"Sorry," Harper says. "I didn't realize she was coming over here."

"I'm sure."

"I really didn't," she says, taking a long sip of her drink. "But it's true. I love what your hands do to me."

Pulling my beer away from my lips, I take a long look at her. The exhausted look in her eyes. The eyeliner that's clearly been dabbed at. The dried remnants of tears.

"Rough day?"

A big breath in, and then, "Yeah. One of my dementia patients passed away. I spent the day talking to their family. It just puts things into perspective."

"Anything I can do?" I ask.

I'm her friend first. Our living situation created a friendship that turned into more, but I will always be her friend first.

"Not really. It's part of the job, you know? They all have a special place in my life, but ... I'll be fine."

"I know, but that's not what I asked," I say.

"You look nice tonight. I like the tie. It matches your glasses nicely," she deflects before lifting her menu and studying it to avoid any more conversation.

*****

The tie. I should have known when she mentioned it at dinner after knowing she'd had a hard day. Plus, it's Friday and Valentine's Day. Nope, we are not romantically involved. She reminded me again tonight, and now she's silently begging for me to do all the non-romantic, naughty things she loves.

The only thing is we don't usually play when liquor is involved.

"You've been drinking," I say. "We don't do things like this after alcohol."

"That's a rule I'm willing to break. Plus, it was only a few drinks and I ate," she says, pulling me by my necktie through the kitchen. Her heels make her legs enticingly long as they disappear beneath a short, pleated skirt and I reach my hand out to lift the back of the fabric. Her free hand pushes the linen down and out of reach. "No peeking."

"What are we even doing, Harper?" I rasp in her ear, as I step close to her and press her chest against the wall of the hallway leading to my bedroom.

"We're playing with fire," she says, and pushes her backside into my groin.

My hands trail up her thighs, lifting her skirt to find the snaps of the garter she wore tonight. She knew what she was doing when she came home to change for dinner. This was never intended to be a roommate dinner. Food was simply a preemptive to an evening of fucking each other's brains out.

I rub slow, calming circles on the tender skin of her bare ass. Her breathing comes out in soft, little pants and as she relaxes her hips against me, I lift my hand away and bring it back to connect with her flesh, the sound reverberating down the hall.

The moan she releases makes my cock instantly hard.

This is a catastrophe. No. A fucktastrophe. That's what this is.

"You're going to ruin me for any other woman who wants purely vanilla, missionary sex," I say, slipping two fingers into her pussy.

"First, there's nothing wrong with vanilla. Second, maybe I'm just showing you exactly what kind of woman you need," she says, dropping her forehead against the wall and sliding her hands up away from her body.

"So now you're the teacher?"

"I like to be the teacher and the student," she says, clenching her muscles around my fingers as I slowly work them in and out of her.

Her breath hitches as I pull them from her body and stick the coated fingers in my mouth.

"You taste ... delicious," I say, making quick work of my tie, opening the knot enough to slip it over my head. Leaning in, I kiss her neck and say, "Hands behind your back, Harper."

A shiver visibly runs the course of her body as the words reach her ears and I watch her skin pebble with goosebumps. Turning her head just enough to see me out of the corner of her eye, I notice the smile. She really likes my tie.

Her arms behind her, I loop the fabric around her wrists. Tightening the knot to restrain her, I wrap the tails around the fabric between her wrists and tie them snugly. She has wiggle room, but it's just tight enough to give us both the illusion that she has zero control.

With just the tips of my middle fingers, I trace lines up both her arms until I reach her shoulders. One hand on the back of her neck, I slowly turn her face toward mine as I step to her side. Harper's mouth opens slightly as her breathing quickens in anticipation, but I catch her off guard and turn her entire body toward me. She lets out a squeal as I bend to pick her up and place her over my shoulder, smacking her on the ass once I've got a good grip on her thighs.

I growl under my breath and step quickly toward my bedroom. This woman is going to be the death of me. Laying her across my bed, her arms beneath her, I withhold all the things I want — like tearing her clothes off and mauling her like an animal. I'm a gentleman, I remind myself. Her tongue peeks out from between her lips and I watch as she pulls her plump bottom lip between her teeth. It's barely a second in time, but it makes me want her even more.

Beginning with her heels, those incredibly tall pumps, I slide my hands up her legs. Her muscular calves that I like throwing over my shoulders so I can go deeper; strong thighs that wrap around my hips to pull me closer; a soft, slender waist hidden beneath a skirt I need to get rid of. Finding the zipper near her hip, I pull to release each individual tooth until it stops and I tug the fabric. She lifts her hips just enough for me to slip the waist over her ass and then down her legs, leaving her in just thigh high stockings and a garter, her pussy laid bare for me to enjoy.

Bringing Harper to orgasm is a beautiful undertaking. She's vocal and mouthy and loves what my tongue does to her, so there's no objection as I kneel on the floor and pull her body to me until she's resting her legs on my shoulders and I'm nuzzling the soft skin of her inner thigh. With each touch, every flick of my tongue, when my lips wrap around her tender clit, she moans louder begging me to do unspeakable things to the rest of her.

"I need you to fuck me. Please, Alex," she cries out. A deep moan tears from her throat as I press two fingers deep into her center.

"You're sure you're ready?" I tease.

"If I were more ready, I would be laying in a puddle."

Standing, I look at her, hands still bound and she's not one bit mad about it. I pull her up to sitting, and as her breasts heave beneath a blue button-down dress shirt with each breath, she looks up at me. I unbutton one, two, three, buttons and outline the ridge of each breast as they strain against the open shirt. There's nothing she can do about what she wants, though her eyes darken with need. I know the look well, and pull my shirt from my pants, unbuttoning it slowly in an effort to make this last as long as possible. I drop the dress shirt beside me, set my glasses on the nightstand, and pull my T-shirt over my head. Then, unbuckling my belt, I pop the button on my slacks, lifting the zipper pull tab and yanking the teeth apart before pushing my pants and boxer-briefs down my legs to pool at my feet and give her full access to my cock.

Without her hands, Harper leans in and licks the tip, then swirls her tongue around the head, and as I pull the hair that's come loose from her braid back away from her face, she pushes her mouth down on me and swallows. Slowly lifting off, she carefully grazes her teeth along the underside of my penis and the sensation is almost too much. Then she goes further, until I'm touching the back of her throat and I just need to be inside her. She has other ideas and as I try to pull back a little, so she sucks her cheeks in.

"If you're not careful ..." I say, my voice low and filled with warning.

Popping off my cock, Harper looks at me seductively, challenging me.

"What? If I'm not careful, what?" she asks, then licks her swollen bottom lip.

Before she can take me back into her mouth, I lean down and kiss her. Pulling her to standing, I break away from her and turn her away from me, walking into her until she kneels on the bed. I grab onto the tie still binding her hands, press her body forward until her bottom is in the air, and lean in to bite the creamy flesh.

Pulling my pants and boxers off my feet, I step away, stroking myself at the sight of Harper positioned perfectly in front of me, to get a condom from the nightstand. Tearing the wrapper and pulling the condom from the package, I glance at the bed. Harper has turned her head to watch me, so I make sure to roll the latex down my shaft slowly.

"You should look in the drawer," she says, her voice hoarse and filled with wanting.

Quirking an eyebrow and tipping my head to the side, I comply. Beside the open box of condoms, she's placed a small velvet pouch and a bottle of lubricant. Lifting the pouch and hanging it from my index finger, I inspect it without opening it. We've discussed. I know she likes her toys. But this is stepping into newer territory for me.

"Is this for you or for me?" I ask.

"The fact you're asking makes me think the latter is something to explore," she says as I slide the baggie open and reach in for the solid metal anal plug. "But I bought it for me."

Tossing the plug on the bed and grabbing the lube, I walk back toward her.

"That looks huge. Are you sure?"

"Yes, please," she whispers.

Placing my free hand on her lower back, I press down until she slides her knees apart and her body lines up perfectly with mine. I caress her bottom, warming her skin to prepare her for what she's asking me to do, and then abruptly stop when she lets out a low moan. My fingers dance slowly down her skin, between her splayed legs, until I find her warmth and slide my thumb in while my middle finger finds her clit and rubs lazy circles on it.

Her breaths come quicker. She's so close. I flip the lid on the lubricant open and squirt a generous amount on her puckered anus as she moans into the bedspread. Using the tip of the plug, I carefully ease it in, feeling her get wetter as I continue to massage her pussy with my thumb.

She pushes back toward me, searching for my cock. Pulling my fingers away, I grab my shaft and guide it into her, pressing slowly forward until I enter her and reach for her hips.

"You are so tight," I groan, feeling the fullness from her ass as I pull out slightly and then push into her again.

"So full," she moans, as I pull out again and then slide all the way to the hilt, filling her completely.

I can't even talk dirty to her right now, afraid it's going to put me over the edge too quickly, so I stay seated deep inside her as her muscles contract around my throbbing cock. It's almost too much to bear and as much as I like having control and she loves giving it to me, I reach to her bound hands and untie the fabric. The satin slips off her wrists as I pull the knot out of the tie and leave the fabric hanging across her back. With her new freedom,

Harper presses her palms into the mattress and lifts her upper body, grinding her pelvis back against me as she seeks relief.

Placing my hands on her lower back, I let her ride me while I enjoy the sensation. Her hair, still braided from our evening out, entices me and I grab it with my right hand, pulling her head back just enough to make her moan. With each thrust back against me, she's finding a rhythm that works for her. Slamming back into me again, I drop my head and inhale sharply, feeling my orgasm building. She quickens her pace and I drop her hair to grab her hips to still her so I can take over, pumping my cock deep into her as she reaches between her legs and rubs her clit.

"Everything ... feels so good," she says. "I need to come. Oh my god, Alexander. Yes, harder."

When she uses my full name, I'm gone. It does something to my brain, in a good way. Tightening herself around me, I feel her muscles contract and begin pulsing as my orgasm hits full force. My body stiffens as I hold her snugly against me, emptying everything I have into her.

Harper collapses onto the bed, her perfect ass still in the air with my cock buried in her pussy, and lets out a satiated moan while I attempt to catch my breath. I touch the plug, wiggling the end with the tip of my finger, and she moans again.

"No more. I can't take more," she says, her words muffled by the comforter. "Everything is too touchy."

"You're sure?" I ask, pressing my body against her.

"Positive." Her response comes as she tightens her vagina around my overly sensitive cock while I'm pulling out of her, and then giggles when I grunt and pull completely out. "See? Everything is touchy."

She rolls onto her side, watching me with a satisfied grin as I pull the condom off and tie the open end in a knot.

"That was different. What prompted it?" I ask, motioning toward her lower half before I set the lube on the nightstand with the little velvet pouch. Her face falls slightly, and I continue with, "I liked it. It felt good."

Pulling my boxers on and then grabbing a pair of grey sweatpants from the closet, I wait for her answer.

"Um ... I read a lot of books. Some have been a little more adventurous than others lately," she says, her cheeks pinking. "I liked it, too. I didn't realize how much I would like it, though."

Covering her face, she groans, then scoots off the bed. This isn't her typical after behavior, but I give her a minute and take care of my dirty clothes, remake the part of my bed that got unmade, and pull on a clean shirt.

Walking down the hall toward the kitchen, I'm hellbent on getting water and a snack for us. The door to the bathroom opens as I begin to pass and Harper sheepishly looks at her stockinged feet.

"I need to put this away and find some pants. I picked up grapes and cheese today," she says. Holding her hand open between us, there's a shiny, clean, plug in her palm. I know I give her an amused look, but she reads it more as a question. "Snacks, Alex. I know you're hungry. Plus, this is kind of the routine we've created for us."

"Do you want water or something else?" I ask, leaning in and kissing her on the cheek.

"Water. So much water," she says, smiling. "All that heavy breathing left me with dry mouth."

We pass one another, but before she gets too far, I turn and smack her firmly on the ass. It prompts an excited yelp from her, and I enter the kitchen with a smile on my face.

Chapter 4

Harper

MAY

"I think I should move out."

Maggie looks at me like I have three heads, and rightfully so because I practically begged her to let me move into her house a year ago when she moved in with my brother. But things have changed since then. For starters, I've been screwing my roommate like a freaking jackrabbit and if we don't stop it's going to end horribly for both of us.

Alex and I have talked at length about how I don't want a commitment. Not from him and not from anyone else right now. I'm just fine going to work, coming home, having sex, going to my own bed, and repeat. Not every night, but it's been more nights than not.

"You're practically in a relationship with him. Why move out? You're doing all the things couples do, Harp, just call it what it is," Maggie says as she places another chocolate design on one of her gourmet cupcakes.

"It is fucking. That's all it is," I say, stealing a piece of a broken design. "What do you want me to do? End up like you and Maverick? You look like you're going to drop that kid any day now."

She shoots me a look that causes me to close my mouth quickly, only to open it again to put more chocolate inside. There's a whole pile of the discarded pieces on the work counter in The Bakery on Main's farm location. I might as well eat them, or she's going to have to melt them again.

"You know what? I think you and Alex are adorable together. However, if you aren't right for one another that's something you can't just create out of thin air. You can't force it, Harper. That's not how love works. I just know he sees you as a person he could settle down with," she says, placing her hands on the counter and giving me her full attention. "Have you found someone else?"

"Someone else for what?"

"You're addicted to Alex's penis. Someone else for sex, Harper," she laughs at me as my mouth drops open.

"No. No I have not."

I hate when she calls me out like this. I really like my sex life. I mean, just last night ...

"So, what's going to happen if you move out?" she interrupts my thoughts. "Booty calls to your old bedroom? And what happens if he finds another roommate? The semester is almost over, but I'm sure there are people still looking for somewhere to stay for the summer."

"I should stay?"

"You should consider putting the sex on ice and figure out what you want to do about the Alex Agenda," Maggie remarks.

The Alex Agenda.

There was never an agenda. There was never a plan to seduce the roommate. It was convenient. He was there. I was there. It's been months of us making naked time a thing, and I'm not unhappy about it. Early on I thought for sure I was going to regret every single interaction. I was positive things were going to get weird.

Despite him wondering if we can take this to the next level and be a real couple, nothing has been weird.

"I'm worried I'm holding him back," I finally admit. "What if the perfect girl for him shows up one day but he's so focused on what we have and don't have that he completely bypasses the opportunity to go for it? I don't want him to be the reason he doesn't fall in love with the right person."

"Fair enough," Maggie says. "I think you should talk to him about your feelings and your friendship. A real conversation, Harper. Not one of those post-coital, it was so good we aren't going to remember what was said conversations. That's how your brother gets me to agree to stupid shit all the time."

I quickly place another piece of chocolate in my mouth without breaking eye-contact with her.

"That's how we ended up with a puppy. Did you know that? He got me all messed up on orgasms and then laid it on real thick about how Sawyer and the new baby need a puppy," she says. "So now? We have a puppy."

Unable to contain my laughter, I cover my face.

"I cannot tell you how much I love you guys. The puppy was a shock, though. I had no clue it was a heat of the moment discussion. He didn't share that tidbit," I say, wiping tears from my eyes.

Handing me a cupcake, Maggie smiles gently like she's about to break bad news.

"You need to talk to Alex," she says, quietly. "Also, your brother would never share that with you. With Bentley, maybe, but not you. He likes to think about you as the innocent twin."

I haven't talked to my other brother in a couple weeks. I should call Bentley and get his perspective on this whole thing. He's had his fair share of strange relationships, and I know for a fact he's been in similar situations, so I ask Maggie if I should text him and request a brother-sister coffee date just as the front door opens.

"No. Whatever you do, don't drag Bentley into this," she says without looking up from the box she's filling with treats.

"Don't drag me into what?"

"Nothing," Maggie and I say simultaneously as my eyes go wide and I don't turn to look at Bentley.

"Cool. I don't want to be part of your antics anyway. You're always stirring shit up," he says. "Mags, Rick wants to know what time you're going to be done."

"When I'm done," she says, glaring at Bentley.

Holding his hands up, Bentley backs up until his butt hits the door.

"I will let him know the hugely pregnant lady is angry," he says, pressing against the door and seeing himself out.

Maggie rolls her eyes.

"He's been ... something else lately. I'm glad he's helping Maverick and Sawyer with the greenhouse while I'm ginormous, but his mouth is going to get him kicked to the curb before this baby is born," she says.

"He could always rent my bedroom when I move out," I say.

"Again, no. Go home. Talk to Alexander. Be a responsible adult, Harper. You don't need to move out. We are not running away from our problems. Repeat after me."

Pushing away from the counter, I sigh heavily.

"Fine. I guess I can do that," I say, resignedly.

"Repeat it."

Blowing my hair off my forehead, I say, "We are not running away from our problems."

"Good. Now get out so I can go see what your brothers need," she says, untying her apron and coming around the counter to face me. Reaching up and taking my face gently in her hands, Maggie says, "I love you, Harper. I don't want to see you hurt and I don't want to see Alex hurt. Essentially, the two of you are the only ones who can decide what the future holds."

*****

What the future holds is apparently me biting my lip and covering my eyes as soon as I walk in the house because my roommate just walked from the bathroom to his bedroom naked while using his bath towel to dry his hair. I wait until I'm sure he's in his room and then make a beeline toward mine.

"Everything okay?" he asks, concerned, when he hears me shuffling through the house.

"Yup. I'm just trying to not look," I say opening my door and stepping inside.

A moment later I realize I should close the door to keep him from coming and questioning me further, but I'm seconds slower than him and when I turn, he's leaning his bare shoulder against the doorframe. The towel is draped low on his waist now and as I'm pulling my tongue back into my mouth from licking my bottom lip, he smirks.

Fucker.

"Trying not to look? What's that about?" he questions, crossing his arms over his beautifully sculpted chest. It's always the nerdy ones. Nerdy, kinky guys and delicate, pretty women are my favorite. "Harper? My eyes are up here."

My head snaps back and for just a second, I think I should just give him the relationship. The sex is so good. I could let myself love him as more than my friend.

"I just ... I had a conversation with Maggie today and ..."

I can't finish the sentence. He's standing there looking at me, waiting for more, knowing there's more. Way more. He was Maggie's friend before she was my sister, and I am so grateful I have her to talk to about this because if it was another friend — which doesn't actually exist because I'm always working or sleeping — I wouldn't trust that friend nearly as much.

"You're going to have to give me more than that to go on," he says, his voice dropping.

"I need you to wear clothes to talk about this," I say. Alex nods, his eyebrows furrowing but I'm not sure if it's confusion or understanding, and pushes off the door to walk back toward his room. Covering my face and attempting to calm down because I don't even know if I want to have this talk right now, it dawns on me he just got out of the shower. I know what he wears after showers. Yelling as loudly as I can, I say, "No grey sweats!"

I hear him chuckle.

"Sure thing," he says from down the hall. "Do we need coffee or tea for this talk?"

"I'll start the kettle," I say and leave my bedroom only to collide with him in the walkway that runs the length of the house. "Oh my god. I need to get it together."

He gives me a questioning look, but then his hand is at my back and he's gently pushing me in front of him toward the kitchen. He's pulling a chair out for me. He's filling the kettle and setting it on the stove. And before he can sit down, I'm talking.

"It's not that I can't see myself with you, we've talked about this, but I don't want to hold you down or back or whatever other direction your perfect match could be coming from," I say.

"Perfection doesn't exist. You know that right?" he asks, pouring steaming hot water into my mug. "It's an illusion. I'm not perfect. You're not perfect. But together we could be."

He's always sensible.

"But what if we aren't and I'm just fooling myself thinking I could handle a relationship right now?"

He sets the kettle on the stove and comes back to sit at the table before responding. He's so thoughtful when we have real conversations, and that's something I hope to find in the next person, too. I'm almost certain whoever comes along next is going to be competing with Alex, in my head, to prove they're worth having me.

"What is different between what we're doing now and a relationship?"

"Because I don't love you like a boyfriend. I love you like a friend ... who provides copious amounts of orgasms whenever I need them," I say. Lowering my voice, I continue, "I sound like such a slut."

His mug stills just before it reaches his lips. His eyebrow arches. He takes a sip. Swallows. Thoughtfully, he sets the mug back on the table ... and pushes his sleeves up his forearms before leaning on the table.

"Do not say that about yourself," he growls, making sure to keep eye contact with me the entire time.

"Why not?" I whisper, challenging him. "It's the truth."

"Who all are you sleeping with?"

"Just you."

"Then you lack the several other partners required to be considered a slut. You are not the definition. You've been with me and only me for months, and the same goes for me with you, so please strike the word from your vocabulary," he demands.

"Professor Alexander has entered the chat," I say, hoping to interject some humor.

It falls flat. I watch his nostrils flare slightly.

"First of all, that's sexy as hell when you say it. Second, yes. I will use my strict professor voice or whatever because this is a lesson I need you to learn," he says, his tone level. "I never have thought of you as that word. You know what you like, you know what you want, and it's fucking hot to have a partner who isn't afraid to demand pleasure for herself."

"But I need to stop relying on you for it, Alex. I want you to date. I want you to find real love. I want you to have fun with other people," I say, much to his chagrin. "I can always add to my collection of toys, but I need a stop date for us."

"We're breaking up? For real?"

"It feels like it," I say, the emotion rising in my throat, choking me slightly. "Even if we aren't really dating, we're not an official couple, yeah ... I think this is us breaking up."

"You won't wait until after my cousin's wedding and come with me?"

Smiling sadly, I shake my head.

"That's still a couple months off. I don't want to string you along just so you have a date to the wedding, Alex. I've been saying I won't go and that hasn't changed," I say.

"I needed to try at least one more time," he says, shrugging as he plays with the handle of his mug.

"Do you want me to move out? I won't be mad if you say yes, but I might need time to figure out where to go. I don't think Maverick and Maggie are going to want me crashing on their couch with her so close to having the baby," I say.

I wasn't going to bring up moving out, but I couldn't help it. He's become part of my daily life and I don't want us not being together to disrupt his routine. Not that it would or should, but you never know.

"We were fine before we let curiosity get the better of us. I don't want you to move out if you don't want to. I would never expect that," he says, and I breathe a little easier. Wiping his finger across the rim of his mug, he looks thoughtfully at me. "What should our breakup day be?"

"Not tonight?"

"Definitely not tonight."

"Tomorrow. It'll be tomorrow," I say, not denying what he isn't saying out loud.

He hears me, just as clearly, and leaves his mug sitting on the table. He stands and pulls me gently from my chair. Trailing along behind him, my hand in his, Alex takes me to bed one more time.

M.L. Pennock

Chapter 5

Alexander

TWO MONTHS LATER

"So, I'll be back next Wednesday. Please don't burn the house down and no parties," I say, throwing the tie in my suitcase.

"I have never once thrown a party in your absence. I can't believe you think I would do that," she says, holding her hand over her heart pretending to be shocked. "You're taking my favorite tie?"

"Don't do that," I warn, feeling the tightness in my jaw as I clench my teeth.

We "broke up" and haven't been together since. That was May. A lot has happened since then. Maggie and Maverick had the baby, Harper took on more cases locally as a dementia care social worker at a nursing home facility, Mags' grandmother — who was Harper's first local client — passed away, I've been stressed out this entire semester of grad school as I work toward my doctorate, and through it all Harper and I didn't slip once. Well, there was an almost around the time I was starting summer classes, but we chose not to burn ourselves and quickly retreated to our own rooms.

"Sorry," she says, quietly acknowledging what she said and my reaction. "It's going to look great with your khakis. You're wearing the long pants, not the shorts, right?"

Normal. We are acting like normal friends. It's not at all strange for me to behave like I wasn't falling hard for her and it came to a screeching halt. I knew the rules.

"I'm taking both just in case," I say.

"What's in this bag?" she asks nudging my backpack with her foot. "And why does it feel like textbooks?"

Folding another shirt and placing it in my suitcase, I shrug.

"Because they are textbooks?" I respond. "I like reading and it's music theory and research for my dissertation. I can't fall behind. Plus, I'm putting together the syllabi for the classes I'm teaching in the fall."

Standing from the end of my bed, she walks to the door.

"Nerdy, kinky boy. Just make sure you take time to have fun, too. Is your cousin going to follow through on his threat to find you an escort?" she asks.

I know she doesn't mean to have a tone, but there is definitely a little jealousy mixed in with curiosity.

After she said for the final time she wouldn't come with me to the wedding, I told her about Danny's idea of finding a stripper for me to bring. She hasn't let it go and has been looking up escort services local to the wedding. It's become a big joke.

"Probably not. I hope not. I'd really rather go alone than put some poor woman through a formal event with me," I say, tossing socks and underwear in my bag. "I don't dance. Not well. I can slow dance, but all the other stuff? No thanks."

Harper laughs and leans against the doorframe.

"You make yourself sound boring, Alex. You're anything but boring. I hope at some point you learn how interesting you are," she says, quietly. "Take some time and go to the beach. Stick your feet in the sand. Enjoy the sun. Listen to the waves. They'll play a lullaby for you at night if you listen closely."

Then she's gone from my door. I watch her walk away, in her dress clothes for work with her sensible shoes and the braid down her back, and it hits me how interesting she is, too.

"Hey, Harp?"

"Yeah?" she asks, turning at the kitchen doorway to look back at me.

"I'll go to the beach. I promise."

*****

My flight landed in Norfolk on time and the car rental went smoothly. Then, I needed to get to Kitty Hawk, which, according to GPS was supposed to take another hour and a half. I took that as a challenge and made it in just over an hour. Pulling into the driveway of the six-bedroom mini mansion my parents and other family have rented for the week, I park the car just after 3 p.m. and take a deep breath.

There's a rap at the passenger window and when I turn my head to look, all I see is ... butt cheeks.

Fucking Danny.

I open the door and climb out as quickly as I can, rounding the front of the car as he's pulling his swim trunks up.

"You're finally here!" he yells.

He's drunk and loud. He's a lot to manage. He's one of my favorite cousins, primarily because he's everything I'm not. Sporty, obnoxious, a ladies man. Your typical "bro" kind of guy. At least when he's off the clock. When on the clock? He's a hot shot lawyer and good at his job. He's somehow single and, now that Harper and I are not together, I will never introduce the two of them. Ever. As long as I can help it.

Reaching a hand out, Danny grasps mine and pulls me into him for a hug. He's sweaty and smells like a mix of sunscreen and tequila.

"Hitting the bottle a little early?" I ask, laughing.

"When on vacation and sending your brother to his death, we drink. A lot."

Wrapping his arm around my shoulder, he begins leading me up the path to the house and doesn't let go when I attempt to turn back so I can at least grab my phone from the car.

"You know he's just getting married, right? She's not a viper and she's not going to steal him away from the family," I say, shoving my hands in the pockets of my shorts and toying with the car key fob.

"I know, but he's my only brother and now I can't just steal him away for bar nights and fishing trips," he whines.

"You're full of shit and need to knock it off," Jayden says, meeting us at the door. "Alex, please don't let this douche manipulate you into thinking I'm going to change much."

Parts of my family are a bit overwhelming sometimes. But, it's the two of them and me on our moms' side of the family. There's also a reason I haven't moved south to be closer to them. Because they're a lot.

"Where's your hot roommate? I thought she was coming with you?" Jayden asks.

"Uh." I press my thumb and fingers against my forehead and rub the confused wrinkles away. "Nope. Harper wasn't going to come with me. I thought Danny told you?"

We exchange a look and then both look at Dan.

"Whoops? In my defense, he told me months ago he was hoping she would come with him, so I might have not changed it from Harper's name to 'guest' like he wanted me to. Penelope is going to murder me, isn't she?"

"So ... beer?" Jayden says looking at me again instead of handling his brother.

I nod but then excuse myself to grab my bags from the car and text Harper to let her know I arrived safely.

Harper: enjoy the debauchery!

Me: Yeah, apparently that's already started.

I slide my phone in my pocket and sling the backpack over my shoulders before picking up the suitcase. Hiking back up the driveway to the house my phone dings again with a text message, so I stop to check it.

Harper: don't come home pregnant you saucy little minx.

Smiling down at the phone, I take a moment to enjoy her humor.

Me: I can't promise anything. We'll see how the week goes.

"Who are you smiling about?"

Jayden is sitting at the top of the stairs to the porch, a beer in each hand, and his big brother face on. He's always been the more down-to-earth of the two brothers, which is why it didn't surprise me when he told me he was finally proposing to his high school sweetheart. They've already been together for a decade, but they wanted to be established in their professional roles. To me, that absolutely makes sense. To his brother? Danny consistently tried to make it sound like Penelope was stringing his brother along, which was never the case.

"So? Who's the one making you smile?" he asks again when I don't respond.

"Um, it was Harper. She was just being silly, you know, and it made me wish she had actually come with me," I say.

He nods, takes a swig of his beer, and then holds the other bottle out to me.

"She broke your heart?" he questions as I sit down beside him.

"Only a little," I admit. "But a little sometimes feels like a lot."

"True."

"But I don't blame her for me getting attached. She's easy to love," I say. "I just wish she was in a place to love me back."

I don't want to spend this week thinking about what we could have had when I've asked her to act like we're just friends. No longer with benefits. I fully understand why she broke it off, and when she offered to move out to make it easier that about killed me. She's the perfect person to share a house with and once we took sex out of the equation, that's what we were back to doing. Sharing a house.

"I get it. Maybe someday she will be," he says. "Just don't wait around for her."

"That hadn't even crossed my mind," I lie, and he knows I'm lying but remains quiet.

"Beach. You need to go get your toes wet and tan up that pasty New York winter skin," Jayden says, switching topics and standing up. "Let's get your shit in the house and then it's time for the ocean."

M.L. Pennock

Chapter 6

Wren

Throwing a bathing suit in my backpack along with three pair of shorts, plus tanks, sunscreen, toothbrush, some underwear, flip flops, and phone charger, I consider the very real possibility that I've lost my mind.

When Brockport fell through and the other schools didn't even give me an offer, I came home to California with my tail between my legs. "Fell through" is a subjective phrase. "Fell through" is what I tell people.

Now, it's been months of working at the college physical therapy clinic and having a difficult relationship with my head coach. She outright questioned what it was I wanted. I told her I wanted more opportunities to prove myself and I felt trying to do that at a different college was my best bet. I'm not just a good player, but a capable coach and need more responsibility.

I think she was more hurt that I didn't come to her before applying for the other positions. What was I supposed to tell her? "Hey, Coach, I want your job since you're getting close to retirement and we haven't had a winning season in three years because you don't think outside the box." That would have gone over beautifully.

Would I have said it that way? Absolutely not. I'm not an asshole.

I know she's been mulling things over since our last conversation about how the recent season went, but I don't want to be the reason she leaves or chooses to retire now. She's aware that we need to make changes and there are only so many hamstrings I can stretch while chitchatting about poor fielding and team building before I say something I regret.

"You're going to be gone for a week, right?" Tasha asks from the doorway.

"Yeah. Are you sure you don't mind dropping me at the airport? I don't want to leave my car in long term parking if I don't have to," I say, zipping my bag.

"Not a problem. Is that really all you're taking? For an entire week?"

Lifting the backpack from my bed and slinging it over my shoulder, I give her a quizzical look.

"It's the beach. I don't need much," I say, as if she's the crazy one.

"You don't want to take real shirts? What about a dress in case your family goes out for a nice dinner?"

"No. I need a vacation, on the beach, and away from here for just a little while. I'm not looking for fancy dinners out or going to museums or anything like—"

"Oh my gosh the Wright Brothers Memorial is there! You should definitely go see that. You might never go back. It's like a once in a lifetime adventure," she interrupts.

"Ew," I say, pushing past her and out of my bedroom. "This isn't a learning trip. This is me on a paddleboard or surfboard in the ocean trying to find the parts of me I'm missing. Even my cousin said all I needed was a bathing suit and a toothbrush, so I feel like I've packed too much."

"At least take a book to read when you're taking a break from the water." She hands me a book and I don't even bother to look at the title before shoving it in my bag. "Plus, it's a long flight, you might get bored."

"Fine. Now, let's go," I say, grabbing her hand to pull her toward the door. "A last-minute trip across the country doesn't need to start with me missing the flight out of here."

*****

I step off the plane, immediately into my cousin's car, and am swept away to a house in Kitty Hawk more than an hour away. It would feel magical if this entire day had not been a travel nightmare and exhausting with my connecting flight getting delayed twice. All I want is to sleep and then tomorrow I'll wake up and stick my feet in the sand.

But the obnoxious jerks next door aren't keen on letting the neighborhood rest. I pull the pillow over my face and scream into it. I make a mental note to buy ear plugs in the morning.

When the bass from the stereo kicks up a notch, I quit.

"I'm going to call the police," I say to my cousin as I walk out of my room and into the kitchen.

"Please don't. We have an entire week here and I don't want to create issues on your first night," Veronica says from across the room.

"Well, something needs to be done. They're ... disturbing the peace. Isn't that a thing we don't like here? It's almost midnight. They're probably scaring the turtles," I say, looking out the window. "Is that a disco ball? On the deck?"

She laughs and shakes her head, then goes back to scrolling on her phone.

"I don't understand why you're all bent out of shape about it. You're not even tired. Your body is operating on time three hours behind us," she states matter-of-factly.

I hate when she makes sense. I don't actually know why I'm bothered by it. But I am. I think it's the stress of life finally catching up to me. I'm used to my quiet apartment and my quiet roommate.

"I'm going for a walk," I say, slipping my flip flops on and grabbing my phone.

"Take a flashlight and don't do anything stupid," she yells behind me as I open the door.

"Me? Do something stupid? Never," I say, and grab a flashlight hanging on the wall beside the entrance.

Before she can say anything else, I pull the door shut behind me and head down the stairs from the deck. It's beachfront and gorgeous. My aunt and uncle bought it years ago and rent the property out most of the tourist season. This week is blocked out for us, though. They're supposed to be having a big family thing with cousins from Veronica's dad's side coming in from all over. So far, it's just me and Veronica, which is great because we haven't seen each other in a few years. We keep in pretty regular contact; we just aren't as close as we would be if we lived in the same state or even on the same coast.

By the time we got back to the house tonight from the airport, it was already dusk. I'm not tired, but travel weary and if I have to listen to the lunatic neighbors party half the night, I'm at least going to sit on the beach while I do it.

Kicking off my sandals and digging my toes in, I shoo away the ghost crabs and sit down in the cool sand halfway between our house and the loud house. I can't tell what the music is they're playing, just that it's music and it's decent. As if they were aware someone was upset about the volume, it suddenly drops.

A quick glance at my watch and I see why. It's exactly 11 p.m.

"There are always people on the beach. Doesn't matter the time of day."

I turn in the direction of a man's voice, but try to remain inconspicuous. Staring is rude and I don't know any of these people. Plus, it's the middle of the night and, aside from these two guys who just walked down from the house next door, I'm the only person on the beach. The last thing I need to do is draw attention to myself, so I turn back to look out in the direction of the inky sea before me as the waves crash angrily against the shore.

Pulling my knees up to my chest, I wrap my arms around my legs and clear my mind, allowing the ocean to settle the anxiety I've carried for weeks.

"See, I told you. Always people on the beach."

Looking up, I lock eyes with a dark-haired man towering over me and my mouth opens slightly. Hands in the pockets of his shorts, his shoulders and chest fill out a polo shirt to perfection, and his jaw ticks slightly in the glow of a flashlight the second man carries.

"Are you okay?" he asks, before removing his right hand from his pocket to push his dark-rimmed glasses up on his nose.

My mouth opens and closes. Then, I suddenly can't see anything as the other guy swings the light in my direction. I fling my arm in front of my eyes and blink to try to acclimate to the brightness after being momentarily blinded.

"Danny, are you high? The fuck," he says. Then he's kneeling in front of me. "Before I was just asking if you were okay because you looked like you were a statue. But now, are you okay for real? He's a dick."

Smiling, I nod and push my hair out of my face.

"I'm fine. I wasn't expecting to lose my sight the first night on vacation, but it's cool. I'm fine," I say, stumbling over all my words. "This is fine."

He is fine. As he lets out a low chuckle, his green eyes sparkle for a moment before he turns to Danny and tells him to turn off the light.

"LEDs, you know. They're great unless you're looking directly at them," he says.

My eyes adjust back to the dark but I can still make out his features in the shadows. When he holds out his hand for me, I forget how to act like a normal person and simply look at it.

"I'm Alex. That's my cousin, Danny," he says, slowly beginning to drop his hand as my brain catches up and I thrust mine into his palm. A crooked smile makes my heart skip and then come to a pause as he applies a small amount of pressure while shaking my hand. A feeling of familiarity sets in. "We're staying up there. You just got in?"

"Wren. I'm Wren. Like the bird," I say, then feel instant mortification because who says shit like that?

"They make beautiful music," Alex says, thoughtfully. "They might be tiny but their voices are mighty."

"Sure," I say. I don't know how words work right now. I'm exhausted and he's handsome. My brain is not what it was a few hours ago when I still had the energy for sarcasm. "Also, yes, I just got here today. Where are you all from?"

Flanking me, Danny sits on my left and Alex settles himself in the sand to my right. My Spidey senses tingle and I'm not sure if it's a warning or because the heat from Alex's skin is radiating into my bubble.

"Here," Danny says. "Well, North Carolina. Not specifically Kitty Hawk."

"Western New York. Buffalo, Rochester, that region," Alex replies. "You?"

"Southern California."

"So, you traded one ocean for another for a week, huh?"

"Basically. It's a family thing. My aunt and uncle own the house," I say, pointing up the stairs to the beach house hidden by the dunes. "It's just my cousin and me right now, but there's supposed to be a reunion of sorts."

"You're Veronica's cousin?" Danny asks. I give him an odd look because, how? How would he know Veronica? These are all just vacation houses. It's not like she lives here full time. "My family has been coming here for pretty much my entire life, so I've gotten to know the neighbors."

"You make things weird, you know that, right?" Alex says, leaning forward to look at Danny.

"It's one thing I am absolutely amazing at other than divorces. It's a specialty."

"Again, making it weird," Alex says.

Leaning toward him, I whisper, "What does he mean by he's amazing at divorces? How many times has he been divorced?"

They both laugh at my expense, but I'm pretty certain the question is valid.

"I'm a divorce attorney. Never been married. Never will be married," Danny says, confidently, as he pushes himself up off the sand. Brushing the excess from his shorts, he adds, "Now Alexander, here, is the marrying type.

If only he could find a woman who likes him enough to split everything in half with when it ultimately doesn't work out."

I glance at Alex as he drops his chin to his chest and takes a deep breath.

"On that note, I think it's time to put Daniel to bed. It was lovely meeting you, Wren," he says, standing from his position beside me. Thrusting his hand between us once again, he's formal with his goodbye. I notice how reserved his mannerisms are and wonder what I missed that changed his whole mood. Instead of asking any questions, I reach forward and meet him in the middle, looking up as he once again towers above me. "Perhaps we'll meet again."

"I'll be here all week," I say, feeling out of place suddenly. It's as if I've met him somewhere before and it's making my brain itch. "I'm sure we'll run into one another."

I watch as they walk off toward the stairs leading back to the house they're renting and dig my toes even deeper into the cool sand. Wrapping my arms around my legs again, I lay my cheek on my knee and watch them ascend. I can't hear the conversation, but there are words being said and I wonder how the beachside discussion would have gone had it been just one of them instead of both.

As their images fade in the dark, I close my eyes and let the sound of the ocean soothe my worries. Are they worries, though? I guess they could be.

My boss is avoiding me. My best friend is rarely around because she's always at the hospital. My boyfriend dumped me for Christmas last year after being the whole reason I started looking for a different job in the first place. All I heard from him was how I wasn't living up to my potential. If I wanted to coach, I should coach the most elite of the elite. Being a physical therapist wasn't enough for him. Me just enjoying coaching and not making it my entire life wasn't enough for him.

I wasn't enough.

That's what I get for dating a sports guy.

Breathing deeply, the smell of the salt hits my senses and brings me back.

He shouldn't have been the reason I was doing any of it. I'm a big enough person to know I was part of the decision making. My need to people please was too much at the time. Regardless, he didn't send my resume and he didn't force me to go to New York.

New York.

Western New York.

I sit up straight.

No. There's no way.

But there's always a possibility.

I bite the inside of my cheek and try to remember where I would have seen him. I was in Buffalo, Rochester, and most of the towns in between because I got lost and then I went exploring. Coffee shop? Gas station? Drinking coffee at a gas station?

Wracking my brain is never going to work. It's done functioning for the day and I need to rest. The beach has calmed my nerves enough to give me some semblance of a good night's sleep, so I stand and brush the sand from my bottom as I make my way back to the stairs and the first night in an unfamiliar bed.

*****

"Wait just a damn minute. You think you know him?" Veronica asks.

Sitting down to coffee with her on the deck, we share a giant cinnamon bun from a bakery up the road.

"Pretty sure. Well, not know," I say around the food in my mouth. Once I swallow, I explain. "He said he's from Western New York and he looked really familiar. It could be my mind playing tricks on me, but ... I think I might have seen him on one of the campuses I interviewed at."

"What came about from those interviews, anyway?"

"Well, I'm still in California, so you can take a guess," I say, lifting my mug to my mouth and taking a sip of hot coffee.

"But I thought Brockport was all wrapped up. Like, you had that job, Wren, and were so excited," she says.

I have always promised myself I will be honest. Now is no different.

"Uh ... before I left to go back to California, I told them I needed to think about it and then by the time I got off the plane I decided moving across the country to coach was ridiculous and I should adjust my priorities," I say without making eye contact with my cousin.

"You have got to be kidding me. Big, strong, mouthy Wren let a guy get in her head," she says. "You let him talk you out of your dream?"

"Nowhere in that explanation did I mention a guy," I counter.

"But I know your tells. You don't get meek and quiet when it's a decision you made. And he broke up with you after you got back!" she scolds. "What the ever-loving fuck, man."

Hanging my head, I feel all the shame I should for letting him talk me into applying to schools out of the state. It was mostly his goading that got me to send my resume to those colleges in the first place. I feel even more ashamed when I let myself recall how his whining about the distance was ultimately what made me turn it down. It's so stupid. I really wanted a fresh start.

"I did let him get in my head, and now I'm paying the price for it. Coach is pissed because I didn't talk to her before flying to the east coast to interview. I just took a few days off and hopped on a plane," I say, popping another piece of roll in my mouth. Swallowing, I add, "I would be pissed at me, too, though. She got calls from those schools asking about me and then I got defensive when she confronted me about it. Neither of us was professional. I wanted her to trust me and then I broke her trust. Then, on top of everything else, I declined the offer and stayed home."

It affected the whole team last season. Everyone felt the disconnect.

"You need to fix it."

"No shit, Roni. I know."

A whistle from the driveway beneath has us both scrambling to the railing in search of the source.

"Heeeeey Veronica!" Danny yells when he sees us. "Long time no see, sweetheart. Y'all coming to the beach today?"

"How did he know I'm here?" Veronica asks without taking her eyes off Danny. "They're never here the same time I am."

"He's Alex's cousin ... and I mentioned my aunt and uncle own the house, so he figured out you're my cousin," I say, noticing a difference in her breathing. "Oh. Oh my gosh, you have a history with the divorce attorney, don't you?"

Without hiding my smile, I face Danny and yell, "We'll be down in a while. Some of us need to caffeinate. We don't thrive on other people's misery like you."

Grabbing his bare chest, he makes a pained expression.

"You wound me, California. Ouch," he says. "We'll see you down there. My nerd cousin isn't much fun and I like surrounding myself with gorgeous ladies."

"You're a massive douche, Danny," Veronica yells. I watch as she bites her lip and considers her words carefully. "Make sure you pack extra vodka in the cooler."

"For you, always," he says.

Danny winks before turning and walking back toward his driveway. My eyes follow the path leading to the stairs, to the porch, and to Alex who is intently watching the interaction. He says something that has Danny running toward the house and then they disappear inside. I wait a few minutes before asking what happened between Veronica and Danny, noticing first the heat that's risen in her cheeks after the slight interaction with him.

"It was a long time ago, okay? I don't want to talk about it right now," she says. "Let's get our suits and get ready for the water. I'm sure you're itching to get out on a board of some sort."

I am, but I'm also interested in what happened with the two of them. If it was a long time ago, I can only assume it was right out of high school.

"Has he always been anti-love?"

"Who said he's anti-love?" she asks.

"He said last night he wouldn't ever get married, so I'm guessing. That's all," I say, opening the door to go in the house from the deck.

"He wasn't always that way," she says, stepping through to the kitchen.

That's a juicy detail, and I would push for more but I know when she's had enough of my questioning just like she knows my tells. I change the topic.

"Meet me outside in ten. I'll grab the bag with towels and sunscreen if you unlock the storage room so we can get the boards out," I say, confidently.

She nods in agreement and walks toward her bedroom as I watch her retreat, her body language showing defeat.

Chapter 7

Alexander

I watch them from the steps without either noticing me as I slowly sip a cup of coffee and welcome the moist, warm ocean air. The way she tosses her head back laughing, completely unaware of how carefree she looks, makes me pause.

Last night on the beach, I know we must have surprised her when Danny and I walked down to the sand. It wasn't intentional.

Wait. Going to the beach was intentional. Making an unsuspecting stranger — a woman — nervous was not.

Sitting there last night, though, there was a niggling at the back of my brain like I'd seen her somewhere before. It's possible she just has one of those faces, but the way her face lights up with joy is making it difficult to believe I haven't met her before.

"Hey, fucker, what are you staring at?" Danny asks behind me seconds before he sits down on the top step to my left. I nod slightly at another house in the cul-de-sac and he lets out a low whistle. "Roni has come home to see me."

"Who?"

"Veronica. That girl from the summer after graduation." The name doesn't ring any bells. I shake my head. He narrows his eyes at me. "Wren's cousin."

"From the beach last night?"

"Yeah."

Realization dawns on me. The girl who broke his heart. The reason he's against marriage, or so he says.

"Interesting. But I wasn't looking at her," I say.

"I bet you weren't. But I am. Excuse me a minute," he says, before bolting down the stairs and jogging over to their driveway.

I can't hear everything that's said. With the exception of him calling her "sweetheart" and her calling him a "massive douche," their conversation doesn't travel on the breeze. It's only moments before he turns and saunters back over to our house.

My eyes trail up the path, beyond my cousin, to the deck where Wren is watching me from her perch at the railing. I consider waving, but I prefer not to seem like a creep.

"Alright, it's time to pack the coolers and head to the beach," he says when he's close enough for me to hear him. "The girls are meeting us down there and you're going to go enjoy yourself, damn it. No nerd shit."

"I have books to read and a huge paper to prepare for. I'll do whatever nerd shit I want to do on this vacation," I say, standing up and taking off into the house slamming the door as his feet pound up the stairs.

There isn't a backpack full of textbooks and notepads sitting in my room for no reason. This is a working vacation if ever there was one.

He slams the door behind him as he comes into the house, panting as he comes to a stop in the kitchen.

"You actually think you'll be able to concentrate on the beach?"

"Yes," I respond, washing my coffee mug and setting it in the drainboard. Walking toward the bedroom I'm set up in, I say over my shoulder, "I'll grab my stuff and be out in a minute. What are we packing in the coolers?"

I'm adamant the distractions won't interrupt nearly as much as Danny assumes they will. I've worked so hard and can't lose focus right now. I know this is technically a break from classes, but I also need to be prepping for the classes I teach as well as the classes I'm taking. I'm used to being on the go all the time at home. Relaxing isn't exactly my speed.

That's what I love about Harper. We're the same in that respect and when we needed to relax, we had each other to unwind with. I reach for my phone, but stop when I realize we aren't together and I don't need to check in with her. We aren't there anymore.

*****

Music theory. My brain is melting. I've been reading for more than an hour and, while I'm fully prepared to learn this book from cover to cover, I forgot how intense some subjects can be. I should be taking better notes, but I'm not. It just means I'll learn it all over again when I sit to annotate later.

Also, distractions. It's not that I'm unable to concentrate. I just keep seeing her. First it was when she was walking down to the shoreline. Then it was walking back to the spot she and her cousin set up to grab a surfboard and they both went out on the water. After that it was catching glimpses of her bobbing on the water, trying to catch a few waves here and there, and then just laying on her board almost like she'd given up.

"How's the studying going? Whatcha looking at?" Danny asks as he plops down in the sand next to my chair.

Reaching into the cooler to grab a drink, he stares at me intently. If I tell him I was looking at the neighbor girl, he's going to act foolish and make it more than it ever should be. I'd rather not put her through that when he gets a chance to talk to her again.

"The water," I say.

"Uh huh. You're sure you're not being a weirdo and staring at Veronica and Wren?"

"Nope," I say, looking back at my open book. "And I'm not a weirdo. It's a beach and I'm looking at the water. Try not to scare the tourists with the frat boy act, okay?"

He makes a face as if I just shocked him with some revelation, grabbing his chest as if in pain, and I notice right away it's the same version of him he gave Veronica this morning as he yelled up to her from the driveway.

"Take that back. It is not an act," he says, then laughs loudly. "I mean, it could be a little bit of an act. Could also be because there's no reason to behave."

"There's always a reason to behave. Your brother doesn't need you getting yourself arrested before his wedding," I say. "We don't want a replay of your parents' anniversary party a few years ago, do we?"

I glance at him, then reach over and take the still unopened beer out of his hand, promptly popping the tab and taking a generous swallow.

"That ... that was a misunderstanding."

"You getting upset with the restaurant owner and peeing in his gas tank does not count as a misunderstanding."

"I plead the fifth," he says, refusing to look at me as he reaches into the cooler between us again to retrieve a new drink. He pops the top and holds it up to clink my can. "Cheers, motherfucker."

Shaking my head, I smile simply because, as much as he's clearly insane, I have really missed spending time with my cousin.

"Cheers."

We sit with the sounds of the water crashing against the shore and children playing. It's several moments before he makes any noise, which means I get some brief uninterrupted time to stare at the textbook in front of me.

"I think that's my cue to go see if she needs a refresher. Those waves are going to eat her alive out there," he says, downing what's left of his beer and pushing up out of the sand.

"You don't even know how to surf," I say without looking up from my book.

"She doesn't need to know that," he says.

He jogs away from me and toward Veronica as she wades in waist-high water holding her board. Squinting against the glare off the water, I see Wren sitting up tall on her surfboard, her face to the sun as her messy chestnut brown braid trails down her back.

Chapter 8

Wren

"That looks like some great beach reading," I say, coming to a stop in front of him.

Alex looks up from the two-inch-thick, hardbound textbook in his lap and shields his eyes as he attempts to look at me. The light bronze tan on his shoulders is quickly turning to dark pink and freckled. I've watched him from the water off and on for the last hour as I've paddled back and forth on my board in an attempt to clear my head. Unfortunately, clearing it is nearly impossible and all I can think about is softball and where I could know him from.

Because I know him. I just don't know how.

"Not really," he states matter-of-factly, the skin between his eyebrows furrowing. Glancing at the open pages, he pauses before looking up at me again. "It's fairly dense and only fun if you like that sort of thing."

"Right. You know, most people come to the beach to enjoy the beach," I say, hiding my smirk by looking out over the crowded sand.

"I'm not like most people, Wren."

His voice drops slightly and a shiver runs down my spine when he says my name.

"I see that," I say, trailing my gaze back to him and swallowing hard. "So, Mr. Not Like Other People, why are you reading a huge textbook on the beach? Student or teacher?"

"Both," he says, slipping a pair of sunglasses over his eyes as a smile sweeps across his full lips. "How long have you been out there watching me read?"

A surprised laugh escapes my lips and I catch myself doing things I wouldn't normally do, like reaching up to play with my hair and cover my smile. This is not the self-assured Wren everyone sees. What the hell is the matter with me?

"Busted?" he asks.

"Slightly," I respond. "I wasn't watching you, though. I was noticing. I'm not used to seeing dudes on the beach reading. Usually it's moms needing a break, reading their novels while dads chase the kids. Plus, that's a huge book. Hard to miss."

He nods, places a sticky note on the page, and closes the text. I'm not prepared for him to stand up.

"Were you that tall last night?"

Raising an eyebrow, he looks down at our feet and then slowly raises his eyes back to mine.

"Pretty sure I didn't grow in the last twelve hours. Maybe you shrunk," he suggests, shrugging.

I pull my shoulders back and stand up straight. Nope, he's still very much taller than me.

"Nah, I'm thinking you were just that tall and I didn't notice," I say, falling in step with him as he meanders toward the water. "What do you teach?"

"College music. Theory, composition, a little scoring and wish we had a music therapy program," he says, crossing his arms as we reach where the sand transitions from dry to wet. While he stares out across the expanse before us, I stare at him. "I'm in a doctoral program now. It's as stressful as I imagined it would be."

"What's your focus?"

"Music education, but my dissertation is on music therapy and how it aids memory and focus in populations with cognitive decline," he says. I raise my eyebrow at him, half a smile on my face. When he turns his head to look at me, his mouth drops open slightly and a half second later he adds, "A friend of mine works with dementia patients and we noticed with her sister-in-law's grandmother that she had less hard days when we played music from different decades she might have been stuck in."

He bites his lip and turns back to staring at the water.

"That's ... that is probably one of the best reasons I have ever heard of for an area of study. It sounds like you're going to do amazing things, Alex," I say.

"What about you?" he asks, veering away from us talking about him. "Are you a student or career woman?"

"Um, I'm a softball player. Well, I'm a physical therapist, but I'm also a softball coach at my alma mater. It was my passion and after graduating, my coach worked with the university to bring me on as an assistant coach," I say. "Her assistant was moving. It's not nearly as impressive as what you're doing. Not by a longshot."

Alex is quiet, and since he has his eyes covered, I can't even tell if he's side-eyeing me or not looking at me at all. Instead, we stand here impossibly close without words. His shoulders are tense, though, and they weren't before I started talking.

"Don't do that," he says, finally.

The words are soft, but the meaning is unmistakable.

"Do what?" I ask, not wanting to immediately submit to this man I barely know.

"Don't make it sound like what you're doing isn't important. It is. You're not just a physical therapist, but also a coach? You're shaping and supporting these young women who probably look up to you more than you realize," he says, catching me off guard. "It's exceptionally impressive."

"Yeah ... well ... so is what you're doing," I sass back.

It's the worst comeback in history, but I'm not great at taking compliments. His light chuckle causes me to smile, just a bit, and I release the tension in my jaw.

"Not good with admiration, are you?" he asks.

"I'm not the best at it, no. I've never been good at receiving compliments. I dole them out like candy on Halloween, though," I admit, though a bit shyly. "I like making people feel good. If providing somebody with a few minutes of happiness means offering a nice comment about their shoes or hair or penmanship, so be it."

Alex laughs loudly, rocking back on his heels and then up onto his toes, as he lets out a whistle.

"Their penmanship? That's a huge compliment considering we're no longer teaching cursive in schools," he says.

He looks at me, smiles broadly, and lifts his sunglasses. He winks at me, and then goes back to glasses on, staring out at the ocean like it was nothing. But it doesn't feel like nothing and I don't want to feel like it was more than nothing. Harmless flirting.

"Some people have beautiful handwriting. It's rare, but sometimes I come across someone worth the accolades."

Maybe he wasn't even flirting.

"I totally get it. Being in education I've seen a lot of horrible penmanship and it really makes me miss when schools focused on that. I get we need to do the math and language arts, but being able to write and read in cursive ... it's an artform. Kids these days are missing out," he says, emphatically.

"You are extremely passionate about this."

"Too much? I can tone it down," he says, smirking.

"Nope. It's the perfect level of crazy. I can handle it."

"So, softball," he says. "Why the 'um' before saying that's part of your career path?"

Crossing my arms, I feel myself close down. Not completely, but enough for him to notice and turn to look at me while we continue talking. I explain to him briefly how I wanted to go into coaching since I was a kid. I'm a natural leader in the dugout and on the field. When the opportunity arose for me to work with the same team I played with and the coach who mentored me through college, I jumped at it. That wasn't a gift I was going to turn down.

"If it was a gift, why do you sound sad about accepting it?"

"You don't do small talk, do you, Alex?" I ask, wondering how we went from a simple little chat about his crappy choice of beach reads to analyzing my choice in jobs.

"I really don't. Some people have said I'm a little intense, and then others who know me really well think I'm just the nerdy guy who talks too much or not enough. I can never get it right. Danny has opinions and they're different every time he wants to throw a jab in my direction," he says, pulling a laugh out of me when he brings up his cousin.

"That must piss you off when he does that," I say.

It would piss me off. I don't know how he deals with family doing that.

"It used to. Danny's more than what you see on the surface, though. The party boy bullshit is just armor. He got his heart torn up right out of college and now this is the Dan we have," he says.

I don't respond out of respect for the situation. Mostly because without asking a lot more questions I won't know enough to make an informed opinion. Right now, he just seems like a self-assured dick, and I don't want to say that to Alex despite Alex being very aware of how his cousin comes across.

Conversation stalls and I know I'm to blame. If I had stayed on topic and told him all the reasons I'm not completely content in my current role, he would probably have me talking about all the colleges I applied to and how I crapped all over my chances of ever coaching full time.

"You okay, Killer? What's the matter?" Danny says.

He stands with his face inches from mine and I jerk backward when my eyes focus. Alex reaches for my arm to steady me before I trip in the sand.

"I'm fine," I say. "I think I just zoned out. Deep in thought. Did you get Roni up on her board?"

"Oh, she got something up, all right," he says, snickering.

"Shut up," Veronica says, walking over to us. "I did nothing of the sort. You're so disgusting. Honestly, Wren, we wouldn't have even planned this family thing for this month if I knew he was going to be here."

The bantering between the two is weird and adorable, and I realize then who he is. The fling. I should have put it together this morning when she said he wasn't always anti-love, but that summer romance she had was so long ago it really didn't cross my mind. My mouth drops open and I look at Veronica, but she glares at me before I can say anything.

"Are you two coming to Jayden's wedding with us or no?"

"What?" we ask in unison.

Roni and I look at one another, a silent conversation passing between us where she is adamant she isn't going and I'm absolutely on the fence and could use a fun night.

"When is the wedding?" I ask, looking back at Alex.

"Friday afternoon," he says, smiling.

"Friday, tomorrow Friday?"

The guys look at each other and shrug.

"Yes, that would be the Friday we're talking about," Danny says. "What, you can't make last minute plans? It's a vacation. You're supposed to be able to just, I don't know, do things and have fun. There is no calendar while on vacation."

"You about done there, Socrates? Making it sound like you're some kind of philosopher," Veronica says. If looks could kill, Danny would be six feet under right now. She huffs out a heavy breath and turns to storm away from us, yelling over her shoulder, "Of course there are calendars on vacation. I hate you."

Exchanging a look with me and Alex, Danny takes off after her. I assume he's going to try to smooth things over, but if he's the summer fling guy he should probably just leave her alone.

"Do you have a dress?"

"I should go check on her ... but, no. I literally threw some stuff in a backpack and boarded a plane. Bathing suit, a few changes of clothes, phone charger, and my toothbrush," I say, watching as Danny attempts to talk to my cousin. "I wasn't planning anything extravagant."

He's quiet as I continue watching, my concern becoming obvious.

"Can I see your phone?" he asks.

Without looking at him, I unlock and hand over the device and then cross my arms as Danny reaches out and touches Roni's biceps, grabbing them carefully and then caressing her skin under his thumbs. I bite my lip to keep myself from saying anything out loud because, man, have I got some thoughts about this development.

"Here you go," he says, placing the phone back in my hand when I hold it out. "Now you have my number and an updated calendar with the wedding details. Oh, and my birthday is in there, too."

Staring at him, I try to grasp what is happening.

"It's not formal, and you don't actually have to come. But, if you aren't busy doing anything else tomorrow evening, there is an extra seat at my table. If you take it, I won't be forced to meet and entertain any of my aunt's friend's daughters," he says.

Smiling at him, I look down at my phone and turn it over in my hands and take into consideration how much a night of dancing is not something I want. But maybe it's definitely something I could use. A moment to let everything else slip away and just enjoy the presence of other people.

I nod, and say, "Yeah, I might be able to make it. I'll have to find a store that sells not formal but nice dresses and ... shoes. All I have are flip flops and running shoes."

"Perfect," he says, pulling his sunglasses down off the top of his head and turning to walk away.

*****

More family has arrived and it's a lot. I'm happy to spend time with Veronica's cousins and aunts and uncles, but, man, I forgot how obnoxious other people can be.

"Are you hiding?" Roni asks, coming into my room. "Because if you're hiding, I'm hiding with you. Why did we say yes to a whole family thing?"

"No idea," I say, looking up from the book I started reading to escape. "Do you guys always leave books in the house or did someone rent from your parents and forget their vacation stash?"

She laughs, but I'm serious.

"They're mine. When I finish reading something that would make a good beach read, I save it and bring it to the house. I swap them out when I'm here and put the ones I remove in the Little Free Library down the street," she says.

"You're such a nerd. So, how did you end up with Danny? You could have mentioned he's the summer fling guy."

"I could have, but it's difficult. We were busy having fun, and then we weren't," she says, climbing up onto my bed and leaning against the wall beside me. "It was a lot of emotions at the time and we both were just starting to figure out how to be grownups."

"You've known him since you guys were kids?"

"Met the summer my parents bought the house, but it was just kids playing on the beach while on vacation when we were all here the same week. We missed out on seeing each other most of high school, and then a few times here and there while in college," she says, wistfully. "Anyway, are you going to Jayden's wedding tomorrow?"

Leaving my finger between the pages I was reading, I close my book and watch her curiously before answering.

"You're not going to tell me all the sordid details of what went on between you and Danny, are you?"

"Nope. Not today. It's more than I can handle," she says, picking at a thread on her shorts. "We'll go shopping in the morning? All of the dress shops near here are probably closed for the day, but we can get up and go first thing tomorrow. We'll hit the bakery again and grab coffee?"

She's carrying a painful memory and I don't want to make it worse.

"Sure," I say. "You aren't coming to the wedding?"

Shaking her head, Veronica doesn't look at me.

"Nah. I'm going to stay in and have family game night with everyone now that we're all here," she says.

Lifting my arm, I wrap it around her shoulders and pull her closer to me. We lean our heads together and snuggle like we used to when we were kids, and I feel her body relax against me as she sighs.

"You're going to be okay? If I go?" I ask.

My biggest concern is I'm going to a wedding with a guy I just met and she also has history with his cousin. It feels strange to not have her come with me, but not icky, and I need to know she's fine with it.

"Absolutely. You need to go have fun. I know you aren't out there in California partying and hitting the clubs. I think I can handle you taking one night of our vacation to go unwind with Alex. He seems like a nice guy," she says. Veronica begins to laugh, and then adds, "I cannot believe he was reading a textbook on the beach though."

"Major vibes. Not bad, but definitely noteworthy," I say, laughing along with her. "Did you know he's going to be a doctor?"

Sitting up straight, Veronica looks at me as if I said something magical.

"A doctor? Are we talking surgeon or something less scary like pediatrician?"

"Music?" I say, a questioning tone because I should have known the first thought when mentioning "doctor" would be medical. "He's a musician. A teacher now and going for his doctorate."

"What's he play?"

"I didn't ask. The textbook today was music theory, though, if that matters," I say.

"Uh ... nope. I don't know anything about music other than I am amazing at car karaoke and shower concerts," she says, falling into a fit of laughter again.

When we slip back into comfortable silence, the house sounds come alive — the air conditioner kicking on, the clinking of glasses and bottles in the kitchen as family enjoys drinks after a long day of travel, and the tapping of rain against the window.

"When did it start raining?" I ask, because I could have sworn there was no rain in the forecast.

"It's not," Veronica says, sitting up and sliding off the bed. "Lover boy is trying to get your attention."

I climb off the bed and come to the window beside her. Alex is standing in the yard below, a handful of pea gravel in his hand, and he meticulously flings a couple stones at my window before noticing me and Veronica.

Unlocking the window and pushing the pane up, Veronica leans against the frame and whistles. Not a "how you doin'" kind of whistle, either. It's ear-piercing and I flinch the second the sound reaches me.

"What do you think you're doing?" she whisper-yells.

"Hi. Hello. Is Wren available?" he asks.

Covering my mouth in an attempt to keep my composure, I step away from the window.

"Maybe. Maybe not," she says. "Can I ask what this is about?"

"What's he saying? I can't hear him," I ask, hidden from Alex's view.

"Nothing. He's just standing there," she says. Yelling out the window, she asks him, "Why are you being weird?"

My phone lights up on the nightstand, and I grab it immediately.

"Would you like to go for ice cream?" I read out loud.

From outside I hear Alex yell back to Veronica, "I am not being weird. I was hoping maybe this was Wren's room and misjudged. I'm sorry for bothering you."

Veronica turns and gives me puppy dog eyes, placing her hand on her heart, and says, "He's so kind. I hope he doesn't turn out to be a serial killer."

"Right. So, I'm going for ice cream. I'll be back in a bit unless you want to come with?" I say.

Shaking her head, Veronica indicates she's staying in for the evening before turning back to the window and yelling to Alex, "It is Wren's room, and yes you can borrow her for ice cream. Don't be a murderer, okay?"

"I will do my best. Thank you!" he yells back.

This should be interesting. I'm going for ice cream with a musician, hopefully not murderer, who's taking me to his cousin's wedding tomorrow and my cousin is acting as comedic relief.

What could possibly go wrong?

Chapter 9

Alexander

"So, tell me about California. What's it like? Palm trees and famous people walking around out in the wild everywhere?" I ask as we wander away from the order window with our cones.

It's a valid attempt to break the ice. I don't know a damn thing about California and she lives there. She's the expert. Twisting her ice cream, she swipes her tongue along the swirl of vanilla and chocolate, and tries to hide a smile that shows in her eyes while her mouth is busy.

I bite the top of the twist on my cone.

She gives me a slightly mortified expression before swallowing the ice cream coating her tongue.

"One, I need to know why you bite your ice cream because that's disturbing. Two, palm trees, yes, famous people not so much. Or at least I don't pay close enough attention to notice. I spend what time I'm not working during good weather at the batting cage or the beach. Swimming, surfing, beach volleyball, all the California girl beach things you can think of," she says before going back to her ice cream.

I nod my head thoughtfully while lapping at my ice cream as it quickly begins to melt down the sides of my waffle cone.

"There really isn't much to tell. I mean, we have hot weather, the wildfires are a constant fear, and I wouldn't mind leaving," she says.

"But where would you go? What would you do?" I ask as we find a bench in the town park. My favorite part about where my aunt and uncle stay is, as kids, we always were able to ride bikes down the road and be free. Ice cream parlors, bakeries, souvenir shops, the park and playground. It's all right here. Once I go home, I'll miss it, but I know in Brockport I'm walking distance to things like this, too. It would be wise of me to remember that when I get home. I briefly realize Wren is looking at me, and ask, "What's better than California?"

Shrugging, she goes back to eating her ice cream, making quick work as the dessert melts faster than either of us are eating.

"I checked out New York. There were a handful of colleges I was interested in coaching at," she says. "It didn't work out."

"Big colleges? Or small ones? There's a difference. I mean, New York is big and we have a lot of schools. Not that California doesn't, but just off the top of my head I can think of at least seven near me," I say. "A coworker has even mentioned the school I work at is looking for a new softball coach. You should apply."

Wren is exceptionally quiet as she continues eating her snack and doesn't make eye contact with me. I nudge her gently with my elbow.

"Brockport is a great area to live," I say with a smile. "We've got coffee shops and book shops and a little art studio and a bakery."

"I knew you looked familiar. I just couldn't figure out from where," she says, and the tone of her voice makes my smile fall. She glances at me and there's immediate regret in her eyes. "No, don't look at me like that, please. I interviewed at Brockport. When we met the other night and you said you were from Western New York it felt like too big of a coincidence. Like there was no way some random guy on the beach was someone I had crossed paths with when I was there in November."

"Did you not fall in love with us? November can be a rough month to visit. You should check it out again," I say. I don't know why I say it, or why there's such urgency, though.

Wren bites her lip. Conversation comes to a standstill and I can't help but blame myself. I'm not used to this. I can talk to people, but when it comes to women, I'm used to Harper and Maggie. They're mouthy and straightforward. Wren is ... not. At least she isn't with me or right now and I hope I get to know her better so she can be open and herself around me, because I get the impression this isn't her normal behavior.

Taking a deep breath, she nibbles at what's left of her ice cream cone before standing and walking to the trashcan across the sidewalk from us, tossing the bottom half of her cone in the bin. When she turns around to walk back to me, she stops and crosses her arms. Lifting her right thumb to her mouth, she gently chews at the skin around her nail while watching me.

"What?" I ask after a beat.

I pop the point of the waffle cone in my mouth and chew as we stare at one another. It's just me and Wren, two total strangers who met but didn't meet last winter.

"It's just ... what are the odds?"

"A million to one," I say without hesitation. "Theoretically, of course. The odds of what?"

"That of all the places and times and dates, you and I are here ... when we were both there months ago and never met. I mean, I can see you in my head. You were standing in line at that coffee place—"

"The Bean."

"Yes, the Jumping Bean! And I was sitting in a booth having coffee because I was trying to ..."

She trails off and I watch her intently, hoping she'll continue.

"Trying to what, Wren?"

She bites her lip again.

"I was trying to figure out if I really wanted to move across the country and leave my boyfriend and everything I've ever known," she says.

Boyfriend. There's a boyfriend. Well, that's okay. If there's a boyfriend then there's no expectations or considerations.

"That was a lot to try to handle on your own, in a coffee place so far from home," I say, relaxing against the bench and crossing my arms over my chest as I prepare to listen. "I can't imagine it was an easy task. You obviously didn't take the job, though, so you were able to make a decision."

Again, she's quiet.

"Are you not happy with the choices you made?" I ask.

"No. Yes? I thought I made the right decision, okay. Originally, I was going to take the job. It was what I wanted. Everything I could dream of at this point in my life and I wanted just a little bit of time to think about it," she says, emphatically. "Then I boarded the plane and I could hear him in my head, gaslighting me about leaving him after he encouraged me to apply for these positions. He was doing it before I left for New York. I let him get in there and I talked myself right out of my priorities. I put the relationship above ... me."

She covers her face and takes a deep breath as I stand from the bench. Stepping into her space, I reach up and pull her hands away from her face.

"So ..." I begin, "call the coach and ask if you can take back your 'thanks but no thanks' on their offer."

"It isn't that easy, Alex. I have no one out there. I'd literally be walking into an entirely new life, completely alone," she says.

Gently wrapping my hands around her shoulders, I stare into her eyes.

"Wren, you would have me."

"But ..."

"But what? The boyfriend?"

She laughs, a hearty, shakes her entire soul kind of laugh, and while I watch her work to compose herself, I get the impression the boyfriend isn't an issue any longer.

"Right. The boyfriend. I said no thanks to the job and within weeks he broke up with me. The boyfriend isn't the but," she remarks. "What if because past me made a dumb decision, I royally messed it up for future me?"

Staring into her eyes, it feels like she's going to regret not chasing her dream more than any guilt she would have if it came to begging for redemption from the softball coach.

"Why New York?" I ask.

There has to be a reason she would choose New York out of all the states in the country, so what is it? It can't be as simple as that's where the jobs were, because there are sports jobs everywhere. Plus, she's a physical therapist, so she could literally go anywhere and work. Instead of answering right away, she fidgets. Her fingers twining together as she attempts to not look at my face.

"If I told you the truth, you'd think I'm insane," she says.

"Try me."

"I found out recently my dad isn't my dad and the guy who is my father was someone my mom met on a business trip to New York," she says. I feel it the moment my demeanor changes and tighten my jaw to hide my reaction as quickly as possible. Quietly, she continues, "I'm hoping I can find him."

Without thinking, I pull Wren into my arms. Her body eases into mine effortlessly.

"I'm sorry," I say, but not for hugging her. "How did you find out?"

"You seriously want to hear my tragic backstory that badly?" she asks, wrapping her arms around my waist and leaning into the hug.

Smiling into her hair, I shrug and hug her tighter.

"We're all a little tragic. This is why I hate small talk. 'How's the weather?' just doesn't have the same ring as 'How'd you find out about your estranged father?' you know?"

We fall into comfortable laughter as she pulls away to look up at me.

"I haven't told anyone. Not even my cousin. She seems to have a lot on her plate now with your cousin here at the same time, so I don't think I'm throwing all of my drama into the mix on this trip."

"That sounds like a good idea. You don't want to push her over the edge or anything. She already looks at Danny with murdery eyes, so I'm not sure what she'd do with this knowledge about your parents," I say attempting to lighten the mood again. "So ... how did you find out exactly?"

Pulling away, Wren turns to stand beside me, touching her fingers to mine before she steps forward, walking away. I take two strides to catch up, my hand brushing the back of hers, as we fall into rhythm with one another and we wander down the path back toward our houses.

"My dad had a major heart attack and, long story short, it resulted in ischemic hepatitis. That turned into the very real fear of trying to find a live organ donor, which of course I was going to see if I was a match because he's my dad. Thankfully, the condition resolved itself because he's a fairly healthy guy and didn't have any other liver issues, but I was already in the rabbit hole and wanted to make sure my mom and I did everything we could to save him. So, I did the tests. Turns out I wasn't a match. For his liver or him," she says. Sighing deeply, I watch her shoulders droop as if the weight of carrying a secret has been alleviated, even if only for a moment. "They do DNA testing and blood typing for all sorts of reasons, and when I got the results, I insisted they mixed up mine with someone else's. There was no way I could have come from him because my blood type simply wasn't possible when combined with my mom's."

I remain quiet, giving her space to share with me anything she would like.

I intentionally move my hand closer to hers, brushing it lightly as a form of encouragement.

"I told my mom and she and Dad sat me down and told me the truth. It was a year after they got married. It had been a difficult adjustment, going from single to married and living together, and a year or so in it was at a breaking point. She was on a trip to Rochester or Buffalo for work, I can't remember which, and met a guy. From the way she talked he was the kind of guy Hallmark movies are made of," she says.

Chuckling, I turn my head to catch a glimpse of her face. Smiling. Head tilted slightly into her chest. Her hair slides slowly across her shoulder, the short strands that frame her face draping just over the curve of her collarbone.

"What does your dad think about all of it?"

Lifting her head up to look at the dimly lit streetlamp lined path in front of us, she slides her hands in her pockets and shrugs.

"He's okay with it. He wasn't right after it happened, but when they found out about me? They worked through their problems in therapy and implemented ideas at home so they could learn how to be a cohesive unit," she says, lifting her shoulders and using her hands while speaking with an authoritative tone. It's clear she was given a version of this speech at some point in her youth. Probably more like multiple times, given her attitude toward it all. Dropping her hands back down and putting them in her pockets again, Wren smiles and says, "So, I saved my parents' marriage, essentially."

"That certainly is one way to look at it," I say, smiling back at her.

"They tried after me, you know? But, I'm an only child," she says, a touch of sadness filling the space between us. "I guess they were fortunate to end up with me."

We continue walking, and once back on the private road leading to our homes-away-from-home, the only noise is that of the world slowly turning in for the evening. I notice Wren fidgeting with her fingers again.

"They found out he was sterile. The literal only reason I'm here is because my mom got mad at my dad and had an affair. I'm the only one, the only child, and I don't even belong to him, and because of that I'm trying to run away from all of it and figure out who the hell I am," she says in an explosion of words I comprehend just enough to understand how much this has bothered her.

She takes a deep breath and I can't tell if she's slowly exhaling or holding it in. Stopping on the side of the road, I grasp her arm and turn her to face me.

"Okay," I say.

"Okay," she repeats. "You don't think this is all a little crazy? Not to mention you've known me less than a day? I don't even know why I told you all of that."

Covering her face with her hands, Wren groans and speaks inaudibly before looking up at me again.

"No. It's not a little crazy. ... It's a lot crazy. That said, I think it's fantastic that you're taking control of something and expanding your horizons because of it," I say. "Look, no one is going to think you don't love your parents because you're interested in where the other half of you came from. I mean, it's cold there way longer than it is warm, and the surfing on Lake Ontario and Lake Erie might not be as awesome as California and North Carolina, but it's pretty amazing that you care enough to give it a try."

As we reach the cul-de-sac, Wren and I stand in the space between our driveways watching one another. I'm unsure how to end this date that isn't a date, but feels like more than a date, so I briefly look over my shoulder at our beach house. Thankfully, no one is looking out the windows or sitting on the porch. Most of the house should be out at Jayden and Penelope's rehearsal dinner, but I begged off. I'd rather be completely surprised tomorrow, and this is their time with the wedding party, closest friends, and their families. I'm just the cousin from out of state.

"What color tie will you be wearing tomorrow?" she asks, quietly. "So, I can attempt to find a dress to match."

"Navy blue with light blue pinstripes," I say, my eyes coming back to catch hers. "It matches my glasses."

"Did you do that on purpose?"

"Not really. It was just the most recent tie I've worn," I say, my mind briefly remembering the last time I used it for something other than wearing. I shove my hands deep into the pockets of my shorts, pushing the thought aside. "If you think you'd like a different color, I'll find one to match in the morning. Just let me know."

She looks at me, narrowing her eyes, before a small smile appears.

"You wore it for a girl, didn't you?"

The question catches me by surprise and I rock back gently on my heels.

"It's okay," she says. "Obviously. We just met, Alex. I have no claim to you or your ties, so it doesn't matter to me one way or another. But if you think a tie is going to make us have a less fun night, you're welcome to find a different one."

My hands clench inside my pockets and I catch myself swallowing hard.

"I'm that easy to read?"

"No, I just took an educated guess."

"Perhaps, we can make new memories with an old tie, then?" I ask, pensive. "It's really one of my favorites and it's still fairly new, so if I don't have to buy another for tomorrow, that would be perfect."

She laughs, and it's a melody I could get used to.

"Old tie, new memories. It sounds like a fabulous evening," she says, reaching out to poke me in the arm. "I should get inside before Roni realizes I'm out here and crashes the party."

I nearly miss what she says as my eyes wander. I watch the way her mouth moves as she chews on the inside of her lip because I'm quiet longer than I probably should be. I can't keep myself from wanting to be closer to her, and my feet shuffle in her direction. There's a pull I can't explain.

"Thank you for trusting me tonight," I say, quietly, as the sound of the waves crashing on the shore reaches us. "And for accompanying me tomorrow."

Reaching out to softly touch her, I slip my index finger beneath her hair and tuck it behind her ear. Time slows down as she tips her head into my palm, her eyes fluttering closed.

"Is this permission to kiss you goodnight?" I whisper, coming toe-to-toe with her.

She exhales, and the warmth brushes my hand as I contemplate how forward I'm being with someone I hardly know. Hardly ... I don't even know her last name.

Leaning in, my free hand brushes the side of her exposed neck, and I place my lips just below her ear. I hear her sigh and know this is as far as it goes tonight.

"Goodnight, Wren," I whisper, close enough for my breath to float along her cheek.

"Goodnight, Alex," she whispers back in the dark.

Chapter 10

Wren

Floating into the house, I go straight to my room and lay down on the bed, placing my arm across my eyes as I rest in the inky stillness. Everyone else has gone to bed or gone out and I need a moment. My skin tingles where his lips touched. My body, heated through in ways it hasn't been in months. Years. Possibly ever.

A noise at the doorway doesn't even interrupt my thoughts, but when she touches my foot, I peek from beneath my arm.

"Good date?" Veronica asks, a shy smile playing at the corners of her mouth. "I wasn't snooping. I just happened to walk past the door to the deck and saw you two outside."

"I don't know if it was a date, but if he asked me to do it again I would in a heartbeat," I say, sighing. She cocks an eyebrow and I realize how it sounds. "Nothing happened. He kissed my cheek before saying goodnight. It was ... refreshing."

Climbing onto the bed beside me, Veronica curls up and places her forehead against mine.

"You okay?" I ask, concerned. Something is off and I don't like it.

"I will be. Just a lot of emotions after seeing Danny. It's been a long time," she says, quietly. "Everyone else went out to look for ghost crabs. I decided to stay in and deal with my ghosts."

I quietly assess the way she subtly changes the subject and play along.

"I need a blue dress for tomorrow."

"What shade of blue?"

"Navy blue or light blue," I say.

"To match his tie?" she asks.

"Of course."

"I know the perfect shop. They open at eight, so we'll get up early," she says, a hopeful tone sneaking through her sadness.

Rolling backwards, Veronica slides her legs off the bed and comes to stand beside me.

"How are you doing your hair?" she asks, propping her hands on her hips.

"Braids? Braided crown? I don't know. I can braid but not very well on myself, so I figured you would do it for me."

"I thought you'd never ask. If the wedding is at two, we won't have a lot of time to get fancy if we have trouble finding the dress."

Sitting up on the bed, I scooch back to lean against the wall.

"If six hours, from the time the dress shop opens until the wedding starts, isn't enough time to find a dress and do my hair, we're doing something horribly wrong. We'll make it all work," I say.

"You're right. It's a wedding, not your wedding. I should only need a couple hours for hair and makeup. We're good. We'll get it all done," she says.

As if that settled the entire conversation, Veronica walks out of my room. I still think she's acting off. She's using dress shopping and doing my hair as a way of doing something normal when whatever history she has with Danny is eating her up. I know she won't talk to me about it right now, so I won't push for answers. If shopping and styling helps her through him being around, that's what we'll do.

I make myself scarce the rest of the night. Showering, shaving, texting my parents to check in. All normal things.

Until I pull up the softball coach's info in my phone.

It's stupid. I shouldn't make this decision on a whim. There's nothing for me in New York. Almost nothing.

And instead of listening to my logical side, I begin an email. I won't send it, but it'll be there while I think it over and contemplate.

Did you not fall in love with us?

That's what he asked me tonight. That's the problem. I fell so in love in the short amount of time I was in Brockport, that I would have started looking for an apartment that day if it hadn't been for my ex. Quietly making my way to the kitchen, I find a notepad and pen in one of the drawers and slip back down the hall to my room, softly closing the door behind me.

For the first time since I left Brockport the very first time I visited, I begin the pro-con list that might change the trajectory of my whole life.

*****

The door flying open wakes me out of a sound sleep.

"The time has come!" Veronica yells.

Standing on my bed, she towers over me as I attempt to pull my pillow over my face. I reach to the nightstand and grab my phone only to see it's barely six in the morning.

"What the fuck," I mutter under my breath. "It's too early."

Flopping down beside me and pulling the blankets up around her shoulders, Roni pushes her head under the pillow with me as I turn to face her.

"It's time to find the perfect dress. Let's find one that's fancy, but not too fancy, and easy for him to tear off you," she says, giggling.

"Did you sleep last night?" I yawn and close my eyes again. Grabbing the pillow, I roll onto my back and leave her laying uncovered. Talking into the fabric, I add, "You're way too chipper for how early it is. I really needed at least another hour of actual sleep."

"I did sleep. But the ocean calls to me when I'm here and I rarely sleep in. Come watch the sun rise the rest of the way with me," she says, crawling over me and pulling the pillow off my face. "Please? It's gorgeous and I know you love a good sunrise. You get all the sunsets on your coast."

I can't argue with her about that. Tossing the covers off, I sit up in the bed and stretch.

"Coffee?" I ask.

"I made a pot to get us started. I'll pour a mug for you while you get dressed."

"You're the best, even if you are a pain in the ass," I say, standing to search my backpack for a clean pair of shorts and tank. "I might need to hit the souvenir shop for a couple shirts. I was not at all prepared for doing anything more than going to the beach."

At the door, she shrugs.

"You can always borrow some of my stuff, too. I pack way more than I ever need. Get dressed. Meet me outside in five," she says as she steps into the hallway.

I'm changed and pulling my hair back into a messy bun before the five minutes are up. Slipping my feet into my flip flops, I open the door to the deck and find Roni leaning on the railing staring off into space.

"You know," I say as I lean next to her and reach for my mug, "You could probably have a whole conversation with him without wanting to kill him."

"I could, but imagining dumping his body into the ocean is way cooler," she says, and I know she's hiding her hurt. Quiet envelops us as we sip our coffee, until she breaks the silence. "I don't really hate him. It's a lot of anger and hurt. He was a playboy and I thought I could change that. I couldn't. It feels like he's still the same Danny from ten years ago. I just wish things had been different."

Slipping my arm through the crook of her elbow, I lay my head on her shoulder while we stare at the big house across the cul-de-sac. All's quiet and dark over there, and I notice the sky quickly lightening. Pushing her gently away from the railing, we walk hand-in-hand to the ocean and have coffee while we watch as the sun creeps above the horizon.

Nestled into the sand, our toes dug in and cradling our nearly empty coffee cups, I let the warmth of the day greet me. It's going to be a good day. I just know it. The list I made last night had more pros than not and the email I drafted, but didn't send, sounds like I'm a person who wishes she chose differently. Not begging for a second chance, but asking for another opportunity to be presented.

And tonight, I get to unwind a little with a beautiful man who seems to expect nothing from me in return. He's given me no indication of wanting more than hanging out, but ... the kiss beneath my ear last night? That's a bit of a mixed signal.

"I think we should go in a few minutes," I say, looking at my watch. "We aren't going to have a dedicated four hours to do my hair and makeup if we don't leave soon."

"Let's go now, then. There's no time to waste," she responds, picking up her mug and standing in one swift motion.

We quickly walk back toward the house, taking care of our mugs and brushing any stray grains of sand from our feet and bottoms before slipping back into shoes. Veronica grabs her keys, and before anyone else is awake we head toward town with the plan to grab coffee and breakfast at the bakery before going to the dress shop.

"So, navy blue or light blue? Or silver?" Veronica asks as she pulls open the door at the formal wear store.

"Any of them. It's going to depend on what looks good and what's within my budget."

"What's the budget?" she asks.

"Uh, under two hundred," I say, stepping up to a mannequin. The halter dress is all sequins and way shorter than I would ever be comfortable wearing. What fabric is showing is silky to the touch and not something I would usually wear on purpose. But this isn't a usual circumstance.

"Right. I'm going to check the sale rack," she says, laughing as she walks away.

Wandering around the store, I find party girl dresses, wedding dresses, first communion dresses, and nothing that would be my first choice. Defeat washes over me as I trail my index finger over the skirts of dresses that are all the wrong color, until I touch a sheer chiffon piece the tenderest shade of lavender.

"It's the wrong color, but the right fabric," I say out loud. Pulling the hanger from the rack, I fall in love with the way the skirt falls, how the bust is shaping without being overly revealing, and the price. "Roni? Come here when you get a chance."

The shop isn't huge, so I'm surprised when I have to call out to her again and when I finally hear a muffled response, I drape the dress over my arm and go searching for my cousin.

"I think I found it," I say, as I walk toward the dressing rooms. "What are you doing?"

I smile as I watch her struggle to get the zipper up on a little black dress. Each side from armpit to hem has a slice of bright red satin and she looks like she's ready to tear a certain man's heart straight out of his chest. Or, she would, if she wasn't hopping around trying to reach the tab between her shoulder blades to finish zipping up.

"I wanted to feel hot."

"Well, you look it. Are you buying it?" I ask as I pull the zipper up the rest of the way and she smooths the snug fabric down the tops of her thighs.

"Probably not. But you could take a picture of me in it and show him," she says as if it's no big thing.

"Only if you absolutely want me to," I say, "but, it's been a long time and maybe that's not the best way to go about this."

She stares at her reflection, contemplating my words.

"Unzip me," she demands. "What did you find?"

"I'll show you," I say, unzipping her dress and stepping into the changing room next to hers.

Off with the shorts and the tank. Forget about wearing a bra with this one. As soon as the silky fabric of the skirt touches my legs, I get a shiver down my spine. Pulling it up over my full hips and slipping my arm through the single strap to create a perfect one-shoulder look, I reach back and slide the zipper into place.

"Are you ready? I need your honest opinion," I say.

Poking my head out, Veronica is sitting on a small couch waiting for me with the black dress lying beside her.

"It's the wrong color, though, so ..." I say as I step out of the closet sized room. "But maybe it will work?"

Roni's eyes widen as she takes in the full look — from the bare shoulders to the graceful sweeping sheer cover. Placing my hands on my hips I turn to look in the mirror, twisting my head as I turn to see the back of the dress in the reflection.

"That's fucking hot," she says. "Like, don't get me wrong, it's conservative and elegant. I think that's what makes it exactly what you need. Who cares if the color is wrong."

"I do. A little," I say, lightly touching the bodice, fingering the ruched details along my abdomen.

"Do you care enough to ask him about it?"

"It would be nice of me to do that."

"Or you could ask him to send you a picture of his tie and you can see how well they go together," she says. "That's the best idea. Because if the tie doesn't match, he needs to go buy a new one pronto. This dress is it."

She stands and walks over to get a closer look, lifting the tag as she spies the length.

"Are you serious right now? This dress is less than half your budget? There you go. It was meant for you," she says, laughing at the coincidence.

"That's how it felt when I put it on, too. I'm buying it. I'll text him," I say. "And now you can figure out the hair."

"But shoes."

"Shoes." I bite my lip. "I hate dress shoes."

"I know, but you don't have to wear them that long. Just for the ceremony and the first part of the reception. Then you're allowed to take them off," she says, as if she's the authority on weddings. "Or, I have a pair of purple Chucks you can borrow."

"Yes. That's more my speed," I say.

Roni unzips the back and I shuffle into the dressing room. Before removing the dress, I pick up my phone and snap a quick picture of my image in the mirror, then a photo of just the fabric. Opening my texts, I find

Alex at the very top of my conversations and attach the second picture to a message.

Me: Will your tie work with this color?

Tossing my phone down on my clothes, I finish undressing and redressing so we can pay and head to the house.

"I really love the color," Veronica says as we walk beside one another to the car. "Hopefully it complements his tie and all. The shoes are a darker shade of purple, but they'll definitely work."

"Why didn't you buy the little, black dress?"

"Because it was going to make me sad and depressed," she says. "Besides, this shopping trip was for you."

"Fair enough. No sense doing something if you know it's going to make you feel that way," I respond.

"Good. It's settled," she says.

As I'm placing the dress in the backseat of her car, my phone vibrates in my back pocket. Then, a second time, before I can get the door closed. When I reach for the passenger door handle, it buzzes against my backside yet again.

Pulling open the door, I slip the phone from my pocket and climb in beside my cousin. Three messages, one right after the other, all from Alex.

"You have a stupid smile on your face," Veronica says as she starts the car, but reciprocates with her own smile.

"He said the color will match the lighter blue perfectly. Then sent fire emojis. And then an apology," I say, snickering.

As we ease into the early morning tourist traffic, she scrunches her nose and questions why he would send an apology.

"I don't know. He didn't say what he was sorry for and I just sent back a purple heart emoji. I'm not reading too much into it," I say, though I feel the heat creep up my ears because my brain sees fire emojis and automatically defaults to dirty thoughts.

I can't read into it. Alex is just a guy — a really nice guy so far — who is letting me tag along to his cousin's beachy wedding. It doesn't mean anything.

Chapter 11

Alexander

"Make sure you have condoms," Harper says loudly in my ear.

It makes my heart seize a little, knowing she expects me to have moved on like that already when we both know I haven't quite gotten there yet and deep down I'm hoping she isn't either. There's still lingering pain for me, even if she's acting like she's fine.

"The ones that are for her pleasure," she adds.

"I never had any problems pleasuring you," I quip, the words sliding out between my tongue and teeth without a second thought as I concentrate on putting my contacts in. "Or were you pretending?"

"I never pretend with you."

Present tense.

"I didn't think so." I'm quiet as I reach for my tie. Glancing at her picture on my phone screen before I turn to the mirror, I clear my throat to get rid of the sudden emotion. "I don't think I'm going to need those tonight, anyway."

"Oh? Is she not interested?"

"Never said that, but I also haven't asked. Plus, we just met. I'm simply giving her an evening out with dinner, dancing, and dessert," I say, wrapping the fabric around into a perfect Windsor knot. "I have no expectations."

She mumbles something under her breath and I quirk an eyebrow as I question what it was.

Sighing deeply, she states more clearly, "You give the best dessert."

Tightening the knot against my throat, I give myself a moment before I respond.

"Harper, what's going on? You didn't want to do this anymore. You ended the benefits package," I say.

I wait for her to fill me in on what's happening in her head. Staring into the mirror while fixing the front of my short, dark brown hair, I continue prepping for my cousin's wedding. It's not my event, but I have to look good for the family pictures. There are always family pictures — weddings, funerals, birthday parties, anniversaries ... there's no getting away from them.

"I don't know. I think I'm just lonely," she says. "I didn't want a relationship, but I don't think I didn't want what we had either."

"Babe, what we had was a relationship. You just ... you refused to call it that. Now we're back to roommates where we're trying to act normal around one another and split the chores like we did in the beginning," I say, careful not to make my tone sound accusatory but it's hard not to. I wanted more with her, but she was afraid that would result in the next step.

Marriage.

Kids.

Game nights with the neighbors.

Going to bed and just sleeping.

Going through the motions and losing herself in the process.

"Maybe it's time for me to move out," she says quietly.

"We're doing this again? Harper, I don't want you to move out," I say. The way she said it, though. There's something in the way she said it that makes me realize this isn't about me anymore. "Unless you think that's what you need. I won't hold you back, but I'll miss you if that's your decision."

I hear her suck in a ragged breath. Then breathing in deeply to clear her nose.

"I'll be home tomorrow," I say, grabbing my phone to start looking into changing my flight.

"Don't!" she yells. "Please, don't. It's not you, Alex. I'm just having a hard time adjusting. And you're right. It was a relationship and I'm an idiot and going back to normal is not possible. It's not. Which is why moving out is probably the best decision."

I stop myself from logging into my account with the airline, but my thumb hovers over the login button.

"Are you sure? Because if we need to discuss this this weekend and create a plan, I'll be on the first flight out tomorrow," I say.

"I'm sure," she says.

We're quiet. I can hear the ambient noise in the background as she works. It's her lunch break, which means she's making notes of things while eating a pack of crackers, maybe drinking a protein shake, and not actually taking a break. She sniffs and clears her throat.

"Harper?" I say to make sure I have her attention.

"Hm?"

"Even though it didn't work out for us, you're going to find someone you can love as much I've loved you. We'll heal from this. Go listen to the ragey playlist I made for you. Finish work and go for a run. Go to Maggie and Maverick's and play with the baby. We are going to get through this and our friendship will be stronger. I'm not going to ditch you because you don't want to play house," I say. "You're literally the only friend I have at this point."

She laughs through her tears.

"That's not true," she says.

"Oh, but it is. Between grad school and teaching as many courses as I can, the only friends I have either work with me or are you. Typically, work friends aren't real friends, so it's you."

"You have Mags."

"I do have Mags. You're right. And how lucky am I that my two closest friends are also women I've dated."

"Ouch, yeah, I forgot for a brief moment you dated my sister-in-law. But it was only like three dates. Do those really count?" she asks, laughing. It's a real laugh, and I can hear the way her heart sings just a little as she picks on me about my brief courtship with Maggie.

"They count at least a small amount," I say. "Because if it wasn't for knowing her and figuring out we were way better as friends, I wouldn't know you, and you're a really amazing human, Harper Rogers. I don't love you just because I had a relationship with you. I love you because you're super cool and down to earth, your heart is ginormous. You feel things so deeply that I sometimes think it hurts to acknowledge them. Being in the line of work you're in doesn't help that."

"Work has been really rough this week," she says.

"I could tell," I reply. Glancing at my watch, I say, "I hate to do this, but I have to go in a minute. Are you going to be okay? If I stay until next week?"

"I will. I'm going to go to Rick's after work. Maybe Sawyer will let me help in the greenhouse. A little dirt under my fingernails should help my perspective."

"That sounds like a great idea. Do me a favor, though?" I ask. "Don't move out before I get home?"

She's almost too quiet, like she was caught in the middle of packing her bags.

"I won't," she says. After a beat she asks, "Alex, is she pretty? Like, not just her face, but her heart? Does she have a pretty heart?"

Adjusting my tie once more, I slide my phone in my pocket and turn to leave the bedroom.

"So far, yes. She's not without scars, either. If we keep in touch after this week, maybe you'll be able to meet her," I say, flipping the light off and pulling the door closed behind me. "I think you'd like her."

*****

I don't know what I was expecting other than a lavender colored dress that fit perfectly with the lighter blue of my tie, but it wasn't a woman dressed like a goddess with a light brown crown of braids and purple Converse.

My eyes trail up her body as she walks slowly down the aisle, her arm casually balanced on Danny's inner elbow, and he tips his head close to her ear. Our eyes meet as I stand to greet her, though she's still several steps away. It allows me extra seconds to enjoy the view, take in her delicate collarbone, the way the little studs in her ears catch the sun, and how she purses her lips in response to whatever my cousin has said to her.

"Save me a dance," he says to Wren before letting her remove her arm from his. He nods in acknowledgement of me.

"He thinks I should be his date," she says to me as soon as he's out of earshot. "He's jealous. Of you."

I tilt my head and scrunch my nose, confused.

"He's an idiot. But I would be jealous of me, too, if I was him, so fair enough," I respond, stepping out of the row I'm seated in so Wren can take a seat. Unintentionally, I catch myself taking a deeper breath when she slips past me. "Your perfume smells like sunscreen."

"That's because it is," she says, giggling. "Can't be too careful when it comes to skin cancer."

"Well played. I spend so much time inside there are days I don't even see the sun."

"That's sad. I don't know if I'm loving the no glasses look, Professor," she says, looking up at me as I take my seat beside her. She reaches out and touches my tie, lifting it to get a better look and then lifting the outer layer of her skirt and laying it against the fabric. "That's a pretty good match. I was worried."

"The Chucks even match," I say, glancing toward her feet. "The plan wasn't for you to spend hundreds of dollars on a dress and shoes, Wren. I'm really sorry."

She smiles sweetly. I'm taken off guard by the shimmer on her cheekbones as the sun warms her face and gives her an angelic glow.

"Borrowed."

"What?" I question.

"The shoes. They're borrowed from Veronica. And the dress was on sale," she says, shrugging. "I didn't even spend half my budget. Oh! And the dress? It has pockets."

She's absolutely giddy about it. I didn't grow up with sisters, but Maggie and Harper always point out when they have pockets in a piece of unsuspecting clothes.

"Women and their pockets," I say, but can't contain my smile or ignore the way my heart flutters slightly.

"So, I can collect shells later," she replies, dead serious.

"Are you sure it's not to collect phone numbers?" I say, noticing one of my cousin's groomsmen eyeing Wren as he walks back down the aisle after seating someone.

Wren wrinkles her nose in disgust.

"Please. I'm here with you, not looking to play the field. We're going to have a lovely afternoon watching your cousin get married to the love of his life and then we're going to eat, drink, and dance as if we've known each other our entire lives," she says, reaching for my hand.

I give it to her willingly, relishing the feeling of her warm skin against mine. My hardened fingers from hours of guitar playing glide between hers. Where I expect to feel smooth, I'm met with tough skin that's been created by months of playing softball. I rub my thumb over the calluses just beneath her fingers.

The moment feels like we've done this before. Maybe my heart and my brain are simply telling me we want more moments like this in general.

"Lots of angry hours in the batting cage lately," she whispers, having caught on to what I'm doing. Motioning to the seaside arbor just a short walk away from us, she says, "It looks like they're about to start."

While the ceremony is relatively short, it's not lacking. I catch Wren wiping a tear from the edge of her eye as the vows are exchanged, and I give her hand a gentle squeeze. She rolls her eyes just enough to be noticed when she turns her head to catch me looking at her.

As predicted, I'm pulled away after for family photos while the rest of the guests wander up the path to the beachside reception center. I watch Wren as she slowly makes her way toward the building and then stands on the deck overlooking the wedding site, giving me time to do what I need to while she enjoys the view of an ocean thousands of miles from the one she's familiar with. The breeze lifts the hair she left down out of her braids and I'm struck stupid as to how we missed connections when she was in Brockport.

"Alex, you're all done. We're just doing photos of Jay, Penelope, and the immediate families now so go on up to your date," my aunt says. "She's pretty. Where'd you find her?"

I smirk.

"I found her on the beach."

"Like a seashell?"

"Or a mermaid."

"A siren?"

"I don't think she's going to lure me to my death, but I'm willing to chance it," I say, smiling conspiratorially.

She reaches out and squeezes my forearm, leaning in to kiss my cheek.

"Go enjoy your evening. You've earned this vacation. I love you," she says and then turns away to go back to the task at hand.

"Love you, too," I say.

I pull my sunglasses from my pocket and slide them into place. Lifting my eyes back up to where Wren stands waiting for me, I push my hands into my pants pockets and take a step toward the girl I found curled up in the sand.

Chapter 12

Wren

Alex's extended family is definitely closer than mine. The number of aunts and uncles and cousins I've been introduced to tonight is more than I can count. I stopped counting. I figured there were maybe a couple on each side, but no. Most of the people invited are family.

They're loud, obnoxious, and know how to let loose. I've met his parents briefly, and then they disappeared, but over all his family is the entire party.

I think I love them.

It's weird. They've each met me, I've been introduced as Alex's date — not girlfriend, not stranger from California, not weirdo he picked up on the beach two days ago — and they just immediately included me in dances and shenanigans.

There's one person here, though, who I wish would forget my existence.

"So, where's Roni? What's she doing tonight?" Danny asks, as he pulls me onto the floor for a slow dance.

"She's home, probably playing Scrabble. You could call her and ask her if she wants to come hang out," I rebut.

"I'm not sober enough for that," he says. "What about you?"

"Sober."

"Completely?"

"Yes. I don't need to drink to have a good time, Danny," I say. "I'm having enough fun without alcohol, thank you very much."

"If I told you you're really pretty and you should come home with me tonight, would you?"

I blow the hair off my forehead that's slowly come out of my braid, step back from him, place my hands on my hips, and stand up straight to look him in his drunk face.

"You seem nice and all, but I'm here with Alex. Maybe show your cousin some respect," I say. "Not to mention you have a history with my cousin and it goes deeper than just a summer fling that ended badly."

He lifts his beer to his mouth and takes a healthy swig. It's guys like Danny who make it easy for me to stay sober at big events.

"Veronica and I will figure our shit out. Don't you worry about it. However, I want to figure you out tonight. Alex is totally oblivious to everything there is to like about you. He always has his nose in some book. You're out of his league. Plus, he's only ever dated brainy chicks and even they don't stick around long," he says.

I look at him curiously, wondering how he can just gloss right over the fact he had a relationship of sorts with Veronica and try to get me to do anything with him. I was really hoping by bringing her up in conversation again he'd tone it down, but apparently not. I'm sure that's one of his attributes as an attorney, but in real life it just makes him look like a dick.

"I guess I'm just not his type then?"

Huffing out a laugh, Danny says, "Absolutely not. You're fucking hot. Not at all his type."

"So, let me get this right ... I'm hot and not smart. Got it."

Reality hits him when I break it down that way and his eyebrows knit together.

"No. No, that's not what I said," he says, sobering slightly. "I didn't say it like that, Wren. You're reading too much into it."

"Right," I say, stepping toward him so the heel of my shoe is on his big toe. He isn't expecting me to speak to him the way I do, but I wasn't expecting to have to defend my intellect tonight. I finish speaking as the song comes to an end, laughing humorlessly as I turn and walk away. He flounders an attempt to redeem himself as I go toward the bar area to find my date. Looking over my shoulder at him, I yell back, "Nice try, Daniel, but you lose this round."

I take my time walking through the reception area where Jayden and Penelope are getting ready to cut the cake and prepare for other traditional aspects of the party — funky chicken dance, bouquet and garter toss, and whatever else usually happens at weddings. Seeing Alex's back as he stands at the bar does nothing to me, but when he turns slightly and I catch his profile in the dim light, a perfect Grecian nose and strong jaw, the way his tie hangs loosely from his neck, my skin pebbles as if touched by an icy breeze.

He twists just enough to look directly at me and I lose my breath. If Morgan Freeman were narrating my life events, he would tell you I thought I was going to melt into a puddle but I did not, in fact, melt into a puddle ... but, holy shit, if one look from anyone could make me want to strip naked and get bent over a bar, it would be Alex and the way he's looking at me from across the room.

Clearing my throat and searching for composure, I take a wobbly step closer to him, and another and another until I finally have my bearings and come to stand beside him.

"Is this seat taken?" I ask.

My attempt to be cute and adorable feels silly, but the way his lips curve into an amused smile makes it worth the embarrassment.

"It's a bar and they took away all the stools, so technically there are no seats. You are welcome to stand with me, though," he says, leaning to bump his shoulder against mine as I rest my elbows on the edge of the counter. "Can I order you a drink?"

His quirkiness is a refreshing quality and I smile at him as my awkwardness dissipates in his presence.

"That would be lovely. A water, please."

"Just water?" he asks, surprised. I nod, knowing it's a party and perhaps there will be judgment, but when with people I don't know, I just don't like to have alcohol. "Water it is, then."

Alex waves to the bartender and requests my drink. Before turning back to me, he cracks the top on the bottle and sets it on the bar, handing me the open container.

"So," he begins. I sense a slight air of jealousy, but wait for him to continue while steeling myself for something like a rejection. "I saw you dancing with my cousin. You looked beautiful out there."

His cheeks flush, as if he's unsure of giving compliments.

"I probably shouldn't have said that," he says, stepping back from the bar and grabbing the loose ends of his tie as if he's holding on for dear life.

"It's okay." I laugh. "Thank you for the compliment. I don't have a lot of reasons to dress up and feel pretty. It's nice to know my efforts are appreciated."

We fall into comfortable silence as the party continues around us like a soundtrack to a movie.

"Danny seems ... nice."

I don't want to insult his family, so nice is as good as it's going to get. Alex lifts an eyebrow and smirks, a look from a man I never used to think was sexy. From him, dressed like that, with his hair perfectly mussed? Five alarm fire.

"... If a rattlesnake is nice, that is," I continue, swishing the skirt of my dress around my legs in a little dance to take some of the attention off my meanness. Dual purpose, actually, because the way he looks at me has body parts throbbing despite the fact I have no intention of doing anything about it.

"You noticed, eh?"

"For sure. You learn a lot about a person in three minutes when they're drunk and let their guard down."

Alex tips his glass and stares into the bottom of his cup, mulling over a thought.

"And what did you learn?"

"That your cousin is a jackass who thinks you're only capable of dating smart girls and therefore implied I am not smart because I am pretty."

The words exit my mouth faster than I can process as Alex opens his to talk, but closes it quickly and swallows instead.

"And then I ground my heel into his toes and let him know he has no fucking clue how smart I am, but that I am the last pretty girl he wants to say stupid shit like that to," I say.

Alex laughs loudly, a truly exuberant sound as it crashes like waves over me and pulls a bigger smile from me. Setting his glass on the bar, he reaches with both hands to tenderly grip my neck as he steps further into my space.

"You're kind of perfect," he says, his eyes darting to my lips before his mouth dips closer to mine.

"I know," I say, breathlessly as his lips connect with mine, a feeling I've only hoped for half a dozen times today as we've shared little touches and wanton glances throughout the afternoon.

My eyes flutter shut as his tongue glides along the seam of my lips, parting them and capturing the bottom lip as he deepens the kiss. I willingly take as he gives and give as he takes. My hands snake up his abdomen and grasp the ends of his tie, holding on tightly because if he lets go of me, I will most certainly fall down. It feels like a short eternity when he gently pulls back, only to place another kiss fully on my mouth, and then lean his forehead against mine.

The rapid beating of my heart matches the panting breaths we both take, and as I open my eyes again, I find him watching me as the flash from a camera catches us off guard.

"Would you like to go for a walk on the beach?" he asks.

"Yes, please, I would like that very much."

His eyes crease at the corners as he smiles and pulls away from me, grabbing my hand along the way to guide me to the nearest door. The warm ocean air wraps around me as we step outside, my hand still in Alex's grasp as he leads me toward the path over the dune.

Stopping once on the sand, I bend to remove my shoes and socks.

"Oh, we're doing this, huh?" he asks, lightness in his tone.

"For sure. Walking in sand in shoes is just silly. Strip," I say, struggling to get my left foot out of its respective Converse.

"Strip. Hm, no. I'm adventurous, but even that is a little too adventurous for me," he quips.

Standing up, I roll my eyes at him but can't keep from laughing.

"You know what I meant," I say. "Shoes have no business being on the beach."

"I beg to differ. This sand gets way too hot sometimes to be barefoot in the middle of the afternoon. But, since it's not the middle of the afternoon, I will concede," he says, toeing out of his dress shoes.

"Curious question. How do your feet not hurt wearing those?" I ask.

Pulling off his second sock and shoving it into the toe of his shoe, Alex shrugs.

"They're the dress shoes I wear to work usually, so they're all broken in and comfortable," he says, picking both pairs of shoes up from the sand and setting them at the end of the path. "Normally, I hate dress shoes. But these are perfect."

Pushing his hands deep into his pockets, Alex nods and steps forward toward the water. The closer we get to the surf, the higher I lift my skirt. This is the part I didn't think about before jumping at the chance for a night walk on the beach — the dress getting wet. I try to stay out of the water as much as I can, but there's still a pull to touch it with my toes, feel it rush against my ankles as we wander aimlessly down the shoreline.

The moon continues to rise above us, adding a sparkle to the ocean I rarely get to see. I stop for a moment to admire her brightness and in that small amount of time, Alex walks ahead of me only to turn around and wait until I catch up. When I do, he reaches for my hand.

Dropping the fabric gathered in my fingers, I take his hand and he leads me toward the dunes.

"How long are you here for?" he asks, sitting down in the sand and looking up at me. "I know you said you're here for a week, but does that mean seven days or ten days? Because getting here in the middle of the week could mean you're not counting the week starting until today."

He lifts his hand and I offer him mine as I turn and crouch down into the sand, my dress forming a mushroom around my waist. I tuck it in under my butt and plop down beside Alex.

"I have a family thing tomorrow, but don't leave to go back to California until the middle of the week," I say.

"Maybe we could go out to dinner before you have to go," he says. "My flight isn't until Wednesday afternoon, so I'm stuck here for a few more days."

"Stuck here, like it's such a bad place to be?" I bump him with my shoulder, but then lean against him and place my head on his shoulder while I listen to the water. "The waves are decent. I wish I could stay even longer to enjoy them."

Alex tips his head to lay it against mine and is quiet. Quietly contemplating something, I'm sure, as he digs his fingers into the cool sand between us.

"I'm sure you have things to get back to, though. Your job, friends, so on and so forth," he says, his voice trailing off.

"So forth such as?" I question. "There's no guy to go back to. I'm in limbo with my career. My friends were 'our friends' and they chose him, except for my roommate who has a superbly busy schedule and a dude."

"Will you be looking into that coaching job again?"

Do I tell him? Do I share that I already emailed the college? I haven't heard anything since sending it before leaving for the wedding and I don't want to get my hopes up, because getting my hopes up about a job because of a guy is exactly what got me into this headspace to begin with.

"I might," I say.

"Dinner? This week before we both go back to our regularly scheduled lives?"

"I would love to," I say as his hand finds mine in the sand.

Chapter 13

Alexander

It's been a month since North Carolina.
I haven't called her.
She hasn't called me.
When I saw her off at the airport and then went in the opposite direction to my gate, I figured it was for the best. She's got an opportunity in Brockport, but I wasn't going to push her for more after only knowing her a week. This isn't a romance novel. Real life doesn't work like that.

"Why haven't you called her?" Harper asks, sipping her drink.

We agreed to a liquid lunch today because I'm stressed about grad school and she had a really difficult intake. A dementia patient who also was the victim of elder neglect. She can't and won't go into the details, but she is well on her way to being fall down drunk.

"Because ..." I say, trying to figure out why. I sigh, lifting the beer I ordered to my lips and taking a long, slow sip. She purses her lips and glares at me. "Isn't this weird for you?"

"What?"

"Us."

"There's nothing weird about getting hammered in the middle of the day with my best friend."

I stare at her. She knows what I'm talking about and it's not that we're having drinks together. It's about our past relationship and her asking about Wren.

"Okay, listen, it's a little weird. I'm working through it," she says. "That said, I'm the one who wanted you to date. I'm the one who said I needed to stop using you as a crutch and I meant it. Are things back to normal? Absolutely not, but we're figuring it out, Alex. I just need you to try."

"I am trying," I argue.

"Call. Her."

"What if she doesn't want to hear from me?"

"Lies. What woman wouldn't want to hear from you? Call her," she says, picking my phone up off the table where it sits on silent between us. Harper puts in my password and I watch as she goes to my contacts. "Wren from California. That's how you have her in your phone?"

"We didn't exchange last names."

"You spent an entire week with this woman and never found out her last name? She doesn't know yours either?" I shake my head. I just put my first name in her phone when I gave her my number. "How is she going to find you when she learns of her unplanned pregnancy? I told you to use condoms."

"You're horrible," I laugh, knowing she's trying to get me riled up. "We didn't even have sex."

"Sad."

"I only kissed her, like really kissed her, twice."

"Really, really sad."

I roll my eyes.

"Look, I already had Danny act like a total asshole about her not wanting anything to do with him and about me not hooking up with her, so you really can't shock me," I say, lifting my drink and taking a sip to keep me from saying anything else. "What are you doing?"

Harper continues swiping her finger all over my phone screen, not acknowledging my question and not even looking up when I say her name. Her fingers stop and her tongue pokes out between her lips as she concentrates on the screen.

"Perfect. Here you go," she says, handing my phone back to me. "She said she'll call you at five her time."

"What am I supposed to say? My hot roommate who I used to bang is trying to play matchmaker?"

Her eyes grow wide as she looks over my shoulder.

"Hey, Ricky," she says loudly as a hand lands on my shoulder and squeezes a little tighter than I consider to be friendly. "Alex said the chocolate stout here is amazing. I'll get you one."

I look up at Maverick — Harper's brother, Maggie's husband, the guy who wanted to murder me and bury me in amongst the evergreens on his tree farm before he realized Mags and I were just friends.

"Alexander."

"Maverick."

"And I'm Harper. Good, glad we got that out of the way again. Remember that girl Alex met when he went to his cousin's wedding? I texted her for him because he's being childish and not talking to the pretty girl he likes," she says. "As if we're in middle school or something."

Rick and I haven't looked away from one another and the relief I feel when he smiles at me is insurmountable.

"Man, do not under any circumstances, tell that sweet California girl about sleeping with my sister. Especially not when she still lives with you," Rick says, smacking me on the back and pulling out the chair beside me as Harper calls a waitress over and orders her brother a drink. "That would effectively end any relationship possibility with what's her name."

"Wren."

"Like the bird," Harper adds.

I cover my face with my hand to hide not only my smile but also my embarrassment.

"Plus, it's not like you're going to have to worry about her knowing I live with you since I'm moving out," Harper says.

Rick and I both stare at her. We talked about this. We agreed she wasn't moving out. The four of us — me, Harper, Maggie, and Rick — even discussed it because we rent the house from Maggie and don't want any of us to end up in a financial bind.

"Don't look at me like that. Either of you," she says. "I'm a grown fucking woman and I'll do what I want. Within reason."

"This isn't within reason," Rick says.

"How do you know? I haven't told you the details yet," she says, and I see the exasperation killing the buzz she's got going.

We wait for her to continue, but she wants us to ask. I don't even want to entertain the idea. I like our arrangement ... even without the sex.

"When and where?" I ask, the rest of the question implied.

"Two weeks. Brian just finished remodeling the apartments above the bakery and gave me first dibs," she says, taking a sip of her drink and looking pleased with herself. "It's two bedrooms and walking distance to everything, plus parking in back and it's above the bakery. Which is next to the coffee shop. Not to mention, the art place. All the places I spend most of my time not at work. It's perfect."

Maverick and I glance at each other. Knowing Harper like we both do, she's been talking to Brian about this for a while, particularly since he's been working on the remodel for months.

"When did you decide this?" I take a chance asking, because I think I can pinpoint when she made her choice.

"Please don't be mad," she begins, and I know I'm right. "You were out of town. It was easier for me to go talk to him about it. I talked to Brian after I talked to you. It just ... happened."

"Wanting to move out and then magically finding an apartment without looking just happened?" I ask.

Rick's attention fluctuates between us like he's watching a ping pong ball be hit back and forth.

"Listen, I don't need to explain it all to you, but I will because you're you and I care about you," she says, pointing her finger in my direction. "First, you need to stop looking at me like you're going to cry. Second, I got off the phone with you. I went to the coffee shop on my way to Ricky's. Brian was there. I said, 'Hey, Bri, how you doin'?' and he said he was doing well but working around the clock to get the apartments ready to put on the market or whatever. I said I might be interested and so he showed me the apartments and I told him to let me know when they're ready to rent. I didn't tell him what was going on between you and me. I didn't allude to troubled waters. I simply told him I was interested in the apartment. He called yesterday and said they'd be ready in two weeks if I was still interested and, you know what? I am. I want you to have the house to yourself so I can come visit for brunch and have bonfires and feel like a I'm in control of my life for a few minutes."

Maverick and I sit quietly as we digest everything she just said. None of us speak until Rick clears his throat.

"I'm really proud of you Harper. This is a huge step and I'm sure it wasn't easy," he says, kicking me under the table.

"Promise you'll still come for fires and brunch?" I ask, because as proud of her as I am, too, it feels like my heart's getting torn from my chest. It's the breakup again, but a thousand times worse. It's wondering how I'm going to manage living alone, not because of the cost, but because I'm going to be alone.

"Wouldn't miss it for the world," she says. "Plus, now that I'm going to not be living there, maybe this phone call tonight with California Wren will turn into something more than just sitting on the beach."

Chapter 14

Wren

"Tell me again why you haven't called him?"

Tasha stands in my bedroom doorway and I know she's questioning my life choices. I've been non-stop working at the athletic complex since fall sports students are back and too many of them haven't been stretching properly. That means I'm starting some of them from scratch and reminding them, not so nicely, of potential injuries.

My softball girls have tried to keep me sane as I continue to work with the ones who are local, playing pick-up games after work and meeting up at the batting cages a few times a week. The exercise has kept my brain busy.

It's kept me from thinking about Alexander from Brockport.

It's also kept me from thinking about how I haven't heard back from the coach out there.

"I don't know. He's probably busy. Plus, I've been busy. We're all fucking busy," I say, vehemently as I wave my arms around in the air.

She raises her eyebrow in my direction and scoffs.

"Busy doing what, exactly? Him. What's he busy doing?"

"I don't know ... laundry, probably. Plus, he's in grad school. That always makes people super busy. Like, you should have seen how stressed he was at the beach after the wedding because he was prepping for his classes and the classes he was teaching," I say, my voice rising. "He was so busy."

"Jesus, Wren, call him already."

"I can't," I say.

"Why not?"

"It's weird. It was only one week. He probably doesn't have my number saved anymore," I try to rationalize.

"One, it's not weird. Two, you said he's one of those nerdy, super organized guys. That information alone tells me he didn't delete your number," she counters.

"I can't," I whine, lifting my pillow to my face and screaming into it.

Part of it is because I just don't want to make the first move. A big part of it. The other part? What if a week of hanging out with a stranger is all it was for him?

"Just text him and quit being a chicken," Tasha says, walking over and picking my phone up from my desk. She tosses it onto my bed in front of me and waits for me to pick it up.

"What if he doesn't respond?" I ask, sadly.

"What if he does?"

I mull it over, this decision based on a question that shouldn't be a question at all because I like him. Even if nothing ever comes of it, I like him as a person and he was amazing and fun to talk to. I want to know how his summer classes went and how the new semester is going. I want to hear about the song he was writing when we went out for breakfast our last morning in North Carolina.

More than all of that, though, I want to hear his voice.

"You should just do it and get it over with. Rip the bandage off," Tasha says. "Or, give me your phone and I'll do it."

"Fine, you do it," I say picking my phone up off the bed. As I go to hand it to her, I flip the device over and the screen turns on. I feel the air catch in my lungs as I read his name in the notifications window. Laughing loudly, I say to her, "What kind of sorcery is this?"

Turning the phone around so she can read the screen, she smiles.

"See, you didn't even need to send a message and he responded. Magic," she says. "What did he say?"

I read it to myself first. Then, the smile twitches at the far corners of my mouth until after I read it again and sigh.

"'I've been extremely busy with school and work, but I've thought about you often. Hopefully you're doing well and haven't called because of your own crazy schedule.'"

Tasha and I look at each other when I'm done reading. She places her hand over her heart and says exactly what I'm thinking.

"You need to call him."

"I do," I say, and then begin typing out a response to him.

Me: I thought maybe you had forgotten about me or deleted my number. Can we talk later? 5ish, my time? I'll call you.

I send it, then read it to Tasha, who has no choice but to give me her friend stamp of approval.

"I need to find something for lunch," I say. "If I don't eat now, my nerves are going to have me for dinner."

Holding my phone, I stare at it as if that will make him text back faster.

"Let's go get sushi and a nice buzz on. Alcohol as a social lubricant, which is exactly what you need since I know you're scared to talk to him," she says.

Climbing off my bed and pulling my sneakers on, I laugh at her. We both know she's joking. We are not young enough to think drinking at 11 in the morning is a good choice. Not that we haven't in the past during the rare mimosa brunch, but she has to work tonight and I apparently have a very important phone call to make.

"If this doesn't go well, then I'll take you up on drinks. But right now, I just need food."

My phone vibrates as I slip it into the pocket of my shorts.

Alexander: 5 it is. Can't wait.

*****

When the time to call him comes near, I start to panic. There's no reason to panic, but I do. Tasha has left for the hospital and it's just me wandering around the apartment with a hundred things I should be doing that I can't even find the executive function to think about let alone complete.

My gut is tied in knots and I start thinking sushi maybe wasn't the best idea when my phone vibrates on the table across the room.

I don't just run from one end of the living room to the kitchen table on the other side of the apartment, I sprint. For reference, it's not that big a space. I jump over the ottoman and nearly land on my face as the phone vibrates again because it's a call not a text or email.

It's a call from a number I don't recognize.

"Hello?" I ask tentatively, knowing full well the person on the other line could just be someone trying to sell me boat insurance or asking about my health insurance, neither of which I need right now.

"Hi. Is this Wren Leary?" I hear.

I wait a beat, my eyebrows gathering to crease my forehead, before answering. I pull the phone away and look at the number again, the area code tickling my brain.

"Yes. This is Wren. How may I help you?"

"Wren! Wonderful. This is Dylan McCabe. ... The women's softball coach in Brockport. Brockport, New York," she says, sounding unsure of herself as she continues speaking as if I don't know who Dylan McCabe is. "Do you have a few minutes to talk? I got your email, but it went to my spam folder and I just came across it."

My mouth forgot how to work. As I try to form words, I walk backward until my legs touch the ottoman and I sit down.

"Yes," I say. Clearing my throat, I say more clearly, "Yes, I have time. I'm glad you got my email. When I didn't hear anything back, I assumed you didn't want to speak to me."

"Quite the opposite. You were my only choice for the position, but you seemed so sure when you declined the college's offer. Are you certain you're interested still?"

"Absolutely. It took some soul searching to realize where I truly belong. I just want to explain what happened," I say.

She chuckles and says she's all ears, so while I have her attention, I give her the short version — the boyfriend, the breakup, the beachy vacation. I leave out the parts about Alex, and I'll leave out the parts about Coach McCabe when I talk to him, but allude to some minor connections in New York because there's the father figure situation I'm hoping to sort out eventually.

"I'm sorry for saying thanks but no thanks when we met last November, and I'm honestly shocked the position is still available, but if you're offering it, I would like to accept," I say.

Coach and I talk a lot longer than I think either of us thought we were going to. She gives me more detailed information on the position and I ask all the questions I can think of. The money and other hiring details haven't changed much, so I'll hear from the college about all that next week. By the time things are situated, and a plan put in place as much as we can manage right now, it's well past five o'clock in California.

But none of that matters.

I'm moving to New York.

Chapter 15

Alexander

It's after 10. She either forgot or something more important came up ... or she really didn't want to talk to me after all.

"It's probably that," I say to Harper. "She could tell it was a girl texting her and now she doesn't want to talk to me."

"Shut the fuck up. She could not tell it was a girl texting her. Alex, you're losing it. You're also forgetting you can call her," she says. "Call her."

"I know I can call her. I just don't want it to be a bad time."

"It's a Friday night and she was going to call you at five. It's fair to say the woman had nothing else going on this evening," Harper scolds, placing her hands on her hips and staring at me as if she's talking to a small child.

Not that I'm not acting like a small child; I just don't want to be treated like one. I glare at Harper, pick up my phone, and type out a message. Before I hit send, I look at her again.

"I would just call if I were you," she says, lifting her hands and shrugging. "If it were me across the country, pining for this handsome bachelor who I forgot to call, I would rather he stake his claim and call instead of sending a stupid message like, 'Hey, I'm sure you're busy, but I wondered if you still wanted to talk tonight.' That's something nerdy Alex would do. Show her dominant Alexander."

My cheeks heat. Dropping my head back against my headboard, I stare at the ceiling. She's right and I know she's right, and I hate that she's right.

I delete the text and tap the phone icon at the top of the chat screen.

"It's ringing. You can leave now," I say, as I place the receiver against my ear.

"Ooh, the professor voice. Kicking me out of your office to talk dirty to your long-distance girlfriend. Love it. She'll be a puddle and begging for you to come visit if you keep that up," she says, stepping backward toward the door.

"She's not my girlfriend. Yet. Now, get out," I say, but smile at her.

"I'm going to bed. I'll set up the coffee maker so you don't have to, lover boy. Goodnight," she says, winking and pulling my bedroom door closed behind her.

"Goodnight," I call out.

As the door clicks shut, I hear, "Oh my god I forgot to call. Alex, I'm so sorry. I completely lost track of time."

"Hello to you, too," I respond, the tension in my shoulders releasing. "You know, you don't have to apologize, right? I'm not upset."

"A little upset? Worried maybe?" she asks. "After all, I am about two hours late calling you."

"I would agree with that assessment," I say, relaxing into my pillows and crisscrossing my legs in front of me. "I'm sorry I waited so long to contact you. I would say it wasn't on purpose, but it wasn't on accident either. It was mostly I didn't know how to start the next conversation."

She laughs and I feel like the weeks barely existed between hugging her at the airport and now. We fall into easy conversation, catching up on the silly and mundane things that life has tossed in our direction recently. It's nearly midnight when she catches me nodding off while still trying to talk.

"Alex," she whispers into the phone.

"Yeah? I'm here," I say, though my eyes won't stay open.

"I know you're there, but maybe you should hang up and get some sleep."

"But what if I don't want to say goodnight?" I mumble.

"Then call me tomorrow to say good morning," she whispers.

"I'd rather you be here in the morning," I say, as my body gets heavier against the mattress.

"Someday," she says, but I've fallen so deeply into sleep I don't comprehend the words.

*****

I wake with a start, my phone on the bed beside me, my glasses still on my face, and my legs stiff after falling asleep in a crisscross applesauce position. Stretching, I try to remember hanging up from my conversation with Wren, but I can't.

Leaving my bedroom, I stroll half-awake into the kitchen and press the brew button on the coffee maker. The house is still quiet — the only noise the faint sound of the air conditioning kicking on — which tells me Harper is either already awake and has left for her brother's or she's still asleep. Scrubbing my hands down my face, I stare out the front window and yawn as the birds in the front yard peck at the ground, a subtle reminder to fill the birdfeeder. At 31, I sound like an old man in my own head, but then I remember how I promised Mags' Gram I would keep the feeders full because the cardinals and wood peckers like it here. On nights I've needed a break from studying and writing music, I've read Gram's birdwatching books so I know which species are coming into my yard. It helps me figure out what kind of food to buy to keep them happy.

"Who are you?" I ask, as a new to me bird lands on the feeder closest to the window. The reddish brown and buffy orange feathers throw me off because the only orange bird I've seen here is an Oriole and he was a jerk. Out loud, I catch myself saying, "Wait here while I get my book. I know I've seen you."

I rush to the living room, grab the book I left on the coffee table, and return to the kitchen window. As I leaf through the book, the bird hops around the feeder like it's waiting for me to notice. Then I land on the page I'm looking for and look back up at her before double checking what I read.

"You're fucking joking," I say, staring at the open page in front of me. I glance up at the bird again and say, "A Carolina wren."

"Is that what we're calling her now? I thought she was from California?" Harper says, shuffling up behind me and peeking around my shoulder to look out the window.

"It's a bird. But I've never seen one here at Gram's feeder, and I stand here almost every morning drinking coffee before leaving for work."

Harper rubs the sleep from her eyes and looks out the window, squinting, and then looking down at the open book on the counter.

"Huh. So it is," she says. "Do you think it's a sign?"

"A sign?"

"Like, from Gram. Maggie and I get them all the time," she says, scooting over to grab a mug down from the cupboard and filling it with coffee. "You're a music and vibrational energy kind of guy, Alex. This isn't outside your realm of thinking."

But, that's the thing. I hadn't thought about it like that. I hadn't thought about Gram asking me to take care of her birds when I moved in here and then the bluebirds showing up the day she died as a sign from her, even after she told me they were her favorite.

"So, Gram's sending me wrens?"

Harper leans against the counter, facing the opposite wall, and shrugs. Lifting her mug to her lips, she pauses, inhaling the scent of fresh brewed coffee. Her eyes flutter closed as she thinks briefly, and I need to look away.

"I think Gram is sending you a message about Wren." When I turn my head to look at her, Harper smiles at me genuinely. "How did your conversation go last night?"

Closing the bird book and setting it up against the cookbooks, I go about getting my own coffee. I make her wait until after I've taken that first sip and watch the anticipation build in her.

"It was good," I say, nonchalantly.

"Good? You give me that kind of build up for 'good'?" she says, laughing. "You're horrible."

"I'm well aware of that. But it was good. We caught up on what's happening here and there. There was a little bit of 'I miss you' and 'I hate that you live so far away.' But overall, it was just ... good to talk to her."

She makes a "hmm" noise and I would question her meaning, but I know her sounds enough to know she's accepting the idea that this is okay. And so am I. I'm okay with my friendship with Harper and whatever is happening with Wren.

"Did you ask her about the softball coach job?" she asks.

"Uh, no."

Harper turns and stares at me.

"That job is a guarantee that you'll be able to see her again. Why wouldn't you ask?"

"It didn't come up?" I say it like a question because no matter what I say, she's going to want to rip into me. It's not that I didn't think about it. I didn't want to ask and have her not want to talk about it. That could have put a major damper on the rest of the conversation. "Besides, what if she hasn't heard from the college yet?"

"Chicken."

"Turkey."

"I can't believe you aren't going to tell her you know Dylan," she says. "Or that you purposely asked Dylan if she had heard anything from Wren. She's going to find out. Women always do."

While that may be true, I'm not going to lie to her about it.

"I honestly didn't want to ask about the job in case she hadn't heard from Dylan yet. I'm not keeping information from her. Harper, I work at the college. I mentioned knowing they were looking for a coach," I say. "Wren is smart enough to understand I probably know Dylan."

"But she's going to be hurt if she finds out Dylan only found that email because you asked about it," Harper says, glaring at me.

I hate when she looks at me like that.

"Don't try to make me feel guilty. I'm not guilty of anything other than knowing the softball coach and knowing the person who was supposed to be hired to also be a softball coach," I say.

She rolls her eyes and pushes off the edge of the counter.

"Whatever, dude, it's your funeral. She's going to find out you know Dylan, that you mentioned the email, and then you're going to have to explain how you orchestrated this entire thing to get her to move here so the two of you can live happily ever after," she says.

"Orchestrated what entire thing?" I ask. "Getting her hired for the job she was already offered once?"

"Yes. That. What?" Harper spins around to glare at me again, but this time it's earned. "I thought she was asking about a position that hadn't been filled. Like she interviewed here and they said, thanks but see ya."

"It's available because she turned it down after being offered the job and Dylan didn't have any other applicants at the time. You can't get mad at me for not giving you all the details," I say. To further my defense, I add, "You've hidden details from me recently and that's not okay, so can we call it even?"

"Fine. Even. Now, tell me everything," she demands, pulling a chair from the kitchen table and plunking herself down to give me her attention.

Sighing, I grab the coffee carafe and refill my mug and hers ... and give her all of it. The job, the dad with health issues, the father she didn't know about. It doesn't matter that it isn't really my story to share. I need Harper to understand the entire thing.

"Wait, so her mom got mad at her dad, came across the entire United States for a work thing, banged a dude, ended up pregnant with Wren, fixed her marriage, and the only reason Wren knows now is because her dad had a medical crisis?" I nod. "That's a Lifetime movie right there."

We stare at one another as her ability to condense all the information down into a simple list works its way through my brain.

"Yeah, it is. Sometimes life is stranger than fiction. Now, wouldn't it be something if it turned out the dad she's searching for was someone we know?" I laugh, because New York is big and that's unlikely.

"That would be a lot to digest," she says. "Okay, so are you going to tell her you know Dylan, then? I need to know you aren't going to keep that information from her."

I play with the rim of my coffee mug, shifting in my seat to uncross and recross my legs. Reaching out to hold my ankle in place I quickly consider all the ways things could go wrong if I don't come forward and share that Dylan and I are kind of work friends.

She's older than me by a decade or more, but when I started at the college as an undergrad, she was one of those people I saw all over campus. She became a familiar face and as I tried to navigate my way through the stress of school and family, I got sucked into her office to talk about my PE credits at the recommendation of my advisor. I'm not the most athletic guy — I work out, but organized sports weren't ever my thing — so nothing sounded interesting or fun. She got me into baseball and softball, which I was able to fall in love with and get behind because of statistics and numbers. Our mentorship started there; our friendship began when I came back with my Master's as a professor.

"I'll tell her," I say without looking at Harper. "It's not that I'm keeping it a secret. I don't want her to think I had anything to do with her actually being offered the job again if that's what happens."

"Dylan didn't say she was going to offer it again?"

"Nah, she holds her cards pretty close. I think the fact I know Wren made it easier for her to not tell me," I say.

As Harper stands to leave the kitchen, she glances down and offers me a sad smile.

"It's going to be okay, Alex. She wanted the job badly enough to reach out and say she made an error," she says. "Now, just think about how, if Dylan offered it to her again, she's going to move here and need a place to stay ... and your spare bedroom is about to become available."

Chapter 16

Wren

We didn't talk on the phone over the weekend or at all during the week, but there were plenty of messages in that timeframe. Nothing too deep or dramatic and I kept the "I miss your face" comments to a minimum, even though I knew they would get me pictures.

I also didn't share my news with him. I thought about it. A lot. The last thing I want to do is tell him about all these life changing events through text messages, so I've been waiting until the paperwork is signed and things are in place. I've been looking for apartments and I've found some, but I don't have a huge savings. The cost of driving across the country alone is staggering, so trying to keep in mind the cost of rent and additional furniture is taking its toll on me.

"What are your plans for this coming week? Anything fun?" he asks when we finally have a chance to talk on Friday.

"Not really. I'm working with the team every afternoon next week, but it's early afternoon at least, and have a full physical therapy schedule. I'm trying to work as much as possible and save up as much money as I can, so ..." I say, stopping mid-thought because this wasn't what I wanted to say, but mindlessly drinking a smoothie my brain and mouth auto connected while thinking about the things I need to do. The information started coming out without my approval.

"So ...?" he says. I hear the question and I want to dismiss it. I can't. Not when he follows it with, "you can move to New York?"

The straw suctioned to my lip pops off. I set the drink down on the desk in front of me and then quickly look around the office to make sure I'm alone. It's a small PT office, so there aren't a lot of people to worry about, but I try to keep my personal and professional life separate. Having my breakfast with Alex while he has his lunch today worked out for us.

"Why would you assume I'm moving to New York?" I ask.

"I'm not assuming. I know."

"What do you mean you know?" I ask, feeling butterflies as they begin to rattle around in my abdomen.

"Wren."

"Alexander."

"When you say my big name it kind of makes this whole country in between us a problem," he says, and I feel my cheeks heat. "Dylan and I had lunch yesterday. She told me she contacted you and you accepted."

It's like hearing a record scratch as my brain comes to a screeching halt.

"You ... had lunch with Dylan. As in Coach McCabe? How do you know her and why would I become a topic of conversation?"

My inquiry must catch him off guard, and why shouldn't it? He's quiet, and I wish I could see his face. I feel like there's a lie and not seeing his face makes it difficult to know if I'm right or not. It could also be the bait-and-switch behavior I dealt with from my ex that makes me nervous and question Alex's motives. I don't tell him any of this, though, because I don't want to come across as crazy.

"We work together," he says, and I can hear the smile in his voice. It should help me relax, but it doesn't. "I got to know her when I did my undergrad work here and then when I came back to teach, we became friends. It's completely innocuous."

Okay, I can understand that. But, how do I fit into the equation?

"That only answers part of my question," I say. "How would she know to talk to you about me?"

I hear him sigh and I instinctively know I was right not to unclench my jaw.

"Am I going to be mad?" I ask.

"I don't think so, but wait to respond until I finish talking, okay?"

"Okay," I say, picking my drink up again so I have something to do with my hands.

"There was the email you sent. You told me about it when we were in North Carolina. Well, I was on campus one day last week and I stopped by to see Dylan, who I have known for years. Literal years, Wren. She's like a mentor to me. That's how I knew they were still looking for a coach. She told me last spring the person she had lined up fell through," he says. "You were that person."

I attempt to respond and he reminds me that I promised to wait, so I quickly say, "mmhmm," and close my mouth.

"So, I stop by and I mention the coaching job. She says she hasn't found anyone yet and is getting discouraged. I suggest she check her spam folder because I knew you had emailed her and she's pretty keen on second chances. We had a quick conversation about how I know you and then she clicked away and boom," he states. "Your email was in there. She didn't tell me what it said, she didn't tell me what she was going to do with the information at the time, and I didn't ask. You getting hired was not my business. Her finding the email was. That's all I did."

I sit with the information for a moment, waiting for him to continue. When he doesn't, I finally speak.

"Why didn't you tell me this when we talked last Friday?" I ask, my voice quiet.

"Because I didn't know if she was going to call you. When you didn't bring it up, I decided I would wait," he says. "But then I met up with her for lunch yesterday and she talked a blue streak about this amazing coach she's bringing in from California and how she can't wait to see what the two of you can do to get the team into better shape. Not that they aren't in good shape, but they're young. They had half the team graduate in the last year, so Dylan's been struggling. She's got outfielders who think they're beauty queens and a second baseman who has a wicked arm and would be better suited in center field."

I bite my lip and spin slowly in my rolly chair, pulling myself across the floor by my heels. Reaching the other end of the office, I turn and heel walk my way back to the desk.

"It sounds like you know a lot about my job," I say.

"Are you mad?"

Am I? Should I be? I don't think I am. If I talk to Roni or Tasha, they're going to find a reason to be mad for me, but right now this was simply him waiting for me to tell him and for that, I can't be mad. I'm not mad at Alex. I'm actually pretty damn impressed he didn't flaunt the fact he helped put Dylan's eyes on my email. Most other guys I know would have definitely strutted around with that knowledge like I owed them a thank you.

Alex isn't like most guys, though.

"No. I don't think so. I'm more upset I didn't mention it the other night. Dylan's the reason I forgot to call when I said I would," I say, chuckling. "We were on the phone a lot longer than I think she planned, but we worked out some details about me getting to New York."

"I like details," he says. Leaving the statement open for me to continue, I giggle like a child. "I also like when you laugh. I like the way your eyes light up."

"I miss your smile," I say.

The swoony feeling that sweeps through me is like a gut punch because he's still almost three thousand miles away. I need to get off the phone before I get emotional about a guy I'm just getting to know.

"When I get there, will you show me around?" I ask.

"I will be your personal tour guide. There will be coffee and baked goods and if the bookshop is open, we'll stop in for your very first piece of Brockport paraphernalia," he says. "Probably a pennant and a coffee mug. It's custom."

I laugh because it sounds silly to me, but I've been at the same college for ten years between my own schooling and now working.

"How are your parents handling your plans for the big move?" he asks.

"Um, that's a conversation we might have to save for later ..." I say.

"You haven't told them yet, have you?" he asks.

"No. Not yet. I want to make sure I have housing lined up, then my mom can't try to talk me out of it," I say. "Because once she finds out where I'm going, I'm afraid she will absolutely attempt to get me to not go. I've already had a guy successfully talk me out of my dreams once. I don't need my mother doing it, too."

"It sounds like you have a good plan. You can fill me in on all the other info later. I need to get to my office hours and you should be having another patient come in any minute now," he says. "Thanks for having breakfast with me."

"Thank you for sharing lunch with me," I reply. "Text me at eight?"

"I can't wait."

*****

Waiting until I have housing lined up was not in the cards when the envelope from Brockport fell out of my bag as I set it on the kitchen counter. It's like I told Alex my plan and Fate stepped in saying, "Fuck that. Let's do this."

"What's this?" my mom asks picking it up.

There is no lying about it. There's no reason to.

"I accepted a job in New York. It's a coaching job at a college," I say, setting my water down on the counter. "I might look into what I need to do for my physical therapy license and find some work doing that, too. In case I need to supplement my income."

The look on her face is not one I was expecting. At all. I don't know why, but I was really hoping once I got an offer and a decision had been made, she'd be excited for me. She knew I was interviewing for coach positions, that I was eyeballing New York state, but it's probable she never thought I would take this step. I've always stayed close to home.

"You're not happy. I know. I can see it all over your face. I need to do this for me, Mom," I say.

Standing in the kitchen I grew up doing homework and baking cookies in, I wish I could have broken the news to her in a way that was any easier than how I am.

"It's so far away," she says, her face stricken. "What if we need you? What if you need us?"

"I'm a flight away. Plus, at most, two connecting flights. It's not that bad," I say, attempting to ease her fears. "I can always fly home for visits and you and Dad can come out there. We have telephones and texting and video calls."

"Why there?"

"Why not? They had an opening for a coach and I want to see other parts of the country."

I keep my tone even, trying not to give anything away.

"Wren Elizabeth, you know why I ask, so don't try to play with me. Why there?" she asks again, and with the use of my middle name, I know I have to come completely clean with her.

When I initially started this journey of finding myself, it was just a dream. I hadn't decided I didn't want to stay in California or with my current team. I was checking the DNA database I submitted my spit to after the medical testing revealed my dad isn't my dad and wondering if I was ever going to have a long-lost cousin pop up in my inbox. I haven't. It's like his family has never taken a DNA test in their lives, which, I suppose, could be a really good thing. It means the potential of being related to major criminals is way lower. That's what I tell myself. Maybe they just are completely okay with not knowing all the percentages of their heritage.

I haven't told her about any of that. You can ask why, but it's honestly because I'm a grown woman and as much as I love my mother, there have always been certain things I haven't talked to her about. Mainly sex, all those times I smoked marijuana in high school, and most recently how badly I want to know who I came from.

I pull her over to the kitchen table and have her sit down. I take the seat across from her, looking in her eyes and holding her hands.

"Mom, I love you and Dad so much. But, there's a part of me that's out there and I'd like to find him. I'd like to know if I look like him at all or if I have siblings or if he even wants to know about me," I say. "And if he doesn't? That's okay, too, but I need to know."

She stares at me, a tear making its way down her cheek, and then slowly blinks as I try to figure out what else I should say.

"You could do all that from here, though," she says, her voice barely above a whisper.

Nodding, I agree.

"I can't argue with that, but I also need a change. This last relationship? He really made me forget who I am. I forgot what I wanted to be and then when I was busy figuring it out, he made me think that's not what I wanted after all. The mind games he played were pretty brutal. I want a clean start and an adventure," I say. "I'll get that in Brockport."

She sighs heavily and, letting go of my hands, grabs a napkin to blow her nose.

"I hate this. You'll be there all alone, Wren," she says. "I won't be able to stay long after getting you settled. You're not going to know anyone."

Biting my lip, I remain silent while she dabs her eyes. First, I'm not expecting her to come out to get me settled. Not because I wouldn't welcome it. I'm just feeling hyper-independent. Second, I do know someone there.

"So, when you and Dad stayed here and I went on that quickie vacation with Veronica and her dad's family, I met someone who actually is from that area," I say.

"A man somebody?"

"Yes."

"And you hooked up with him and now you're moving across the country?"

Staring at her, open-mouthed, it takes me a second to regain my composure to explain everything to her. Asking her to not speak until I am done, just like Alex did to me earlier, is way less intimidating than I expect, but I need her to hear me out. Her abiding by my request? Unheard of, but there's always an exception.

As I finish explaining to her how Alex and I met, that he recognized me and I recognized him, I attended his cousin's wedding with him and he was a complete gentleman, that we've kept in contact, and that we absolutely did not "hook up," she looks more at peace with the idea that I know a dude in New York.

"I'm still in the process of figuring out the logistics. Once I know, you'll know."

"Are you going to get settled before you try to find him?"

My thoughts pivot from Alex to my biological father, and the fact I have so little to go on.

"I'm not even sure how to begin looking. You don't remember anything about him, Mom. It's going to be difficult to find out anything when you can't even remember his name," I say, feeling some sort of emotion rise up in me that I haven't made peace with yet.

"That might have been misleading. Things were pretty rough after you found out and Dad's health was not okay, so I may have omitted some information," she says.

"You … what?" I say staring at her. "What sort of omission."

She slowly begins shredding the clean napkin she picks up. Long, slow rips. Delay. Delay. Delay.

"Mom?"

"Uh, yeah. I know his name. His first name, at least," she says, and I feel my body go cold. She lied? Before I can open my mouth, she raises her hand to stop me. "He's a veteran, but that part you knew. He served during the Gulf War. The first one. Desert Storm. I was newly in admin for Veterans Affairs and there was a conference in New York. He came as an advocate for the people he served with. He volunteers at the hospitals, spends his time with the old guys from World War II and the men who served closer to his time in the military."

"You're using present tense. Do you … have you kept in touch with him?" I ask before finally closing my mouth and swallowing.

She shakes her head vehemently, her eyes wide as if the question alarms her.

"No, actually, I just —" she says, stopping and sighing. "I sometimes get caught up wondering where he is and it's like I haven't moved beyond that weekend. So, things come out as if I still know him."

She's lied to me once, why should I think she's telling the truth now?

"I swear to God, I haven't spoken to Will since the morning I left him sleeping in that hotel room, Wren," she says, lifting her hands in defense. "I don't know his last name. All I know is he was from Western New York."

"What part? It's a large section of the state, Mom," I ask, feeling my gut react as she casts her eyes downward. Raising my voice, I ask, "Mom? What part?"

"Brockport ..."

We sit in stunned silence, her because she's known all along and would have to tell me. And me? Because if he's still there I might have already met him. How many places did I go when I was there for those couple of days? The coffeeshop. The bakery. I stopped by an art studio called TopCoat. The bookshop. I was all over the college campus.

"Of all the places you would find a coaching job ..."

"How old is he?" I haven't asked a lot of questions out of fear that it would hurt her and Dad if I wanted to know more, but now I want to know all of it. Everything. "Was he older than you? Younger? What did he look like?"

"Wren, stop. You're going to try to overload yourself on information I don't have. Those questions, I can answer, but I really didn't get to know him well. It was a weekend, and we weren't exactly talking the entire time," she says.

Horrified, but amused, I smile. Then laugh. And when I stop laughing, it's because I'm crying and she's left her chair to come to my side of the table. She pulls me from my seat, turns us around and sits down, yanking me onto her lap to hold me like I'm an infant. Maybe I am. I'm still just a child. Her child. And Will's. I can't get my emotions under control. I've held in everything — every thought, feeling, and question about this man.

As my breathing finally begins to regulate, she tucks my hair behind my ears. Looking me straight in the eyes she says something that makes me cry harder all over again.

"Every time I look in your eyes, I see him all over again," she says, a tear tracing down her cheek. "He gave me the greatest souvenir from that trip. He gave me you."

Throwing my arms around her, we hug in silence until I hear my dad enter the kitchen. I hear the sound of paper being picked up and unfolded.

"You told her where he is?" my dad asks. His tone unalarmed, like he knew this day would finally come, just not how it would happen.

"I told her where he was when we met. Now, it's up to Wrenny if she wants to find him," she says over my shoulder. "It shouldn't be difficult. She's moving to Brockport. Our girl is going to go coach some top-notch softball."

Turning my head, I catch a glimpse of my father as he steps up behind my mother. He places a gentle, solemn, kiss to the crown of my head and whispers in my hair.

"I see that. You're going to be amazing out there, kid. I can't wait to see you in action," he says. "As for Will ... well, if you find him, I would like to thank him for creating such a cool person for me to love and raise."

Lifting my head so I can see him, the first thing I notice is a smile. Not a sad one. Pride. He's so proud of me. And why wouldn't he be? He's my dad.

"You aren't mad?"

"Mad? Hell no. I was mad almost thirty years ago, but we resolved that. I'm grateful now. The past is the past, and if we didn't have that, we wouldn't have you," he says. "Even if my health hadn't gone haywire, we should have told you long before now. But, honestly, once you were born, it didn't matter who made you and I sort of forgot."

"You forgot?" mom asks, a bemused smile making its way to her lips.

"Poor choice of words," he responds, chuckling. "It was no longer something at the forefront of my mind. We had a baby and she was perfect. There were better things to be concerned with than who she was biologically related to. Now, it's a little bit of a different story."

That's putting it lightly, but Mom and I agree. I stand from her lap and hug my dad. I think he needs one from me as much as I do from him and his big bear arms hold me snug against his chest as he kisses my head again.

"When are you supposed to start out there?" he asks.

"A few weeks. Coach McCabe wants me to start working with the team right after Labor Day. I'd like to be there with a week to get settled before diving in, but I haven't found an apartment yet," I say, shoving my hands in my pockets and walking over to lean against the counter. I need some distance, and I need them to have physical closeness with one another right now so I can see with my own eyes they're okay.

It's not every day you learn your only child is moving across the country or that they are going to be in potential biological father territory. It's a lot for all of us to come to terms with, but they've also had time to know his name and his possible location, whereas I have not.

I'm okay. I just keep telling myself I'm fine as we continue to talk about my move, my new job, and looking into how to use my PT license in New York. Things are proceeding as normal.

"And what about this man you met in North Carolina?" my mom asks, glancing at Dad. "You said he's also in the area you're moving to."

"Coincidence?" my dad asks, raising an eyebrow at me, knowing full well I don't believe in them.

"I don't know her," I say, smiling. "But, yes. It's pretty crazy. His cousins and Veronica actually used to vacation at the same time in the Outer Banks right next door to one another. He was there for one of the cousins' weddings when I went out last month."

"What's his name?" Dad presses. "Is he a decent guy? Does he have a job or is he a bum?"

I cover my face with my hands to hide the smile. It's been a long time since I was grilled by my father about a guy. He got to know the last one I was with and wasn't super impressed with him, but then again, in the end, neither was I.

"Alex. Yes. He's a music professor at the college and working on his doctorate. Not a bum, promise," I say, pushing off the counter. "Is the interrogation over? I should probably get home and start trying to find a place to live and pack. Alex gave me the name of a local guy with apartments available, so I have a call in to him and waiting to hear back. I have no idea how I'm going to move across the country when I hardly survived moving across the county from here."

My mom pulls me in for a hug and kisses my cheek as Dad kisses the side of my head.

"We'll figure it out," she says. "We always do."

Chapter 17

Alexander

Finishing up a summer class while prepping for the beginning of a new semester of teaching and also working on the data for my thesis has me running from one end of Monroe County to the other nearly every day. But today, I'm sitting at the nursing home with Harper and we're playing music from 1937 — Tommy Dorsey, Bob Crosby, Frank Sinatra.

As I sit in an activity room with a half dozen residents who grew up hearing these styles, some of them seem a little more cognizant of their surroundings. There's a little more ... something in the room with us. Could it be the puzzles? Sure. But last week they were doing puzzles without music and most of the same people sat nearly motionless for the hour I observed.

Today, I rolled in a record player I found in the basement of my house along with a box of old vinyl that Gram had obviously stored down there years ago. It's like a time capsule. I'm grateful Maggie is okay with me utilizing what I've discovered. Once I'm done with this project, anything that needs to be restored will be and then it's going to my office.

As Frank croons a melody today, I watch one of the elderly women slowly tap her foot on the floor as she touches a puzzle piece. She picks it up. Brings it close to her face, then sets it back on the table. She taps her finger on the piece, then picks up another and places it beside the first, tapping the interlocking edges together. She smiles at herself and I watch as she becomes obviously pleased. She continues tapping her foot on the floor in time with the music.

"Huh. Interesting," I say, quietly and to myself as I take notes.

"What's interesting?" Harper says in my ear.

Glancing at her, she lifts her head from her ereader and gives me an expectant look. She's on her lunch break, but chose to spend it with me. Not because I need a babysitter, but she was either going to sit in her car and read or sit in the breakroom and read. The location was the only thing to change.

"Things are happening," I say. "She's more lucid."

She looks in the same direction as me and when I look at her out of the corner of my eye, I watch the smile form.

"That is amazing," she says, quietly. "She usually won't even attempt to feed herself."

As I continue observing, I see more of the same from a couple other residents. It's not groundbreaking, but it's a start. I take notes about the songs playing, who's responding to the tunes, and how. Is it just a foot tapping, or is there a head nodding? Is someone who was sitting doing nothing during one song suddenly participating in some way? What changed between the two songs to elicit a change in behavior? While music therapy is used in a lot of ways and in a lot of places, it hasn't been used here. It hasn't been utilized with these people. My goal is to find out how it can make life better in this home — between old recordings and eventually by introducing instruments and, potentially, my own composition pieces.

Harper taps my leg and stands up, tipping her watch so I can see the time. Lunch is over.

"See you tonight," she says, before wandering away toward one of the nurses. I watch her cross the room and feel a sense of pride bloom in my chest as she says to the woman in white scrubs, "I think he's onto something."

The nurse looks at me and we share a smile as Harper leaves. I go back to observing, giving myself another twenty minutes before winding down for the day. An hour of observation for each music genre or decade seemed to be adequate when I was putting together my research proposal, and considering I'll be doing several of these activities, an hour per session was my max.

As I begin placing my pens, notepad, and laptop into my bag, my phone vibrates in the pocket of my slacks.

Brian Stratford: Since Harper is moving into the apartments, does that mean I can tell people you have a room for rent?

I read the message and try to comprehend, but I'm trying to figure out if I should tell Wren there's space at my house if she's still looking for somewhere to rent. I'm stuck between wanting to repaint and make sure there's no sign of a woman having lived with me and being lazy while dealing with the possible fallout.

The phone vibrates again.

Brian Stratford: Because I have someone looking for a place. I would set her up in my apartments, but Harper has one and the second one got scooped up this morning by a lady who works at the college.

He's got my interest. I just gave Wren his info, so maybe she was able to get the other apartment he had ready, but her living next door to Harper would make for a very interesting dynamic.

Me: *A lady who works at the college? Anyone I know?*

Brian Stratford: *Probably not. She works in student affairs. But if you're renting out Harper's room, I've got another person looking.*

I shove the phone back into my pocket and finish gathering the records and player before responding. Waiting at the door for the nurse who was overseeing activities today to pass, she wheels my foot-tapping puzzle woman past me. A cool, papery touch to my hand catches my attention. Looking down, her cloudy blue eyes stare up at me as she brings her other hand to cover and clasp my fingers.

"Thank you, young man" she says, her voice a hoarse whisper filled with emotion. "I love to dance. Come visit again."

"It's my pleasure. I'll be back in a few days with something else," I say.

"Wonderful."

It is, isn't it, I think as she drops my hand and the nurse pushes her through the door and down the long hallway. Maybe what I'm doing will have an impact on her, at least in the short term.

Falling into step behind them, I make my way around the nurse's station and then make a right down the hall to my exit. The heat of the day warms my face and as I finish putting everything in my car, my phone vibrates again.

Brian Stratford: *If you don't like the person I send your way, I'll have the next unit ready in a few months.*

Me: *Sure. Send them my info. It'll help with the bills for a bit if nothing else.*

*****

By the time I make it home for the evening, the sun has nearly set. I'm ready to pass out, but between spending most of the evening in my office on campus and part of the morning at the nursing home, I need to shower.

"Do you want food?" Harper asks as I trudge down the hall past her bedroom. "I made mac and cheese."

I stop, take two steps backward, and look into her room. There are bins and boxes. She's clearly been busy since leaving work this afternoon. I don't mention it. I've come to terms with her decision to move out, but that doesn't mean I have to like it. Regardless, when the time comes, I'll help her move her stuff to the apartment and try to keep my thoughts to myself.

"Boxed or homemade?" I ask.

"Homemade. My mom's recipe."

"I'm showering and then eating," I say, a yawn escaping.

"Do you think you'll be able to stay awake that long?"

Shrugging, I continue my way down the hall, past the small extra room I use as a home office, to my bedroom. I drop my laptop bag on the bed, set the record player and box of records down on a small work table, then proceed to slowly unbutton my shirt.

"You okay?" she asks from the doorway.

Tossing the shirt on the back of my chair, I pull my undershirt from the waistband of my pants and then over my head.

"Not really. I'm exhausted. Today wasn't a lot but it was a lot. I don't know how you do it every day. Being there with them and not feeling ... sad."

Loosening my belt and pulling it from the loops, I catch her eye. It's not on purpose. She's standing in my room; I just want to go take a shower and she knows that.

"It's easy for me. It was a change from working with kids. I get to see the end of a life typically lived well instead of the beginning when they haven't had a chance to live at all. I hated watching kids struggle. At least this way, I get to hear the stories from their entire life because they've had an entire life."

It's this moment when I really understand why our relationship worked for her and I almost wish things were the way they were months ago when we were a way to relieve stress for one another. Almost.

I watch her swallow as I undo the button on my slacks, her eyes flitting to where my hand rests and my cock twitches.

"We can't," I say, softly.

"I know," she responds, lifting her gaze to mine. "It's been a long week. I'm still trying to let go of old habits. I'll heat up dinner for you."

Harper slips out of my bedroom, leaving me confused. I could have just kept having fun. We didn't have to have more. I didn't have to have more.

But ... I did. I do. I want more and Harper isn't the one to share that with me. I keep talking myself through all the truths and the whys as I close the bathroom door and strip off the rest of my clothes. The rush of warm water washes over me as I step beneath the spray, helping to bring some clarity to the situation.

Harper is going to move out in the next week. My classes start in two weeks. Wren is moving to town in less than three. Brian has someone interested in an apartment he doesn't have ready. I need to paint Harper's room and should probably deep clean the bathroom and the kitchen.

I'm still running through the mental checklist of things that need to be done at home, work, and school when I step into the kitchen. Pulling a clean T-shirt over my head, I hear a car pull out of our driveway.

My water bottle has been refilled and there's a note beneath it. I pick the paper up and stare at it, feeling the emptiness of the house surround me as I read her words.

"Gone to Rick's. Sawyer needs help moving plants for the weekend sale. See you tomorrow."

There's a bowl of mac and cheese sitting on the table nestled between a spoon and a napkin, and before I bother to sit, I go back to my room to grab notebooks and pens. As a second thought, I add my phone to the pile of materials and head back to the kitchen.

Spreading my work out on the table in front of me, I begin going through my data, taking bites of food between pages and glancing at my phone every now and then. When I look at my watch and the clock shows it's close to eleven, I take in the mess of papers I've created and the half-eaten bowl of macaroni I pushed to the side. Data for my research, lesson plans for the classes I'm teaching this semester, and the music theory text I've begun to keep with me at all times just because are scattered about.

The faint sound of my phone vibrating pulls my brain in another direction and I lift papers and books until I find it buried where I set it down two hours ago.

Wren's name flashes on the screen and before answering, I look at my watch again.

"Hey. I didn't expect to hear from you tonight," I say as soon as the call connects.

"Hey," she says, but there's something off in her tone.

"What's wrong?" I ask on instinct.

"I called that Brian guy you told me about, the one with the apartments," she says, her voice rising. "He got back to me, but said he just rented the last apartment he has available and won't have anything else for a few months at least. I'm kind of screwed."

"There's got to be other places close by," I say, beginning the process of picking up my papers.

"Oh, yeah, I know there are. Brian was really helpful and gave me the number of a person with a room for rent, but he wasn't sure when it would be available," she says. "The guy's ex-girlfriend is in the process of moving out and into one of Brian's apartments. So, I figured I would go ahead and try this number he gave me. The thing is, as soon as I typed it into my phone your name popped up."

"Shit," I respond.

"You think?"

"I can explain," I say, setting my papers back on the table.

Scrubbing my hand down my face, I try to figure out how to make sure she understands Brian's misguided ex-girlfriend comment.

"Yeah, I figured you would be able to since you never once mentioned a girlfriend, or even living with a woman. That seems like it would have been an important detail to toss in there between the miss yous and wish you were heres we've been exchanging for weeks. Weeks, Alexander. Weeks."

While she's talking, I begin pacing the living room, until I feel stifled and make a beeline for the door leading to a screened in front porch. I give Wren time to take a deep breath, I wait until I know she's done talking, and as I sit in the oversized armchair Maggie left at the house, I realize the absolute best thing to do is tell her the complete truth.

"Harper and I were living together because we both needed a place. One of my best friends, Maggie, owns the house. Maggie is Harper's sister-in-law," I begin. "We weren't in a committed, serious relationship, Wren. We never defined our relationship."

I hear her let out a low groan, a slow, "oh," when it clicks.

"She's one of my closest friends, and Brian referring to her as my ex is a bit of a stretch since that implies we were exclusively together. Now, I'm not going to say that wasn't something I wanted at one point, but that's not been the case for a while now," I say.

She's quiet. As I wait for her to say something — anything — a yawn sneaks out. I was not planning on having this conversation so soon with her. At least, I was hoping it wasn't something that would be brought up prior to her moving to New York.

"I'm a fairly level-headed person, Alex. If you say you haven't been with her in a while and she's actually moving out, fine. Great," she says. Her voice suddenly takes on a quality that sounds equally as exhausted as mine. "It doesn't solve my issue of not having a place to move to. You knew I was looking. Why didn't you just tell me you have a room available in your house? I'll pay my share. I'm not looking for any handouts. My last resort is staying with Coach McCabe until I have something."

I start laughing. It's not funny as in humorous, but I'm just tired enough to see how ridiculous it is that I didn't tell her. Why would I withhold that information from her? Especially when I knew she was searching for a place to live out here. I give myself a couple beats to think about it as I regain control.

"I didn't want to come off as creepy. Or needy," I say. "How was it going to look to you if, because of me, Dylan reached out to offer you the job and then I magically had a fully furnished bedroom for rent. Wren, that feels like the premise of a horror movie not a stable friendship or relationship. It didn't feel right."

Laying my head in my hand, I rest my elbow on the arm of the chair and prop my feet up on the ottoman in front of me. Slowly I feel my body begin sinking into the comfort of the chair when she speaks again.

"Fair," she says, her voice softening. "But now I need a place to stay. Alex, my job starts in eighteen days and I have nowhere to go."

"So come home to me."

"Promise to not be a serial killer?" she asks, reminiscent of our evening wandering with ice cream in the Outer Banks.

I hear the smile in her voice and match her energy, saying, "Scouts honor."

Chapter 18

Wren

How did we already end up at the end of August? The last several days have been a whirlwind since I left California for New York and I haven't been able to stop my brain long enough to catch my breath.

It's only been two weeks since the decision was made to move in with Alex.

No. That's not exactly correct. I'm not "moving in" with him. I'm moving into the house he also rents. I've talked to Maggie Rogers, who owns the house, and will sign the lease when I arrive. We decided the best choice for the time being would be a month-to-month agreement since it's a bedroom with shared common spaces and with a man. It felt like the better option, because what if Alex and I don't mesh as housemates? I don't want to be stuck in a lease with a friend I can't cohabitate well with. Because we're friends. Nothing more, nothing less, at this point in time.

My dad is weird about the whole situation, but I don't have time to be. Not the lease situation. The Alex Situation. That's what he's been referring to it as.

"So, the Alex Situation is interesting."

"When you get there, what's the Alex Situation going to be like?"

"Keep your mom informed about the Alex Situation so I don't have to worry."

"I don't know if the Alex Situation is the best idea."

I asked him to please stop, and he has for the most part. Catching himself now and then and rephrasing his choice of words has been refreshing to watch.

But ... I do wonder how the Alex Situation is going to play out.

As if on cue, my phone rings, cutting off my audiobook.

"What's up?" I ask by way of answering.

"How long until you're going to be here?" he asks, sounding mildly out of breath, and I resist the urge to ask what he's doing.

"The GPS says twenty-two minutes, but I take that as a challenge and plan to beat it by five at the very least," I say.

He laughs, and a shiver slides through my body at the depth of his voice. Blood throbs where it hasn't in weeks and I refuse to think about what he's done to me without realizing it.

"Just be careful. It's a beautiful day out and with people returning to campus, it feels like there are more cops hanging around town," he says, lowering his voice. "I just don't want you starting your adventure here with a speeding ticket."

Ugh, he's sweet and sexy.

It's starting to feel like the Alex Situation is definitely going to be a situation.

"I will make sure I do the speed limit. Now, can I get back to my book? You interrupted at a very good part," I say.

"Oh, really," he says, his voice dropping even deeper than before. "Is it the part where he slowly climbs up her body, beginning at the foot of the bed, trailing his fingers along her legs until she drops her knees and opens up for him? Is she whimpering while waiting for him to give in and place the flat of his tongue against—"

"Alex! Oh my God, you need to stop," I say, slamming on the brakes and coming to a standstill mere inches from the car in front of me. My chest heaves from the adrenaline and the anticipation of what he was saying. "You ... I need you to stop."

He chuckles.

"So, you don't want to hear about—"

"Nope. No. Not right now. No, thank you. I need to concentrate on not dying in a fiery car crash while you talk filthy little things over my car speaker," I say in a rush. "Nope."

"See you in fifteen," he says, a deep laugh touching all my sensitive parts all over again, and then the line goes quiet. Seconds later my book picks up where it left off.

"Take a deep breath and let go of the fear. All it does is hold you back," the narrator says. "It's time to take control of the situation ..."

*****

The GPS indicates I need to turn left off the main road leaving the village, then a mile down my destination will be on the right. As I slowly roll down the street all I see are trees, until I come over a small crest and there on the

North side of the road is the most adorable little ranch style house. There are flowers out front and bird feeders. A Blue Jay flies off as I pull into the driveway and park beside a Chevy Equinox that matches my own.

"Interesting," I say to myself.

Taking a moment to pause my book, gather my water bottle, and pick up the couple of coffee cups that need to be thrown out, I prepare to step out of my car and into the first day of my new home. Before I can get the door open, Alex appears from behind the house. I take in the sight — dirt on his hands, dirt smeared on his forehead, a filthy T-shirt and cargo shorts ... and bare feet.

Climbing out of the car, I drop my trash and water bottle on the seat and step around the door to get a better look at him. It hasn't been that long, but it's been too long at the same time, and I don't know how it's possible to feel like time stood still while moving at lightning speed.

He pushes his glasses up higher on the bridge of his nose and then I get the biggest smile, a wordless greeting, as he rushes toward me. Wrapping his arms around my waist, he lifts me into the air against him in a tight hug. My arms encircle his shoulders as I hang onto him as if it's been years since we saw one another and I don't want to let go.

"I have missed you so much," he says, his voice a low growl, as he slowly begins sliding me down his body until my toes touch the ground.

My fingers find their way into the hair at the back of his head and I tenderly grasp his neck, feeling way too many feelings for so early in the day. For not knowing enough about him.

"I'm here now, though," I say, smiling up at him as my arms slip down his biceps and I slide them around him, pulling his body against me again for another hug.

He smells like sunshine, sweat, and mud and I fall in love with the scent. Kissing the top of my head, his chest rises and falls with a deep, relaxing breath as we stand in the driveway in this weirdly familiar embrace. I'm not used to it but have missed it so strongly it was going to pull me across the country one way or another. Job or no job, I think I was going to end up here at some point.

But, at the same time, I really hope I didn't just complicate the Alex Situation more.

No, that's not true. I absolutely want to complicate it. I want to complicate it in the worst ways. Right now. But no. I stop the thoughts from coming at me. I can't get carried away with what this isn't. This is a new friendship.

We're just ... roommates. That's all we are right now. That's all we've alluded to this being, despite the couple of kisses in the Carolinas. I have an entire career to focus on and so does he. We don't have time to be more.

"What do you have that needs to come in right this second?" he asks. "I'll start grabbing bags."

His chest vibrates against me as he talks and I absentmindedly squeeze him tighter. The months between North Carolina and now were long, and there's a need inside me to not let go of him.

"I don't even know. It's mostly clothes and books and empty coffee cups."

So many coffee cups.

"And I haven't peed since Erie."

"Pennsylvania?"

"The one and only. I hit that last rest stop before New York, grabbed another coffee, some gummy worms, and sunflower seeds, and was on my way," I say, looking up at him.

I notice his fingers trailing tiny circles on my back and it feels like my heart is glowing.

"Bathroom is through the kitchen and down the hall. First door on the right. Go. I'll get stuff from the car," he insists. Kissing my forehead, he pushes me away and immediately goes to the back of my car. I stand still, staring at him, shocked at the way he just took matters into his own hands. When he notices I haven't moved, he says, with a slight growl in his tone, "Bathroom."

"Yes, sir," I say. I turn and hightail it toward the house without a clue where I'm actually going, but refrain from stopping to ask for more detailed directions. I can feel the heat in my cheeks and don't want him to have any idea how his voice affected me. Or maybe it's that I don't want to admit out loud that it affected me at all.

I enter the breezeway through the front door and stop immediately. It's a large open area with a set of stairs leading to what I assume is a basement and directly in front of me is a door to the backyard. While the inside door is open, there's a screen door allowing a gentle breeze to waft through and the scent of freshly dug dirt infiltrates my nostrils. It's not that I'm not used to smelling dirt — my life is spent on a softball field — but this is farm dirt and it's Alex. It's the way Alex smells. He doesn't smell like the ocean and cologne like he did the last time I saw him.

The ocean was always like my second home, but this? I can get used to this.

The back hatch of my car slams and I realize I have hardly moved and, while the anticipation of his voice deepening makes my body react in ways I'm not accustomed to, I still need to use the bathroom. I jump up the steps to my left and through the main door of the house into the kitchen. There's a hallway to my right and I walk the few feet until I come to the first opening.

I close the door just as Alex enters the house.

It's so childish, but I feel as if I'm hiding from him. Is it because everything is new and I'm adjusting? Probably not, I tell myself. It's absolutely because I need to give myself time to get my hormones in check. I take my time washing my hands and then splashing my face with water to help calm my nerves. My phone vibrates on the counter as I'm drying my hands and I pick it up, answering as I lift it to my ear.

"Do you want everything to come in?" he asks.

His voice echoes beyond the bathroom door, so I slowly open it and begin walking back down the hall toward the kitchen.

"Eventually everything will need to come inside," I say.

Reaching the doorway, I lean against the frame and watch him as he stands at the sink, looking out the front window.

"True," he says. "I wasn't sure if you wanted to bring things in yourself or if it was okay if I do it while you start unpacking."

"You're welcome to do it, but I'm a big girl. I can handle it," I say, watching as his shoulders stiffen.

Alex turns to look at me, still holding the phone to his ear as he leans against the counter.

"I never said you can't handle it," he says, taking a step toward me.

I stand my ground, phone to my left ear, and cross my right arm over my chest, clasping my bicep and holding on so I don't start talking with my free hand.

"It was implied," I say, goading him.

He steps closer. This is no longer friendly territory and I'm well aware of the tension in the room. We created it over the course of weeks with texts and phone calls. He thinks I'm being a brat. He takes another step.

"I would never imply you're weak, Wren," he says, and I swallow hard at the sound of my name leaving his lips.

"You're growly and I like it more than I should," I say, the words slipping out of my mouth before I have a chance to think.

His eyes widen and darken as understanding hits him. His bare toes touch the tips of my sneakers as he steps into my personal space and I straighten my spine to look up at him. Pulling the phone from his ear and ending the call, he reaches for my phone as well, and slides them both into the pocket of his shorts.

"Don't tempt me to use it too much," he says, leaning in and kissing just below my ear.

I stop breathing and let the feeling wash over me as my body heats. Holy shit. I can't move, and thankfully the doorframe continues to hold me up, because without it I would be a puddle on the floor. Where was this Alex in North Carolina? Or even on the phone?

Roommates. We're roommates, I remind myself.

He knows what he's doing, too. I catch a glimpse of his smile as he pulls back slightly, before he leans in again.

"Second door on the right. I'll get more stuff from the car while you start unpacking," he says before stepping backward and turning to go out to the breezeway.

I smirk and cover my face as I watch him walk away, pulling at his waistband to adjust his shorts.

Chapter 19

Alexander

"Yes, she's here. No, you can't meet her yet. Please don't let yourself into the house and scare her," I say.

"But it's my house!" Maggie yells, followed by a giggle.

I blow out a heavy sigh. I helped Wren get everything from her car into the house. Since she was going to head over to campus after calling her parents to let them know she was here safely, we left all the softball equipment in the back seat. She's hellbent on getting a feel for and memorizing where everything is before her first official day. I offered to walk around campus with her, but she's adamant she wants to do it herself and I give her a lot of credit. I would have jumped at the chance if someone who knows that campus inside and out offered to show me around when I first started college.

She's not starting college though. She's starting a job. Not only that, this has been a huge change for her. Between flying out last year for interviews and then taking nearly a week to drive across the country on her own, I guess learning her way around a school isn't so big in the grand scheme of things.

With that in the back of my head, the decision for me to go find some work to do was made. I left before her, and before anything else could happen. There hasn't been any kind of discussion as to "us" and I don't dare mess up her new job and her new life in New York. She's my roommate, and we're definitely attracted to one another, but I don't want another Harper.

"Why do you have me on speaker? I'm well aware it's your house."

"And I need her to sign the lease."

"Damn it." She laughs loudly and it's obnoxiously loud in my car. "I know you don't need me there, but she also was getting ready to go see about meeting up with Dylan and watching the team practice. Do you want to come over tonight?"

"I know you well enough to know you aren't gatekeeping the new girl, Alex. Plus, you're on speaker because I'm prepping for events this week and can't find my earbuds. I can't hand my stuff off to anyone. Delilah and Genevieve are swamped, and Sawyer is busy with the greenhouse right now," she says by way of explaining she won't come over unannounced because her hands are full. "I'll call Wren and set up a time."

I make a mental note to get her extra earbuds for Christmas.

"Perfect. Now leave me alone, I just got to the office and I need to use my brain," I say. It comes across meaner than I intend, particularly since I meant it to sound funny and I absolutely had a clipped tone.

"Don't be grumpy just because you're horny," she says, laughing.

"Who's horny?" Maverick says in the background.

"Alex. Wren just got here and he needed to escape to the office to get his boner under control."

"Poor guy."

"Poor guy? Man, you're all alike," Maggie says, laughing. "He's gone way longer than you have not getting any, so I don't think you can commiserate."

"After we had the baby, we didn't for—"

"Are the two of you done making fun of me, yet?" I interrupt loudly. "Because my ego is starting to feel a little bruised."

They continue talking amongst themselves in the background. I need to get out of my car and try to get a little work done, so I just yell over them that I'm hanging up and will talk to them both later.

"Bye Alex!" Maggie yells, and then the line goes dead.

Throwing my backpack on over my shoulders so my hands are free, I grab the record player and a tote of vinyl LPs and slam the door shut with my foot. I was in such a rush to leave the house after taking everything else out of Wren's car that I threw on the first shoes I could find — a pair of flip flops I left in the breezeway after getting back from Jayden's wedding. I rarely wear sandals, but I didn't want to take the time to wash the dirt from my feet and then let them dry before putting socks and shoes on. This is fine.

"Mr. Makris, do you need a hand?" I hear the voice behind me to my left, so I turn slightly and find Dylan coming up beside me. "You look like you're … stressed. I'm not used to seeing you stressed."

I ask her to take the record player off the top of the tote, and it makes the load light enough I can carry on a conversation while walking. She asks me about my research and I ask about fall training as we walk to my office in the music department building.

It's not uncommon to see her on this side of campus considering she lives close by and unless it's snowing or raining, she walks or bikes to the athletic center. I just wasn't expecting to see her today.

"Maybe you should come get on the tee and work off your frustration," she says. "Release some endorphins and help you relax a bit."

Before responding, I set the tote down and unlock the door to my office.

"Were you planning on putting that in there?" she asks, motioning to the slightly cramped space.

There are a couple chairs that have books piled on them, the bookshelves are filled with texts and folders of loose music, it looks messy and I know it's a lot at first glance.

"I have enough room. I'll just have to rearrange a few shelves," I say, shrugging. "I should probably take the drum set home. It takes up a lot of space and I don't play in here. Or I'll take the records back home with me after I'm done today."

"I would start with putting the drums somewhere else," she snickers. "Plus, you play guitar. Where are all of those?"

"My babies? They don't live here. With one exception, but she stays in her case when I'm not playing," I say.

The look we exchange is comical and complicated. She understands the clutter. It's not the first time she's been in my office. She also understands that I know where everything is when I need it. Could I be more organized? Yes. Do I want to be more organized? Also yes, but I haven't taken the time.

"What time is practice?" I ask by way of changing subjects, even though I have rarely asked about her practice schedule in the past. While waiting for her response, I start unpacking a few of the records I wanted to listen to so I can make notes for my research, but look up again when she doesn't speak after a few beats. A smile from her throws me off. "What? Isn't the team practicing today?"

"Nothing. You're just very interested in softball these days."

"I like some sports, Dylan," I say.

"Oh yeah? Not usually this much though," she says, smirking. "When is Wren arriving?"

Busted.

"It has nothing to do with her," I say, standing up straighter. "But ... she's here."

Instead of arguing with me, she turns and walks out of my office, only to poke her head back in at the last moment.

"You're a shitty liar, but I figured. You're weird today. Drinks on Friday. We'll talk then," she says, and disappears again.

*****

    I make all the excuses to get as much work done in my office as I possibly can. After a morning filled with intro classes and freshmen students, then working in Gram's gardens while waiting for Wren to arrive, I should have taken the rest of the day to work on nothing at all. Every plan for the semester that I need to have ready is ready. My grad classes are in full swing and I'm on track to finish research by December so I can put my dissertation together and defend it next spring.
    Really, I didn't need to come to the office.
    I couldn't remain in the house or go back to the garden, though. I needed something that was repetitive and that is music. It's the thing I need to feed my soul and calm my mind. There's too much going on in there.
    Kicking off my sandals, I reach into the case beside my desk and pull out the acoustic guitar. It was the first one I bought with my own money, and I keep her in my office because I have her twin at home. Yes, I have two identical guitars — both Martin LX1E — and I don't think that's a bad thing. It's like the girls who have multiple copies of the same book because one is to read and one is signed … except I don't keep either of my guitars as trophies. They get equal play time.
    Propping my feet up on the windowsill, I pick at the strings. Nothing new comes out, just noise. It's not a song, just notes. I've been playing them over and over for weeks. Eventually they might be paired with lyrics, but I have to feel it first.
    I'm deep into playing the notes on repeat and quickly add more. Repeat. Write it down. Play again. They're still just notes, though.
    This has always come naturally to me. I've been doing this long enough the music flows from my fingers and I continue plucking away at the strings until I hear her clear her throat quietly as if she was trying to interrupt but not be invasive. I left the door open; it's an invitation, but I didn't expect anyone to accept.
    "That's pretty."
    I lay my hand across the strings to soften the noise before turning in my chair. Wren's hair falls in waves across the front of her shoulder, lighter brown streaks where the sun has bleached out some of the color running

through the shortened locks. She's cut it since North Carolina. I wasn't expecting that.

Her brown eyes sparkle in the wake of a setting sun as the rays filter in through my window. Then she smiles and something stirs inside me.

We aren't going to be able to just be roommates. Not when she looks at me like that. Not when we react to one another the way we do.

Not when I've missed her as much as I have.

Being roommates was never going to work.

"You found me," I say, finally breaking the silence.

Shrugging, she smiles slightly and then lets it fall.

"Coach might have clued me in to where you call home away from home and walked me over on her way back to her house," she says softly. "I was able to get some practice time in before officially starting next week, so I'm happy. I considered just going back to your house, but figured I would see if you were still here since Dylan showed me where your office is. I didn't want to be rude."

"Home."

"What?" she questions, her brow furrowing.

"It's not *my* house. It's home. It's your home now, too," I say, adamant about this fact.

Her lips part as if she's going to respond and then thinks better of it. Standing up, I prop the instrument against the wall and come around the end of my desk. Leaning against the front of the table, I cross my arms over my chest and my legs at my ankles, and take her in for a minute before elaborating. I wasn't prepared for conversations since the rest of the staff in my department left for the day hours ago. I was well inside my head before she walked in.

"I'm aware," she says. Stepping into the office and clasping her hands behind her back, she leans against the small wall space beside the door.

She mimics me and crosses her tanned legs at the ankle, the definition of her quads and calves becoming a turn on I wasn't expecting. I've seen her wearing less. This is somehow sexier than watching her paddle around on a surfboard in a bikini.

"I just want to be sure," I respond, attempting to keep myself from wondering how it would feel to have her thighs wrapped around my ears. We stare at one another as she swallows hard. "I don't want you to think of it as my house just because I lived there first. That's silly. Maybe right now it doesn't feel like home because you aren't settled in yet, but I don't want you to think of it as anything but that."

She looks down at her feet briefly, scuffing the toe of her sneaker against the floor like she's rolling a pebble around with the tread.

"I'm that transparent, huh?" she asks, then looks up at me through her hair that's fallen across her face. "I don't mean to make it sound like it doesn't feel like home, but you're right. It's because I just got here. I can guarantee I'll call it your house at least a few more times before it's home to me."

Nodding, I accept the answer.

"This feels weird. Being in your office," she says, looking at the musical paraphernalia I have hanging on the walls. "You're an actual professor."

I look around the space. Everything here is mine, from the guitar to the books to the photos on the wall. But in reality, the professor part isn't mine yet.

"They might call me professor but I'm more an 'instructor' right now. They can call me doctor soon enough," I say, smirking. "Hopefully."

"They will. How is your research coming?"

"It's been a lot," I say without elaborating on the emotional toll. "Are you ready to go home?"

She raises an eyebrow at me.

"The sun is almost set and I'm exhausted. I assume you are as well between driving all morning, unpacking, and then hitting up practice. So, I'll ask again," I say, raising my eyebrow back at her in response. "Are you ready to go home?"

I don't mean it any other way than going home to the house we share, but my voice unfortunately says something different and I catch my tone as I complete the question, as I watch her chest rise and fall rapidly.

"Yes, please." She looks at me and pulls her lips in as if that will help her take the wanting away from her words. "I mean, yes, I'm ready if you are. Do you need help carrying things to your car?"

Pushing off the desk, I step into her space. She allows me, keeping her arms behind her back as I close the distance between us. I can't keep myself from touching her face, allowing my finger to follow the curve of her cheek, tucking her hair behind her ear. Her breath hitches as my fingertips trail down her neck and my thumb presses beneath her chin until she lifts her eyes to look at me.

"Are we going to be able to handle this?" I ask, my voice deep as I speak quietly to her.

Wren's eyes soften as she blinks, the corners of her mouth turning up slightly with a shadow of a smile.

"We're going to have to try. If we can't, we'll have to figure it out as we go," she says. "Let's go home."

Chapter 20

Wren

Staring at the car in front of me as it slowly pulls forward through the green light, I can barely wrap my head around the book I'm listening to. It turned on again as soon as I started the car when Alex dropped me back at the athletic complex, and I don't have the wherewithal to turn it off. After another of his naughty escapades which absolutely was mutual, it isn't lost on me the irony of listening to a self-help book about being in control when he has me on the verge of losing it all.

We're roommates. I keep telling myself that's what's happening. We. Are. Roommates.

But ... it's already more than that. This is way more than roommates and it was before I even moved across the country.

As I drive back to the house from campus, I'm glad my new home is far enough away that it was easier to drive than walk today because if I had to ride back with Alex, I don't think either of us would be ending the night on a responsible note.

"How's the Alex Situation?" my dad asked when I called home to let them know I had arrived in Brockport earlier today.

At the time I didn't lie. The Alex Situation was fine, he helped me bring things in from the car, and then he left to let me start unpacking before venturing out to see what's up with the team. Easy peasy.

If I were having that conversation now, I would not be able to be honest. The situation is no longer in friends only territory and I am struggling to know how to handle it.

I know how I want to handle it.

That can't happen.

Why can't that happen? I ask myself.

"Well, self, I don't really know why that can't happen. I just know I should not start out my new living arrangements by banging my roommate," I say out loud as I sit at the next red light. "Not even if I really want to, so I just need get out the vibrator and take care of it myself."

As the light turns green, I look both ways to be certain the coast is clear and that's when I notice the truck in the turn only lane beside me. There's a man in the passenger seat staring at me with his window open and I am forever grateful that I don't have mine open, too. How embarrassing would that be for a total stranger to hear me talking to myself, especially about that.

I smile and press the gas pedal, hoping I make it back to the house without any other incidents. I follow the GPS again as I get through town and pull into the driveway, parking beside Alex's car that matches mine. He's not out front and I'm grateful because I need a minute to collect myself before going inside.

I hear the shower running as I walk through the door and make a note to figure out dinner soon. I'm not sure where anything is or if there's a place to order from that's open. I'm unsure of everything right now because he is in that shower and it's the one place I want to be, too, and emotionally I'm right back where I was in his office.

Yearning.

Wanting.

Needing.

I hurry down the hallway toward my bedroom and close the door.

Walking across the room, pulling my tank and sports bra off as I go, I grab a towel from the stack on the dresser and wrap it around my chest. I secure the fabric and then slip my shorts and underwear down, kicking them off and into the basket I've set in the closet for dirty laundry.

While I wait for the shower to be free, I grab out clean clothes and sort through a box of things I need to put away still.

"Sometimes this door doesn't latch tightly and it opens on its own when the windows are open," he says. "Gentle breezes and whatnot."

"I closed it," I say, standing in the middle of the room, still holding some of the items I was sorting, and staring at Alex as his body fills the space in my doorway. As I stand there in a towel becoming more aware of my nakedness, he's seemingly unaffected by the interaction.

"Right. But it's an old house. The doors don't always swing all the way shut and latch, so sometimes you need to push them closed tightly," he says, looking at my hand and smirking. "Especially if you want privacy."

"Privacy?" I question slowly.

It takes me a solid second to turn my head and look at the massager I'm holding. The vibrating muscle massager. The very one I use on my back and calves after softball that could potentially double as something else. I can feel my face heat the moment realization hits me.

"This is not what you think it is."

"Isn't it, though?" he retorts, raising an eyebrow.

"Fair. It could be, but it is not."

"Would you like to demonstrate what it's used for then?" he goads.

I close my eyes, hoping my heartrate slows down, because I'm wearing only a towel and even though there should be nothing sexual about this, it's very, very sexual. It's been sexual since the moment he hugged me this afternoon. The smirk tells me everything I need to know the moment I open my eyes.

He's enjoying the hell out of this.

But so am I.

"I would very much like to, but I need a hot shower and some clean clothes," I say. In a final act of defiance, I step up to him, pressing my body against his while holding my towel in place, and finish with, "After that, you can lay on your belly on the bed and I'll show you exactly what it's used for."

I watch him swallow hard as his eyes darken slightly and I slip past him to the hallway. As I enter the bathroom, I look back down the corridor but all that remains is Alex's bedroom door closing softly behind him, separating us.

If I wasn't sweaty and disgusting from running around the softball field with Dylan and the team, I would have found food before showering. The thoughts about how hungry I am keep running through my head as I massage the shampoo into my scalp. Food will keep my brain from thinking other things, like wandering to the image of Alex standing in my doorway in a grey tank top and bright orange gym shorts.

Consequently, my shower is the quickest one I've taken in a long time.

It's also one of the fastest orgasms I've ever given myself because there is no way I could step out of the bathroom or my bedroom still so wound up without making a stupid decision that ends with him between my legs. If I can take care of the issue and get through the rest of the evening without incident, that will be best for everyone.

"Are you hungry?" he asks as I emerge from my room in a fresh shirt and run shorts.

I jump at the sound of his voice and look toward his door at the end of the hall. It's closed and when I turn to look the opposite direction, I catch him waiting for me at the hall entrance in the living room.

"I didn't mean to scare you," he remarks.

"You didn't," I say too quickly.

He tilts his head to the side, looking at me like he can see through me, and maybe he can.

"I startled you, then. Food? There's a Mexican place down off Main Street that has the best birria tacos I've been able to find around here," he says. "I'll drive so you can look around and try to get acquainted."

Wrapping my arms behind my back, I grasp my elbows to stretch my shoulders. His eyes drop from my face to my chest and I clear my throat.

"Dude."

"Maybe don't stand like that," he says, shrugging as he shoves his hands in his pockets and turns into the kitchen.

"You're never going to be able to come to any softball games or practices to hang out with me. We all stretch that way at one point or another," I say, dropping my arms and following him out to the breezeway. "Are sandals okay?"

"Sandals are fine," he says, slipping into his own flip flops. "And I didn't say anything about anyone else standing that way. Just you."

"Don't be a misogynist."

"I'm not a misogynist. I love women. I absolutely do not think I'm better than them. However, I might be slightly territorial. Maybe a little possessive," he says, grabbing his keys from his pocket and starting the car from inside the house.

"Who said you get to be territorial over me?" I counter, my anger flaring a little.

"Who said I don't get to be?"

"It's about to be me. I'm not property. The last guy who tried to be possessive didn't end so well once I got my head on right," I say as I step up to him. In an attempt to convince myself and him that we haven't changed our relationship status to anything other than friends, I add, "We're roommates."

He's taller than me and I can't decide if I like it as much now as I did on vacation. He looks down at me and smiles, then brushes hair out of my face. He keeps doing that, and for an independent woman who doesn't take anyone's shit anymore ... I enjoy it immensely. Anything to feel him close to me after weeks apart.

"I know. I keep reminding myself," he says, sadly. "I like us, Wren, and I want to get to know you more, because there's so much more to know. Let's go have dinner. I'm not trying to be any of those things. I'm sorry. I didn't mean to be an asshole, but when it comes to banter, you've become my favorite partner."

"You're mine, too," I say, quietly. I haven't had conversations with anyone else the way I do with Alex. He's fun to talk to and keeps me asking questions. If it weren't for him, I probably wouldn't even be in New York right now. As he turns and I follow him out the door to the car I say, "I'm glad you're driving. I'm having a margarita tonight."

The drive to the restaurant lacks enthusiasm — I look at the storefronts as we drive down Main Street and plan for what I want to check out first after I've settled in more tomorrow, but other than that our conversation stalls into comfortable silence. We make two turns and are at the restaurant, are inside and seated within minutes, and a fresh margarita is placed in front of me shortly thereafter.

"I have classes all day tomorrow so you're on your own to explore. When do you officially start at the college?" he asks, sipping on a glass of water.

It's small talk and chatting about normal things, and I'm okay with that, until he asks out of the blue.

"Did you ever find out more about your family history or figure out a jumping off point?"

My mouth drops open slightly, because it's not something that was top priority. Getting here was; finding Will was not. That's when I realize I haven't told him about the last big conversation I had with my parents before leaving for New York about who my father is.

"Um, yeah, actually. My mom knows his first name and some extra details, but I'm not quite ready to talk about it," I tell him. "I just got here today and it's already been a pretty crazy last few days. I want to get settled before I tackle another huge thing."

The last week in California was spent obsessing over packing what I needed immediately, moving any of my larger items back to my parents' house so Tasha could utilize the space I no longer occupied, and scouring the Internet looking for "Will Brockport Army Veteran." Because a search engine was going to come back immediately with the answer to my paternity questions.

"That's understandable," Alex says. "You've got so much going on right now, I don't blame you for putting that aside. Sometimes you have to choose what's most important for the moment and obviously getting situated here takes precedence."

Our food arrives and through bites of rice and tacos and licking the salt off the rim of my glass, I ask him a thousand things about the town, what kind of community there is, if there are events I should have on my radar, and so forth. Alex happily answers all of them as if he's my personal tour guide.

"I grew up here, so I kind of have a handle on what's going on," he says when I apologize for the litany of questions. "If I don't know of something going on, Maggie will. If she doesn't, just go to the coffeehouse. Between the flyers on Brian's corkboard and the way those guys gossip, you'll never be bored."

"What about when it gets cold and snowy? Does everything shut down?"

He looks at me like I've grown an extra head.

"Absolutely not. Sometimes that's the best time here. Apples and pumpkin picking in the fall, Christmas trees right after Thanksgiving ... like I said, you won't be bored if you're looking for something to do."

"Do you cut your own Christmas tree?" I ask, raising an eyebrow. Even though I know he was working in the garden behind the house when I got here, I can't imagine Alex with an axe or chainsaw. "Because that's something I'd like to see."

Popping a chip with salsa into his mouth, Alex gets a twinkle in his eye. Or maybe the tequila is hitting my bloodstream.

"I haven't, but I will take you to pick one out this year. I go to Sugar Shack. It's Maggie's husband's business."

"Are you, like, friends with all the small business owners in town?" I ask, laughing. Every friend he's mentioned seems to have a store or property or is related to someone who does.

"A lot of them are. It's not intentional," he says, playing with the edge of his napkin. "I started playing the open mic nights at the Jumping Bean as soon as Brian and Greg announced them. I needed an outlet and they provided one. I knew Maggie from high school, but she's a few years younger than me, and I met her business partner when we dated briefly. They own The Bakery on Main."

"Wait, you dated Maggie? Our landlord?" I say, surprised.

"It was three dates and no attraction like that. Her personality is top notch and I'm nothing like her type."

"But you also had a thing with Harper, who is Maggie's sister-in-law?"

He begins to speak and must think better of it as he closes his mouth, pursing his lips as he ruminates on the thought he thought he should share. I give him a moment to think about it more.

"Yes. I did that."

"Are there any friends of yours you haven't dated or banged?" I quip.

"You," he deadpans.

"Just me?"

Neither of us can keep from laughing.

"Uh, no, more than just you," he says through giggles. "Those two are the only two I've had any sort of romantic relationship with so far."

"So far? You're sure?"

"Pretty sure I know who I've been in a relationship with," he says, chuckling, "but yes, I'm sure."

I nod and go back to nibbling on my chips because I don't actually want to keep having this conversation. I know where my feelings lie with Alex and I know there's a touch of jealousy lurking behind the mask I'm wearing right now. If I don't stop asking or joking about it now, the alcohol will do the job of creating a bigger issue. I don't drink often, but an emotionally charged conversation while drinking? That's a recipe for disaster.

"Hey, man, how you been?" I hear Alex say as he stands from the table. "I saw Murph the other day and he said you'd gone out of town for a Vets retreat with some of your guys. Glad to see you back home."

I glance to my right and see a pair of green cargo shorts and Teva sandals. I don't try to eavesdrop, but they're standing right beside the table, so it's really difficult to not listen.

"I got back yesterday. It was a good visit with all of them, but Rick needed some extra hands at the greenhouse so I'm back on landscaping duty," the man says.

His deep voice sends a jolt through me and I look up at him. His greying hair is cut short and styled, a ballcap in his hand, he's wearing a plain white

T-shirt under an open button-down shirt with the sleeves rolled up almost to his elbows.

"Well, hello," he says to me, smiling. The skin around the edges of his eyes crinkle and he reaches out a tanned arm, offering me his hand to shake. "I'm Will."

"Will." I say his name quietly like it's a complete sentence because I don't know how else to say it. I don't know how else to react as a full body shiver tears through me.

"Sorry, poor manners. I should have introduced you," Alex says, looking back and forth between me and Will as I continue to sit and they stand. "Will, this is Wren. She just moved here and is starting at the college. She's a new softball coach working with Dylan. Wren, Will."

"Hi," I say, then slowly shake my head as I get my bearings, and reach out to take his still extended hand. "It's nice to meet you. I think we were at the same stoplight earlier."

"California plates?"

"Yes, that's me," I say, smiling.

His smile somehow shines a little brighter before a hint of sadness touches the edges of his eyes and he lets go of my hand.

"I used to know a girl from California. That was years ago though. I don't want to keep you kids from dinner, just wanted to stop over to say hello," he says. "It's nice to meet you, Wren. I'm sure we'll be seeing each other again if you're hanging out with this fella."

Not once did I think to stand up, but I also don't know if my legs would support me if I tried. Instead, I remain in the booth and smile and return the sentiment. As Alex and Will finish their quick conversation, I take another sip of my drink and try to not overthink.

Because I'm pretty sure I just met my dad, but he has no idea I exist.

Chapter 21

Alexander

Wren's been quiet since I interrupted our dinner to talk to Will. I hadn't seen him in the last couple weeks between getting ready for the new semester and his trip with the group he volunteers with. When he walked into the restaurant, I didn't want to be rude and not talk to him.

The ride back home is nearly silent as she nibbles at her thumbnail. Though the trip isn't far, every once in a while, I hear her sigh heavily as she looks out the window at the buildings we pass on the way back through town. She doesn't say anything as she gets out of the car and meanders back into the house, waiting for me in the breezeway to unlock the door.

Comfortable quiet is what I'm accustomed to with her.

This isn't comfortable quiet, though.

Something is wrong. I can feel it as deeply as I've felt the connection to her from the day we met.

But I give her space to adjust. I push open the door and let her enter home first, and as she passes me, she whispers a barely there "thank you."

Confused, I shake my head and step up into the kitchen, hang my keys on Gram's key board, and start setting up the coffee maker for tomorrow morning. I like stopping into the coffee shop, but I reserve that for a mid-day pick-me-up if I need it. When Harper lived with me, we shared the entire pot every day. Since she moved out, I've had to resort to brewing less so it doesn't go to waste.

Does Wren drink a lot of coffee? Enough to start making a full pot again?

It's a silly question because I know if I make a pot of coffee she'll drink some. I saw the numerous cups she brought in to throw away from her trip. I stop mid scoop, set the measuring spoon down, and go to her room.

Knocking gently, I wait for her to respond, and when I hear a faint, "Come in," I open the door to find her curled up on the bed.

Crying.

Pushing my glasses up on my nose, I push my hands in my pockets. I'm unsure of the next step I should take, other than feeling like I might be responsible.

Wren shimmies her way up to the headboard and wipes her eyes quickly.

"What's up?" she asks, as if her strong façade will hide anything.

I furrow my brow and look at her, as I lean against the doorframe.

"Today has been a lot," I say.

She nods.

"I have to get up early, so I'm setting up the coffee maker. Do you want me to make a full pot so there's some for you when you get up?" I ask. Without giving her a chance to respond, I attempt to give her a rundown of my schedule, but it's different almost every day of the week, so it's almost pointless. I tell her anyway. "I teach at eight and ten tomorrow morning and then have my own classes in Rochester in the evening. I don't always come home between since it's easier to get work done in my office instead of dragging it back and forth all the time."

Looking at me curiously, she sniffles and wipes at her eyes again.

"Coffee, yes. If you make a full pot, I'll likely drink whatever you don't," she says. "If you don't come home, when do you eat?"

"I have protein bars and usually pack a salad or something for my in between time."

"Do you have a slow cooker?"

"I do not. Harper left her pressure cooker here, though, so sometimes I use that."

"I'm buying us a slow cooker. There's no reason to not have something better than a salad and protein bars," she says.

"A slow cooker sounds like a great addition to the house," I say. I know she might not want me to ask, but I need to know. "Why the tears?"

Wren grinds the heels of her hands into her eyes before responding.

"You'll think I'm stupid. It's a dumb reason to cry."

Shrugging, I say, "Try me."

Taking a big breath and letting it out slowly, her face is filled with exhaustion from emotions and travel and who knows what else.

"At dinner I said I wasn't quite ready to talk about all the 'who's your daddy?' stuff, but that was before dinner was interrupted," she says, pulling her legs in and sitting cross-legged.

Grabbing a pillow, she presses it into her abdomen as she sits up straighter and I don't miss the smoothness of the motion. This is a comfort thing for her, and I shift my weight from one foot to the other in preparation for what she could be about to tell me. It doesn't have anything to do with us, per se, but I can feel her anxiety from across the room. The energy has shifted.

"What about dinner changed your mind about talking about it?"

"Will."

"He's a really nice guy. You'll get to know him. He's like everyone's uncle around here," I say, smiling to ease her tension.

"The man my mother slept with was named Will."

"That's quite the coincidence," I say, my brows knitting together.

She sighs, slightly exasperated.

"I don't know her."

"Know who?"

"Coincidence. Jesus, the Alex Situation is getting weirder by the moment," she says under her breath, clutching the pillow. "Stay with me, here, okay? Mom's Will was a Veteran, Alex. She said he volunteered all the time with guys he'd served with and the older generation vets, like World War II and the like. I found out a few weeks ago, my mom's Will lived in Brockport. None of this—"

"Wait," I say, holding up my hand as I try to catch myself up because I'm still stuck on her calling this "the Alex Situation" and how I've become a situation. "Are you saying it's possible Will, my Will who is like another dad, is ... your actual dad?"

She pulls the corner of her lip in between her teeth, widens her eyes, and tilts her head all as if to say, "Yeah, stupid."

"A little bit. He said he once knew a girl from California," Wren says. "I don't want to go assuming things, but he checks all the boxes."

I motion to the bed and she nods, scooting over to make room for me to sit next to her. Out of all the things I was expecting when I met a girl in North Carolina, this was the furthest thing from my mind. When she told me why she had been looking for jobs in New York, my area of New York, the possibility that her biological father was kicking around here felt like a slim possibility. The fact Harper and I recently joked about how crazy it would be if the dad Wren was looking for was a guy we know hits me like a ton of bricks.

Because that's exactly what's happening.

I wrap my arm around Wren's shoulder and pull her close to me. She drops her head against me and I feel her relax into my side as we sit together silently staring at the wall across from us.

"I don't know what I should do," she says quietly before a yawn sneaks out.

This is a sticky situation. On one hand, I think she should definitely talk to Will and find out if her mom is the "girl from California" he referenced. On the other hand ... this is a lot of new to happen in a short amount of time.

"Maybe ..." I begin, then take a deep breath. "Maybe you should just live your life for the time being. Get used to a new schedule, new job, new people, before tackling the possibility that William Murphy is your dad."

"That's his last name?" she whispers. Then as if trying it on for size, she mumbles, "Murphy."

"It is," I whisper back. "His brother is Father Murphy down at St. Peter's. So, if Will is your dad, your uncle is a priest."

We turn our heads to look at one another. The tears on her cheeks have long since dried, but the weariness is ever present as the weight of life presses down on Wren. I can't make this less heavy for her.

"You're right. I think I should get adjusted to being here before pursuing any of the impossible leads I currently have," she says, her voice small. "I don't think I'm going to mention it to my mom yet either. I don't want her to react. ... Poorly. I don't want her to react poorly. She's going to react no matter what when I do find out who he is. I just don't want to get her curious and then have it not be Will Murphy from Brockport."

I nod, and pull her a little more snugly into my side so I can carefully press my lips to her forehead.

"I think that's a good idea for now," I say.

As if we've spent time like this a hundred times, Wren slides her arms around my middle, twisting her body enough to get a good grip on me. I slide my free hand along her arm, encircling her to let her know she's safe here.

*****

When my eyes fly open, the room is dark. Wren and I have maneuvered ourselves down from how we had been sitting before sleep overtook both of us. Her back is to me, pressed up against my front, and as I try to carefully pull my arm from beneath her head, she sighs in her sleep. I roll toward the edge of the bed and sit up, careful not to wake her, and quietly find a lightweight blanket in the closet to cover her with.

I don't want to leave her, but I also don't have an alarm clock in her room, my phone is in the kitchen, the door is still unlocked, and as I step into the kitchen, I see the coffee maker only halfway set up for morning. Locking the door first, I finish prepping coffee for morning which is now only a few hours away, and grab my phone on my way back out of the room.

Though I'm used to living with someone, I'm not used to living with Wren. We just started this adventure. And as I step into the hall on my way back to my own bedroom, looking at my phone to set the alarms on it so I don't oversleep, I run right into a half-awake girl who is supposed to only be my roommate.

For now.

She's my roommate for now.

"Are you coming back to bed?" she asks, sleepily. Rubbing her eye and yawning, she reaches for my hand and pulls me back into her room.

"I guess I am. I just want you to know I do have my own bed," I say, chuckling.

"I know. You can sleep there tomorrow," she says, crawling across the covers to her side.

"My intention was not to fall asleep in here," I say as I lay down beside her.

Wren curls up on her side facing me and I watch her eyes flutter shut as another yawn tries to pull her back into sleep. Her arm lays naturally across my abdomen and mine goes behind her neck as if on instinct.

"It wasn't my intention to develop a crush on my roommate before he was my roommate. But here we are. Plus, I don't want to be alone tonight," she says, sleepily playing with the hem of my shirt.

"As long as we're on the same page," I say, not hiding my smile in the darkness of her room.

Her fingers gently caress the skin beneath my shirt at the top of my shorts and my body reacts to her touch. The featherlight hint of her fingertips as they stroke along the ridge of my hip draws a sigh from me that I don't mean for her to hear.

"Are you okay?" she questions. It's not concern, but the traces of a giggle I hear as I make a mental note that she knows exactly what's happening here.

"I'm perfect," I respond, pulling her closer to me as I close my eyes.

Wren snuggles up against me, carefully rolling her hip to place her knee on my thigh, and it's unnatural how natural all of this is — waking in the night and then coming back to her bed as if I belong here with her, having her head fall heavily against my chest as she makes herself comfortable with me ... it's all like it was meant to happen.

It's scary.

I've tried to have this once before.

It didn't work out well last time.

I was burned hard from it even if I didn't allow her to see how badly it hurt, even if she's still one of my best friends.

Wren is supposed to be my roommate first. This was not supposed to be happening.

And the more I tell myself that the less I believe it.

When I hear her gently snoring, I reach my arm up and brush the hair from her cheek. The room has started to lighten and I know soon enough my alarms are going to ring. I'll have to pull myself away from her embrace and try to leave the house.

If it's at all possible, she'll still be sleeping when I leave. I don't want morning to be awkward for either of us. How would I leave for work if she's awake? Do I kiss her? Do I give her a high five? Do we just pretend like we didn't have a PG-rated evening in her bed and go about the day like we're just friends?

Also, are we just friends?

Do friends sleep together? As in really sleep?

My brain doesn't turn off as I lay beside her and run all the scenarios through my head. I try, but even closing my eyes and just breathing, not thinking about anything at all, doesn't work. I'm still not sleeping when my first alarm starts blaring.

I quickly swipe it to "off" and unwrap Wren from my side, pulling the blanket up around her shoulders so she hopefully doesn't wake from the lack of body heat beside her again.

My shower is cold and coffee hot as I step out back to check the garden before leaving for work. It's barely seven in the morning and the dew is heavy on the grass as we slowly begin being tugged toward autumn. I pull a few tomatoes from the vines and check the squash before realizing I don't have time to commit to the task this morning and will have to worry about it later. Carrying the tomatoes and a single small eggplant into the house, I set them on the counter, fill a travel mug, and turn toward the table where my bags are waiting.

"Have a good day," she says in the quietest voice I've heard from her yet.

Standing at the doorway near the bathroom, Wren wipes sleep from her eyes and her tank top rises just enough to show me a sliver of tanned, toned skin above the waistband of her sleep shorts.

Swallowing, I walk across the kitchen, set my coffee on the table, and step into her space. It's exactly the same position we were in yesterday after she got here and was getting settled, the moment I realized I needed to leave the house and let her have space because I needed it, too. But now? Now I want to be in her space more than anything.

Looking up at me, she smiles shyly. I kiss her temple, the scruff on my unshaved cheek causing her to bristle slightly as it brushes against her smooth skin.

"Take some time to get to know the house and then hit up the bakery. Maggie will probably be there this morning if you want to talk to her about the lease," I say. "I'll be back around nine."

"This morning?"

"Tonight. You're on your own all day, but text me if you need anything. I'll be near my office until four-ish then in Rochester."

She nods, accepting that I'm not coming home between teaching and taking classes. I drag myself away from her and sling my laptop bag over my shoulder along with another backpack filled with my own schoolwork, snacks, and water bottle. Wren steps over to the table and picks up my coffee mug, holding it out for me, and instead of saying thank you, I lean in and kiss her tenderly on the lips for the first time since North Carolina.

*****

"What the hell is wrong with you?" Harper yells into the phone. "You were in her bed and did nothing?"

"I didn't think you were going to go all Team Wren so quickly, especially without meeting her first, but yes. Slept in her bed and did nothing."

She lets out an exasperated breath.

"Just wife her," she says.

"Can't wife someone who isn't ready to be wifed. Plus, kind of difficult to wife someone when you aren't even dating them. Also, why are we using the term 'wifed?' Maybe 'partnered?'"

"Are you a cowboy? You're going to partner her? Stop being weird. Also, officially. You're not officially dating her, but it sounds like you're unofficially dating her."

I shrug, though she can't see it, and go back to organizing the books on my shelf. After the drum set and record player vying for the favorite spot in the office, I opted to take the drums to one of the classrooms where we'll actually use them this semester. After that, I don't know what I'm going to do with them.

"So, when do you think you'll officially start dating?"

Arranging two books in alphabetical order by author, I wait a beat before answering.

"I'd like to wait and see where we end up. How does that sound?" I ask.

I value Harper's thoughts. I didn't think I would ever be going to her for her opinions on my dating life, though, because she was my dating life. However, she knows me better than even Maggie in some respects, so I'm willing to listen.

"Just don't wait too long. If she's as amazing as you've led us all to believe, I might steal her from you," she says.

"You wouldn't," I say, as my hands still with a book in each. "Harper, that's not fair."

She laughs maniacally, and when she finally stops to catch her breath, I hear, "Nah, I've got my eye on a different girl on campus. Well, not girl. I mean, yes, she's female, but of the woman variety. Never mind. She's around our age."

Going back to my task, I place two more books where they belong before I finish for the time being. All my books are visible, in order, and dusted. I like the way they look on the shelf and wish I had done this when the spring semester first ended so I could have appreciated the organization all summer.

There was a lot going on at that point in the year, though.

"Who?" I ask, realizing Harper hasn't given me a name.

"Angela? She's in student affairs, but moved into the apartment next to me. Or, I moved in next to her? Brian rented to us days apart, so she's my neighbor," she says, sighing a little. "She got stuck in the crappy complex on the other side of campus when she moved here in March, but now she's my neighbor. My cute neighbor."

Interesting development.

"And is she gay? Or even gay-ish, like you?" I question.

It's never been a secret that Harper is bisexual. She just hasn't had a relationship with a woman in years. I'm starting to think this was a big part of her "I'll ruin your life" mantra when I was trying to get her to stay with me — because settling with me when she hadn't actually found her person isn't fair to her or me, and I know that now.

"Not sure. It hasn't come up, but she's pretty and smart and flirty, so I'm going with bi-panic and just hoping for the best," she says.

"Maybe she'll be your penguin. Remember when your brother was on a whole soulmates kick a while back after watching PBS Kids with the baby? Maybe there's something to it," I say, trying to be nonchalant.

"Yeah, maybe," she responds quietly. "I should let you go. I have to finish some paperwork and get out of here. Happy Thursday! A long weekend is almost here! Oh, that reminds me, are we doing a picnic at your place or Maggie and Rick's?"

Long weekend and picnic wasn't even on my radar, so I tell her we should do it at her brother's since Wren just got here. I don't want to overwhelm her the first weekend she's in town.

"Good point. I'll let them know we're definitely doing it at their house," Harper says, followed by a string of words she smashes together right before hanging up on me, "Talktoyoulaterloveyoubye!"

Staring at the phone on my desk as the screen goes dark again, I say to my empty office, "Love you, too."

Chapter 22

Wren

I'm not sure what the rules are as far as me going into the backyard, but I'm going to take my chances. There's a beautiful bench by the flower garden and a huge vegetable patch. My mom grows what she can, but has never really had much of a green thumb. I've always had better luck when it comes to veggies than she does and that's okay ... I assumed my natural love of plants was something I picked up from my dad.

Until I realized he didn't really have a natural talent for things that grow either.

Sitting on the bench, I curl my legs beneath me and steady my coffee cup on my knee as I breathe in the warm September air. Alex's shoes were wet when he came in an hour or so ago before leaving for work, so I was prepared for the dew and the bits of cut grass to cover my feet.

It's not the beach, but it'll do.

Closing my eyes, I straighten my back and let the sun warm my face. I savor each moment and listen closely to the sounds of nature all around me — the breeze rustling leaves that are already turning gold and red, a Blue Jay squawking, the low hum of a bee somewhere nearby.

Footsteps coming through the grass is what causes me to open one eye and peek between my lashes.

Work boots, dirty jeans, an equally filthy T-shirt adorn the man striding through the lawn as if he owns the place.

"Good morning. I wasn't expecting anyone out here when I pulled up. Sorry to intrude," Will says as he reaches where I sit. "Wren, right?"

"That's me," I say, shielding my eyes from the sun and looking up at him.

"I don't mean to interrupt your time alone. I was going to check the flowers and make sure we don't need to replace any of Gram's mums. I'll just be a minute and then out of your hair," he says, smiling in a way that makes my heart stop.

I can see what drew my mom to him, if this is the same Will. He's charismatic without being in your face about it.

"Graham?" I question, unsure who he's talking about. "I thought Alex lived here alone. He talked about Harper, but didn't mention another guy named Graham."

Will smiles again, the laugh lines deepening in his cheeks around his mouth as the ones beside his eyes wrinkle.

"Not Graham, like the cracker, but Gram, g-r-a-m. She's Maggie's grandmother. This was her house and she shared it with Maggie before Mags moved in with Rick and started renting it to Alex," he says, pushing his hands in his pockets and playing with what sounds like a set of keys. "Before Gram passed we put in new flower beds and the garden."

I lift my right hand and make a motion as if to say, "gotcha," but I don't really got it. However, I'm starting to understand how close Alex is with everyone. It's not just a closeness between his family members like I saw when we were in North Carolina. He's close with ... everyone.

"So, you just stop by to check on the flowers now?"

I'm trying to figure out how it all goes together, and maybe it's just too early because if Alex lives here now and Maggie owns the house, why doesn't Maggie check the flowers?

Will tips his head and looks at me like he's figuring out a complex math problem before speaking again.

"Maggie's husband owns a landscaping business. I help him out from time to time. Gram was good people and I've been around Maggie pretty much her entire life, so between kind of being like an uncle to her and also doing the landscaping thing to stay busy between other jobs ... I occasionally stop to check on the flowers," he says. A mischievous twinkle in his eye catches my attention as he follows up with, "Sometimes, if Alex isn't around, I pick some of the vegetables for myself, but that's between us. Half the time he can't eat everything we grow and he takes it to my brother down at the church."

I nod, enjoying the story time he's regaling me with.

"Can I help?" I ask, the words slipping between my lips before I realize I'm asking them. But I double down. "Can I help check the mums and the garden?"

"Absolutely. Come on," he says, motioning for me to follow him as he wanders toward the flowers to begin his inspection. "Gram loved all the flowers, but once the summer blossoms died off, I know she hated seeing how brown everything was. Mums help to brighten it up back here."

As he checks the flowers and dead-heads the ones that are done for the season, Will shares with me stories about cutting down trees out front and putting in flowers there and how, as Gram's health deteriorated, it became more and more important to everyone involved to get the gardens out back done and ready for her. It was just one more thing to help her enjoy life as she was slipping away.

"Alex tell you she's the reason he's doing the research he's doing?"

"He mentioned it, but I didn't realize it was Maggie's grandmother he was talking about. She really made an impact on him, huh?"

That glint in his eye strikes again.

"She had an impact on everyone. Don't think she won't affect your life in some weird way, too. Gram just had that way about her," Will says. "Well, the flowers are looking good. I don't think we'll have to replace any, but if there are any other colors you think you might want, let me know."

As he begins walking toward the vegetable garden he stops and turns toward me.

"I can't shake the feeling that we've met before. You look so much like someone I knew. It's uncanny," he says, mostly to himself, and I force myself to stay quiet. "Do you like tomatoes? There are a few ready. They'd be great on a sandwich."

I just want him to keep talking. I feel like I'm discovering a missing piece of myself and I can't even tell him — not yet — so I say, "What kind of sandwiches do you like?"

"Me? I've always been partial to mayonnaise and tomato on toasted sourdough. That is peak summer sandwich making," he says.

"That's it? Mayo and tomato? No meat? No lettuce?" I giggle.

His eyes grow wide.

"You haven't lived until you have a mayonnaise and tomato sandwich with tomatoes fresh from the garden. Let me guess, you grew up on grocery store tomatoes?"

"I mean, that's where the tomatoes were. I'm sure my parents could have found a farm stand or something, but I guess that wasn't a priority," I say, tipping the rest of my coffee into my mouth. Swallowing, I look into my empty cup. "But with this whole garden here with all these tomatoes, I don't have a reason not to try a fresh one on a mayonnaise sandwich."

"Well, kiddo, you're in luck," Will says, setting a large Beefsteak tomato in my hand before plucking two more from the plant. "Now, let's check the squash ..."

I know I'm going to go in the house and make a tomato sandwich as soon as he leaves. The problem is, I don't necessarily want him to leave yet.

"How did you and Alex meet, anyway?" he asks moving from squash that isn't ready yet to a plant that clearly contains melons. As he pulls a cantaloupe off the vine and sets it beside his boot before moving on to the next set of leaves, he adds, "That guy doesn't get out much. Always has his nose in a book or playing a guitar."

Reaching down into the leaves, I copy Will's movements — pushing the large green canopy aside to search for ripe fruit and when I find one, I point to it and ask if it's ready. He nods and I pull just enough to snap the vine.

"The Outer Banks. He was there for a wedding and I was there for a family thing. We kind of hit it off. I had already been looking to relocate to Brockport, so when he said he lives here it was hard to ignore," I say, holding the melon in one arm and picking up my tomato and coffee mug with the other hand.

"That's ... wow. Right place, right time, I guess," he says, picking up the fruits and vegetables he harvested while we chatted.

"I guess so," I say. "How much more do you have to do out here? I was thinking about another cup of coffee and then going down to check out town. Alex told me to stop at the bakery to see Maggie."

"I'm just about finished. I'll leave these for you two. There wasn't much today so I won't thief any for Murph's guys."

"I'm sure Alex won't mind if you do. I know I don't have a problem with it," I say, as if my opinion bears any weight. "At least take one of the melons and a tomato or two. That way they can have tomato sandwiches, too."

"You're a good kid, Wren. Someone raised you right," he says, wistfully, the smile reaching his eyes after a few seconds. "I should get going so you can go on about your day. Mags should be at the bakery by ten. She was getting ready to take the baby to her mom's when I left the shop."

I nod as we walk toward the house. Will begins to round the edge of the garage with his pickings when I call out to him once more.

"Maybe we can pick vegetables again in a few days?" I ask. "I'll bring an extra cup of coffee."

"I would really like that," Will says. Once again, a smile brightens his cheeks. "Have a beautiful day, Wren."

"You too, Will."

*****

Between running to the store to pick up some things for my bedroom, extra grocery items Alex didn't have, a slow cooker, stopping at the bakery to finally introduce myself to Maggie and sign my lease, and setting up my practice net to get some batting in, I have completely turned off my brain by the time I hear his car pull in on the other side of the house.

I'm mid-swing when Alex pops out the backdoor, leaning against the side of the house to watch me. His body language is tense, brows furrowed, as he watches me. But he's watching me, and that's the part that unravels me a little. I'm used to college guys teasing and acting foolish around the girls their age, but this is different.

I am not used to full-grown men looking at me like they want to tear my tank top off and devour me when I'm dripping with sweat from a workout.

Or maybe I only want this full-grown man to be looking at me like that.

Finishing off the bucket of softballs beside me, I pick up the container and walk toward my practice net. Cleaning up my mess, I contemplate being done for the night when he clears his throat.

"You made dinner?"

"It's just frozen meatballs and sauce from a jar," I respond, throwing a couple more balls in the bucket.

"Thank you. Did you eat yet?" he asks, stepping over and reaching to take the bucket from me.

"I had a cupcake mid-morning from Delilah and Maggie's bakery. Then I made a mayonnaise and tomato sandwich late this afternoon," I say.

He's quiet as I step past him to set the tee inside the backdoor to the breezeway. I catch him giving me a strange look as I slide the backstop up against the backside of the garage.

"Is that a thing you learned in California or ..."

"Will stopped by this morning. He let me help him check the garden."

Alex smirks, then nods his head.

"Did he take stuff this time?"

"Of course. But I told him he had our permission. He acted like you don't know he does that, though."

Carrying the bucket, he follows me into the house and sets it down beside the tee. The movement is so rehearsed and smooth it's as if we've done this before. I close the door and lock it for the night before we walk together up the steps to the kitchen.

"That's because he either doesn't realize I pay attention to what's growing or he knows I know and it's just an unspoken agreement between us that he can help himself. It doesn't matter which it is, as long as the food doesn't go to waste. That's why I take a bunch to Murph's. I know it'll get eaten," Alex says, lifting the lid off the slow cooker and stirring the meatballs. "Pasta or subs?"

"Subs," I reply, stifling a yawn. "I bought rolls and provolone."

"Are you even going to stay awake long enough to eat?"

I shrug, but grab the plates from his hand and set them side by side before putting a roll on each. We work quietly, making our plates and then sit at the table. I pull my feet up in my chair and sit crisscross, stretching my knees and quads to keep the muscles from getting tight too quickly. Plus, it's comfortable.

"How were the tomatoes?" he asks when he's halfway through his sub.

I've barely touched my food, my hunger dissipating as soon as I sat down. The yawn was just a precursor to the exhaustion hitting full force once my butt was settled in the chair.

"They were good. Fresh from the garden is something I'm not used to. Will pegged me as a kid who grew up on grocery store everything, and he's not wrong," I say. "This is a nice change."

"I'll cut up the melon and put it in the fridge for tomorrow," he says.

I'm not sure how long we sit, eating our dinners in silence as the sound of crickets play outside the front window. As the evening winds down, I can feel my eyelids growing heavy and am surprised when Alex stands from his place at the table and picks up my nearly empty plate. I haven't touched it in the time it's taken him to make and eat a second plate of food, so I'm not offended when he scrapes the couple bites that are left into the garbage.

It's not that I'm not used to a man helping in the kitchen. My dad does, but he isn't the most self-sufficient person, either. My mom is the one who does a majority of the cooking and after meal things.

Watching Alex confidently manage the space heightens my awareness of him, and I watch intently as he places the leftovers in a container and sets them in the refrigerator. The extra rolls go in the breadbox. The crock is gently placed in the sink and water run to loosen any stuck-on sauce. And then I watch as he pumps soap into his palm and washes away anything left behind on his very capable fingers.

As he wipes his clean hands on a dishtowel, Alex strides toward me. He sets the towel on the table and, placing one hand on the back of my chair and the other on the table in front of me, leans into my space.

"You're going to fall asleep sitting there. Go take a shower and get to bed," he says, his breath warming the top of my forehead. His words reach my ears seconds before he kisses the top of my head.

It's his voice and the quiet demand mixed with his sincerity that stirs something even deeper inside me again. I'm too tired to argue with him. I'm too tired to keep my filter in place. I'm too turned on by watching him clean up the kitchen to not say something that could backfire.

"Are you going to join me?" I ask.

Looking up into his green eyes, I catch the moment his pupils dilate slightly and feel the energy in the room shift. It's a static electric charge that gets stronger every time he's close to me. It's happened since the first goodnight we shared, standing between beach houses. I know he feels it, too, and I know that's why he left when he did yesterday after I got here. It's taken us both by surprise how quickly we went from, "Hey, person I just met. I hope you aren't a murderer," to, "I think we should get naked together but not actually tell each other that's what we want."

But, good fucking lord, I want to get naked with Alex.

I'm tired of neither of us voicing what we want.

"In bed? Or the shower?" he asks after a moment. It was the longest moment and I sincerely wondered if I had asked him to join me out loud or kept that as an inside thought.

Not an inside thought.

"Both," I say, looking up at his questioning eyes.

He reaches into my lap and lifts my hand, pulling me to standing. He wordlessly leads me along behind him toward the bathroom, turning off the kitchen light as we enter the hallway. Two more steps and he's standing on the tile floor, flicking the light on, then turning to face me. I watch as he drops his gaze to my bare feet and silently drags his vision up my legs. I feel every inch he isn't touching and on instinct, squeeze my thighs together, creating pressure where I long for his touch.

His eyes continue to climb higher, inspecting my fully-clothed body as if there isn't a shred of fabric on it, until he reaches my face. Alex reaches up with his free hand and, with his thumb, pulls the corner of my bottom lip free from my teeth before wiping the dampness away.

He pulls me toward him and I go willingly, his mouth connecting with mine as his touch registers at the hem of my shirt. Turning his head slightly he deepens the kiss as my shirt slides up my abdomen. Lifting my arms above my head, he breaks our connection and slips the tank up and off my body. His mouth is on me again in an instant, the heat of the kiss multiplied after a brief hiatus and I hope he never stops kissing me with such fervor.

My hands find his belt, pulling the tail out from where it's nestled in the loop against his hip. My tongue finds his as I loosen his belt and swiftly unbutton his dress pants. He bites my bottom lip as I release the zipper and pull the fabric apart, not touching the expanding bulge between us.

Reaching between us, I pull his dress shirt from his waistband. Without breaking eye contact, slowly I unbutton it from the bottom to the top, pushing it off his shoulders until he shifts and the shirt pools at his feet leaving only a T-shirt between my fingers and his flesh.

"I'm impatient," he says as he pushes my shorts down my waist until they drop to the floor.

"I see that," I say. "But foreplay is the best."

His mouth discovers mine again as he loops his arms around me only to reach the solid back of my sport bra. His fingers touch, touch, touch, sliding along the band to find nothing to pull, and his frustration begins to climb as he hooks his thumbs beneath the fabric.

"It zips. In the front," I say, pulling from his lips and giggling as I open my eyes in time to see him roll his.

"Sporty chicks always have crazy contraptions," he says.

"And how many sporty chicks have you been with?" I ask, only a little serious.

"Including you?" he asks as his hands slide along the edges of my top, his thumbs beneath the elastic band as he studies the zipper and prepares to take us out of the realm of second base. "Just you."

"Just me?"

He lifts the tab and slowly — painstakingly slowly — pulls the zipper down as my breathing hitches. My nipples pebble as the fabric separates and grazes the sensitive skin, or maybe it's from the way he's looking at me.

At me. Not my breasts. Alex is staring directly into my eyes as he pushes the fabric away from my now naked chest and it makes me ache for him more.

"Just," he says, dipping his head to take one taut nipple in his mouth to tease, releasing it, completing his sentence, "you," and quickly pulling the other between his teeth.

On a sharp intake of breath, he wraps his arms around my waist, his tongue twisting and circling the sensitive buds as I let out a low moan. My fingers find his hair as his left hand holds me in place and his right slides down my belly to the top of my underwear. Lifting his head, I pull Alex's mouth back to mine as his fingers gently slide between me and the last bit of fabric on my body. His large hand cups my vulva, and as he pulls my tongue into his mouth, he slips a finger deep inside me. Slowly he works one finger in and out of my throbbing pussy until I ask him for more. He pulls the fabric down my legs, baring all of me to him before adding another digit. Hooking his fingers along the front of my vagina, Alex coaxes the beginnings of an orgasm from me. He nips my bottom lip and dips his head back to my breasts as his thumb finds my clit. Gently teasing the nub, he rubs small circles that quickly send ripples of pleasure throughout my body. The amount of stimulation is overwhelming in the best way. My leg begins to shake and he holds me up, pressing my shoulders back against the wall for extra support. As my breath begins coming out in shallow bursts, I drop my head forward into his hair and release a deep moan.

"Do you want to come for me?" he asks.

I can't speak. All that comes out of my mouth is an affirmative grunt and, as if he heard a silent command for more, he adds a third finger and drops to his knees to pull my clit into his mouth. The sight alone could make me orgasm, but then he reaches up with his free hands and carefully twists one of my nipples as he flicks his tongue across my clit and simultaneously finds the spot inside me that unleashes the loudest moan from my body.

"Oh ... my ..." I can't finish the sentence as my orgasm pulses through me, radiating down my legs while he continues to pump his fingers in and out of me, drawing out every last drop of energy like he's making up for all the bad sex I've apparently been having since the day I lost my virginity.

My fingers twist in his hair as he slowly pulls his from my body and then I stare at him in awe as he places each digit, one by one, in his mouth to clean them off. Alex trails kisses up my belly as he comes to stand in front of me, a satisfied smile on his face.

"You look less ... sleepy," he says, kissing my collarbone.

"Do I?" I ask. Placing my hands on either side of his face, I pull him in to taste myself on his lips.

"More relaxed," he remarks, taking his glasses off and setting them on the counter beside the sink.

Smirking, he reaches behind his neck and, grasping his T-shirt, drags it up over his head and off his arms. Our eyes connect again and I touch the waistband of his slacks, pushing them from his hips. I want to be more bold and tell him everything I want, but I wait for him to carefully slip his boxer-briefs down his legs and watch as he kicks his discarded clothes into the pile with mine.

It feels like an eternity getting to this point, but then he's stepping away from me to turn the water on in the shower and I get to see his tan lines in all their glory. He turns back to me in time to catch me raking my gaze across his entire body and when I notice him watching me, it sends a shiver up my spine. He's not looking at me like a guy looking for a fun night with his roommate.

This man wants to worship me.

He takes my hand and, kissing my palm, pulls me closer to him before stepping aside to let me get in the shower. He sets two washcloths on the built-in shelf then enters behind me, pulling the curtain closed. The warm spray of the water releases any ache left in my muscles and I allow the heat to trickle down my hair and across my breasts before pulling my hair back and soaking it thoroughly.

Alex doesn't take his eyes off me as he wets a cloth and begins to lather it with the soap I left in the shower after I washed up yesterday — it's citrusy and fresh, the kind of soap used to wake up all your senses. With his free hand, he touches my cheek as if in awe before pressing the cloth to my shoulder and carefully washing my body. Every inch. Methodically. Lovingly. As if he's waited forever to give someone this kind of princess treatment.

And he chose me.

Turning us around so he can wash my back, he gently touches my shoulders until I lean forward against the shower wall. The cloth slides down the center of my back, across the swell of my hip, and then over the round of my ass as it juts out toward him. Unintentionally, I let out a moan as he drags the cloth up my inner thigh and against my most sensitive areas. He does it again, only this time he means it and I press back against his hand.

Reaching behind me, I search for his cock with an urgent need to reciprocate. I find what I'm looking for and, gripping him harder, pull my hand along his length. A sharp inhale from him is all the encouragement I need to slide my hand back down as he grows harder against my palm. He pushes his hips forward, the head of his penis pressing against the soap-slicked skin on my backside, and on the next stroke I rub my thumb across the tip of his cock.

The deep moan he releases creates a bigger need in me to bring him to release. Pumping him in my fist, I start slow — my hand sliding gracefully until I can feel the short curls surrounding him and then back up to the tip and again — until he grips my hips and his fingers dig into my skin in an attempt to keep some semblance of control. Rubbing my thumb just below the head of his cock, his fingers tighten more offering a dose of pleasurable pain. Alex leans down, laying his forehead between my shoulder blades, allowing the water to soak both of us as my motions quicken until he's breathing heavily.

"If you don't stop soon, I'm going to come all over your back, Wren," he grits out just above the sound of the shower.

I squeeze his cock tighter and clench my thighs at the visual of him orgasming with me for the first time. Tipping my head back and holding myself up against the shower wall as he kisses my shoulders, my focus shifts to making him come as quickly as I can. Gripping the tip, I tightly massage it, twisting my palm over the head and then back down the shaft as his arms wrap around my abdomen.

"Fuck," he breathes out. "Again."

I comply, as he drops his right hand to the apex of my thighs and slides his middle finger into my slick center.

"More," he demands, as I drop my head forward against the cool tile.

He doesn't realize how close I am or the way the noises he makes affect me. His fingers emulate the motions I'm making, the speed and rhythm, and I gasp as my orgasm hits low in my belly. I grip his cock tighter as a wave of pleasure rolls through my body and barely register that his left hand is wrapped around mine and stroking his cock faster as he continues to rub my clit.

"Holy shit," I say, my thighs clamping shut as I lean back into him.

"Are you ready?" he asks.

I can't form words, but nod my head as he slides his hand behind mine. I release him as he presses himself against me, his cock warm and thick as he places it on the small of my back.

"Please," I say, my skin pebbling at the thrill of begging this man to come for me.

I feel his hand as he pumps his cock — once, twice, a third time — against my skin and then he goes still. A groan tears through him. His head drops to my shoulders again. He slides both his hands up my abdomen, holding me close to him as we catch our breath, his chest heaving against me and his heart beating hard enough for me to feel it against my back.

The moment went from just having fun in the shower to physically and emotionally intimate in a matter of seconds when he pulled me against him. I'm not the only one to feel that change, a fear that is swiftly pushed away as he kisses below my ear and nibbles my neck.

"I think, and correct me if I'm wrong, we just defeated the purpose of taking a shower. I'm dirtier now than I was when you got home from class," I say, smiling as I drop my hands to grasp his.

Hugging me more snugly, Alex laughs. It's a deep, honest sound. I'm not used to that, but I'm going to get used to it. For the first time ever, I don't feel like my body was just for his pleasure.

"I think you aren't wrong and now we both need to use your fancy soap," he says, standing up straighter. He moves his arms so they cover mine and pulls me closer into a tight hug. "But we might want to be quick."

His body has shielded me from the water and the moment he steps us back into the spray I know why we need to rush. The cold hits like a polar vortex and I take a deep breath. Alex grabs both washcloths and gets them damp before adding soap. He quickly washes away any evidence of himself on my back before switching spots with me and washing himself with the unused cloth. I scrub my hair and rinse off before swapping spots with him again.

As soon as the water is off, we grab towels and dry off enough to get out.

Kissing me once more before we walk down the hallway, I realize I need to know one thing.

"Are you still going to come to bed?"

Alex looks at me questioningly, a frown marring his beautiful features as he adjusts his towel where it's tucked in at his waist. The crease between his eyes deepens as he puts his glasses on and I find myself explaining.

"I mean, that—" I say pointing back toward the bathroom, "happened and I don't want things to be weird or just about that unless that's what you want, so if you don—"

He shuts me up quickly with his mouth on mine, teasing my tongue and biting my lip softly as his fingers circle my neck and his thumbs lift my chin toward him.

"Stop. I'm just going to grab a clean pair of boxers and then, I'll be in your bed. All night."

"All night," I repeat.

"All night."

Chapter 23

Alexander

All night.

The words are on repeat as I slip into a clean pair of underwear and brush my fingers through my damp hair.

How long has it been since I spent multiple nights in a bed with someone? Undergrad, maybe? Even then, that was a rare occurrence. Any relationship I've had has been single-night weekend sleepovers. I have never lived with a girlfriend with the exception of Harper, and she never stayed in my bed after our first night together.

I never slept in hers.

It's already getting late, and I have to work tomorrow. I'd rather stay home, in bed, with Wren, but that can't happen. I opt to give myself a few extra minutes in the morning by pulling my clothes out for the day, setting my watch on the nightstand, and placing my glasses beside it. Everything I would do if I was going to crawl into bed in this room. But I'm going to Wren's room.

Turning the lamp off as I pick up my wet towel, I walk back toward the bathroom. I'm used to being quiet in the house, not because anyone ever complained, but because everything else sometimes feels so loud. Wren doesn't notice me in the doorway as I stop in to collect her towel from the end of the bed on my way through to the bathroom.

Her confusion when I come back into the room is cute and comical.

"I know I had a towel," she says, looking on the floor and then lifting the comforter to scan beneath the bed.

"I already took care of it," I say.

She stands upright, straightening her shoulders, and her stress melts a little from her features when I shrug and smile.

"I could have hung it up. I was going to. I needed to brush through my hair. The cold water made it all knotty," she says, overexplaining. "Why are you looking at me like that?"

"Like what?"

"Like 'Aw, poor Wren'," she says.

"Nope. That's not how I thought I was looking at you. Is this better?" I ask, cocking an eyebrow and crossing my arms over my chest.

"Um, not so much. I like when you look at me like you want to devour me, not when you have your judgy teacher face on," she blurts out.

"Get in the bed, Wren."

She giggles as I walk to my side of the bed and pull the covers back. Rather than getting in the bed, she watches me intently as I climb in and get comfortable. Tossing my left arm behind my head as I lean against the pillows, I motion with my right hand for her to join me.

"Were you waiting for an invitation?" I ask, as she curls into my side and I scoot down the mattress.

Sliding my arm beneath her neck, she lifts up enough to turn off her bedside lamp and get comfortable again, wiggling her butt against my lap.

"Just wanted to make sure you were in the spot you wanted."

"You need to stop moving. This is supposed to be just friends spooning," I say, a yawn escaping.

"Just friends spooning isn't a real thing," she says.

"Sure it is. See, we're doing it right now," I say, draping my arm across her hip and pulling her closer to me.

"Just friends shouldn't include a boner in my butt cheek."

"Shouldn't doesn't mean couldn't."

The room goes as silent as it does dark and I wonder if she's already drifted off. Her exhaustion was apparent during dinner and I really didn't have any intention of keeping her up late. She caught me off guard with that question when I told her she should get ready for bed. Not in a bad way, though, because I want to get to know every inch of Wren.

If she'll have me.

I need to remind myself that even though she isn't Harper, I also don't know if she's ready for something more than what's happening right now. Snuggling, making out, and apparently making each other orgasm repeatedly in the shower.

I listen as her breathing slows and her body relaxes against me. Sleepily, her hand pulls mine closer around her and I nuzzle her head, deeply inhaling the intoxicating scent of her shampoo as I seek to fill the space between us.

*****

Sneaking out of my own house is a new concept, but I want Wren to sleep. Knowing she doesn't technically have anything going on today makes it easier to quietly slip out of bed, kiss her forehead, and gather my things for work.

Does that mean I don't want to wake her from a sound sleep and watch her fall apart for me with my mouth firmly planted against her clit before I leave? No. It actually takes all my self-control to not wake her up. Will I attempt to do that tonight? Possibly. I'm a gentleman, though, and going to let her lead the way.

By the time I get to my office, I want to turn around and go back home to her. Nothing else happened last night, but knowing she'd be there when I woke up made it easier to sleep. I was content, and despite normally being content, this is different. I can go about my life happily distracted by the things I need to do, the routine, and the few friends I have. Falling asleep with someone I feel connected to? Her letting me fall asleep with her? This is not my normal contentment.

It's euphoric.

As I turn the corner to my office, I come face-to-face with Harper whose eyes immediately widen.

"Oh my God, you got laid," she says.

"Did not," I reply, unlocking my office and swinging the door open for her to enter.

"You only look this calm after sex, Alex," she says. "I would know."

"Again, did not," I say, stepping in behind her and closing the door. "Not really."

Her eyes flit between me and the closed door.

"Right, you're at work. I'm reducing my volume. So, tell me what happened," she inquires while planting herself in my chair behind my desk. She props her feet up on the table and crosses her arms, waiting for me.

"Isn't this weird for you?"

"No."

Setting my coffee, backpack, and laptop bag down on the desk, I sit on the edge of the chair across from her. Leaning forward with my elbows on my knees, I clasp my hands in front of me.

"Nothing major happened. We just had some fun. She had a long day, I had a long day, she was practicing her hitting when I got home, we had dinner, and then took a shower," I say.

"Together?"

"Yes."

"So, you had not sex sex and it was really good," she explains for herself to understand without me having to explicitly tell her.

"That's definitely how I would describe it," I say.

Staring at my hands, I let the room go quiet. I have so much to get done and after I get through today we have a long weekend I would like to enjoy, but I also don't want to kick Harper out of my office.

"Where did you sleep?"

Looking up at her, I see hope in her eyes. Hope for me. It's an involuntary movement when my mouth curves into a smile and she reciprocates.

"Her bed."

"I love that for you, Alex," she says.

"Same," I say. "Now, as much as I love being interrogated first thing in the morning before the coffee has really kicked in, I need to get ready for my Friday seminar."

Harper pulls her legs off my desk and pushes herself to standing.

"Yeah, yeah, I know. Big bad professor guy has to be prepped for class. I honestly just wanted to stop by on my way to work to let you know yes to cookout at Rick and Maggie's. We're planning Sunday. You don't have classes Monday, but Maggie and Delilah are open for normal business Monday. They aren't doing holiday hours since school starts next week and all the PTO moms want cookies and cupcakes for the teacher's lounge."

"Perfect. I'll touch base with Mags and see if there's anything I can bring. Is Will coming?" I ask, hopeful he and Wren will have another opportunity to visit.

"Is Will coming? That's a silly question," Harper says as she rounds the desk. Placing a kiss on my cheek, she adds, "He'll be there. I heard he talked my brother's ear off about his morning meeting with Wren."

Kissing her cheek in return, I give a look.

"In a good way?"

"Like in a, 'Rick, I swear I know her from somewhere,' way and I didn't dare mention the possibility of ... you know."

I open my mouth to congratulate her on keeping hers closed, but think better of it.

"I appreciate you not telling Maverick what we're all wondering," I say, pulling her in for a quick hug. "It really means a lot to me, because I have no idea where she's at with all of it. I don't think she's even mentioned having met Will to her mom."

We never had that conversation last night. We talked so quickly about Will and the garden I didn't even think to ask if she had thoughts on him being her biological father before we were moving on to eating dinner.

"Of course. I know this is a sensitive topic and I don't want to do anything to hinder Wren's search for her father," she says moving toward the door and placing her hand on the knob. "Plus, I still think it would be absolutely wild if he was her father because, seriously, what are the chances?"

Shoving my hands in my pockets, I watch her open the door and step through before saying, "Slim to none, but slim nonetheless."

"True. I'm outta here. Loveyoubye!" Harper's out of sight and around the corner by the time I stick my head out into the hallway.

Scrubbing my hands down my face I turn back to the desk, take a sip of my coffee, and pick up my guitar. I have a little more than an hour to get into teacher mode and it doesn't seem like nearly enough time. My nervous system needs a slow down; my brain needs to do something routine. Strumming the same chords on repeat. Over and over. Trying to fit in where I know the song. It's not one I usually play, but I know the tune and just keep playing.

Over and over.

I must play for forty-five minutes, closing my eyes to feel the vibrations from the guitar as I pluck the strings, trying to remember the song. I know the tune and somehow even without knowing the words I can hear the entire thing, adjusting the chords as I go until it sounds right. As soon as it feels perfect, I start again.

"Oh my, my. You've got it pretty bad, huh?" Dylan says from the door. I stop playing, laying my hand flat against the strings, and look at her, quizzically. "'Ordinary.' That's what you're playing. Did you not know the song?"

"I had no idea. I just started playing and couldn't figure out what song it was so I just kept playing until it sounded right."

"I like her," Dylan says.

I nod, propping the guitar against the bookshelf and then tipping back in my chair. Lacing my fingers together behind my head, I stare at her.

"I like her, too."

"I know. We've got a scrimmage next Friday. You coming?"

"If she wants me to."

Dylan rolls her eyes.

"I want you to. This isn't about Wren. This is about you. I want you to help the girls with a playlist they can use during warmups. Sort of a team building thing," she says. "It was Wren's idea."

"A little AC/DC? Some Ozzy?"

"Or Benson Boone and Alex Warren, since you apparently already know some of his stuff. They're into all sorts of music, so swing by a practice next week and chat with a couple of the ladies. Just make sure it's appropriate for all audiences. The last playlist we had got me called to the college president's office," she says, pushing up out of her seat.

I laugh remembering the game I went to last season that got her in trouble.

"Some songs are definitely better suited for the bedroom instead of the ballfield, that's for sure." I chuckle.

"Hilarious. Just keep laughing, but remember I'm putting you in charge now so if something is amiss, you get to go see the president," Dylan says, laughing along with me.

She reaches out and I meet her hand halfway, offering a firm handshake.

"No worries. I'll start putting something together and stop by practice on Tuesday," I say.

We exchange a few more niceties until I realize I'm going to be late to my class if I don't hurry. Dylan walks with me, leaving me near the room my students are strolling into, allowing me to fall back into my ordinary routine. I watch each of these people enter the room, waiting until it's my turn, and my phone buzzes.

Wren: I hope you have an extraordinary day.

The smile comes on its own as I realize ... I'm okay with not having ordinary.

Chapter 24

Wren

"My parents are in Rochester," I say out loud after I get off the phone and catch Alex staring at me.

This was not the plan. They were going to drive out in October once I was a little more settled and bring some of my bigger things — my bike and boxes of books, my giant reading chair, things like that.

"That's great! They came out to surprise you?" he questions, standing shirtless with his hair still mussed from our shower while he diligently works on the food we're taking to the picnic.

I love that he's excited about this because I really want my parents to meet him. For one, it'll make my dad less apprehensive about me living with a guy he doesn't know. The Alex Situation is turning into more of a beautiful, symbiotic relationship, which I've tried to explain to my father. He's still leery of it. As he should be. He's a dad and worries.

My mom is less weird about it. Unfortunately, she could get more weird very soon.

I'm still in shock they came to New York for Labor Day weekend. On a whim, no less, which is not like them.

"Alex, we're getting ready to go to Maggie's."

"I know. I'm mixing a pasta salad. I'm aware where we're going. Text them the address so they can meet us there. Or we can wait and they can ride with us."

I smack my palm against my face and groan. His brain is still cloudy after our early morning together. He is the best alarm and I crave him, but now is not the time for his grey matter to fail me.

"Alexander," I say sternly and he turns from the counter to look at me, deer-in-the-headlights eyes and everything because I don't call him Alexander ... and when I have his reaction has been a little more feral than this. With his attention on me, I say, "We are going to Maggie and Maverick's for a picnic. Did you forget who else is going to be there?"

His eyes grow impossibly wider as it becomes clear what I'm talking about. Or at least, I thought it was clear until he responds.

"Oh. Oh! I don't want you to get upset. I know Harper is going to be there, but—"

"You're adorable when you're hopeless. Alex, Will is going to be there. Will."

"Shit," is all he says.

I nod, trying to figure out if it would be acceptable for me to bow out of the picnic. I could have Alex tell them I have cramps or need to finish unpacking or anything else that will give me an escape. But that's not how I want to be. I want to spend time with the friends I'm trying to make here. I want to meet more of Alex's friends. It sounds crazy because of their history, but I really want to meet Harper.

And I want to spend time with Will.

I bite my lip, feeling overly emotional because it's suddenly all so overwhelming. Alex wipes his hands on the kitchen towel he has draped over his shoulder and steps toward me. Tossing the towel on the counter, he takes my face in his hands and tips my head back so we can see each other's eyes. He walks me back until my shoulders touch the refrigerator door and I have nowhere else to go. Then his mouth is angling toward mine and he's kissing the fear and overwhelm out of me.

"Good," he says, placing his mouth on mine again.

My fingers find the top of his hips as they peek above his boxers and the jeans that ride low on his waist.

"That's much better," he says, pulling away from me again.

"I don't know what's better, but okay."

"You are. You were sounding a little freaked out," he says, smiling.

He presses a gentle kiss to my forehead and slides his hands down my arms to hold my hands.

"I am freaking out," I say, closing my eyes and dropping my head back against the fridge, feeling the weight of the potential situation.

"But why? So, your parents are here and Will is going to be at the picnic. Who better to give you confirmation or not than your mom?" he says, and I slowly open one eye to look at him. "If he's not *the* Will she created you with, you can mark him off your list and keep looking."

"That doesn't make me panic less. I've been secretly hoping it's him because he's just so nice, Alex. If it's not him ... maybe I shouldn't keep looking."

"You're putting all your hope into one person you met five days ago. Why?"

I wait a beat to respond because I don't have a response.

"I put all my faith into you a day after we met and, to add insult to injury, barely knew you when I moved out here. It's kind of my signature," I say, smiling to help the delivery.

"You're cute when you're sassy, but don't lose the plot. Your mom will know if Will Murphy is her weekend fling and your dad," he says, his eyes turning as stern as his voice.

I briefly wonder if his students see this side of him and if it's ever caused a problem.

"Plus, I want to meet them. This is some major Band-Aid ripping and maybe it's best to get all of it over with at once," he says, stepping back. I miss him immediately. "At this rate they're going to get here before we leave for Mags' so at least they get to meet me first and then everyone else."

Sighing, I step away from the fridge as he goes back to mixing the salad. I pour what's left of the morning's coffee into my mug and reheat it. I share what's left with Alex, handing him the mug as I take over putting the lid on the salad to place it in the cooler filled with ice and extra drinks.

"Did you buy more juice boxes?" I ask, counting the number in the cooler.

"I did. Figured between Maggie and Maverick's kids, Fisher and Delilah's kids, Fisher's sister's crew ..."

"How many people did they invite?" I realize I never asked and between us and everyone he listed so far that's already almost twenty people. "Maybe we should have made a bigger salad."

"The entire family. Don't worry about food. You forget Fisher is a restaurant guy. He always brings too much," he says.

I roll my eyes at Alex.

"I can't have forgotten. I didn't know."

His mouth opens but I raise my hand to quiet him before he can apologize.

"I guess I know where date night is going to be."

"Date night? Are we going to have one of those?" he says, deadpan.

I immediately wonder if I've misread the entire situation. Rather than bring it up right away I go about getting the kitchen picked up while he switches laundry. It's our first weekend living together and we've already fallen into routines that are so domestic.

This isn't roommates.

This isn't even friends with benefits.

Finishing in the kitchen, I wander back through the house to the bedrooms, stopping in mine to make the bed. I put the pillows back where they belong and fold the quilt. Alex brought it in last night because it was chilly, so once folded I pick it up and carry it to his room.

I haven't been in here yet. Not because he doesn't want me in here, but because I haven't had a reason. Setting the quilt on the end of his still made bed, I let my eyes wander. A guitar on the wall, his diplomas from high school and his undergraduate and graduate schools on either side of the instrument, a framed picture of his parents on his dresser. A bottle of cologne, drum sticks, guitar picks, and a hair brush. A stack of textbooks with pages flagged, and I recognize one as his beach read.

I touch the quilt I've laid at the foot of his bed. It doesn't look like it belongs in here.

Regardless, everything is in its place.

Neat. Tidy. Minimalist. Nothing like his office where he's maxed out most of the small space.

How's he going to feel when all of my stuff gets here? Where am I going to put it?

Turning back toward the door, I jump finding him standing there. Leaning against the door, he fills the frame and watches me, but is not judging. It's curiosity.

"The quilt," I say. "Where does it go?"

He points to the closet and I move to pick it up.

"It's okay there. The nights are going to keep getting cooler so we'll probably want to just leave it on the bed. Your bed," he says, pausing. "Or my bed. Our bed?"

I swallow and leave my fingers dangling, the tips touching the fabric, as he watches me.

"Is this moving too fast?" he asks, finally.

"Do you think it is?" I respond, wondering how he is asking the same question I was going to.

"I don't think something can move faster than it's meant to. When something feels right, works well, and fills all the voids I didn't know were there, I think it's going to happen even if we try to slow it down," he says quietly, choosing each word carefully. "But maybe I don't want to slow it down."

"I don't either."

"You fill all the voids," he says, and I notice his eyes fall to the quilt, my fingers, the bed.

"Are we sure we don't want to casually date first?" I ask, an attempt to inject humor into a heavy conversation.

"I mean, we could, but we skipped a bunch of steps already. Backtracking seems a little silly at this point."

It's not like we met and jumped right into bed. We talked, danced, walked, played on the beach, and talked for hours on the phone with a country dividing us. I ached for him without admitting how much I missed him, even though I only knew him for a week. We condensed what some might take years to do into a couple months getting to know one another. He knows about my dad, and that's something I haven't even shared with my cousin, the person who was one of my closest confidants as a teenager. To casually date now — slip out of one another's beds and go out for dinner as if we aren't together, to not be committed — doesn't make sense.

"It's not really logical, is what you're saying," I finally respond, catching his eyes as he looks back up at me.

"Yes. It's not logical at all. I already know I want you to be mine and only mine," he says, his voice low and serious, making him completely unaware of the way my body responds to him when he talks like this. It ignites a need we literally don't have time to address and I shift uncomfortably. "Problem?"

"Nope. We'll handle it later," I say, my voice slightly higher than it should be. He gives me a devilish grin as I step toward him with the intention of leaving his room.

"You sure?"

He cocks his eyebrow at me and I fall a little harder when he tugs his glasses off to wipe the lenses on the shirt he grabbed from the clean laundry. He doesn't take his gaze off me as he softly rubs each lens between his thumb and middle finger. When I look at him, I notice the smirk. Always a little, knowing, smirk.

"Something on your mind?" he asks.

"Not really," I say in an attempt at nonchalance. "Just thinking about what it's like to get rubbed like that. You're really good at it."

He can't keep a straight face and as I slip between him and the doorframe, he presses into me, leaning into my space to kiss me like he more than likes me.

*****

"Your parents are on their way here now? That's awesome," Maggie says taking the pasta salad dish from my hands.

Alex and I explained briefly how my mom called not even an hour ago from the Rochester airport and I panicked.

"I don't like being a burden on people and it feels like springing on you guys that there will be more people coming than expected is … burdensome," I say.

It stops me from saying anything more when Maggie bursts out in laughter.

"Burden? Stop, please," she says, looking around her very full kitchen. Dishes are lined up on counters, packages of hot dog and hamburger rolls are stacked on the table, and there are teenagers running after toddlers. "We believe in chaos around here these days, if you hadn't noticed. Two more mouths to feed won't relieve us from the number of leftovers everyone is being sent home with. Hopefully Murph's guys are hungry tomorrow."

I swallow hard at the mention of Murph, Will's brother. I haven't met him yet.

"Is Murph coming today?" I ask. Glancing at Alex, I find he's more concerned with dipping carrot sticks in ranch and eating them while checking out the rest of the food than anything we're talking about.

"He is. He and Will are already out back with Maverick getting the fire ready if you two want to grab drinks and go out there. I'm just about set in here," Maggie says as she rearranges a shelf in the refrigerator.

"Are you sure you don't need help?" Alex asks, coming to stand beside me again.

My phone begins ringing in my back pocket. I excuse myself as I see my mom's name flash on the screen and hope they haven't gotten lost. When she called earlier, they had just deplaned and were headed to baggage claim. Then a text came in while they were waiting at the car rental area to tell us to go on ahead of them and they would meet us here instead of making us wait.

"Is she okay?" I hear Maggie say to Alex.

My back is to her and I'm halfway into what I assume is their living room before Alex responds.

"She's just got a bunch of things on her mind. There's a lot going on right now, you know?"

I refocus and answer my phone, knowing if I don't right now it's going to get sent to voicemail.

"Hey, were you able to find your luggage?" I ask as soon as the call connects.

"It took a bit, but we found it. According to GPS, we are almost to the address you gave me," she says.

"Five minutes, but I'm going to see if I can beat it," my dad says in the background.

"If you're that close, I'll wait outside for you," I say, feeling my excitement begin to creep in. It's only been a week since I left California, but it feels like forever since I've seen my parents. The uneasiness of the possible situation that is brewing dissipates for the moment as I poke my head back into the kitchen and, covering the mouthpiece on the phone, tell Alex they're almost here before I go out the front door to meet them in the driveway. "I didn't bring my car, but Alex has the same one just a different color so when you pull into the driveway and see the thousand cars but not mine, that's why."

She chuckles and it's a welcome sound. We're going to need to figure out phone calls with the time difference.

"Sugar Shack Landscaping?"

"That's the place," I say, unable to keep the smile from my voice. I listen as the car crunches on the gravel and then lift my arm to wave. "I see you!"

"I see you, too!" she exclaims, and then hangs up on me as my dad comes to a stop beside Maverick's work truck.

My mom practically ejects herself from the passenger seat and grabs me around the waist in a tight hug, lifting me up on my toes.

"You could have let me put the car in 'park' first, Anita," my dad playfully scolds as he comes around the back of the rental and scoops me up. "How are you, my sweet girl? Are you settling in?"

My voice is muffled against his shirt, the smell of the cologne I've known my entire life filling my senses with familiarity, as I say, "Getting there."

"It's been a busy few days since I got here. I didn't expect to see you two until at least next month," I say, stepping back and sliding my hands in my pockets.

"Well, we wanted to come visit before trekking across the country with a trailer full of things," my mom says sheepishly. "This way we can see how much room you're working with."

I noticed my dad's eyes flick to something behind me and don't have a chance to turn and look before feeling Alex come up beside me. Placing his left hand at the small of my back, he reaches out his right arm to shake my dad's hand.

"Hi, you must be Wren's dad. I'm Alex. It's nice to finally meet you," he says, keeping his hand protectively on my back as he and Dad exchange quick pleasantries. Mom looks at me, trying not to smile but failing spectacularly as Alex then introduces himself to her. "I'd love to say Wren's told me all about you both, but not really. I think it's been kind of a whirlwind since she got here."

My mom grabs my arm and pulls me away saying, "I want to hear all about it." Then more quietly, she adds, "He's cute."

I feel my cheeks heat as I turn my head to look behind me where Alex and Dad remain. I can tell by the way my father crosses his arms over his chest and widens his stance that he's about to grill Alex about anything he can before Alex tries to escape. This isn't the first time I've seen my parents pull this, but it is the first time I'm not afraid they're going to scare him away.

"Yeah, he's pretty handsome," I finally respond.

We wander off toward the backyard where Maggie said tables and tents were set up along with snack foods and coolers filled with drinks.

"He's been good to you since you got here?"

"Oh yeah, the best," I say, knowing she has already figured out we're more than simply sharing a house.

"Just use protection, Wren," she says, causing me to gasp, as she stares out at what must be the pine tree farm. There are greenhouses nearby, but there are hundreds of evergreens reaching out across the property. "I thought this was called Sugar Shack? And your friends owned a landscaping company?"

"I haven't been here long enough to know the details, Mom. It's definitely a landscaping company. It's also a Christmas tree farm. Maggie's husband Maverick owns it and his friend helps out when their daughter is in school, Alex helps occasionally. It's a whole family operation," I say, wandering toward the coolers marked 'water.' I grab two bottles and turn back toward my mom. "I'm sure 'sugar shack' comes into play somehow. Maybe because the bakery has an onsite location?"

I'm rambling, but that's how I usually talk to my mom. She usually rambles right back at me. Only this time she's looking beyond me.

"It was Sugar Shack before they started tapping the maples on the other side of the property and over at Gram's, but now the farm is living up to its name," he says, opening the cooler I just closed. "Glad you could make it, Wren. Did you go back out to pick more tomatoes yet or are you doing that tomorrow morning when Will comes over for coffee?"

My mouth splits into a smile while I watch the color drain from my mother's face, until I turn and realize that it isn't Will talking in third person. They just look and speak very similarly.

"You must be Father Murphy!" I say, reaching out my hand. "Were the veggies okay? Will said he was bringing them to you after he let me help with the garden."

"They were perfect. Thank you for sharing," he says, taking my offered hand. "I heard you were told about the secret family recipe — toasted tomato and mayo sandwiches. Did you try it?"

I laugh, feeling myself relax into the newness of meeting Murph, as I also carefully watch my mother, who has yet to step closer or say anything as she watches the interaction.

"I did. It was better than I anticipated and I do believe I'm a fresh from the garden tomato convert."

"My mother would be so proud. My brother out here doing the Lord's work," he says, winking at me. Motioning toward my mom, he says, "And who is this?"

I make quick introductions and it's as strange as one could expect, right up to the point of my mom blushing and telling Murph he looks a lot like someone she knew once.

I pull my lips in and force myself to be quiet as Alex and Dad make their way into the yard mid-heated conversation about the Yankees and Red Sox.

That's not a conversation I care to get in the middle of and thankfully they're nearly finished as they reach us.

"Murph, Yankees or Red Sox?" Alex asks.

"No, thank you," Murph responds. "I don't take sides in baseball. That's a conversation to have with Will. But I am a Buffalo Bills fan to my core."

"Will?" Mom questions, her eyebrows wrinkling at the bridge of her nose.

"My apologies. Will is my brother. He loves baseball. I'm a football guy. Makes for lively get togethers anytime of the year," Murph says. "He's around here somewhere. I'm sure he'll turn up and you'll get to meet him. Usually, he's helping Rick with the grilling or chasing one of the little kids around but he might have taken a drive out back to the greenhouses. He said something earlier about bringing up some mums for Wren."

"But the ones at the house look fine. That's what he said the other day."

"I'm just the messenger," Murph says, raising his hands and chuckling, he steps back from our small group.

As we find our way over to a table to sit, Murph walks back toward the grill and I take the moment to ask Alex who all the other people are roaming around. He begins pointing at each one and giving me and my parents a run down on who they are, where they live, work, what business they have, how many kids they have, and I can't hide my curiosity as he shares information with me. I want to know all of them. I want to have this family like he does. It's always been me and my parents and no one else, really. Big gatherings like this weren't the norm for me growing up and as I sit with that knowledge, I begin to miss a childhood I didn't experience, through no one's fault. It just wasn't how I was raised.

"You know everyone, huh?" my dad asks.

Alex shrugs. "It's a hazard of living here. Wren will hopefully get used to it."

"I did not grow up in a super close-knit community, that's for sure," I say, taking a sip of my water. "At least it didn't feel that way. I had a few close friends and things, but nothing like this. It might take a while for me to really settle into the idea of everyone knowing everyone."

I watch as Maggie and another woman come out of the house carrying platters of food, followed by two teen girls also with their arms full, and stand to go in that direction. Alex questions me with a look and I let him know I'm going to go help.

"Want me to come with you?"

"No, that's all right. Sit and visit. Let me do this," I say and lean down to kiss his cheek.

As I stand, I see Maggie and the woman she was walking with staring at me. Maggie is smiling; the unnamed woman is judging. I can see it on her face and, as I walk closer, I feel the judging even more. She doesn't know me and I'm apparently in her territory.

"Can I help bring more things out?" I ask by way of breaking the ice.

Looking between me and her friend, Maggie seems to be gauging the vibe. Gently with the palm of her hand, she shoves her friend and tells her to get walking.

"Harper," Maggie whispers to me as Harper walks ahead of us.

"Oh, that explains the look," I say, saddened that this was our first interaction. "Is it okay I'm here? My parents and I can go back to the house and I can get them settled if it's going to be a problem."

Maggie opens the back door and we enter the mudroom off the kitchen.

"Harper is just being Harper," Maggie says loudly. "She's not really a bitch."

I know my eyes open wide and I'm suddenly uncomfortable. Maybe this wasn't a good idea.

"Nope, I'm not," Harper says as we walk back into the expansive kitchen. "Why? Who thinks I'm a bitch?"

"Harper, Wren. Wren, Harper. There, now you're all introduced. Still so weird the guy I dated then dated my sister-in-law and is now dating my new tenant. This should be illegal," Maggie rattles off as she arranges fruit onto a clean platter, stopping to shove a strawberry in her mouth.

At the same time Harper and I respond, "So weird."

"But," she continues, "we were never 'dating,' okay? We didn't do the whole being exclusive thing."

"But you were exclusive, were you not?" Maggie asks.

"I wasn't fucking anyone else, if that's what you're asking," Harper says, shrugging, and I clamp my mouth closed to keep from laughing.

"Close enough to exclusive, if you ask me," I say, adding more vegetables to another tray.

Maggie holds her hands out in my direction, and says, "See, she gets it."

"However," I continue, "if the two of you never agreed to be exclusive, I don't think it counts. That sounds more like a relationship of convenience."

The room is quiet as I continue putting cauliflower on the tray. They are both staring at me when I look up and, for a second, I again wonder if I should go home, until they look at each other and smile.

"Yeah, I think she's going to be good for him," Harper says.

"Thanks? I think?" I question, acutely aware of the fact I'm having this conversation with the ex-girlfriend of my new boyfriend, or at least I think he's my boyfriend now. "Yes. Thank you. I hope I'm good for him. So far, he's been pretty good for me, too."

"I mean with a dick like that—" Harper begins and cuts herself off as she looks at me. "Never mind."

"Yeah, good save, Harp. Jesus, if there's one way to scare her away from all of us, it's definitely like that," Maggie scolds as we walk single-file behind her, each of us carrying a tray of something, out of the house to add to the arrangement of foods available under the party tent.

Stepping into the sun as it crosses over the house to the backyard, I shield my eyes and notice Alex sitting beside Will, across from my parents, and I stumble. Alex is up out of his chair as quickly as I correct my steps. My dad and Will both stand up and make movements toward me, but Alex reaches me first and they sit back down after seeing I'm fine. Tenderly removing the tray from my hands, Alex turns to my side and presses his hand to my back like he did when meeting my parents not long ago.

"What's going on? Over there?" I ask, my voice hushed. "I can carry that."

"Just a few people getting to know one another," he says. "You can carry it, but I'm carrying it now."

"Alex, I wasn't planning on them meeting Will when I was in the house. He was nowhere to be found when I went in there and I come out and they're all getting cozy," I say, the panic finding its way into my gut.

He sets the tray of veggies down beside the one filled with fruit and turns back to me as I watch the table across the yard. Will stands up and reaches his hand out, shaking my dad's hand and then taking my mom's, and that's when I see her face.

I see it.

The recognition.

The knowing.

The intimacy.

She hasn't said a thing, she couldn't possibly have, or I'm sure there would be more happening. I don't know what kind of more, but it would be more, wouldn't it? Some yelling? A heated discussion at least?

"I think ... it's going to be fine. Will has some more mums for the house and he's coming over for coffee tomorrow morning, right?" Alex asks. I nod. "So, make today be about getting to know new friends and enjoying the last long weekend before you're thrown into work and save all the concern for tomorrow. I'll make myself scarce so you and your parents can visit. How long are they here?"

"Good plan. I have no idea; it didn't come up. Also, I met Harper. Officially."

Alex's face pales. I smirk.

"Apparently, she and Maggie think I'm a good fit for you. Plus, there was something about your, uh, member," I say, trying to keep the conversation as appropriate as I can considering there's a sudden barrage of children hovering around the snacks.

"Oh really?" he asks, and I can see the need to be nosey is slowly wrecking him. "What about him?"

"Not much. I assume the intention is for me to become better acquainted with him, but Harper stopped herself before she said too much and made it more awkward," I say. "She might not think it was, but it was already pretty awkward."

He laughs loudly and wraps his arm around my waist, pulling me close. "I'm sure it was," he says, kissing me quickly before leading me away. "Come on. You still need to meet everyone else."

And I go willingly because I want this. I want this entire life.

Chapter 25

Alexander

I wake with a start. It's dark. Wren isn't in bed.

Then, as I lay back against the pillows, I hear it. The muffled sound of a bat hitting a ball.

Thwack. Thud.

Thwack. Thud.

And again, but this one is louder, harder, more aggressive.

It's my cue to get out of bed. Pulling a pair of grey sweatpants on over my boxers, I pad down the hallway. As I push my arms into a hoodie, I leave the hood up to keep me warm against the chill of the September morning, and make my way slowly to the breezeway. The sound is louder now with the back door left open and a cool breeze slipping through the screen door.

I don't go outside. Instead, I wait in the doorway and watch as she tosses a ball up in front of her, waits a beat, positions her feet, rocks, lifts up slightly, and then swings. The sound of the bat connecting with the ball is like a gunshot in the silence of morning. Then comes the thud as the ball flies into the net and bounces against the side of the house.

She reaches into the five-gallon pail beside her and produces another fluorescent yellow softball. Again — toss, position, rock, lift, swing — only this time I notice her shoulders and hips as they rotate in perfect union with the bat. The ball produces another thud.

Propping the door open, I sit on the step. Leaning my elbows on my knees, my bare feet in the wet grass, I clasp my hands together as I watch her in the half-full moonlight while she takes everything out on the ball.

Again.

Her breathing is heavy. Her cheeks are wet. Her feet are just as bare as mine, as she stands there in a fitted tank top and mid-rise running shorts, looking like she belongs in a sporting goods ad instead of sliding into home plate. In the dim light beside the door as it spreads out toward her, I can make out the flushed color of her skin from the cold and physical exertion. Sniffing deeply, she picks up another ball and goes again.

Thud.

"How long have you been out here?" I ask in the quiet.

"Not long enough," she replies.

"Want a sweatshirt?"

"No."

Another ball. Thwack. Thud.

"Need a hug?"

Silence. Her shoulders droop as she drags the bat behind her and comes to stand in front of me.

"Yes."

Looking at her, I push myself up and wrap her in my arms where she promptly falls apart. She doesn't tell me why, or which of her thoughts caused the need for a middle-of-the-night batting session, but I also don't need an explanation.

I know I'm not always the most emotionally available person, but for her I am. Somehow, for her I am.

"Yesterday was a lot."

She nods, squeezing me.

"It was heavier than we realized."

"Uh huh."

"But, I'm here to carry it with you. I'll always be right here with you, Wren."

She takes a shaky, deep breath in, and buries her face against my chest.

"You can't promise me forever, Alexander. It's too soon to say always."

"Maybe," I respond. "But I don't want to wait until it's too late."

In the silence, we hold one another a little longer, until I feel her body grow heavier against me. The sound of the bat bouncing on the solid ground behind me is the even bigger clue that her energy has given out. Glancing down at her, she's nestled her cheek against my chest and is almost sound asleep.

"Hey," I whisper. "Let's go back to bed."

"Mmhmm," she responds.

Slowly I pull her with me as I step into the house, her feet coming with us reluctantly as I guide her back to the bedroom.

"My feet are grassy," she says, climbing between the sheets.

"We'll worry about it in the morning," I say, tucking her in.

She yawns and rolls onto her side away from me. Before leaving her to close and lock the outside doors and settle down for the rest of the short night, I lean in to kiss her head, hoping I've done enough to help her sleep well.

"Forever and always," I say, hoping she hears my promise to her.

*****

Her parents arrive before nine in the morning after staying at a hotel nearby. I haven't slept since Wren and I went back to bed, so the coffee was already brewed and a cup poured for each of us when they knocked on the front door.

"She's alright, though?" Anita says after I finish explaining why Wren is still in bed. "Did she tell you what was bothering her?"

Tony has yet to come in the house, taking his time to explore the backyard after expressing his jealousy at Wren's green thumb, and then finding out I'm also a skilled gardener.

"I think yesterday was overwhelming for her. She met a ton of new people, you guys surprised her, and we were on the go all day. That's overstimulating for anyone, but for someone who just moved here and is thrown in the mix of smalltown life it's amplified," I explain.

I grew up here and haven't gone far without turning around and coming back, so it's not that I have experience myself being tossed into a different village of sorts. However, I've witnessed students who have melted down from the stress of moving away from home for the first time and having their lives upended right after jumping into college. It's the same concept. The only difference is Wren is working at the college, not living there.

"She said Will is coming over this morning," Anita hedges.

"He is. I figured while you, Tony, and Wren visited and worked out what you're bringing out next month, Will and I can start working in the garden," I say, attempting to give them all the space they seem to be asking for. "Apparently, he's bringing more mums."

"I saw the ones he picked out for Wren. Where do you plan on putting them?"

It's not something I've put thought into. But I tell her Will probably already has an idea where he wants to plant them so I'll follow his guidance.

I can tell she wants to say more. She fidgets and wiggles in her seat at the table.

"You look like you want to say something but don't know how," I say, walking across the kitchen to refill her coffee.

She winces, pulling the corner of her bottom lip in between her teeth like Wren does when she's trying to find the words she needs.

"Has she told you about her father?" she finally asks, very quietly while watching the door in the living room that leads to the hallway. "Her biological father?"

"She's told me about as much as she knows," I say, turning to replace the pot on the burner.

Anita takes a deep breath and releases it slowly, then picks up her mug and allows herself the time she needs by taking a long sip of her coffee. I hear the breezeway door open and footsteps coming into the house, assuming Tony will be joining us finally.

Staring into the mug, she says, "It's Will. Will is her biological father and I know my kid well enough to know she figured it out, but needs confirmation. It's been almost thirty years since I've seen him, but when I met Murph I was confused because he looked and sounded so much like Will, and then ... then Will came and sat at the table with us. And I couldn't even talk, because for the first time since that weekend I was staring at my daughter's father."

"I'm what?" Will says.

"Finally!" Tony exclaims coming up into the kitchen behind Will.

Anita and I both turn as Will stands just inside the doorway to the kitchen. He takes three more steps into the room and looks at the two of us. I follow his gaze as he lifts his eyes to the doorway across the room where Wren waits, wrapped up in one of my way-too-big for her hoodies and a pair of leggings, her hair thrown haphazardly up into a knot. She looks like a goddess. A slightly confused and exhausted goddess, but goddess nonetheless.

"He is? I wasn't imagining the way you looked at him yesterday?" she asks, her arms relaxed and at her sides as the sleeves hang down beyond her hands.

"I'm so sorry. I—" Anita begins. Taking a deep breath, she tries again. "I'm not sorry. It's not logical to be sorry about this."

"I mean, it's a little logical," Will says. "What do you mean I'm her father?"

Anita stares at him, then looks at Tony pleading for some help, and when she gets none, she says, "I left New York and found out two weeks later I was pregnant. We were careful, but not careful enough."

"Did you even try to find me? It's been twenty-nine years and four months. Did you even once try to find me?" Will asks, his voice rising slightly.

Tony's excitement is dissipating as the realization of what is happening hits home.

"I didn't know how to find you, Will. Google didn't exactly exist in the mainstream."

"You could have called the VA, Anita. They would have been able to find me," he says, his voice filling with more emotion.

I've never seen Will upset. A little frustrated once in a while, sure, but his ears are turning a bright red. He throws his hands up and clasps them behind his head as he walks over to the kitchen window. Staring out at the front yard, he watches the birds as they come and go at Gram's feeders. Blowing out a breath he was holding, the rest of us are silent as he absorbs the information. Sliding his hands forward, he grips the brim of his hat and pulls it off his head. Scratching the top of his head, he then replaces the hat and I can honestly say I've never in my life seen him so discombobulated.

"I did. Do you know how many 'Williams' are in the veterans' system? I didn't know your last name. Oh, his name is Will and he volunteers," Anita says, a tear slipping slowly down her cheek. I see the regret in her eyes as she comes to terms with the years they lost, that Wren lost. "They didn't know how to find you and I certainly wasn't going to tell them why I was looking for you. I wasn't going to tell them how my marriage was on the rocks and I came home from a business trip pregnant after a weekend with a stranger."

Turning and leaning against the counter, I watch this man who's been like an extra parent to me most of my life, shatter. I see his features change from frustration and sadness to understanding.

"I have a daughter," he says, his face reflecting the incredible weight of the moment as he looks at Anita. Then, turning his focus to Wren, he says, "You're my daughter?"

"That's what I'm learning, yeah," she says, her voice barely above a whisper, shrugging but not making any move to come into the room. She plants herself firmly on the other side of the threshold just inside the living room. "I guess it makes sense why you thought I reminded you of someone you used to know, especially after I mentioned I was from California ..."

Will stares at her, the flicker of recognition growing even stronger.

"You look like your mother."

"I know," she says. "But I look like you, too."

They fall into silence again, quietly sizing one another up, wordlessly comparing their features. It's not uncomfortable, but I feel like an outsider. I know Will, I'm falling in love with Wren and still getting to know her, and it's all happening in my house — well, it's our house — so I'm suddenly not quite sure what I should be doing with myself.

"She's a really good kid," Tony says, interrupting my thoughts as he walks to the table and picks up his coffee mug.

Will crosses his arms and stares at Tony as if he wants to say something but doesn't want to hurt his feelings.

"I know she is," Will says, confidently. "I could tell the minute I met her. Plus, she's got to be a good kid to move cross-country and deal with Alex. He can be a lot sometimes."

I turn my head in slow motion to glare at him.

"Don't you dare drag me into your family matters like that," I say sarcastically.

"Why the hell not? You're the one sleeping with my daughter," Will says, lifting his arm in Wren's direction

Wren gasps and Anita covers her mouth after a snicker sneaks out.

"She's wearing your sweatshirt. I'm not stupid, Alex," Will says.

"This is why I called it the Alex Situation," Tony says, confidently throwing his two cents in.

"I think I need to go check the garden," I say, pushing off the counter. With my mug gripped tightly in my fist, I shuffle toward Wren. She steps to the side to allow me through and whispers that I'm going in the wrong direction. Kissing her cheek, I say, "I'm grabbing a sweatshirt. I think you should get some coffee and go talk to your mom and dads."

She smiles at me.

"My dads. That sounds so strange, but I have a feeling it's going to be okay. Right? It's going to be okay?"

"Sweetheart, it's all going to work out," I say.

Chapter 26

Wren

Alex kisses me on the cheek again as he comes back through with a clean hoodie and a pair of socks, grabbing his mug from the coffee table on the way out of the house. I watch helplessly as he walks between all my parents on his way to the breezeway. He leaves the door open and sits on the bottom step putting his socks and boots on, stands to pull his sweatshirt on, picks up his coffee, and steps out of view.

"Wren," my mom says.

"Maybe we should all sit?" I suggest, hoping they'll be in agreement. "I just want a chance to pour a cup of coffee before we do this."

They respect my wishes and as I fill a clean mug, I hear the other chairs slide across the floor as my dad and Will each find a spot. There are only four seats at this table and as I turn back, I take a deep breath. The men have situated themselves on either side of my mom. It feels like I'm facing the firing squad, as I pull my chair out and sit across from Mom while noticing Dad and Will each slid their chairs slightly closer to her instead of all of us being equidistant from one another.

I sit, pulling my right leg up to wrap my arms around my knee.

"So," I begin. "I don't think any of us thought you would be in Brockport."

"But I live here. Why wouldn't I be in Brockport?" Will says, looking genuinely confused until a small smile forms.

I laugh, grateful he's taking this so well for the time being.

"I've had plenty of time to get used to the idea that I had another dad out there somewhere. They have known for ... twenty-nine years," I say, motioning to my parents. "You've known for ten minutes. Are you okay?"

Will lifts his coffee mug, pauses before taking a sip, and for a brief moment I watch his eyebrows scrunch together and then relax.

"I think if I wasn't okay with the idea of and meeting a child I fathered, I would have already walked out of the house," he says. "When your mother and I met, I wasn't in a good place. I know she and her husband — your dad — were off to a rocky start. We talked about all those things. Never in a million years did I think our weekend together would result in a baby, but I'm not stupid enough to know it wasn't a possibility."

I prepare myself for the next hardest question, because I'm ready for it if he wants to go through with confirmation.

"Would you feel better if we did a paternity test? So you know for sure that I'm yours?"

I watch his face, and his expression doesn't change.

Looking at my mom, Will says, "Anita, did you sleep with anyone other than me and your husband?"

I hide my smile because now is not the time to think this is funny, but it is humorous all the same. Here's this man I just met barely a week ago asking very personal questions about my mother's sex life and I'm really glad he's the one asking, not me.

My mother's jaw goes slack and for a split second I wonder if I should be worried.

"No, Will," she says, her eyes softening. "You were the only other one."

"So, if it's just him and me, one of us is her biological father. How do we know it isn't Tony?" he asks.

Noticing the other three mugs are nearly empty, I get up from the table and grab the coffee carafe to give them a warm-up as my mom begins telling Will about my dad's health problems. While listening, I set the coffee maker up again and turn it on for a fresh pot, knowing this conversation could last a while.

I sit quietly, hearing the story I already know and filling in details here and there.

"Then, without talking about it as a family, Wren had the testing done to see if she was a match should an organ donor be needed. She wasn't a match, but her blood type also isn't possible if she came from me and Tony," Mom says. "I knew, from the moment the pregnancy test turned positive. So did Tony. We ... we weren't in a place in our marriage at that point where a pregnancy would have happened."

Will, listening intently, gets a confused look on his face for a brief moment, and then it clicks.

"You two hadn't ...? Like at all after you got back from New York?"

My mom shakes her head. My dad looks at Will and shrugs.

"Shit was difficult. The stress we put on ourselves right after getting married took its toll," he says, sadly, and I know despite all the work they've done it still hurts that they started off in such a tough position. "There was very little of that happening. When we found out about Wren, we got ourselves into therapy and worked on our marriage so we could be the best us for her."

Fully invested in my parents' story, Will leans forward cupping his mug between his large hands, and chews on the inside of his lip.

"But you made it through all that. A lot of people don't. A lot of people wouldn't even make it through finding out the baby isn't theirs," he says, and both my parents nod. "You should be really proud of yourselves."

"We are," my mom quips.

"Good. Is it just Wren? You and Tony didn't have any other kids?" he asks.

My mom glances at me, knowing I'm aware of the struggle they went through to give me a sibling.

"We tried. We went to specialists and doctors and … it just didn't happen. We decided we were happy to just have our little bird. It seems the only way we were getting one was by way of you," Mom says, holding back tears. "I just wish you'd been able to see her grow up from the beginning with us. I'm sorry we didn't try harder to find you, but I had such little information to go on. I'm so sorry."

Will reaches out and covers my mother's hand with his. It's the first time I've seen them touch since shaking her hand yesterday, but this is more than a handshake. It's intimate. It's lost lovers meeting for a fleeting moment. It's gentle. This touch is a quiet okay for a history he wasn't part of. My dad notices and the skin around his eyes crinkles at the edges as a small smile forms while he watches the interaction. It's as if he knows something I don't and I'm unsure how I feel about that.

"Do you have any other children?" Mom asks, her voice low.

I respect that she cautiously approaches the question because it could change the course of my life. It would be wild to not only meet my father but also find out I have a brother or sister. But Will shakes his head slowly, staring down into his mug. I'm still an only child.

"I never settled down with anyone. I've got Murph's guys at the church and working here and there with Rick. I've kind of become the surrogate uncle to a lot of kids around here, Alex included. Plus, I still have my Vets. They keep me busy," he says, but I can hear it in his voice. I can feel how much not having his own children was not part of his plan. It's not regret as much as resignation that it never happened.

"But now you have me and I'm your child," I say, overcome with emotion. "I'm yours and I want to know Murph's guys, too, and get to know you and be part of your life."

Will's head snaps up when he hears me.

"You are part of my life," he says. "You became part of my life the night you moved here and I met you at the restaurant. Even if you weren't part of me, Wren, I was going to know you because you're here. Even if by some weird turn of events you turned out to not be my daughter, you're still stuck getting to know me because I'm everywhere in this community."

As tears stream down my face, I don't bother wiping them away. Mom hands me a napkin, but I just hold it between my fingers, crumpling it in my fist. It's my emotional support napkin.

"The thing is, though, you are mine. I don't have a single reason to believe you aren't. And I sure as hell am not going to put all of us through a paternity test when you already know Tony isn't biologically related and, with the exception of me, your mom's been faithful to him. You're mine. You look like me and your mother, but you look like mine, too," he says, pulling his wallet from his back pocket to retrieve a black and white photo of a young girl.

Then he sets a photo of a young him and Murph on the table, and at the same age I could have been his twin. I pick the photos up and carefully examine them — my father, my uncle, and my grandmother, and we all look so similar.

The resemblance takes my breath away.

It all takes my breath away because now I can fill out the other side of my family tree with accurate information. I have an uncle, I have grandparents whose names I can learn, I have a bigger family when a few days ago it was just me and Mom and Dad.

I have an extra dad and he wants me in his life as much as I want him in mine.

And my life has never felt more full.

"Now that we've gotten all of that out of the way, would you like to go plant your new flowers with me?" Will asks, standing from the table to put his wallet back as he steps closer to my seat. He holds his hand out and I look up at him. "There are also tomatoes to pick. I heard all about how you tried the sandwich and liked it, so let's go fill a basket."

Placing my hand in his, I let him help me up from the chair. It doesn't surprise me when he pulls me into a hug. What does shock me is how it feels natural. Normal. He hugs ... like a dad.

A sob chokes me on its way out of my throat and he pulls me in a little tighter. It's only been a few years since Dad's medical complications led to me finding out Tony isn't my real father, but it feels like my heart has been waiting to connect with the other half of me for so much longer and this hug, this man, completes that. The tears won't stop, and Will just holds me as the front of his shirt slowly gets more damp. That's when I feel their arms, too. Mom and Dad and Will. All of them surround me and hold me up, because as much as I'm excited to get to know Will, this is so much more than I bargained for. Yesterday was a lot. Today is more.

"Why Wren?" Will questions, his voice muffled as I'm still in their hug huddle.

I lift my head slightly, turning my face to see my mother's eyes, and they sparkle a little as she looks up at him.

"You said Carolina Wrens are your favorite," she says. "Because they're good for gardens and symbolize hope. Tony picked it. It helped us heal. If nothing else, we wanted her to know she had a little of you even if you never met her."

"It fits her perfectly," Will says, smiling down at me.

My dad hasn't spoken much since they came in from the garden, but when I excuse myself to change while everyone else goes outside, I hear him and Will talking. I can't make out what they say, nor does it matter. I think the biggest thing is they communicate. I don't want there to be animosity, and I'd be wrong to think that once the dust settles there won't be any at all, but I can hope. Maybe having open lines of communication will make this transition easier for all of us.

Honestly, I hate that my existence is because my mom cheated. I don't like the idea that Will was "the other man" or that my dad and mom had so much negativity between them so early in their marriage that instead of talking, she hooked up with another guy.

If one good thing other than me can come out of this situation, I think it's going to be that we all work together. It's not that I want them to work together for me — I'm an adult now so it isn't like they need to navigate a young child finding out all of this information and then dealing with the potential fallout from that. No, I want us to all work together because I think deep down, my dad truly is thankful they have me regardless of the circumstances, my mom has made peace with herself for stepping outside their marriage, and Will has craved having a family of his own so much and for so long he's made everyone part of his family.

As for me? I think I just want to get to know my father, get to know my boyfriend, and play ball.

My back is to the door when Alex pokes his head into my room and clears his throat.

"Figured I would find you in here," he says. "Where do you want the mums planted."

Even if I didn't sleep in this room last night, it's where my clothes are so it's still my room. We're figuring out the logistics and once I really sit down to make a list of what I need from California, logistics are going to be even more important.

Pulling my T-shirt down over a sport bra, I turn to look at him.

"It's not my yard," I say, apprehensively. "I'm not sure where we should put them. Does Maggie have an opinion?"

"Nope, she said yesterday to have you decide."

"That's way more responsibility than I want right now," I say, laughing as I pick up Alex's hoodie and walk toward the door.

He doesn't move, so I step into his space only for him to drape his arms over my shoulders and kiss my forehead.

"We need to stop having big, overwhelming days. You haven't even been here a full week and already you've got a brand new big kid job, a boyfriend, another dad, and now people are demanding you choose where to plant the fall foliage," he says.

"The only thing missing is a collection of flannel in my closet and an unplanned pregnancy."

"I can remedy that for you," he interjects. "The flannel. For now."

I smile at him, enjoying the humor he finds in little things, loving the way we have melded into one another's lives so quickly.

"Everything has definitely been more than I bargained for, that's for sure, but I'd rock some flannel for you if it appears in the closet," I say. "As for the flowers, how about out front so everyone can enjoy them?"

I look up at him and he nods, then presses his lips to mine, his tongue tracing the seam until I open up for him. He deepens the kiss momentarily, just enough to make me need more, and then pulls away leaving me wanting. I groan at the loss.

"That kiss had potential. Me not being able to stop myself from locking you in here and bending you over the dresser can wait until later," he says, nipping my ear.

"That sounds like a really good way to alleviate stress," I say, my chest heaving slightly.

"I will do anything you want me to do and more tonight. But for right now? I'm not taking any chances of getting in trouble with your mom and two dads today."

"You're really enjoying saying I have two dads." I giggle. "You're such a weirdo."

"But I'm your weirdo and you love it."

"I love you," I say, the words slipping out without any effort to hold them back.

"Always and forever, Wren," he says, kissing me deeply again before topping it off with a nip to my bottom lip, taking my hand, and dragging me back down the hall to go plant flowers outside. Turning back for a beat he smiles and says, "I love you, always and forever."

Chapter 27

Alexander

NOVEMBER

I sit staring out the window in my office, the door closed and locked so it looks like I'm not even here right now. Thinking back on the last three years, it doesn't seem possible all the things I've taken to task in that timeframe. When I decided to apply for the doctoral program in music, I knew I wanted to have the PhD after my name. I wanted more out of this career.

Two and a half years later, I've completed all the prerequisite work, taken the exams, created and had the dissertation proposal approved, and started my research. My advisor and the committee were interested in what I was researching, and knew I would be considering more than just how music affects dementia patients. I'm looking at the psychological implications. So, when I started digging into my formal research — the book stuff and peer reviewed journals — I knew I would be finding more information in psychology texts than anywhere else.

I think my advisor was less surprised by that than I was. She's notably a musician, but also a known psych nerd and married to the head of the neuroscience department at the hospital affiliated with the university. My dissertation is the thing she's excited about right now, and I'm excited, too, but the hardest part is coming up. I have to put all the information together.

Confining myself to my office on campus before and after teaching for the last several days is the only way I've gotten most of my research put together in a cohesive manner. I'm coming to the end of my first set of observations at the nursing home, seeing the light at the end of the tunnel to my semester. Harper's ten-bed dementia unit proved to be the perfect size for a study like this and I'm grateful every resident's family was onboard and saw the validity in this research when I proposed the idea to the facility.

I'm starting to spiral, stuck in my thoughts when a text comes through.

Harper: I just want you to know I can see your office light is on and your car is still in the parking lot.

I turn on the small library desk lamp and then get up, walk to the door, turn off the overhead lights, and go back to my desk.

Me: You've been misinformed of my whereabouts.

After Wren's official first day at the college, we fell into a routine that gave us mornings and evenings together. I'd show up to scrimmages and practices; she'd stop by for lunch in my office on days I had late classes to teach or would be in Rochester for the evening. We worked together with the team to come up with their spring warm-up and walk-up music, she has consistently let me bounce ideas off her about this research. Tonight, I know she has a batting practice she's running with the team before finishing up for the fall and preparing for spring training.

She knows I'm here.

No one needs me right now, least of all Harper.

But I need me to get focused.

I turn notifications off and place my phone in the desk drawer before going back to the notes in front of me. The observations, the changes in behavior when playing music from various decades, stand out. They have from the beginning. The classical music, the calm music, the hip hop and rap, the old country music ... all of it.

For the next three hours I pore over the research, wondering if I can go deeper without losing sight of the reason for my study. And I can. It's a dissertation, yes, but by the time I'm completely done I want it to be polished and publishable if at all possible. I want to help families like Maggie's. I want to help the Grams out there who get lost in a time that no longer exists.

I've watched how some of the residents respond to the music and it gives me hope that I'm not wasting my time. The music brings them back from somewhere, and if they're not wandering through the past, it simply brings them joy. They smile, they function better, those who can will get up and sway or dance. The initial observations have my advisor and her husband curious about my findings.

Before long, the white board beside my desk is littered with Post-It notes as I add information to my outline and build the body of my research from the conceptual skeleton. I know I'm attempting to do too much at one time, but it feels too important to stop in the middle of the process and go home.

It also is very probable that I'm sitting on campus organizing the most complicated paper of my career because my girlfriend isn't home yet and I don't want to be in the house alone.

Our house is quiet when we go home at night. We're entering after busy days and exhausting schedules. Tony and Anita were here for a little more than a week helping move Wren's stuff in and getting her, and by default me, organized. We added a bookshelf to what is now the spare bedroom, rearranged my room to make it our room, put some things in the office and basement to store them, and finished off the growing season by picking what was left.

Every night while they were here, we had a family dinner with Will. Every week regardless of her parents being here or not, Wren makes time to have dinner with Will at least one night. Usually, they get together when I'm in Rochester, and as much as I hate to miss the chance to see their relationship grow I'm okay with them not including me. They need to get to know one another. I get my time with Will when I want it, just like I have for the last twenty-five years.

It might only be the beginning of November, but Wren and I need to have the conversation about Thanksgiving — if she's going to California, staying here, if her parents are coming here, if we're going to Maggie and Maverick's, if we're staying home ... It's our first holiday together. I get along with my parents, but they haven't been the "host a holiday" type since I was a child and usually go away on a trip. Now that I'm grown, I don't have the luxury of dropping everything to go with them, and the last time I actually spent any time with them at all was at Jayden's wedding.

This is why I cling so tightly to friends like Maggie and Harper, Maverick and Will, and now Wren. The blood of the covenant, you know?

Glancing at the board, I take my glasses off and press the heels of my hands into my eyes, rubbing the tired away. The clock on the wall above the chair tells me it's nearing ten at night and the exhaustion immediately makes sense. Sticking my pen behind my ear, I open the desk drawer and reach for my phone.

Seventeen missed calls from Wren.

Six from Maggie.

Nine from Will.

Text messages from all of them including Harper.

Wren: 911 Call me immediately.

My heart rate spikes. I press the call button while shoving my wallet in my pocket and grabbing my jacket. She answers before the end of the first ring.

"My dad's been life flighted," is all she says.

"I'm on my way," I say.

We live three minutes from where I park on campus and yet it feels like time moves too fast and too slow all at the same time as she tells me how her mom called. Her father collapsed and was rushed by ambulance to the closest hospital. They don't have a cardiac unit capable of handling what they think was happening. With his previous history, they made the decision to immediately send him by helicopter to the best cardiac hospital in the area.

I still have her on the phone when I pull into the driveway and she meets me by the car.

"I have to go. I need to go to California, Alex. I have to go home," she says, frantically.

Pulling her to me, I try to console her, but I haven't been in this position before. I haven't had emergencies. I've had a pretty regular and boring life.

"What do you need me to do for you?"

"I don't know. I don't know anything. Mom called me back when they decided to airlift him to Cedars-Sinai, but then we hung up when she got on the highway. I haven't heard anything in about an hour," she says, clinging to my shirt. "At that point she was thirty minutes out from the hospital, maybe more depending on traffic."

"Okay, so let's go in and find flights out there while we wait to hear from her. I'm not letting you go alone," I say.

We make our way out of the cold and into the house, pulling out her laptop to book flights from Rochester to Los Angeles with the least number of layovers possible. Finding a flight out by tomorrow morning is easy, but when it comes to deciding on a return flight, that's where we struggle. We've looked at return flights, changing the airline, leaving from a different airport, and spent the most amount of time considering if taking the last flight out is smart or not.

"What if he's not okay by Sunday night? You need to come back. You have classes Monday, Alex," she says, then checks her phone for any new messages from her mom. "Oh my god, you have classes tomorrow. You can't come with me."

"I can cancel if necessary," I say, knowing I have never in my life canceled a class before. My students also know I'm not the kind of professor to cancel without a really good reason. I like my schedule.

But this is more important than my schedule.

"We can book return flights when we know. Let's just get something out there and we'll figure out the rest when we know how he's doing," I say softly, rubbing her back as she clicks the button to book the flights.

In the time it has taken us to get this far with planning, everyone who called and texted me has been responded to. Will has checked in to see if there's anything he can do. The girls and Maverick have done the same. There's nothing anyone can do right now and it's going to be that way until we hear back from Anita, which puts all our decisions up in the air.

Her phone rings as she's putting in my credit card information.

"Mom?" she asks, her phone on speaker.

The response is a heart-wrenching wail, the kind only created by the loss of someone you love so intensely nothing could tear your relationship apart. It's the final breath of a 30-year marriage and I feel my heart drop to my stomach as the reality of the situation hits Wren and she releases a gasp.

"No. No, Mom. Mom? No," she says, her face stricken with the severity of what has transpired. "I'll be there as soon as I can. I'm booking a flight right now."

"Wren ... he's ... gone," Anita sobs into the phone. "I got here ... and he was gone. We were having dinner out at our favorite restaurant and now he's just gone."

I lift Wren up from her chair and sit in her spot, pulling her back down on my lap, wrapping her into my arms as the tears begin to slide down her face.

"Mom, what do you need me to do?" Wren echoes the question I asked her not even an hour ago, the same question everyone else has asked as well.

"Come home," Anita says, drawing in a shuddering breath. "Other than that, I don't know. Just ... come home."

Chapter 28

Wren

Alex holds my hand as I greet friends my parents have had for years and extended family who have come from across the country to pay their respects to my dad. I've been numb since last Thursday. I barely feel it when he pulls his hand away from mine, but I know it's not there anymore and look at him between mourners.

He's wiggling his fingers and clenching his fist.

"You were squeezing. My fingers were starting to lose feeling," he says, giving me a sad smile.

"Sorry," I say, blankly, unsure how else to respond.

"I'm going to grab a water. I'll be right back," he says, reassuring me. He speaks quietly to my mom, checking on her like he's been checking on me — constantly.

He's been a consistent source of strength for me since I moved in and now I'm leaning on him even more. Part of me hates that I'm taking more than I'm giving, but I can't carry my heaviness alone. Not right now. He told me to let him handle the things I couldn't, and I've allowed him to. I've handed over responsibilities I can't manage right now like calling Dylan to let her know what happened the night Dad died. I was busy throwing clothes into a bag and he stood watch, calling her to say I wouldn't be able to work on Friday, that we were flying out in the morning.

Dylan met my dad when they were in Brockport two weeks ago. He wanted to see where I was working and what I was doing. He's always been invested in the sports I play, and when I got really serious about softball, he was my biggest cheerleader. He was at every game, made sure I was at every practice and turned the headlights on more than once when I wasn't ready to bring it in and go home. That was our connection. Dylan heard all about it when Mom and Dad were in New York, and when Alex told Dylan why he was calling she said go. She'd manage things on her end.

I feel his presence before he's close enough to touch me and I wait for his arm to come around my waist. When it does, my body falls limply against him as a fresh wave of hot tears trickle down my already splotchy face.

"Do you want to take a break?" he whispers against my hair.

I shake my head "no" and brush the salty rivulets away. I close my eyes and breathe in deeply during a lull in friends and family. I'm still focusing on breathing when large, masculine fingers wrap around my wrist. Opening my eyes, I fall into Will's arms, sobbing and unable to hold any of it back anymore. He leads me out of the viewing room, Alex following a short distance behind as my mother watches along with my aunt, Veronica's mom, who arrived over the weekend.

Will holds me up, consoling me as I fall apart just out of view of everyone else while Alex stands guard in case someone comes looking for me. Will shushes me, rubbing his hand in a circle over my back, as he gently tells me it's going to be okay.

"How, though? How will it be okay?" I ask.

He pulls back from me, holding me away from his body just enough to see my face, and he smiles.

"I don't know. I had very little time to get to know Tony, Wren, but one thing that was abundantly clear to me is he loved you and your mother with every piece of his soul. He'll send you signs," he says. I attempt to speak, my eyebrows knitting together, and he stops me. "Listen, I learned a lot from Gram and she always believed in signs, so if you think I'm out of line tell me."

"I don't," I say. "I don't think you're out of line, but I wish I knew what to watch for, I guess."

"He'll let you know," Will says, pulling me in to kiss my forehead. "In the meantime, we're here to be strong for you and your mom."

Leaning into him again, I wrap my arms around his waist and take a deep breath. My nose fills with the scent of his cologne and I'm grateful he and Dad wear different scents.

"We should go back out with Anita," Alex says softly behind me. "Veronica and Danny just got here and it's almost time for the service to start."

"Danny is here? With Veronica?" I ask, shocked because that's a development I didn't expect.

"He sent me a text when their flight got in. I didn't know anything until then," he says, stepping to the side of me opposite Will. Looking around me at Will, he adds, "I didn't even know Will was coming."

They flank me as we walk back out to where my mom stands and Veronica sees me. She moves swiftly through the room to hug me and then offers a fist bump to Alex as Danny follows behind her and shakes his cousin's hand.

"Hey, man. I'm really sorry about Wren's father," Danny says, solemnly. "When Veronica told me he passed I wasn't about to let her come out here alone."

"Family sticks together," Alex says, pulling Danny in for a quick hug. "Danny, you remember Will from when we were kids?"

Dan and Will size each other up, one clearly unsure why the other is here, as Veronica and I watch.

"Sure do. It's good to see you, sir. It's been what, fifteen years?" Danny says.

In the months since accepting my job on the east coast, I've tried to fill Roni in on the Two Dads Situation since we were finally able to move on from the Alex Situation. Though I have gotten to know Will well over the past several weeks, I wasn't sure he would be ready to jump on a plane and come to my dad's funeral. I also shouldn't have thought he wouldn't do that for me and Alex.

"Wren's extra dad? That Will?" Veronica says. "Man, seeing you two next to one another you can't hide the resemblance."

"I'm missing a story, aren't I?" Danny says, looking around our small circle.

"You usually are," Alex says, laughing.

We stand quietly, the silence awkwardly infiltrating along with the melancholy tones of funeral home music. The overbearing scent of roses and gladiolas begins to get to me and I wonder if Dad would even want all of this pomp and circumstance.

"I hate this," I say to no one in particular. "He wants to be cremated, but we're still going through all of this. Why?"

As I'm questioning the decisions my mother and I made, she walks up beside me and slowly pushes me closer to where we're sitting. Alex sits behind me; Will behind my mom. Danny and Veronica are beside Alex. Veronica's parents beside me.

The family all falls in line and together we say our final goodbyes.

*****

Mom and I took a little extra time following the service to privately say those last few words we had for Dad. We left Will's rental at the funeral home and the four of us drove together to the restaurant, meeting everyone else there. I asked again why we were going through the trouble of an open casket and my mom reminded me of the three of us discussing all of it when Dad had his heart attack a few years ago — the health issues that led me onto the path of finding Will.

"We're honoring his wishes. Nice funeral in a timely manner, then cremation," she says as we reconvene in the kitchen at my childhood home in sweats and non-funeral clothing.

"I know we're honoring them, but I'm just confused," I say, pouring hot water for a mug of tea. "How long until we have him back?"

"It'll be a few weeks," she says from the table.

I walk to the counter facing her and lean against the cabinets.

I'm back to numb after the luncheon.

The only thing keeping me grounded is Alex's presence and right now he's off somewhere with Will trying to get a hotel room, which is stupid.

"Can't Will just stay here?" I ask as I wade through my thoughts.

"He can, if it's easier for him," she says.

"Did you bring all of my softball gear to New York?" I ask, jumping from subject to subject.

"Dad kept a set of everything here. It's in the garage," she says. I stand up straight as soon as she says "garage" and my feet instinctively move in that direction. "Wrenny?"

"Hmm?" I respond without looking at her.

"Don't break any windows."

I leave the room, my feet bare and my mug of hot tea in hand, in search of a physical release. I need something. I need to get it all out. I need to not be numb.

I set my tea down on top of the standing freezer and rummage through the cabinets in the garage labeled "Wren's Sports Stuff." Amongst the lost soccer balls and a random lacrosse stick, I find a tee and a bat and what looks like a brand new bucket of fluorescent yellow and pink softballs. Carrying everything to the back yard, I find he had my spare net set up still and I wonder if he was sneaking out to rip a few balls once in a while after I left.

Signs. Will said he'd send me signs, right? Maybe this is one.

Tossing everything on the ground, I hit ball after ball into the net as hard as I can until I have nothing left to give. Each thought comes and then I hit the ball as hard as I can as if that will make it better. As if, if I hit it harder it will bring him back.

He loved me no matter what. He never once got mad about Will. He allowed me to grow and chase my dreams.

But he left me before letting me show him how much I loved him back. Twenty-eight years wasn't long enough.

"It wasn't long enough!" I scream, hitting another ball into the side of the house. "I want more time!"

When I collapse to the ground, I notice my mom sitting in a chair on the deck watching me. There's no telling how long she's sat there, watching as I come apart at the seams.

"There wasn't more time. He gave us everything he could, Wren," she says, the exhaustion in her voice hovering just beneath the surface.

"But why didn't they try harder to save him? Why?"

"You think they didn't? They worked on him for as long as they could, sweetie," she says. "I don't know all the details, and regardless of all my years working around medicine or medical terminology I don't want to know them. Not this time. He had no detectable heartbeat regardless of their efforts, Wren. He was gone before the helicopter landed."

I curl my body around my legs, pulling my knees into my chest. Unlike her, I want to know the details and I ask what else she knows because there's got to be more. It feels like there's always more.

"He was still young. The medical examiner's findings came back with a complete blockage of the left anterior descending artery," she says. She rattles it off like the words have been on repeat in her head, and they most likely have been. "They call it the 'widowmaker' for a reason."

"There was no way for him to survive? They didn't test him for that possibility after everything else?"

"Considering the other health issues, it was unlikely for him to survive," she says. "The focus was on the liver problems after his last heart attack, so I don't recall them running any tests for this. Trust me, Wren, if they could have saved him, they would have. He would have done anything to live for you. For us. You need to believe me."

We sit in silence. She watches me carefully as I chew on the end of my thumb; I watch her watching me.

When I break the quiet, all I say is, "I love you."

"I love you, too."

"I'm going to move back home," I say.

"The fuck you are," she responds.

Throwing up my hands I steel my resolve and double down.

"I'm an adult. I can move back here if I want to," I say. "You can't stop me."

"I might not be able to stop you, but I know two men who would be devastated if you picked up and left them," she says. "I'm not saying stay for them, but I do think you should consider them. You also have an entire team of girls and a head coach who need you. Your dad told me all about how impressed Dylan is with your coaching and the ideas you have for the girls and how responsive the team is to you."

Huffing out a sigh, I pull my legs back into my chest, then wiggle around until I'm sitting crisscross.

"What would you be coming back to, Wren?" she asks, solemnly. "Dad's gone. You have a future in New York. Don't come back to this and break apart everything you've worked so hard for. That is the last thing your dad would want."

"Fine. But I don't know how I feel about leaving you here all alone," I say, finally.

She laughs at me. It's the realest laugh I've heard from her since before Thursday and I'm comforted by the sound.

"I think I'll be okay for now. I still have work to keep me busy," she says. "For now."

"Promise you'll tell me if you're having trouble surviving?"

"Cross my heart, kiddo. You do the same."

I nod, and in the softness of the evening I hear a car door close. Then a second one. Alex calls out for me and I yell back to him as he finds his way through the house to the deck.

"Apparently there's a convention or something in town because there isn't a single hotel room available for a fifteen-mile radius," he says as Will comes to stand beside him. "So, is there a couch or air mattress Will can borrow for the night?"

I look from Alex to my mom to Will.

"I can sleep on the floor if nothing else. I just need a pillow or a rolled up blanket," he says.

"Nonsense. There's a spare bedroom all made up," my mom says, looking up at Will. "Plus, I think you being here for a day or two with Wren will be good for her. Despite the circumstances, she can show you where she grew up."

Will crosses his arms over his chest, separating his feet as if he's standing and watching a game from the sidelines. I see him contemplate the idea of staying in the same house as my mom, and I notice the moment he accepts the invitation.

"I won't be any trouble," he says.

"I didn't expect you would be," Mom says, standing from her seat. "Come on. I'll show you where your room is."

As my parents — as Mom and Will — go in the house, Alex makes himself comfy on the steps to the deck and gives me a knowing look.

"Feel better?" he asks, motioning to the equipment behind me.

I shrug.

"Eventually. This was just to work through the anger," I say. "It sort of came up out of nowhere."

"Anger does that sometimes."

We're quiet together while I consider the conversation I had with my mom.

"I kept asking why they didn't try harder to save him. She told me there was no way. It was too late."

"Unfortunately, that might have been better than them bringing him back, Wren. Tony was too full of life to be on life support or come back unable to do things he loved."

I nod, but it's in recognition of the facts he's presented, not because I want to accept them as reality.

He watches me, tapping the fingers of his right hand against the opposite leg as he leans his elbows on his knees.

"Missing your guitar?" I ask.

His head tips to the side, his eyes questioning.

"Your fingers. You do that when you get overwhelmed sometimes or bored. Usually, it's when you're stressing about something. But I know from watching you play that you're mentally picking chords," I say, a soft smile forming on my lips as I push up off the ground and walk closer to him, nestling my hips between his knees. Leaning down to kiss him, I ask, "What are you playing tonight?"

"'Perfect.' Ed Sheeran."
"Good song."
"I'd like to dance with you to it someday."
"Someday? Not today?"
He shrugs. I smile.

Wrapping his arms around the backs of my thighs and pulling me closer to him, he snuggles against my belly, breathing in deeply.

"Someday soon," he says.

Chapter 29

Alexander

Tony's been gone just a few short weeks and, while Wren's schedule has slowed down a bit as she and Dylan wrap up from their fall practice schedule, I'm busy trying to plan for exams for the classes I teach. I've finished all the exams I need for my doctoral program and continue to meet with my advisor and the residents at the nursing home. For the next several months, I'll be finishing my research and writing the bulk of my findings before defending my dissertation in the spring.

Wren and I have fallen back into a routine, but with the holidays fast approaching, she's been doing volunteer work with some of the girls. It's part of her plan for team building and teaching them about working together. Some afternoons I get home and she's nowhere to be found. I've quickly learned that if I text her saying I'm home, she'll tell me where she is.

I don't need to know where she is, though it is nice on days like today when she says she's at the bakery and I have a need for cupcakes. As soon as I read her text, I get back in my car and head to town. Pulling into a spot in front of the shop, I quietly make my way through the door, the bells jingling softly, and begin perusing the display case while waiting for Maggie or Delilah to come out front.

"You're positive she's over him?"

"Alex was just an exercise routine," I hear Maverick say.

"That doesn't make this any better," Wren replies.

I stand frozen at the counter, listening but also trying not to listen.

"How does that make any of it better?"

An oven door opens and closes. A baking sheet clatters against a countertop.

"Look, we all know casual sex happens between consenting adults and it's normal-ish. I'm not saying the situation they created for themselves is right, I'm just acknowledging it happens," Maggie says. "Could it have been more? Sure, but it definitely wasn't going to happen unless they both wanted to be miserable five years from now."

"How can you be so sure of that?"

"They're too alike. Plus, she's batting for the other team these days."

I snicker at Rick's use of sports terminology, but it's the rest of the conversation that has me concerned.

"Hey, Alex!" Maggie says extra loudly as she comes out from the back of the bakery. "What's up?"

She tries to act nonchalant about the conversation she correctly assumes I overheard.

"I needed cupcakes," I say, smiling. "Also, what's the plan for Thanksgiving? Am I bringing cheesy potatoes or something else?"

Wren appears in the doorway, and the second she sees me she looks guilty of something. Maggie shifts uncomfortably, looking from me to Wren, before she starts putting cupcakes in a box. I didn't tell her how many or what flavors I wanted, but she gives me a mixed half-dozen.

"Cheesy potatoes. I know Sawyer and Gen will eat the heck out of them," Mags says. "Unless you want to bring something else."

"That's fine," I say, my gaze shifting from Wren back to Maggie as she rings up my order.

"Are you going right home?" Wren asks, moving toward the counter. I nod and she continues, "Maybe we could do take out for dinner? We didn't plan anything for this far into the week and I'm kind of wanting tacos."

"Of course," I say. "What time are you heading back to the house?"

"Soon. The girls from the team already left with cookies for Murph's guys so they have them for dinner. Will is at the hospital visiting one of his guys," she says. "I just wanted to help get cleaned up here since the girls and I made a bigger mess than Maggie and I anticipated. I can ask Rick to drop me off."

"Nope. Go home. Maverick and I can handle this," Maggie says.

I see Wren's trepidation and I don't like that my presence is what caused it. I don't like beating around the bush and whatever they were talking about seems to have her in her head.

"What happened?" I ask.

Rick leans against the door to the kitchen, eating a cookie I'm sure he wasn't supposed to be taste-testing.

"My sister started it," he says through a mouthful of chocolate chips. "She was in here running her mouth, asking questions she shouldn't be asking and talking about your penis again. Made it awkward."

I take my glasses off, cleaning the lenses on the soft cotton of my untucked dress shirt beneath the peacoat I threw on.

"You have your professor face on," Maggie says.

"I don't have a professor face."

"Yes, you do," Wren says, and I watch her cheeks flush. "Maybe we should go home for this conversation."

I nod, picking up the box of cupcakes.

"Are you riding with me?" I ask, knowing her car is still in the driveway at home.

"Yes, please," she says, quickly untying her apron. She lifts the fabric over her head and hands it to Maggie who gives her a quick hug and a thank you for helping with the baking as I wait by the door.

Wren comes around the end of the counter, wearing a pair of black softball pants with a green belt and tall, hunter green socks to match covered with a pair of slides. Her Under Armour T-shirt with the college logo and "Coach Leary" embroidered on it is tucked in, giving her a professional look I suddenly want to defile. I hold the door open and she steps through, pulling a hoodie on as she steps onto the sidewalk and turns to me.

"It's nothing. I'm just being really sensitive," she says.

"Do we want to do this while standing on Main Street?" I ask as I walk past her toward the car.

I'm irritated. The history I have with Harper and my continued friendship with her shouldn't be affecting my current relationship like this. Harper is living her life, chasing the girl next door, so why she feels the need to poke and prod Wren, I'll never understand. I know Harper well enough to know she's not jealous, but without knowing exactly what she said I'm not sure how to approach a conversation about it with her.

Pressing the unlock button, I open the back driver's side door and set the cupcake box on the floor. Closing the door again I notice she hasn't moved from the sidewalk.

"Get in the car, Wren," I state, matter-of-factly.

"Bossy, aren't we?"

"Yes. Yes, I am. Get in the car."

"I feel like I'm not getting the full Alexander experience," she says, crossing her arms.

She used my full name and that's when it hits home what Harper was probably talking about with my girlfriend.

Pushing my hands into the pockets of my dress pants, I step toward the sidewalk, and prop my left foot up on the curb. Pushing myself up, I take two steps and come toe-to-toe with her, and while our height difference isn't extreme, I tower over her in this moment. Wren's tongue darts out to dampen her bottom lip and there's a brief moment of contention where I think she's going to create an argument just for the sake of arguing. Is she going to pick a fight with me because I have a little bit of a dominant side she hasn't fully seen? We have yet to argue and I have enjoyed not fighting with the woman I love, but I'm smart enough to know arguments will happen.

I just don't want the first one to happen in front of The Bakery on Main where all the neighbors are friends of mine and, by association, friends of Wren's. I also know where this conversation could lead and I would definitely prefer we be at home for it.

Placing my face closer to hers, I stare at her for a beat, gauging where her head is at.

"If you would like the, quote, full Alexander experience, end quote, I suggest you get in the car, Wren," I say, feeling the muscle in my jaw tic.

Turning, I walk to the passenger side door and open it, waiting for her to come to me.

"I just want you to know, I'm going to need the full story at some point," she says, ducking under my arm and climbing into the car.

I close the door and take a deep breath as I walk around the back of the car to give myself a few more seconds to bring my blood pressure down.

"Sweetheart, there really isn't much of a story and anything Harper told you might have been blown out of proportion to get a rise out of you," I say, pushing the ignition and putting the car in reverse to back away from the sidewalk.

"Seems it's gotten a rise out of you, too, and you don't even know what she said," Wren points out. "But I can tell you, if the blindfolding and toys are true, I'm game. I would even agree to some gentle spanking."

"She said I spanked her?" I look at Wren incredulously.

She's quietly facing the opposite direction and looking out the window as I turn at the stoplight, making my way around the block and back through town on our way home.

"I didn't say she said that. I'm saying I wouldn't mind it," she says, finally. "We don't talk about former relationships, Alex. We haven't. The last man I was with …"

She trails off, still staring out the window as we pull into the driveway at home.

"What about him?" I ask, lowering my voice as I try not to think about Wren with someone other than me. Then the realization seeps in that the last person she was with might not have been a good person. "Did he do something to you?"

Her head turns and she looks at me, and it's a look filled with love. As she gently shakes her head, I feel my shoulders relax slightly.

"No. He just never gave me a chance to explore … things. It was the most basic sex of my life. There was no excitement. There was no putting my needs first," she says. "Then I have Harper, who I really do like, talking to me and Maggie about her current sex life and dropping hints that she knows all the intimate details about you. Then she's asking about the nightstand and I'm clueless. And that's just really difficult to deal with."

I'm quiet. I should apologize, but how do I apologize for something that was part of my life before Wren was in it? Or maybe I don't want to apologize because if sex was boring for Wren before, maybe this will help her express what she wants with me.

"Is our sex life mundane?" I ask.

"It wasn't. When I first moved here and we jumped from flirting with the possibility to actually dating, it wasn't boring. But you've been stressed, I've been trying to manage my emotions about my dad's death, because grief is really fucking hard for me, and I'm trying to have a relationship with Will. I'm trying to stay as busy as possible because you're busy and everything is hard, Alex," she says. Brushing tears away before they can fall, she says again, "Everything is hard. I just want our sex life to be not something I need to worry about. I want you to make me forget how everything is hard, even if it's just twenty minutes at a time."

"It's usually more than twenty minutes," I say, chancing a glance in her direction and she snickers.

"I know it is, but I think back to the first time in the shower and how attentive you were. I think you pulled back not knowing what I want," she says, picking at an invisible thread on her black pants.

I can't explain it, but I know she's right. I did pull back. Despite an explosive beginning to our sexual relationship, there are times I hesitate, unsure if she wants more, and then I don't push her boundaries. Harper always told me exactly what she wanted, she voiced her needs to me, and Wren doesn't. I don't want to compare the two, but Harper also opened my mind up to more than what I had experience with previously. If it weren't for Harper, Wren and I probably wouldn't even be having this conversation.

Twisting in my seat, I reach for and touch her chin until she turns to face me. I hold her chin between my thumb and fingers and refrain from kissing her plump lips, though I want to ravage them.

"If you want me to know what you want, you need to talk to me. Before, during, after. I need you to tell me what feels good and how to make it feel better," I say, watching as her eyes grow wider. "I don't just want to have sex with you; I want to make love to you slowly and gently, pulling every ounce of pleasure out of you until you can't put two thoughts together."

She continues to watch me, never pulling away, but I notice when the muscles in her jaw release and her body relaxes.

"I want to fuck you until you scream my name. I want to hold you while you drift off to sleep after you're completely spent from orgasm after orgasm," I continue. "Wren, I want to wreck you in the best ways but if you don't tell me it's good, I think it isn't. Your pleasure is of the utmost importance to me."

Wren shifts in her seat, her thighs squeezing together just slightly as she slides one leg against the other. The amber flames of a setting sun shine through the window, lighting the interior just enough for me to notice her pupils dilate and her chest lifting heavily with each breath.

"I think we need to get out of the car, Wren. There's not enough room in here to do what I want to you," I say, tracing my thumb along her bottom lip.

"What do you want to do to me?" she asks, her voice coming out on a breath.

"I have a new tie I'd like to make some memories with."

The moment the words leave my mouth, Wren smiles.

"Do I get to wear the tie?" she asks, innocently looking to see which necktie I'm wearing today.

She should know exactly the tie I'm referencing. She bought it for me after she moved in and said it was to replace the one from my cousin's wedding since I had left that one in North Carolina. She just doesn't know I left it on purpose. That part doesn't matter. It's the past.

I squint and purse my lips, then get out of the car without answering her, adjusting myself before reaching into the backseat for the cupcakes.

She hasn't climbed out of the car yet and peers at me from the front seat as I bend to pick up the box.

"Alex?" she questions, giggling. "What are you going to do with the tie?"

"You'll see." I close the door and circle around to hers, opening it and offering her my hand. Pulling her out of the car, I press her up against the back door, letting her feel how aroused I am just at the thought of making her come again and again. Placing my lips on her neck, trailing my tongue up to her earlobe, I say, "I'm almost certain you will enjoy it."

Grabbing her hand, I urge her to follow me to the house, closing her car door with my foot on our way.

We're hardly inside the breezeway when I turn and grab the back of her neck to pull her into me, my mouth hotly crashing against hers while walking her backward toward the stairs. I set the box on the table beside the stairs and roughly pull her to me, needing her more than I think she realizes. Both my hands trace down her waist, over her hips, and around her muscular thighs until I break our kiss while tightening my grip on her legs and lifting her up. Wren wraps her legs around my waist and wastes no time reconnecting our mouths as I navigate the stairs, thankful I left the door unlocked for my brief trip to the bakery.

Slamming the door shut behind me, I walk us over to the counter and set her down, my hips still tightly nestled between her legs. I brush the growing bulge in my pants against the snug fabric of her softball pants and she releases a soft whimper. I trace my fingers up under her sweatshirt, lifting the fabric until Wren pulls it off over her head and I can untuck her polo shirt. My fingers dance lightly along her belly, my short nails tickling as I push the fabric up her abdomen. She leans back, placing her hands on the countertop behind her to hold herself up as I bend down to trace the center of her belly with my tongue.

"Shirt. Off," I demand, and she responds by tossing her work shirt on the floor next to her sweatshirt. I return to tracing her body with my tongue until I reach her bra. "This one, huh?"

"I forgot how much you liked it," she says, her tone sassy as I finger the tab that rests between her breasts. I slowly unzip the fabric until it comes apart and I can continue my assault up her chest with the tip of my tongue, leaving her breasts covered but available to me as her breathing quickens.

Sliding her hips closer to the edge of the counter, I press mine into her harder. As I reach her neck, Wren releases a deep moan.

"Do you want more?" I ask, pressing my pelvis into her again and grinding against her.

She pushes herself against me in response as I guide my hands along her sides until my thumbs caress the underside of her breasts. I'm careful not to touch her nipples, wanting her to beg me to pay them any attention. I lock eyes with Wren and I can almost hear her pleading with me to touch more of her. I flick my thumbs beneath her sports bra a fraction closer to those taut buds, then pull away.

I slide my coat down my shoulders until it slips off my arms. I turn away from her, leaving her wanting on the counter, nearly half naked, while I hang my coat on the back of a kitchen chair.

"Alexander Makris, get back over here," she says, losing all patience and coyness as she demands my attention.

Turning back to her, I slowly begin unbuttoning my navy blue dress shirt, only to find her missing the last thing covering her breasts. She slowly twists her nipples between her thumbs and forefingers as she waits for me to return to her.

I come to her slowly, enamored at the sight of her on our kitchen counter and loving the hell out of her giving herself pleasure. As I reach her, I bend toward her breasts. Replacing her fingers and taking one nipple in my mouth, I flick my tongue across the pebbled flesh. Wren places her hand at the back of my head, urging me to continue as she twists and pulls the other. I gently bite her skin and she sharply inhales just before letting out a deep moan as I release her and move to the other breast, giving it equal and ample attention.

As I stand with my shirt fully unbuttoned, I loosen my tie and don't take my eyes off her face while I pull it over my head. Standing tightly against her, I take her hands in mine and wrap my arms around her back, slipping the satiny fabric around her wrists and tying them together.

"Comfortable?"

"Uh huh," she says, staring at me. "But what about my pants? And your pants?"

"I'll take care of everything. I'll take care of you." Wren looks at me as though she doesn't believe me — as if no lover has ever put her needs first. No one, that is, but me and she's incapable of making that distinction right now. "Do you trust me?"

She nods.

"Say it."

"I trust you, Alex."

"Good girl."

I reach down and pull her shoes from her feet, dropping them on the floor, then lift her legs to wrap around my waist once more. Lifting her from the counter, I carry her into the living room and lay her back on the plush, oversized reading chair in the corner. Lifting her right foot, I push the leg of her pants up and grip the top of her knee-high sock, stripping it from her body slowly until her toes wiggle free. Her left foot is next, and as I toss the cloth on the floor I bend her leg, kissing up the calf until I reach the back of her knee. Grasping around her thigh, I place my knee on the chair between her legs and press myself down onto her, opening her hips as I settle myself against her core. She arches up, wanting to feel me more as I suckle her breasts and feel her writhe beneath me.

Releasing her leg, I sit back and slowly unbuckle her belt, pull the button free from its snap, and slip the zipper down.

"Since when do you not wear underwear?" I question.

Her cheeks redden and match the flush across her chest.

"It's been a couple weeks. You hadn't noticed," she says, shyly.

Placing my lips on her hip bone and following the dip toward her mound, I make it known how much that saddens me.

"I'm so sorry I've been neglecting you," I say, kneeling on the floor.

Resting her thighs on my forearms, I reach around and pull the waistband of her pants over her hips until her nakedness is on full display. The fabric is taut around her knees, impeding my ability to taste and touch, and I quickly remove them. Rolling Wren onto her side and then up onto her knees, I press against her inner thighs until she opens them for me more.

Standing, I take in the sight of her spread before me, hands bound with my tie, perfectly prepared for me. Unbuttoning the sleeves of my shirt, I slide it off and add it to the growing pile of clothing. My undershirt is next.

I kick my dress shoes off and remove my socks. Then, walking closer to her, I unbutton my slacks as I reach out to touch her soft bottom.

"Spanking?" I question. "You're sure?"

Her response is a moan as I gently caress the round of her ass, allowing my fingers to explore and leave feather-light touches along her vulva. My calloused fingers graze the sensitive skin. Standing behind her, my right hand dips between her legs as my left carefully rubs calming circles on her buttocks.

Then, as she softly moans a "please, Alex," my hand lands quickly where calm was and she releases a surprised yelp followed immediately by a deep moan as I caress the sting. She presses her body back toward me, trying to claim my fingers and I give them to her. Pushing two fingers deep into her pussy, I feel her body shudder as if a chill cascaded down her skin and gooseflesh appears. Bending down I carefully bite her exposed bottom, then heal it with a kiss, before preparing her with my palm again.

Wren grips the satin tie, still tightly wound around her wrists, as she pushes back onto my fingers. Turning them inside her, she tightens her muscles, panting my name as I massage her. Her juices coat my fingers as I pump them into her while rubbing circles on her bottom. I feel her squeeze my fingers, then relax, and again cry out in pleasure when my palm connects with her skin.

Kissing the pinked skin, I release my zipper with my free hand. Freeing my cock from the confines of my pants and boxers, I stroke the length while watching her body consume my hand. Spreading the precum around the head of my shaft, I step out of the fabric pooled at my feet and kick it to the side.

Removing my fingers, Wren moans sadly.

"No. More," she says.

"No more? Are you giving up on me?" I ask, as I switch hands and use Wren's dampness as lubricant. Stroking faster, I kneel behind her, burying my face in her pussy, the stubble on my face harsh against her tender skin. She pushes her body harder against my mouth as I trail my tongue from her clit up her slit and then dip it into her core. Her moans reach my ears. "Are you sure no more?"

"I didn't ... say no more," she says.

I'm well aware of what she said and what she meant.

"Pretty sure you said no more," I say, biting her thigh. "I can stop. You just need to tell me what you want."

Lifting my head to see over her in the downward dog position, I catch her eye.

"I need you," she says.

"I'm right here," I reply, reaching between her legs again to stroke her clit.

"Alexander," she says, breathlessly, grinding back onto my hand searching for release. "Please."

I wait for her to continue, pressing my face between her thighs again as I lift her hips up so I have easier access to her sweet center.

"Please, what?" I demand, swiping my tongue up her slit again.

"I need you to fuck me. Please, give me your cock," she manages to whimper.

Pushing up off the floor, I kneel between her legs and position the head of my cock at her opening, rubbing it along her slick skin, using it to tease her clit on each pass. She moans with each touch, each breath silently begging me to enter her fully. She instinctively pushes back, hoping to gain purchase as I hold myself still in my hand and allow her to claim me unsheathed.

Seating myself deeply inside her, I still my body and allow her to adjust. Feeling her muscles clamp down on me, I attempt not to move and reach out for her hands, gripping her wrists. I pull her harder against me, then slowly pull out, only to slam my hips back into her.

"More," she cries out.

Holding her bound wrists in one hand, I grasp her hip with the other and pump my pelvis into her, slowly, then more forcefully. I pull out, and kiss her lower back as she whines that she misses me, and I bury myself deep in her all over again until she's arching her back and screaming my full government name.

Pulling her hands back toward me, I unwind the satin tie and release her wrists. Her arms fall limp at her sides as I slowly stroke my cock in and out of her. Wren pulls her knees up under her, unseating herself from me, and rolls to her side before guiding me back between her legs.

Gaining access again, I connect us at the hip and hold myself above her.

"You look happier," I say, dipping my head to kiss her collarbone.

"Thanks. Turns out I just needed to be tied up and fucked really good," she says, a tired smile making its way up to her eyes. "But if you don't come soon, I'm going to start thinking it wasn't good for you."

"You would be very, very wrong," I say, placing my mouth on hers. Then, closer to her ear, I say, "I need to know where you want it, Wren. Do you want my cum deep inside you?"

She nods, scraping her nails down my chest until I connect my mouth to hers again. My tongue separates her lips slightly and I pull the bee-stung bottom lip into my mouth, deepening our connection as I wrap my arms around her back, pinning her to my chest and the chair simultaneously. With her lips occupied, I pump my hips harder until her mouth falls open in silent satisfaction.

"Where do you want me to come?" I ask her, needing to hear her give me her consent.

"In me. I need to feel you in me," she cries out, bringing me to the brink.

I rock my hips into her again and try to hold out to give her more pleasure. Willing myself to not find my release yet is fruitless as she wraps her calves around my waist, allowing me to drive my cock deeper. I feel the ridges of her vagina tighten around me and I can no longer hold back. My body stills as my cock twitches and I empty myself into Wren.

My mouth finds hers as we lay in the darkening living room, catching our breath, until she gently nudges me off her. Flaccid, I slip out of her and curl up with her back to me as she takes my hand in hers and quietly kisses each finger.

"Thank you," she says, softly.

Moving her hair away from her neck, I kiss the tender flesh below her ear. "For?"

"For showing me you love me in everything you do," she says. "Even when I let someone else get in my head, you remind me it's you and me. It's just been difficult lately."

I realize this is the side of Wren I needed to see. I've had every other version of her but this one, and despite knowing I want her forever, this connection seals the deal. Not because she's begging and pleading, not because she's being submissive, but because she's giving herself over to me. When she so badly seeks control in every other aspect of her life and can't find it, she has me. When everything else is spinning out of control, she can tell me what she wants and expect to receive exactly that.

"How can I make it easier?"

"I don't think you can. I just ... I just need you to love me through it."

*****

Sweatpants, hoodies, *Practical Magic*, and Mexican take-out.

Those are the only things she wanted after we cleaned up, collected our clothing from throughout the house, and settled in for the evening.

"I'm so glad I had my parents bring this out from California," she says, giggling in the afterglow as she sits crisscrossed on the overstuffed, oversized reading chair. "It came in handy tonight."

"It can come in handy every night if you want," I say maneuvering a scoop of rice into my mouth. I raise my eyebrows at her hopefully. Swallowing the bite, I add, "Or every other night."

"Alexander," she says, watching me carefully to see if I'm serious.

I look at my lap, then at her.

"Don't talk like that unless you mean it," I say.

"What is it about your big name? And please tell me it doesn't work like that every time someone uses it."

I bark out a laugh and shake my head.

"Absolutely not. It's a very specific reaction to very specific circumstances. I don't know how to explain it," I say.

"It was just a random discovery?" she says.

"It was deliberately done by someone who noticed something and now it's apparently a thing," I say, trying to skirt around the who and what knowing she will connect the dots. "How I discovered this very intimate reaction to hearing you say my name doesn't matter. I like the way my full name sounds in your mouth when I'm buried deep in you, Wren, and that's the thing I want you to focus on."

She stares at me, understanding and reading between all the words I say that I don't want to talk about how this came to be. Unfortunately, I know she's figured out it was Harper. Fortunately, she's just petty enough to want to take that power and make it her own.

"So ... If I come home from work and feel all stressed and messy, and I say your big name you'll know I need all the attention? Is that one way this can work? Because I could get behind that," she says.

Getting up off the chair, I walk out of the room. Returning a moment later with the box of cupcakes from The Bakery on Main, I sit back down.

Pushing my glasses up further on the bridge of my nose, I open the box and try to decide which one I want while I contemplate how to respond to her inquiry.

"If you come home stressed, I want you to talk to me about it. I want you to talk to me about your day, your feelings, your thoughts, the good things, the silly things, the hard things. I want all of it, Wren," I say, lifting a red velvet cupcake with vanilla bean buttercream out of the box. "But, once you talk to me about all the things, I always want to help you through it and hear you moaning my name after."

Choosing her own dessert — lemon cake with a red raspberry buttercream with fresh berries — Wren purses her lips and looks at me, squinting, like she's mulling it over.

"'Kay. Deal."

"Also, I want to marry you, in case that wasn't obvious," I say, looking away from her stunned expression as I bite into my cupcake.

Chapter 30

Wren

"He just dropped that on you during dinner?" Will says on Wednesday.

We meet up for coffee a couple mornings a week before I head to the college. The Jumping Bean is usually quiet right after they open and with Alex going to campus extra early to work on his dissertation, it gives me a little more time to spend with Will as we navigate our new relationship. A relationship made even more complex with my dad's death.

"Should I kill him? Lots of places to hide bodies around here, Wren," he says, his tone only half joking.

He drapes his right arm over the back of the booth and raises his eyebrow above the steaming coffee he holds close to his lips. I smile and lift my mug of chai, taking a deep breath in for the spices to warm me before that first sip.

"If you kill him, you can't have a son-in-law who already thinks of you as one of his own parents. You've known Alex so much longer than me and he fully respects you, so I think murder is not the option we should be going for here," I say. "I was surprised, but not, you know? We fell into doing life together so easily."

As I finish talking, Will is grinning and understands that I am not in any way opposed to Alex saying he wants to marry me.

"I did tell him I think we should take our time, though. We've rushed everything else so far and maybe we should wait with a wedding. Give ourselves a few more months, maybe get through Thanksgiving this week and our first Christmas together, you know?"

"Good plan. What if he's a horrible gift giver? You can't be settling for that," Will says, the corner of his mouth lifting into a smirk as he glances at my hands. "You're being smart. Not to mention, getting engaged and actually having a wedding are two different things."

"Plus, he didn't actually propose," I say, noting that it was simply a statement that he *wants* to marry me.

Switching gears, I bring up Thanksgiving again knowing he usually spends the day with Murph. He's told me about his "family brunch" with Murph's guys and how after that he goes to the VA hospital to visit anyone there for the holiday. In the past he hasn't had a reason to not do those things.

But now there's me. I don't want him to change his plans or his life because I've come crashing into it. I just want him to know having time with him matters to me.

"Any chance you'll be stopping by Maggie and Maverick's? Mom will be here, but I want to be able to spend some of the holiday with you, too," I say.

At the mention of my mom, his eyes widen and his mouth falls slightly open for a few seconds before he closes it again and looks down at his napkin.

"What are your plans for tomorrow? Are you and Alex going to be at Maggie's all day or go over noon-time?" he questions.

I shrug, because I don't think it's been discussed in detail. My assumption is we'll be there for an early dinner since Maverick and Sawyer will be opening the tree farm the next morning for the holiday season.

"I'm not sure, but if there's something else I have to do in the morning, I don't think anyone is going to miss me if I show up a little later than planned."

"Want to come to the church with me and serve brunch? I've been getting a lot of crap from Murph's guys about having not met you," he says. He quickly follows up with, "They're all decent people. They just don't have homes. I wouldn't put you in a position that would make you uncomfortable."

"I'd love to," I spit out, feeling my heart flutter knowing he wants to introduce me to my uncle's group. "What can I bring? Would you be opposed to some of the girls coming to help? I'm really trying to get this philanthropy thing with the team off the ground."

"Murph and I have that part under control," he says, relaxing into the booth and lifting his mug in salute. "You and your girls just need to show up and show off how well you flip pancakes."

*****

Alex walks into the house from school with an armload of groceries and a guitar case slung over his back. He kisses me on the cheek as I stand at the kitchen table folding a load of laundry and without asking how my day was, begins asking questions I don't understand.

"Crock-Pot?" he asks.

"What about it?" I respond.

Pulling a bag of diced potatoes from the grocery sack, he holds them up and looks at me.

"Those are potatoes, not a Crock-Pot. Use your words," I say, snickering.

"Usually, I do the cheesy potatoes in the oven because it just makes sense to me. That's how I've always done them. Then, I was scrolling on the Internet as one does when avoiding productivity, and I came across a recipe for my cheesy potatoes but done in a slow cooker," he says. "I'm thinking, to make life easier when we get to Mags' house, I'll just do them like that and we can plug it back in to stay warm when we get there."

Placing one of his dress shirts on a hanger and hooking it over the doorframe to the living room, I nod.

"I don't see why not. Unless you're afraid they'll taste different," I say. "What time are we supposed to be there, anyway?"

"Around one, that way the baby is down for a nap long enough that if he's woken up by everyone being loud, he won't be too grumpy," he says, and I stare at him. "That's what Maggie said. Plus, I think she's full of it because I have yet to see that baby grumpy."

The first time I saw him with his friends, I understood how close he is with them all. They're the epitome of found family, especially since his is never around. But when he talks about Maggie and Maverick's son, Ashton, it triggers something that hasn't ever been a concern of mine.

"What?" he asks.

"I think it's really sweet how much you pay attention to your friends and their kids, that's all," I say, trying to remember the last time I talked to Tasha. It's been more than a month. At least. With the exception of a quick visit at my dad's funeral, we've hardly talked since I moved to New York.

Stepping into my space, he takes the leggings I was folding from my hands and sets them back in the basket.

"I think it's really sweet that you noticed I like their kids. But I think the bigger question is," he says, placing his hands on either side of my neck, "do you like kids?"

"Is this conversation going to turn into a 'how many do you want?' kind of conversation?" I ask, swallowing hard.

It's not that I've never thought about it. I just haven't had anyone I wanted to have kids with ... until Alex. But I haven't voiced that. We have too many things happening to consider that aspect of life along with how new our relationship still is and his recent declaration of wanting to marry me. Plus the little conversations here and there about wanting to buy a house but not wanting to give up the area we're in.

"It doesn't have to," he says, leaning in to kiss the corner of my mouth. "Maybe it's something we could consider talking about soon, though."

"Where is this coming from? Is it the stress or the fact you're over thirty?"

He shakes his head.

"Neither. I just want everything with you. Life. Babies. All that stuff," he says.

I reach up and hold his wrists as he lays his forehead against mine.

"I want that, too. Let's get through the holidays. You have so much on your plate right now," I say. Giggling, I add, "Plus, getting busy and trying to make a baby this week probably isn't a good idea with my mom flying in tonight. Also, I'd need to come off my birth control first."

"Anita knows how babies are made. We could be really quiet and just practice a lot for the time being. You can stop taking your pills when you're done with this pack," he says, walking me back toward the living room and pinning me against the doorframe. "When does her flight get in?"

"No, Alex, because that would mean next week," I say, laughing as he nips and nibbles my neck. "We are not making a baby for Thanksgiving."

"Christmas?"

"What has gotten into you?" I ask, amused by his sudden change of behavior.

Lifting his head, he rests his forearm on the doorframe above my head, and kisses the tip of my nose.

"My cousin sent me a copy of the photos from his wedding, and I didn't realize until I saw the way you looked at me in those pictures and the way I looked at you that I have been madly in love with you almost from the day we met," he says, and my heart begins pounding in my chest. "I looked at those pictures and it solidified that I want the rest of my life to be with you. I knew it before, but this picture makes me want to make it official."

He slides his phone from his pocket and unlocks the screen. Immediately, I'm thrown back to the moment the photographer captured us standing at the bar — he stands with one foot crossed over the other, his knee slightly bent, as he relaxes with his elbow on the counter looking at me with a smile as I stand in front of him, looking up with a smile to match, while I hold his tie in my hand. It was after dancing with Danny and our eventual escape to the beach where he kissed me for the second time and it felt like I never wanted to kiss anyone else ever again.

"Okay," I say.

"Okay?" he repeats.

"You want to make it official," I say, looking up at him and grasping his tie. Pulling him closer to me. "Okay."

"Just so I'm understanding, you're saying yes to marrying me? Like a real yes, not a 'that sounds like something for five years in the future' yes?"

"You might want to ask properly, though," I say. "You've told me you want to marry me, but you haven't asked."

"Wren Elizabeth Leary ... will you please do me the honor of being my bride?"

"Yes," I say, pulling him down to meet my mouth. "Yes. A hundred times, yes."

As Alex pulls away from me, he lifts his guitar case from his back and sets it on top of the laundry basket, opens it, and lifts out a small, vintage, blue crushed velvet box.

He opens the top to reveal a sterling silver ring with a single small ruby set in a cluster of diamond chips. My breath is stuck in the center of my chest and I force myself to release it.

"It's gorgeous," I say, my emotions welling up inside me as the excitement begins to bubble.

He removes the ring from the box and takes my left hand in his, carefully sliding the band along my fourth finger. Once it's in place, Alex lifts my hand and kisses it, then takes my face in his hands and kisses me like I'm his reason for being.

Coming up for air, I look at my hand and then ask him where he found it. It's not the typical diamond engagement ring we've been trained to expect, and I love it even more for being unique.

"I had a little help," he says, kissing me once more before stepping back.

"From whom?" I ask, holding my hand out to watch the kitchen light dance along the facets.

"Uh ... the church."

"Murph?" I ask, my eyes widening. "Why would Murph have a ring like this?"

"Well, Will and Murph. It was their mother's," he says. "They wanted me to have it because they knew how I felt."

I laugh, because of course they knew how he felt. I told Will this morning.

"When did you see Will and Murph?" I ask, to satisfy my curiosity.

I try to go back to folding the laundry, but can't stop looking at my ring — my grandmother's ring — and wondering what she was like and wanting suddenly to know everything about her.

"Last week. I stopped by for coffee with Murph and the church organist and Will was there," he says. "I think that trip out for your dad's funeral took a lot out of him."

"What do you mean?" I ask, looking at Alex as he begins putting the groceries away.

"I mean, he was very honest about how much he wants to make up for all the years he didn't have with you," he says. Closing the freezer and leaning against the counter, Alex crosses his arms over his chest. "He was very open about not wanting us to take advantage of being young still. Because being young means nothing."

"And from that conversation he and my uncle just handed over a family heirloom and told you to propose?"

Reaching behind him, he grasps the edge of the counter and lifts himself up onto it. Clasping his hands together between his knees as he lets his feet swing, he stares at me.

"Will and I talked when we were in California, Wren. He knew then how I felt about forever with you," he says. Meeting my gaze, he adds, "Him and Murph giving me the ring to ask you with was something they wanted to do. They've known I planned to ask you."

"So, Will being surprised when I told him this morning about you telling me you want to marry me was a ploy? Because he seemed genuinely surprised for a guy who supplied you with the ring to ask me," I say, hiding my smile behind the shirt I lift to fold.

Placing the T-shirt on the pile in front of me, I look at the ring again — how it sits against my skin, just slightly loose, and how the light dances off the cut of the ruby. I'm not much of a jewelry person except for the occasional pair of earrings, but this piece fits me. It's petite and perfect.

"He's good at keeping secrets, Wren," Alex says. "He doesn't want us to wait for the sake of waiting if we know we belong together."

I nod, and as another thought comes into my mind about the holidays and tomorrow at Maggie's our conversation flows in a different direction. It's easy, and I enjoy it. Alex helps me take care of laundry and I double check that the spare room is tidy for my mom while he gets dinner ready.

An hour later, I'm on my way to Rochester to pick my mother up from the airport, very aware that I have a ring on a very specific finger.

Chapter 31

Alexander

"Anita, how are you?" I say as Wren and her mom walk in the house. I pull her into a hug and she squeezes me back. "How was your flight?"

"About as good as a flight across the country can be," she says, allowing herself to laugh. "I'm just glad to be here with you two. You're sure you don't mind me staying? I can always go get a room at a hotel."

Wren picks up her mom's bags and carries them to the bedroom.

"Mom, we wouldn't have offered if we didn't mean it," she calls from down the hallway. "Are you hungry?"

Anita picks up her purse, walking toward the spare room, while I start grabbing leftovers from the fridge and a plate from the cabinet so she can have something to eat. It's not late, but I'm sure she's exhausted from traveling. Plus, we have a full day tomorrow. Wren's going to help with brunch, which will give me the morning to put the potatoes together and work on a composition piece. Original score isn't part of my dissertation, after all, but when I took my guitar to the nursing home recently, some of the residents gravitated toward it and showed a definite interest. One of the women asked to play, and though I was unsure because it's my baby, I went with my gut and handed my guitar to her. The plan all along was to introduce instruments to them for therapeutic reasons, so I couldn't very well bring it and then not let them play. I knew it was the right decision when her eyes started to shine with recognition and her fingers remembered what to do. Even though frail and fragile, they plucked away as she created her own tune.

That gave me an idea, though, and it's something I haven't actually done in years. I prefer the guitar, but I've stepped out of my comfort zone and started playing piano again when I'm at school. Since I knew I would be asking her to marry me sooner rather than later, I wanted to begin composing a piece to have played at our wedding, or for our first dance, or whenever she wants to listen to it.

"What are you thinking! Married? You've known him less than a year, Wren," Anita exclaims, breaking into my thoughts as Wren walks back into the kitchen.

I see the moment Wren's emotions turn from shock to devastation that her mom is questioning her decision to marry me.

"Wow. I wasn't expecting that reaction," Wren says, forlornly.

"I wasn't expecting you to run away from home and marry the first guy to come along," Anita says.

I stand against the counter holding a plate of food, unsure if I should step in and say something or if I should allow them the time to talk alone.

"You hardly know her," Anita says to me, angrily lashing out. "Why would the two of you want to rush into something like marriage?"

I open my mouth to talk, but quickly close it and set the plate down when I realize she really isn't looking for an answer. Besides, my answer might not be what she's looking for. Does she actually want to hear me say I've loved Wren since North Carolina and, though it seems like things have moved very quickly, I never want to let them slow down with her? I want to keep doing things at the speed of life every day with her daughter.

While I continue to figure out if I should give a response, Wren has already started talking for us.

"I don't want to wake up tomorrow and wonder what if. Life changes in the blink of an eye and I don't want to not take chances. I don't want to get to the end of my life and wish I'd done it differently," she says, her voice softening after the initial hurt and anger. "You of all people should understand."

"But, Wren, you barely know one another!"

"I don't want to wait until it feels like the right time. When is the right time to know you want to spend forever with someone? Is it after six months? A year? Five years?" she asks, rhetorically. "Sometimes … sometimes it feels like there will never be enough time to do all the things I want to do. I'm going to take advantage this time and say yes to Alex and marry this man and not regret the fact we did it outside of some ridiculous timeline."

Anita's face falls just a bit, as if the pain she's feeling about the moment is less about Wren and I becoming engaged and more about the ghost in the room. The loss she's still reeling from, that Wren is still overcoming, and that Will and I have been attempting to support both of them through.

"Dad loved Alex. Will gave his stamp of approval. Two of the most important guys in my life already said this was okay. All Alex had to do was ask. I was going to say yes no matter when the question came," Wren says.

Holding her hand out, she continues, "Mom, this is my grandmother's ring. We have good men who care about us. I have to stop playing things safe at some point and take a leap of faith."

Anita reaches out to touch Wren's hand and I, a fly on the wall, smile like a fool who's hopeful this is the one and only bump we will encounter.

"You took a leap of faith when you moved here. How many more leaps are you going to take before it's too many?" Anita says softly.

"Mom ..."

Headlights flood the living room as someone pulls into the driveway. Despite not having plans for more company tonight, heavy footsteps fall on the stairs up to the house from the breezeway, there's a slight tap on the wood, and then the kitchen door opens. Forgetting I asked Will to swing by to grab food from the freezer I picked up for tomorrow's brunch is more than a bump.

Will finds Wren and Anita standing in the kitchen looking at his mother's ring together.

"Uh ... I can come back," he says, eyes wide, and begins to step back out of the house.

"Oh no you don't," Anita says, whipping around to glare at him. "Get in here."

"Yes, ma'am."

"Don't 'yes ma'am' me. You knew about this?"

"Anita, I can explain," Will says, holding his hands up as Anita takes a step back from Wren and crosses her arms over her chest.

Wren steps over to me, pressing her shoulder against my side as I wrap my arm around her.

"Go on. Explain," Anita says.

"So, is this what it was like growing up with her? Can I expect this from you, too?" I ask, my mouth close to Wren's ear.

She giggles and says, "I mean, Dad never 'yes ma'am'd' her, but I imagine this is how it would have gone."

As we watch Will and Anita have words — nothing harsh by any means, but definitely a case of trying to understand where each other is coming from about the wellbeing of their newly engaged daughter — I notice a change in the way the room feels and wonder if Wren feels it, too.

It's been a solid ten minutes of them discussing the intricacies of knowing who "the one" is and the theoretical timeline for marriage. In the midst of her saying we should have waited longer, Will loses all composure and raises his voice.

"Damn it, Anita, would you have rather she slept with him and he never heard from her again? Would it have been better if she used him for a fun weekend and then left? Or how about him realizing he wanted more but couldn't bring himself to go find her? Because, out of the two of us standing here, I'm the only one who knows what that is like," Will yells.

Brushing his hand down his face, Will turns away from us. His shoulders lift with a heavy breath. As he reaches a hand up to wipe at his face again, he adjusts his ballcap, and then steps toward the door.

"I just stopped by to let Wren know to be at the church around nine tomorrow morning and pick up the extra bacon from the freezer. Sorry I caught you all at a bad time," he says, leaving us speechless as he walks out of the house.

Wren looks up at me as the front screen door slams followed by the sound of his truck door. I wait for the engine to roar to life, but it doesn't. Kissing Wren on the temple, I unwind my arm from her.

"I'm going to go check on him," I say quietly and she nods.

Throwing a jacket on as I leave the house, I walk carefully over to Will's truck and climb up into the passenger seat. We sit together quietly, staring at the back of my car in front of us, as he softly cries.

"If it weren't for Tony, I would have gone to find her, you know? She didn't tell me she was married until our second night together, didn't wear her wedding band because they were fighting, and when I found out ... well, there was no way I was going to California and be the reason they split up and went through with a divorce," he says. "Not when I wasn't sure she would even want me."

He takes a shaky breath.

"I shouldn't be encouraging you two to get married so quickly," he says, taking his hat off and tossing it on the dash. Scrubbing his hands through his salt-and-pepper hair, he groans. "But, I see how much you love my daughter and how much she loves you in return. I don't want you to wait just because of some stupid etiquette type nonsense."

Listening to him, I truly begin to understand why Will has been single all these years.

"She was the only one for you?"

"The one and only. I didn't want anyone else, but I wasn't going to ruin her marriage to have her," he says. "It was only a few days together. No one has ever stuck to my insides like she did. When you know, you know, Alex. I guess that's why I see no problem with you and Wren moving so quickly in your own relationship."

"We appreciate you for that," I say, unsure of what else to say now that I have a plethora of new knowledge.

"The worst part is, Tony was a pretty great guy. I know I was part of it, but I really hate that she cheated on him."

I snicker, because it's just a weird conversation. But I also could see Will and Tony being closer friends if they had had the chance.

"I'm glad I got to know him a little and that he held no hatred for me. When I met him, he was nothing but kind and generous. Grateful, even, because of Wren. Anita is hurting so badly from losing him, and I know that, but I don't want her hurt to keep you kids from finding your joy," he says, facing me in the dark. "Her grief, Wren's grief, it's going to come and go and ebb and flow, but don't let it smother the light you bring to one another."

Chapter 32

Wren

"Pancakes, coming in hot!"

I slide another tray of perfect, fluffy pancakes onto the tall countertop in front of three very hungry, dressed in their best, homeless men. Murph's guys. Though I'm far from religious, I love that my uncle is absolutely out here doing this kind of work and probably would be even if he wasn't actually a priest. He's just a very humble, down-to-earth man who wants to do good for others, and I can't fault him for that.

"Will, your girl is really good at this. She should come to lunch more often," one of the men says, taking a large forkful of pancakes into his mouth before reaching for the bottle of Sugar Shack maple syrup.

"Yeah, well, that's up to her. She's got a busy schedule, you know. She's a big-time college softball coach," Will says. Sipping his coffee as he sits on a barstool over by the island counter, Will grins in my direction before turning back to the men sitting around him.

"Please, continue laying the compliments on me. I need all I can get," I say, turning back to the stove.

Once Will left last night and Alex came back in the house, Mom went to bed. I heard her crying. I should have gone in to talk to her.

I didn't want to. I didn't know how to.

How do you ask your mom if she feels remorse over one man when she's in the center of grief over another? It's so complicated and after Will's admission, I really needed to let everything cool down before attempting to talk to either of them about it.

But then Alex came to bed and told me what Will said and, even though I was already putting the puzzle pieces together, it all made sense. More than that, though, I realized the electric feeling in the air when they're near each other is not just in my head.

Walking up beside me to check on the bacon, Will leans in close.

"Is your mother okay?" he says quietly.

I shrug, and I don't want to make a scene, but ...

"She cried herself to sleep last night."

He mutters under his breath a curse word, probably quieter than he normally would have given our surroundings, and moves the bacon from the pan onto a plate covered with paper towels. Before saying anything else, he turns off the heat and moves the greasy pan off the hot burner.

"I didn't mess things up for you and Alex, did I?"

"Nope. Whatever is between you and Mom is between you and Mom. I trust you both to not put me in the middle," I say, flipping the next batch of pancakes. "I do think you two need to talk, though. Whatever is going on has nothing to do with me and Alex getting engaged."

Will sighs deeply, sips his coffee, and turns to lean against the counter beside the stove.

"You're right. And I will talk to her."

"She'll be at Maggie's later."

"I will talk to her *not* at Maggie's."

"Will. Come on. Just rip the bandage off and have whatever conversation with her you need to have," I say, pointing at him with my spatula as I talk with my hands. "You care about my mom. You care about me. Just ... talk to her and tell her about all the caring. It's not like you two don't text each other to talk about me. Jesus, you had my dad on speed dial and talked constantly from the day you met him up until the day he died."

He smirks.

"Tony was a good guy. In another lifetime, I do believe we could have been best buddies," he says. Pushing off the counter, he leans in to kiss the side of my head before walking out of the kitchen. "Don't worry, sweetheart, I'll talk to Anita."

I stare after him as he disappears down a hallway that leads to the sanctuary, but I don't follow him. Just like me and Mom, I think Will is hurting, too, from losing my dad and I want to allow him time. We all need time.

"How are we doing over here?" Murph asks as he comes up beside me with a box of scones.

I'm briefly distracted when my former second baseman, but new centerfielder, walks into the kitchen with a younger man I haven't met. She's chit-chatting as she hands him a plate and asks if he wants coffee, and he shyly smiles as he accepts.

"Did you go to the bakery while I was making breakfast?" I ask accusatorially bringing my attention back to Murph while looking at the box in his hand.

"I absolutely did not," he says, his eyes twinkling as he opens the box and removes one of the pumpkin spice scones. "I went to the coffeehouse, not the bakery, and Brian made me take these since he's closing early today."

I say a dismissive, "uh huh." I take the box while handing him a full plate of hot pancakes. Then, as he attempts to take a bite of the scone in his hand, I hand him the plate of bacon and go back to finishing making the pancakes, leaving him helpless with both hands and his mouth full.

"Let me help you, Father Murphy," Bree says, coming around the counter to take the plates from him.

I catch the new younger man's eye as he smiles at Bree and Murphy's interaction. He's definitely new here, but it's colder and Will has told me sometimes new faces pop up during the winter months. I'm assuming this is one of those cases.

Regardless, there's plenty of food for another mouth. My goal this morning was to make enough for the guys to take some with them. They get hungry between their visits with Murph and now that there are also scones from Brian, there will be extra for them to take.

Through the course of several conversations about Murph's outreach, I've learned he tends to make box lunches for anyone who needs them. It's not a church outreach program, though. It's just Murph. As a collective the church does plenty, but these guys who come for brunch and lunch tend to shy away from what the church typically offers. They don't want to be preached at and they aren't always looking for services to help them get back on their feet. What Murph does, though, reminds them they're human and important. They just don't have homes. Sometimes, the stigma of being unhoused is worse than being unhoused. Murph takes that out of the equation. He keeps the group small so he can counsel individually if they need him to, and it's out of pocket not church coffers ... really, it's Murph and Will having coffee and snacks with friends.

"So, Uncle Father Murph," I say to get his attention once he's handed the plates to Bree. He steps back over to me and I ask, "Why do you do this? This little tiny outreach?"

"Everyone is welcome in God's house, Wren," he says, "But not everyone in God's house is welcoming."

"I get that. Not everyone has empathy," I respond, flipping the last of the pancakes.

"And you need empathy to work in outreach. These men remind me of Will after he first got out of the service," he says. "It was just us, our parents had been gone since his senior year of high school, and when he came home, I needed to take time to help him find the light again. War, being in the military, all of it, hurts everyone. These men, unfortunately, also understand that."

"Was Will ever unhoused?" I ask while wiping down the counter.

"For a short time," Will says from the doorway. "I couch surfed and Murph gave me a place to land for a bit."

"But then you went to college?" I ask.

"Will went to college?" one of the guys asks. "I never would have guessed he was book smart, too."

"I'm all kinds of smart. Know a lot of stuff about a lot of things, but yes, after getting out of the service, I didn't have anywhere to go, so I ended up here with my brother," he says, lifting his mug in Murph's direction. "Once I got my bearings, I started volunteering and after a while I put the G.I. Bill to good use. I had planned to go to school, but the military was the best option for me at the time. I served my country and then, because of my degree, my country helped me serve my community."

"This is all new information for me," I say, and I wonder if my mom has any idea at all. The entire time I've been here I haven't once asked my father if he works or where he works.

"I'm in engineering, some architectural design, but I don't work for anyone. I've been smart with my investments," he says. "I have my own business, Wren."

"Does Mom know?" I ask, only for the question to ricochet through my head a second too late. "That's a dumb question. I'm sorry. It's really not her concern."

Will's smile creases his eyes and he lets out a hearty laugh that gets everyone's attention, including Bree and Murph's new guy who were in the midst of their own conversation.

"When I met your mother, I was just starting my college adventure. I didn't have much to tell at that point and she was already so much more successful than me," he says, and I watch his eyes shine as he talks about my mom. "I wasn't sure what she saw in me that weekend, but I'm glad for whatever it was. I'm thankful, and, after all, isn't that what we're supposed to be celebrating today? Things we're thankful for?"

*****

When Will and I finally arrive at Maggie and Maverick's, we're the very last ones there. Walking in, Alex lunges for me, wrapping me in a hug like he didn't quietly violate me in the best ways before the sun came up this morning. He drags me away from the door and hides me in the corner of the mudroom off the kitchen as he kisses me senseless. We have yet to tell anyone other than Mom and Will about the engagement, and I get the feeling he just wants a few more minutes with me before anyone else finds out.

"Are you all right?" I ask, pulling away from him and leaning against the wall to catch my breath. My hands press gently against his chest as my fingers softly rub the fabric of the flannel shirt he put on over a T-shirt.

"I'm perfect." He leans in to kiss me slowly again, his large hands resting on my waist until he slides them down the backside of my jeans. Grabbing me by my bottom, Alex lifts me up onto my toes, pulling me tight against the front of him. Our mouths still somewhat connected, he says, "Maybe we should sneak back home. I think I forgot the something."

I laugh, the sound soft, as I take notice of the thickness pressing into my belly.

"The something, huh? I think you're going to have to get yourself under control, lover boy," I say. "There are too many friends around for us to bail so soon after I've gotten here."

"There's a whole tree farm out there. We could tell them we're going to find the one we want for Christmas." I shake my head, because I don't think that would work, and mention that I really think someone will want to come with us and it will result in us actually leaving with a tree today instead of the intended quickie he's implying. He kisses my nose, reaches down to adjust himself, and says, "Good point. I love you. Let's go visit. I'll explore your forest later."

I laugh loudly as we walk out of the mudroom and, while I'm a little sad to not be sneaking away, this gives me the chance to be reintroduced to

Maggie's parents and Maverick's entire family, plus a plethora of children running about, as food is prepared and football is watched. I attempt to make my way around the house talking to everyone and even find myself on the floor playing with Ashton at one point.

"What do you do between the fall season and spring training?" Harper asks when we find ourselves alone a couple hours later.

We're the only ones in the kitchen creating cocktails for anyone who wants them, and though I'm not a huge drinker, Alex is driving us home so I'll allow myself one or two. Harper is busy whipping together a pineapple bourbon lemonade while I'm making the simpler vodka cranberry with Maggie's home canned cranberry juice.

"Train. I just keep training. Dylan and I are working on a plan for where to start since I'm still new to the team and several of the girls are new this year," I say. "I miss just playing for fun, but this is what I've always loved doing. I'm working on getting the team more involved in community activism, but it's been slow. Bree, one of our outfielders, was the only local girl to show up at Murph's this morning."

"Weren't you a physical therapist back in California? Any of that happening here?" she asks, dipping a chunk of pineapple in her drink and then taking a bite out of it.

I smile at her, but not really at her. It's more the fact I figured that's what I would be doing out here, too.

"I've considered it. I'm not sure yet, though. I'm afraid if I add too many things at once I'll leave no room for personal growth. I love coaching and playing, I've loved working in physical therapy and sports medicine, but I don't know if I want to pigeonhole myself just yet," I say.

"Well, what about a rec league so you can play for fun while coaching and then teach people how to stretch properly? You have all the credentials for it," she says, sipping her drink.

A recreational league isn't something I had given any thought to before, but now ...

"Do you know who runs the Little League program? Or is there an adult rec league here you were thinking about?"

Harper shrugs.

"Is that something you would want to do?" I ask, staring at her. Getting a goofy grin on my face, I ask more pointedly, "Harper? Do you want to play softball with me?"

She lifts an eyebrow at me over her drink glass, and then lifts one shoulder.

"It would be great for stress. If I know anyone who needs to destress, it's my sister," Maverick says walking into the kitchen. "She played Little League, you know?"

"I never would have guessed," I say.

"Is it because I'm tall-ish? Or the makeup? The makeup throws people off. They always pegged me as a cheerleader, but I grew up with brothers. One of whom is a total dick and tried using me as a tackle dummy when he thought he wanted to be a football player," Harper says. "I still haven't told Mom and Dad about that, by the way."

Maverick's cheeks redden. Grabbing the grill tongs, he makes a move toward the mudroom and backdoor.

"That was Bentley's idea. Don't you dare tell Mom it was mine," he says, stepping from the kitchen to the mudroom. We hear him talking to someone, and I'm surprised when I hear, "I'm so sorry. I didn't mean to interrupt. Just need to go check the brisket on the smoker."

What surprises me even more is when my mom and Will slip past Maverick.

"Hey, you two. Need a drink?" Harper asks.

"No, thank you," Will says, lifting his ballcap to brush his already short hair back before replacing the hat on his head.

Harper looks at him with an odd expression.

"What about you, Mrs. Leary? Beverage?"

I tilt my head and look at my mom. Something is off. Then I look at Will. Something is definitely off.

"Sure. What are you having, Wren? It looks cheerful," she says.

"Vodka cranberry," I say, grabbing a glass and pouring for her. "Are you okay? You look a little flushed."

Her eyes go wide and Will suddenly is very interested in going outside to talk to Maverick. He touches Mom's arm before he turns to leave the house, a gesture I've seen before just not between them.

"Wrenny, we need to talk about something," she says as I'm mid-pour.

I stop. I set the bottle of vodka down. Harper chokes on her drink and then exits the room immediately.

"What's going on and should this be a conversation we have at my house?" I say, splaying my hands on the counter in the center of Maggie's kitchen. Loud cheering erupts from the living room and I can only assume the Bills scored. Waiting for the noise to lessen, I take a deep breath before asking, "Do I need to worry?"

She smiles at me and it reaches her eyes, but it lacks the warmth and comfort I need after having so many major life events happen in just a few months.

"I'm selling the house and moving out here," she says.

I turn my head slightly and look at her out of the corner of my eye, grasping at the complexity of the situation. Where do I even begin?

"Okay, so selling the house. That's fine as long as you're sure. Moving out here. Fantastic, I would love to have you closer. But …" I say, giving myself a moment to catch up with the thoughts racing through my head like where is she going to live and why she didn't talk to me about this before now and why was she hiding with Will.

"There's nothing keeping me in California. I don't want to stay there and have to hop two or three planes just to see my kid for a weekend. The house is lonely, Wren," she says calmly. I don't know how she's so calm. "It'll take some time for the house to sell and close, so I won't be out here until early next year. I assume, anyway."

"That will give me and Alex time to configure space and make sure we have room for your things. This'll be fine," I say, feeling less apprehensive knowing it's not a case of she's here now and not going back to California. "The basement is huge and technically is an apartment in itself, so maybe we could talk to Maggie and—"

"Stop," she says, holding her hand up. "We will figure that out later. Right now, my plan is not to crash your relationship by moving in with you and Alex. It's hard enough starting out somewhere new, and then starting a new relationship, without your mother moving in. I want you two to have your space."

Taking a deep breath, I wonder how long she's been thinking about this. She told me after Dad's funeral she was okay, but something changed. Maybe it's grief, or healing, or healing from her grief.

"This is a big decision so soon after losing Dad. Are you sure?"

"Positive. Your dad and I had already been toying with the idea before he died, Wren. We just didn't want to make it look like we didn't trust you to be on your own," she says, stepping up to the counter. Standing across from me, she copies my stance — hands on the countertop, fingers splayed, but then she pushes her hands forward and covers mine, touching my ring carefully. "We had talked about it with Will, as well. It was important to your dad to give you and Will time to get to know one another, but he also wanted us to be able to foster a connection with him. And we have, through phone calls and text messages and you."

I nod, letting myself acknowledge this is not a rash choice my mom is making, but something that had already been in the works.

"Is that why you and Will were acting strange?"

"Yes," she says, a little quicker than I expected. "We were discussing the house and me moving here. I didn't want you to find out from someone other than me. That wouldn't be fair."

"Agreed. So … does this mean you're not mad anymore about me and Alex getting engaged?"

She leans her elbows on the counter, her hands still covering mine, and drops her head down.

"I am so sorry about last night, Wren. I absolutely overreacted and reacted in the wrong way. I wasn't upset about the engagement and I am so happy for you two, it was just somewhat unexpected, you know?" She looks up at me and I lean into the counter. Turning my hands over, I hold onto hers, seeking connection more than anything. "You're right about not being on a timeline. It shouldn't matter how long you've been together if you truly love one another. I just want you to be happy."

"I am happy. Life is stressful, but I'm happier than I've been in a long time. I've got Alex and Will, I'm making friends, Harper wants to start a rec league team from the sounds of it. It feels like I've finally figured out where I belong."

"You were built for small town life, eh?" she says, smiling, as Will and Maverick walk back in with the pans of meat they took off the smoker.

"Of course she was. It's in her DNA," Will says as he wraps an arm around my shoulder and kisses me on the top of the head. "Just like her green thumb."

I pull my hand out from under Mom's and reach across the front of me to pat Will's arm. Maggie wanders into the kitchen looking like she's on a mission until she spies the scene before her. Her gaze softens and then I watch as her eyes lock onto my left hand.

"Wren."

"Maggie."

"Is that a ring? Like a ring ring?"

Alex, who was walking in behind Maggie, stumbles as she comes to an abrupt stop. I glance at him and he smiles back at me.

"Yes," I say, holding my hand in front of me.

"Oh, my goodness," she says loudly, holding her hands up in front of her mouth before rushing over to the counter. Reaching out for my hand, she says, "Let me see."

Mom and Will step to the side, allowing Maggie and Harper in their spaces to ask all their burning questions — was it romantic, how did he do it, when am I shopping for a dress, and so many more, most of which I haven't even thought about. A very brief rundown of the last twenty-four hours later and the entire house is hugging me and Alex. When I emerge from a group hug I'd been pulled into on the other side of the room with Harper and Maggie, I see them.

My parents.

Standing there across the room, Will drapes his arm around my mom's shoulders, pulling her close as he leans against the counter behind them. My mother and father watch me celebrate one of my happiest occasions and all the while the memory of my dad lives freely in the moment with us.

Everything feels like it's falling into place.

Chapter 33

Alexander

The last few months have been a blur. Christmas came and went, we welcomed the new year in with friends, new semesters of school and work started, and we celebrated Wren's birthday in February. Each week I watch as Wren's relationship with Will gets stronger and, since her move out East, Anita and Will's relationship has grown. It's like life decided this is what we are doing and all the pieces are moving into place.

The universe has perfectly orchestrated all of it, and I've come to the realization I can't imagine it happening any other way.

A mug of hot tea sits idly in her hands as she watches the birds flit around by Gram's feeders in the front yard, their bright colors loud against the snowy backdrop. I kiss her on the cheek, bringing her out of a fog she momentarily slipped into while sitting nestled in a blanket on the front porch.

It's her first winter in New York and I love watching her love the snow while it falls soundlessly from the sky as the sun begins its ascent. Landing along the edges of the yard where the plows have banked it, the fresh flakes cover the dirt peeking out of the piles, making everything appear clean again.

"Everyone keeps asking me when we're setting a date for the wedding," she says. "It's only March. We just got engaged. I didn't think we needed to decide on a day yet, but maybe we should."

"Who's everyone?" I question, knowing her mom and Will are content with waiting for us to open the conversation.

"Dylan, Harper, Bree, the entire team ..."

I walk across the small sitting area and take a seat in the chair opposite her.

"Every practice, one of the girls is asking when the hot music teacher and I are going to tie the knot."

Leaning forward, I place my elbows on my thighs and clasp my hands together between my knees.

"They do not call me 'the hot music teacher'," I say, smiling.

"Not to my face, at least. But I hear them talking in the locker room and the freshmen definitely have noticed you," she says, sighing. "I don't even know how to plan a wedding. What are we doing, Alex? I don't have a clue how to do this."

Looking at her, she's exhausted. It's not just tired from keeping each other up late because we don't see one another otherwise ... this is a bone deep exhaustion from running herself ragged in the recent months. Right after Christmas she applied for her license to practice physical therapy in New York. It came through in February and she immediately started seeing clients a few days a week at a clinic in town. She's going eighteen hours a day lately and doesn't sleep in if she can help it.

Spring training started almost as soon as the fall season ended and she's been keeping up with morning and evening practices while also fitting in physical therapy patients, getting her mom moved into an apartment just outside of town, and me.

I've got my own crazy schedule, so as much as I hate how busy she is, I hate that I'm no less busy. This morning, I have to go to Rochester to finalize plans for defending my dissertation and then have to teach this afternoon.

The fact we get any time together is amazing as Wren's also doing as much team building outside of softball as she can with the girls.

"What if we don't set a date?" I question.

Lifting her eyes up to me, I find confusion.

"We should set a date, Alex. That's what's expected. And I don't want an eternal engagement, either. I want to be married to you."

"When have we ever done what's expected?" I ask. It isn't that I'm trying to be difficult. I'm making a point, though. "When?"

She pulls the edge of her bottom lip in between her teeth and nibbles on it. I don't want to pressure her to do something else unconventional, but I also don't want her to stress out about a big wedding or pleasing everyone in our lives. We won't ever please everyone. Sliding off the chair to my knees, I crawl across the floor to her. Taking the mug from her hands and setting it on the small table beside her chair, I grasp her hands in mine and kiss each fingertip.

"When was the last time we did something expected of us? As a couple? With the exception of holidays and showing up to birthday gatherings," I say.

"We haven't. We have been the most unconventional in the span of our very short relationship."

"Right. So why start playing to people's expectations now?"

She shrugs.

"I don't want to let them down. They all want to see me in a white dress and walking down an aisle," she says.

I nod, because I know. And I'm very aware that's what *they* want — Maggie, Harper, Delilah, Anita, Veronica, even Will and Murph ...

"But what do you want?"

"I want you to defend your dissertation and I want to win the championship, and then I want to get married in the pitcher's circle while your students play the song you've been composing and my girls cheer us on from the dugout."

The words flow out of her so smoothly it seems she's been thinking about it a lot. This is the first time she's told me, though, and the smile that breaks through after she stops talking, followed by the exhausted giggle is what makes my heart beat faster.

"If that's what you want, let's do it."

"But what if we don't win the championship game?"

"Are you going to not marry me if you don't win? What about if they don't award me my doctorate?"

"I didn't say that," she says, her voice sad. Maybe it's because she's thinking about those two very real possibilities. Or maybe it's because she thinks I'm taking what she said out of context. I didn't though. I'm simply playing devil's advocate here and making sure I understand where her head is at.

"I'm aware, but I needed to be sure you're sure you want to do this with me. So, even if you don't win, or I don't get my doctorate this year, I'm still going to meet you in the circle at your chosen time or after the championship game," I say, pulling myself up to kiss the tip of her nose. "White dress optional."

"I love you forever and a day, you know that right?" she says.

"I love you, always and forever."

*****

"Well, it looks like everything is in order, Alex. You should be set to defend this in early April," my advisor says at the end of our meeting. "It's been a real pleasure watching you grow through this research. I wasn't sure when you first proposed the project. The previous research was a great foundation, but showing the difference in behavior of the residents based on the kinds of music is pretty amazing."

I sit across from her, her desk between us, and touch my index and middle finger to my bottom lip. I'm deep in thought, wondering if it really is good enough.

"What's wrong?" she asks.

I shake my head.

"Nothing."

"Alex, I've gotten to know you well these last couple of years. Are you doubting your ability to present this?"

"Not at all. I'm just ... I'm just having a difficult time believing this is real."

She nods.

"I remember that feeling all too well. I understand. But it is real. This is good research. Your methodology works, your premise is spot on, your research proves even more how different styles of music affects those with brain related illnesses. I think the implications are greater than dementia, though, and I hope you'll explore that with additional research."

I scrub my hand down my unshaven face. It feels like a thousand years have passed since Wren and I talked this morning.

"I'll get everything submitted to the committee and schedule my defense," I say. "I want to give myself enough time to make revisions if necessary."

She said early April, but that could be any time the first week or two and then I need to submit the final manuscript.

"I have a checklist," I say absentmindedly.

"Alex, you're doing amazing things. I can't wait to see what you accomplish after this," she says, standing to come around the desk.

I stand as well, knowing our time is up and I need to get the rest of my work together. Wren will be away for spring training in Florida starting Thursday and won't be home for more than a week. The only thing that will keep me from going stir-crazy is going to be working on this and grading midterms. It's likely I'll have everything submitted before the end of spring break because when I have nothing else going on at home, I work more than I do when the semester is in session.

"I appreciate all the guidance you've given me," I say, shaking her hand as my mind runs through the reality that in about six weeks I could be adding "Dr." to the beginning of my name.

And Wren's name. I feel a smile work its way across my mouth as I realize our conversation earlier means we will be Dr. and Mrs. after graduation.

My advisor opens the door for me, I sling my backpack over my shoulder, and step into the small hallway outside her office.

"As always, it's been a pleasure," she says, smiling as she closes her door.

*****

I stroll back into the house following my meeting to find Wren in a full panic. Walking down the hall to our bedroom, I catch Harper sitting on our bed watching Wren as she mumbles something under her breath.

"This is … interesting," I say quietly as I lean against the doorframe. Looking at Harper, I point at Wren, who's standing in front of the dresser. "What's going on?"

"Something about lucky socks. You didn't tell me she was leaving Thursday. Angela keeps talking about break, but I didn't even think about Wren having a practice on Friday in Florida."

"Angela?"

Harper rolls her eyes at me.

"The girl next door who works at the college. I told you about her forever ago. There's been a development," she says.

I raise my eyebrows at her and glance in Wren's direction right as she pulls the dresser drawer out and dumps it on the bed.

"Ah ha! There they are. Told you I would find them," she says, triumphantly spinning around with a pair of familiar navy-blue knee-high socks in her hand, waving them in Harper's face. When she notices me standing in the doorway, she rushes over to kiss me, "You're home! How'd it go?"

"First things first … lucky socks?"

"They're more a comfort item than magical. I wash them during the season if I wear them. Don't worry. I'm not gross," she says, going back to the bed to begin picking underwear and socks up off the comforter to put back in the drawer. "I usually only wear them for spring training games, and if I don't wear them, they're in my bag with all my gear."

"How'd they end up in the regular sock drawer instead of with your softball stuff?" Harper asks.

Wren and I share a look. I feel the heat creep up my neck as Wren's cheeks flush pink.

"You know what, I don't need to know. I'm just really glad you found them and that you get lucky while wearing them," Harper says, punctuating her sentence with laughter. "What's the second thing?"

It's just enough to bring me back to Wren's question after my mind quickly wandered to the image of her meeting me at the door the other night in that pair of knee-highs, wearing my favorite tie, and nothing else.

"Right, the second thing. Everything is looking good for an early April defense. I'm going to schedule with the committee, reserve the lecture room, and then over break while you're away I'm going to polish everything to shine and submit it," I say, pushing my hands down into my pockets. "Then I can focus on building the presentation, practicing, and probably writing some new music so I don't go completely nuts doubting myself."

Harper looks at Wren and then looks back at me.

"You're going to be amazing, Alex. They're talking about hiring a full-time music therapist at work because of the way the residents responded to your research. Some of the staff just saw you coming in and playing music, but those of us who were in the activity room every single time you've been there know what kind of impact you're having," Harper says. "Like that first day in the activity room when Mildred put puzzle pieces together? Or the day Frank was having outbursts when you started with classical music and then you switched to reggae after asking where he was from and he calmed down within minutes? We all knew Frank grew up in Jamaica. We didn't realize he wasn't fully lucid, and it chilled him out so quickly I was even in shock. This isn't something you should doubt yourself about."

I know I'm doing good things. Part of me wishes I was doing more, though. More than just going and playing music and watching the reactions. More than taking notes and hoping it gets me my degree. More than —

"The research is solid, Alex," Wren adds, her voice quiet. "You've spent months working with this group, and now your research is almost done. Don't let imposter syndrome get you now."

I drop my head and stare at my dress shoes. My legs are crossed at the ankles and I'm still propped against the doorframe. When I look up at my future wife, I know what she sees.

A scared kid. Someone I keep locked away most of the time.

"It's just hard sometimes," I say, pulling my left hand from my pocket to wipe the dampness from my face. "I was this kid who wasn't going to amount to much. I just wanted to play music. My parents cared but didn't care. Whenever I decided I wanted to try something, they threw money at it until I was tired of it. Sports, science camps, art projects, all of it. I just never got tired of music."

"And now, here you are, about to be a doctor of music stuff ... and you're making a difference in people's lives," Wren says, stepping up to me and standing with her bare toes touching my shoes. She pushes up on her tiptoes, kissing the tear off my stubbled cheek. "You're making a difference and it's not because they threw money at a hobby. It's because you're an incredible human who writes love notes on slips of paper and jots down lines between classes. Your entire life is written in sheet music."

M.L. Pennock

Chapter 34

Wren

This is the first time Alex and I have been away from one another since I moved to Brockport. I would be one hundred percent full of shit if I told anyone I was doing okay sleeping alone. We've been in Florida for The Spring Games less than twenty-four hours and already I want to go home.

It's got nothing to do with my team or the other teams or Florida. I just miss him.

However, I'm trying to focus and be a decent coach on this trip because, even though I'm not the head coach, Dylan and I tend to share the load.

"That's another line drive to right field," I say to Dylan as we stand on the third base line. "Every single pitch she's hit goes low and looks like it's going to take the pitcher's knees off. Does she realize this is just our warmup? Was she hitting like that at home off the machine?"

I worked more closely with other players, so I hadn't really noticed all the nuances of each girl. But as much as I've worked with Bree, this is one thing I haven't paid much attention to.

"Yup. She doesn't like to pop them up," Dylan says, blowing a bubble with her gum. "When she was in high school, I watched her take a couple girls out. Not intentionally, of course, it's just how the ball came off the bat. Lots of bruised shins and thighs from that one."

We stand mirroring one another — feet hip-width apart, arms crossed, eyes forward — as we chat about each of our girls. It's still early Saturday morning and after flying in Thursday night, none of us really wanted to get up and to the field yesterday or today, but it's nice to be out of the twenty-degree weather New York is getting hit with. The only exception being I would have been snuggled in my bed with Alex instead of in a hotel room with an unreliable air conditioner and nauseous from the heat and lack of good sleep.

I sent Alex a screenshot of my weather app early this morning and he responded in kind. It was the first "I miss you" of the day.

"Alex said you two were finally planning a wedding," Dylan says, seemingly out of left field.

"Planning is a term I would use loosely. We talked about a date, but that's about as far as we got."

"What's the date?"

"Our conference championship game day. Tentatively."

Dylan turns her entire body to look at me. It's not quite a horrified look, but it's close.

"And what if we make it to the championships?" she asks, narrowing her eyes.

"Wedding after on the field," I say, smiling brightly. "I have every intention of us making it through and winning."

"We have a lot of players who are still kind of new to college play. I'm not saying we won't, but I'll be pleasantly surprised if we make it out of our regular season in one piece," she says. "And there's no guarantee where that game will be held."

"So, no notes about the wedding?"

She shrugs and crosses her arms over her chest.

"I think May is a beautiful time of year to get married," she says. "But maybe have an actual plan. Wait until the other team leaves, stuff like that."

Dylan laughs, but I agree with her.

"In all honesty, he asked what I wanted and I just blurted it out. I didn't think he was going to take me seriously, but the more I think about it, the more I love the idea of getting married on the field. I've spent my whole life playing ball, so it just makes sense. Even if we don't make it to the playoffs or the championship, I'm planning for May 9 at a ball field. Any ball field," I say. "I'm not a church wedding kind of girl."

"Which is hysterical considering your uncle is a priest," she notes, raising an eyebrow at me followed by mirthful laughter.

"Touche. But, in my defense, I didn't know I even had a priest uncle until a few months ago," I say.

"We just going to stand around chit-chatting all day, ladies, or are we going to play some ball?" the Homeplate umpire says as he saunters over to us.

Neither of us move as he walks closer and then stops to create a triangle out of the three of us. He places his hands on his hips, his umpire mask dangling from his fingertips, waiting for us to give a response.

Dylan and I look around at our girls and at the other team, which is also warming up, before looking at each other.

"Are we not playing ball right now? Because I'm pretty sure everyone is here to play. We were waiting for you. We know how you guys like to get yourselves all pumped up before a game," Dylan says to him.

"Well, you two seemed to be deep in conversation and we need to get this game started," he says. Holding his hand out to Dylan, he introduces himself, "Trevor."

"Coach Dylan McCabe. This is my assistant coach, Wren Leary," Dylan says as I reach out to take his hand. She checks her watch and lifts her arm to signal our girls to bring it in. "We're ready whenever you are, Trev."

Turning away to hide my smile, I jog in line with a few of our players as they head toward the dugout our team has been assigned. I'm more than ready to get this game underway. It's only been a year, but I've missed the competitive play. Our fall games were more like scrimmages, which was a great way to see how the team worked together.

Being the "home team" we take the field first and even though I know Dylan has her doubts about this season, I coach through each inning side-by-side with her and am impressed as each time we give feedback, the team takes it, utilizes it, and adjusts. They're asking questions as we're giving observations, and when we're back out in the field at the top of the fifth inning, we're finally on the scoreboard.

My goal as a coach is to make sure my team is teachable. I want them taking the criticisms and the suggestions and applying them to do better, and I hope that's something that helps them not just in softball but in life. Before going back out onto the field, I mention to our center fielder that our opponent has a few girls next in their lineup who like to hit high and deep, so she needs to look alive out there.

"Coach, I always look alive," Bree says with a wide smile before turning and running to her position, double Dutch braids trailing behind her.

The first batter hits a grounder to left field for a base hit. On an attempt to steal second when the next batter swings for a strike, she gets tagged out. Dylan and I both congratulate the team on the play and then rein it in as our pitcher eyes her target. She releases the ball and the bat connects, sending the ball straight to center field, but too low for Bree to get under before it bounces.

With one out and one on first base, the next at-bat is the one I've had my eye on. I motion to Bree to back up a little and wait to see if I'm making the right decision.

"What are you thinking?" Dylan asks, watching me closely.

"If she hits like she's been hitting, it's headed right to center field and Bree will get us our second out. If I'm wrong? She gets a double out of it and we try to make the next play at home," I say.

As I finish speaking, we watch the ball leave our pitcher's hand and the runner on first lead off seconds before the bat lifts the ball high and directly toward center field. Cocking my head to the side, I watch as Bree jogs a few steps in and positions herself to catch the fly ball. Almost as soon as it lands in her glove, she's whipping the ball as hard as she can to first base. In the rush of the moment, I hear the ball slam into our first baseman's glove as the runner is lunging for the bag and she tags her for a double play.

Dylan turns to me and smiles.

"Good call on having her move back," she says. "This team just might surprise us yet, Leary."

*****

We're into our third day of games, playing two games a day, and the girls are still kicking ass. Winning? Not necessarily. Learning? Absolutely.

"How'd it go today?" Alex asks me when I call home around 9 p.m.

We've texted and called when we can, but he knows my game schedule and I know he's trying to tie up all the loose ends with his research now that everything for his dissertation is scheduled. With all that is going on, bedtime really is the easiest time to talk.

"It went … okay. The morning game was good. We were up most of the innings, but lost it in the last by one run. This afternoon's game was a complete mess," I say. "So much a mess that Dylan and I are meeting for a drink in a few minutes. I'm headed down to the hotel bar."

"That's really not good," he responds.

"I can promise you, though, we aren't going to be talking about how bad it was. I want to focus on what we did well and see how the team can learn from the ass whooping they got today," I say, stepping out of my room and pulling the door closed behind me. "There's no point in rubbing their faces in the mistakes that were made. It won't make them play harder or better. Can't change the past."

He snickers and I hear what sounds like his glasses getting set down on the kitchen table. Then there's an unmistakable sound of papers shuffling.

"How was your day? You worry about mine, but you're at home with snow and research so I know it's not all sunshine and roses," I say as I wait for the elevator to arrive and whisk me away to the bar.

He lets out a deep sigh, followed by a groan.

"Maybe I shouldn't be a doctor. Maybe I should just be what I am and not worry about the other stuff," he says, and it feels more like he's talking to himself. "I'm so close to done, Wren, and it feels like it isn't enough. Like I'm never going to know enough about it and even though the research is good, is it good … enough?"

Hearing him talk like that breaks my heart because I know how much he's wanted this degree and how hard he's worked. An image of him sitting on the beach with his music theory textbook flashes in my head and I smile at the memory. Remembering him talk that first time with me about what he was researching, makes me hope he never gives up.

"Right before a big breakthrough, we all think we're doing the worst and that it's all pointless. Alexander, you have busted your butt to get where you are. You. No one else, and you deserve this new title," I say, knowing full well he's not going to believe me. As I reach the ground floor of the hotel and the doors open, an elderly woman steps to the side to let me through before she enters the car and it hits me. "If you won't do it for yourself, do it for Gram. Do it for all the grandmas you've met during your research. They, and their families, want you to succeed as much as I do, except they have personally benefitted from your research. Do it for them."

Dylan waves as she sees me walk through the lobby from the elevator bank and motions to the bar. I lift my hand, displaying my index finger to let her know I need another minute. As I walk closer to her, she says she'll order a drink for me while I finish up.

"Sometimes I hate how good you are for me," Alex says in my ear as I'm mouthing "thank you" to Dylan. "It would be easier to give up."

"Same, but you're stuck with me," I say.

"Always and forever?"

"Forever and always."

"I have a little more work to finish up before I call it a night. Plus, you have your coaches meeting, so I should let you go," he says. "You'll be home Sunday?"

"I will. The college is picking us up at the airport and then I'll be home after that. As long as we don't have any delays, I'll be home in time for sweatpants and dinner."

"Don't talk sexy to me when you're not close enough to do something about it."

I feel the blush creep up my neck as I look down at my shoes to hide my smirk.

"There are ways around that, you know," I say.

He gasps in mock horror.

"Wren. Are you suggesting we engage in," he says, then lowers his voice to a whisper, "telephone sex? Like in the olden days?"

Without warning, laughter erupts from me, a deep belly laugh that causes me to cover my mouth to get myself under control as people nearby begin looking in my direction.

"Maybe? But when you put it like that, maybe not," I say.

"God, you're my favorite human ever. I love you so much. Go have a drink with Dylan and I will whisper dirty little things to you later," he says, his voice filled with complete sincerity.

"I love you, too."

As the phone goes quiet, I slip it into the back pocket of my jeans and walk into the bar. Even at 29, I feel odd being in a bar. It was just never my scene in college, and judging by my lack of comfort it's still not my scene.

"Hey, over here," Dylan says, waving to me from a table. "I know it's loud in here, but at least it's a little quieter in the corner."

Pulling my phone back out of my pocket, I set it and my wallet on the table and settle down in the chair directly across from Coach McCabe. Before me sits a chilled mug filled with a dark amber liquid. As I reach for it and the smell hits me, I feel my stomach turn.

"Are you okay?" she asks, lifting her own glass to her lips. "You look like you're going to puke."

"Uh, yeah, I think I need some food before I start drinking that," I say, pushing the drink away from me. "I just don't do well with alcohol on an empty stomach, you know?"

"You sure you aren't pregnant?" she asks, deadpan. The look in her eyes is both curious and hopeful.

"Why is that always the first thing people think?" I ask. Dylan shrugs. "It wouldn't be the worst thing, but, no, the likelihood of that is very slim. I've been on birth control since before Alex and I met, and even though we want to start a family, it's not happening right now. I'm just not a big beer drinker. The smell of the hops or whatever sets off my gag reflex sometimes. Probably comes from years of collecting cans and bottles for fundraisers."

Dylan nods with complete understanding, then reaches across the table to slowly slide my glass over to her side.

"Let's get food and a fruity drink for you," she says. "Then figure out a plan for the rest of our games."

"I don't want them to feel shitty about how they played today," I say without pretense. Waving down a waitress and putting in an order for a chicken Caesar salad and a margarita, Dylan waits patiently. As the waitress walks away, I launch back into our conversation, saying, "They didn't play poorly, but they were definitely not in the game this afternoon. We can use it to our advantage."

She raises an eyebrow at me, takes a long sip of her beverage, and then lets out a sigh.

"Okay, Leary, let me hear it."

So, I give her my game plan — the positive reinforcement with a dose of tough love. My version of running laps until you want to die, only fun. Team building exercises and campus-wide scavenger hunts once back home. Everything my coach in California thought was pointless because she believed the team could be good without being a family. "They just need more time in the weightroom" was a favorite saying of hers.

"They aren't communicating with one another enough. Did you ever do trust falls in high school?"

"That was a long time ago," she says, laughing. "But, yes. We used to do them off the bleachers. I still don't know how that was ever safe. What's your point?"

Taking a deep breath, I hope I'm not going about this the wrong way.

"They need their own version of trust falls. I'm not talking about them falling off the bleachers and expecting someone to catch them, but some of these girls have never had someone catch them at all and it shows," I say. "My dad was always there after a rough game to catch me, Dylan. Want to know why Bree does all the volunteering and is always early and stays late for practices?"

"Because she's an overachiever with a superiority complex?"

I cover my face with both hands and slump in my chair.

"No," I say loudly from behind my hands. Uncovering my face, I add, "Not at all. You've never noticed how none of her family comes to games? She's never once mentioned family. We know she grew up locally because we have access to her school records, you saw her play in high school, and no one shows up. She's close enough to the other girls, but they don't hang out. They're kind to one another, but she's the peripheral friend. We have a few like that."

"She's a loner. So?"

"Dyl, no one has ever caught that girl, so she just does it all herself. She's early because she loves the game, but she stays late because she picks up the slack from some of the other girls who know Bree will do it. She's done every volunteer opportunity I've given them as a team building exercise not because she needs to bond with the team, but because she doesn't want to let all of us down," I say. "She's a junior in college and holding herself together with KT Tape and a need to be needed."

I stare at Coach McCabe, praying something sinks in.

"She's going to break from carrying the weight of all of us if we don't get this team to lift each other up, on the field and off. Our game play is good. We aren't going to lose all season, but even if we did, I don't care. You didn't hire me just to win. You saw something else in me last year when we met."

Dylan wipes her thumb down the side of her mug, clearing the condensation off the glass as she contemplates what I've just said.

"Nope, you're right. I saw a kid who knew how to play with hustle and heart. I didn't care what your record was when you were a player or even when you were coaching in California. It was useful, but not the deciding factor," she says, lifting her glass to take a sip. "Okay, Leary. Let's do it your way."

Chapter 35

Alexander

By the time Sunday rolls around, my paper has been finished, edited, and in the hands of the committee members for four days and I just want my fiancée back home.

"Hey, we just got to baggage claim," she says as I answer the phone.

"Perfect. I've got a few things to finish up here and then I'll head over to pick you up. I can't wait to see you," I say.

"Can we get take out for dinner? I'm starving," she says, then pauses. "Unless you cooked."

I look around at the cluttered table and the few dishes in the sink. There's a load of laundry I haven't folded yet.

"I have not cooked. Take out sounds great," I say, reaching for the basket of clean clothes. "Figure out where you want to order from and we'll call as soon as we're home."

"You're sure? I hate the idea of wasting money on take out if we have food to eat at home, but I really just want a hot shower, clean hoodie, sweatpants, fluffy blanket, maybe a movie, and you."

"Sweetheart, I will make all your dreams come true. Go do what you need to do to get all of you home and I will see you in less than an hour," I say. "I love you."

I hear her audibly sigh and feel lighter, knowing she's almost here. It wasn't as long a separation as after the Outer Banks, but the anticipation of seeing her has my nervous system buzzing.

"See you soon. I love you, too," she says before disconnecting the call.

Dropping the phone on the table, I busy myself with folding the clothes I've worn throughout the week before depositing the full basket on our bed.

I'm grateful Wren called from the airport. It gives me a chance to hide the project I've started. I take time putting the architectural drawings Will left with me on an old table down in the basement that belonged to Gram. Beside those drawings lie the purchase agreement for the house. She knew I was going to be focusing on my dissertation while she was gone, but I didn't tell her I planned to talk to Maggie about the house.

We don't want to rent forever, but we also love where we're at. Maggie doesn't want to be a landlord, even though the extra income is a nice perk, so I made a suggestion that Wren and I purchase the house from her. This way the house stays in the family and she knows the buyer. Considering her grandparents built this house and Maverick taps the maple trees on the property, that last part is important to her. It's important to me, too, since Gram entrusted her home to me when Maggie started renting it out.

Harper thinks I need to tell Wren about the house as soon as she gets home. Maggie is firmly planted in her opinion that it's romantic I'm waiting.

I'm not really doing it to be romantic. I want all the financial information and the conceptual designs Will is finalizing to be done before I tell her I took our little conversations in passing and am making it a reality. There are so many working parts right now — her softball season is just getting under way, I'm finishing my degree, we're planning a wedding to the best of our abilities, and now the house.

Then there's babies. Will and Anita were deep in discussion about how the new rooms could be used for their grandbabies and I had to remind them, while Wren and I do plan to start a family, it might be a ways off.

Staring down at the drawings, I can see all the changes in front of me. The walls being built, the rooms being filled with kids, even the basement being transformed into something more magical than dusty storage rooms and a root cellar.

Walking back through the room, I click the lights off and go upstairs to finish picking up the kitchen and leave for campus.

A short while later, I pull into the parking lot at the athletic complex. I'm fortunate enough to get here before the bus arrives and I take the opportunity to let the car warm up while I wait. She's been in Florida for a week with tropical weather and is coming back to New York where we finally saw temperatures reach 40 degrees for the first time in months. Waiting beneath the overhang of the complex entrance I notice a dark figure — dark jeans, work boots, a heavy jacket pulled around his slender frame, and a stocking hat covering a ball cap on his head. Despite looking familiar, I can't place where I would know him from, so I sit tight waiting for the bus while keeping an eye on him.

The bus pulls up in front of the building and before I can get from my car to it, Wren, Dylan, and a few of the players are off the rig and waiting to unload.

"What can I help with?"

She turns at the sound of my voice and I wrap my arms around Wren's waist, pulling her away from the group to welcome her home. Her lips quickly find mine and it makes a reunion after the time apart that much sweeter.

"I missed you," she says before pulling my mouth against hers again for another quick kiss. "We need to unload all our equipment and take it inside. I'll come back tomorrow and help Dylan organize before practice."

"Consider me your ball boy. I'll carry whatever you need me to," I say.

She smiles and rolls her eyes as we turn back to the group.

"Here ya go, ball boy," Dylan says, tossing a bag in my direction and laughing. "Get moving."

"Aw Coach, don't be so mean to the cute music guy. He's kind of scrawny," one of the players says, hoisting a backpack onto her shoulders over top of a hoodie. She's got a helmet strapped to the front of the bag and three different bats sticking out of the side pockets. "Maybe we should give him a lighter bag."

Standing beside me, Wren giggles.

"You must be Bree," I say, holding my hand out and smiling. "It's nice to finally meet you. Officially."

"This tells me Coach Leary has talked about me at home. Hope she hasn't been too mean," she says, shaking my hand, but also looking around me toward the door to the building.

"Mean? Nah. Super impressed? Absolutely."

She looks from me to Wren and back again, before nodding.

"Thanks Coach," she says quietly. "I'll take the ball bag and your bag in, if you want."

"I can bring mine in, but if you don't mind grabbing the other that would be helpful," Wren says. Raising her voice above the noise of the bus, she adds, "Listen up! Everyone needs to carry something in. Tomorrow, we start fresh for the rest of the season. Get home, get some food, get some sleep."

As a group we make quick work of getting everything back into the complex and stored away in the equipment room. Once the team equipment is put away, the girls slowly begin leaving. It's not late, but the travel after a full week of play and being away from home has several of them ready to go home.

"Are we doing any volunteer stuff this week?" Bree asks as Wren locks the room. "I want to make sure I have it on my calendar."

Keys in hand, Wren turns to her and smiles. But I know her smiles. This isn't a happy to have help smile like when she talked about Bree coming to Murph's brunch in November.

"I'm creating a plan with Coach McCabe to get the whole team involved in something. I'm not sure what yet, or even how since it's been like pulling teeth. I'm actually feeling a little discouraged," she says, pushing her hands into her jacket pockets. "Did you have something in mind you wanted to do this week?"

Bree bites her lip as I watch the conversation unfold.

"I was thinking we could talk to Father Murphy and see what his guys need. Gavin mentioned with winter being hard they're a little low on staples, so I was hoping we could go shopping ..." she says, her voice trailing off. "If it's not too much to ask."

Wren looks at me, concerned, because neither of us know who Gavin is, but he's obviously someone important to Bree. Her entire demeanor has changed from razzing me out by the bus, as well. I see the moment Wren decides we're doing this this week and nod as I excuse myself.

"Hey Coach," I say, entering Dylan's office down the hall and sit down in the chair opposite her desk. I want to give Wren and Bree a moment to talk; this is a warm place to land for a few minutes and gives me a chance to catch up with Dylan since we haven't had a lot of time to talk. "How was it last week?"

She yawns first, then shrugs, leaning back in her chair and tapping a pen on the top of the desk.

"You know, it was softball. We had some good plays. We had some not good plays. Teambuilding. Your wife insisting on trust falls. It was interesting."

I bark out a laugh.

"Trust falls? Like where you actually fall and are supposed to expect people to catch you? I didn't know anyone still did those."

"Essentially, except not. I think she's reimagining it because she can't think of a better phrase. So basically, she wants to get these girls to open up a little more and trust one another. Because how can you know your team has your back if you can't trust them? Right?" Dylan chews on the end of her pen. "I'm giving her free rein to do it and lead us in some sort of direction. They might not win all the time, but they are all winners."

"You sound like a motivational poster."

"She's wearing off on me."

We smile at one another and then I notice her gaze shift.

"Hey, there you are. The girls have all left to get food and go sleep before they have to worry about classes tomorrow. Are you ready to go home?" Wren says quickly, placing a hand on my shoulder. "You guys okay?"

Dylan smiles broadly at her, then at me, and nods.

"Yes. I was just mentioning to Alex how you've rubbed off on me. We'll meet tomorrow to talk about the volunteer stuff and how we're going to get these girls to work together a little more?"

I tip my head back to look up at Wren, her smile glowing despite being tired.

"For sure. I'm ready to see what they can do," she says, looking down at me.

We say goodnight to Dylan knowing she's going to spend more time in her office before leaving for home, likely mulling over some of the things she and Wren talked about while out of town.

"Food?" I ask as we push through the complex doors and I press the remote starter to get the car heated.

"Burgers or burritos?"

"Both?"

"You are my favorite person on the planet. There's no way I was going to be able to choose between them," she says, moaning as she speaks and reaching out to hold my hand as we walk through the parking lot.

*****

We pulled into our driveway, food in hand, and Wren immediately went to take a shower to "get the travel smell" off her, she said. I didn't think she smelled like anything but herself, however I can appreciate the sentiment.

I set up a floor picnic in the living room and queue up a movie while waiting for her. All the big lights are off and the lamps are turned on, casting the room in a muted glow. I'm just setting drinks down when I hear her pad down the hallway and stop in the doorway, looking over the spread before her — burritos, queso and chips, burgers, fries.

"I'm never going to eat all this," she says, sighing. "I was definitely starving when we ordered, but now that I see all of it ..."

"We'll save the rest for tomorrow," I say, motioning for her to come into the room and take a seat. "Tell me about this new teambuilding initiative. Dylan mentioned trust falls?"

Wren covers her face as she gracefully folds her legs together in front of her. Uncovering her eyes, she quickly pulls her damp hair over her shoulder and proceeds to skillfully braid it. Twisting a hair tie around the ends, she then reaches for a french fry while making me wait for her answer.

"It's not trust falls as much as it is learning to be vulnerable with one another. Every single person on the team is good at, let's say, three things. But they are equally bad at at least one other thing. I want them to learn what everyone is bad at and connect with others who can help them be better at it. It's weird, I know, but that's also what the volunteering stuff is for," she says, quickly biting the fry in half and chewing.

"I don't think that's weird. It's good to be vulnerable if you're in a safe group."

I take a bite of my burrito and stare intently at her. She swallows hard and looks at her hands. A lamp positioned slightly behind her offers an angelic glow around her head and shoulders, and I catch myself sighing deeply, not because she's beautiful and perfect for me ... but because she is my safe space.

"Is that why this is easy for us? We're safe for one another? We can be vulnerable?" she asks, tipping her head slightly and looking at me.

"I think that's a big part of it for us. Finding the person you fit well with and want to spend time with isn't simple. So many of us spend forever looking for that person, when maybe we just need to take a vacation and let it happen by chance," I say. Shrugging, I attempt to find something else to say, but I don't have anything.

"I was so afraid I scared you off because I was too open and vulnerable with you when we first met," she says, lifting another fry to her mouth and nibbling at it. "I wasn't pining for you, but I was worried that whatever I felt wasn't reciprocated, even though every second with you felt like it was meant to be."

"That's because it was," I say.

Lifting myself up, I reach out for her. Wrapping my hand around her delicate neck I pull her toward me and gently kiss her lips, the edge of her mouth, across her jawbone, until I reach the sensitive spot just below her ear.

"It was absolutely meant to be. I think both of us being open to the fact we aren't perfect has been good for us, just like it's going to be good for the girls on your team to understand they have an entire support network. They just need to be receptive to it," I say, sitting back down and picking my food up again. "Now, tell me how being vulnerable fits in with volunteering?"

"I want it to be more meaningful than baking cookies for the food pantry. I love that Bree has helped with things at Murph's, and she's made a connection with this Gavin guy, but they're all intelligent sports girls. I was doing some research and found out the summer rec program is in need of a softball program do-over," she says, and I am trying to follow, but she's brought up three different things in the span of one breath.

I narrow my eyes at her, contemplating how to have her focus on one thing at a time.

"I hate when I'm talking and you look at me like that."

"You're going to have to spell it all out for me slowly because I'm lost," I say.

She takes a deep breath and pushes her food aside.

"I want the girls to reboot the summer softball program because there hasn't been enough support for it. Baseball, yes. Softball, not so much. Even if it's just running clinics for girls who need something to get involved in until we can get it off the ground and play other teams. That's the long game," she says, pulling her legs up to her chest and then pulling the front of the hoodie — my hoodie, which is apparently now hers — over her knees.

"You want to start with a softball clinic? I think that sounds like a fantastic idea. You can manage it and the team can run it," I say.

Laying her head on her knees, Wren looks at me like she's relieved and scared.

"What's the matter? This is a really great concept. It's not out of the box thinking, but it is out of the box coaching because I know Dylan has never done something like this," I add. "Hopefully the town rec department will see the importance of having a good softball program."

"Nothing's the matter. I just hope the team is up for it," she says. "I know Bree would be on board and a few other girls, but the rest of them are who I'm worried about. I was thinking about checking with student affairs and finding out how we can safely get the word out to the elementary, middle, and high school, but it all just seems like a lot to take on."

"It is a lot to take on. Most of the college students leave campus for the summer and go home," I say, knowing that I was rarely on campus during the summer when I was a student.

"I already thought about that and looked at everyone's location. With the exception of a couple, everyone else is pretty local, but I wouldn't expect all of them to want to do it. I hope they will, but doubt it'll happen."

I question what she means. Why wouldn't they want to help with this? They were all little kids playing ball once, too.

"Trust me, I hope I'm wrong. I get the impression some of them don't appreciate my way of coaching. Like I should worry only about the sport and the way they play and not worry at all about them as people," she says, shrugging. "Not everyone is like Bree who wants to help, sometimes for the sake of helping and sometimes because she needs us to need her. I really just want them all to know I'm invested in them and want to help them all succeed."

Standing up and putting trash in an empty bag, I start clearing our dinner mess up while Wren relaxes for a minute.

"Do you think starting a new adult rec league team would be overzealous of me?" she yells from the living room.

Setting leftovers on the counter by the sink, I back up until I can see her through the door and stare at her.

"How many things are we putting on our plate for this spring and summer?"

Biting her bottom lip, Wren stands up, picking up a few more things to bring to the kitchen, and looks at me sheepishly.

"A few more?" she says as if it's a question. "I know we have a lot going on. Current season, dissertation, wedding, now these new things I'm thinking about ... but it's not bad to be busy, is it?"

I lean in to kiss her, taking the leftovers from her hands.

"I have something to show you," I say.

Emptying my hands and leaving everything on the kitchen table, I grab her hand and pull her with me through the kitchen, into the breezeway, and then to the basement.

"I really wish we could do more with this area of the house. I don't want to ask more of Maggie, though. I know a lot of the stuff down here is Gram's," she says, as I flick the light on at the bottom of the stairs.

Smiling, knowing what she's going to find, I flip a second switch. The lights over the old kitchen table come on, illuminating the drawings Will gave me. On top of them are the papers for the sale of the house.

"What is this?" Wren asks, her fingers touching the architectural drawings. She glides her fingertips along the paper until she reaches the purchase offer Maggie and I drew up. "Are you—? Wait. Are we buying a house? Alex?"

I want to say something cute or funny, but don't.

"Yes," I say.

"We're buying a house. We're buying our house?" she says, picking up the paperwork to read it more closely and then looking at me in disbelief. Glancing down at them, she takes more notice of the large drawings. I give her time to digest the information. "These are building plans. Alex, what's happening right now?"

I hold my breath unsure if it's a good or bad "what's happening" until I hear her giggle and point to the bottom corner of the drawing.

"My dad drew up plans for an addition to our house that wasn't our house when I left for Florida."

"Um, your dad is a very useful guy," I say, smiling.

"Yeah, he is," she says, a small sad smile on her lips. "I think that's the first time I've openly called him my dad. I always call him Will."

"I know," I say, pulling her into my arms. "He is your dad, though, and I know where your head is going and I just want to say, Tony will always be your dad, too. You're not replacing him by calling Will 'dad'."

Setting the papers on the table and turning in my arms, Wren wraps her arms around me and holds on tight.

"I know I'm not replacing him," she says, her breath warm against my shirt. "I'm ... adding to him. I think Will and I fit together so easily not just because he's part of me, because nature versus nurture and all that, but because he's so much like Tony. I love them both. They're both my dads. And how lucky am I to have had so much time with Tony and now also get to have time with Will?"

"It's still difficult. No one is going to tell you otherwise," I say, kissing her forehead. "Grief is going to hit when it wants to."

"And it does. I've just learned to feel it and move through it," Wren says, gripping the back of my shirt in her hands. "Did I see correctly that he's planning on adding on through the spare room?"

"That is correct."

"Did I also see correctly he labeled it 'grandkids playroom'?" she asks.

I feel the slight rumble of her laughter as I lift my head up, turn slightly, and look over at the drawings.

"That was not an approved label. I just want you to know your parents were very adamant about rooms for babies and I told them we weren't there yet," I say. "Despite how much I want to start a family and how much we've talked about it, I'm glad I agreed with you. I think you're right and waiting a bit is a good idea."

Pulling back, Wren looks up at me and, as her eyes soften, all I see is love and appreciation.

"We've got so much going on right now, adding a baby would be a lot. I want time to love you without the stress of grad school and brand new jobs before we make babies," she says, smiling. "But, I'm willing to enter into serious discussions for when to start trying."

Chapter 36

Wren

I'm not even sure where to begin.

The last several weeks are kind of a blur.

We've had games and practices, and we've won a couple. However, even with losses under our belts and the team feeling discouraged, the girls were amazingly receptive to the ideas I had for increased volunteer opportunities. I've heard from more than a few of them that being able to take a break from school work and switch their focus from school to philanthropy once a week has given them a deeper appreciation of ... everything. A lot of them have been helping where Murph's outreach is concerned, especially Bree. She usually comes with me for coffee on Thursdays because her classes are later in the day. As a group, there's been quite a bit of shopping happening to build supply kits for Murph's guys as well as the unhoused community at large.

Working together off the field has definitely impacted how they interact on the field. Bree no longer is the only one to stay and pick up after we're done, and on a few occasions, I've taken equipment back to the athletic complex only to return to the field and find the girls still tossing a ball around.

Playing. Like kids.

That's when I knew I was certain about getting involved in the youth softball program if it still existed in some capacity or getting it started up again. Talking about it during a family dinner one night, Harper said she was still interested in an adult league, but that I should reach out to Angela in student affairs to get something going with the local schools. The premise being maybe she has some connections.

So, I dropped by her office one day.

And, now we're in the midst of taking registrations for a few softball clinics over the summer, including traveling to the City of Rochester to work with kids there. The programs are more sandlot games than structured clinics for the time being. If there's one thing I'm relearning through this experience as a coach it's that kids should be allowed to play and have fun. That's how they learn.

When helping me set up the information for the events, Angela wanted to know how much we're charging for registration so she could include it on the flyers. I refuse to charge a registration fee the first year. While I'm sure we're going to have kids who are financially okay, I'm not going to let finances be a reason someone doesn't get to play and learn a new skill.

Alex and I are covering the cost of having shirts made for the kids, me, and my girls, and we're supplying snacks and lunches. The consensus of the team was to also purchase meals to send home at the end of the day for anyone who needs it.

Needless to say, it's going to be a busy few months once our season is over, and not just because of more softball.

At home we've been busy figuring out the house plan with my dad and mom popping in frequently to talk about the scope of work for the addition. The house is officially ours, so we're just waiting on permits to start the actual work with Dad and Maverick really running the show.

Though he'd rather be working with the guys on house prep, Alex has been squirreled away in one office or another as he finishes getting ready for one of his biggest moments in this lifetime. He has spent countless hours prepping for his defense and here we are, finally at the moment.

I'm sitting in the hallway outside a large conference room waiting for him, because when it's finally done, he's absolutely going to collapse and I want to be here with him regardless of the outcome. He's supported me through every change I've had to make in the last nine months and I'll be damned if I won't sit here for as long as he needs me.

"Whatcha doin'?" A quiet voice says and I look up from my book to find Harper poking her head around the corner. "How long's he been in there?"

"He just went in a few minutes ago. I'm not sure what to expect, so it could be a while."

I pat the seat beside me and move my bag so she can sit down. Plopping into the chair, she hands me a cup of coffee and then takes a sip from her own.

"You drove all the way out here for him?" I ask, lifting the cup to my mouth and not turning to face her.

"I did. I know how hard he's worked on this, I know how hard I've worked with him at the nursing home on this, and I know sometimes his support system needs support, too. So, I'm here, because I love you both and I'll raise hell if they don't say his research is acceptable," she says, shrugging.

"Alex is a perfectionist and he doesn't stand for errors so I'm guessing he's going to get an acceptable with minor or no changes."

I laugh, covering my mouth because I'm unsure how solid the doors to the conference room are and I don't want to be the reason he gets distracted.

"Definitely a perfectionist."

"Enough about him. Bring me up to speed on the wedding plans," she says.

This is actually a tough topic because there are no plans. There were, but weren't, and …

"I think May is just too soon. It's literally a few weeks away and if he has to do revisions, it's that much more stress to do it all," I say.

Harper nods, but remains silent.

"I understand. You've known each other less than a year, been engaged a few months, and apparently both want to take over the world considering all the stuff you're involved in. You have to do what makes you happy," she says. "What makes you happy?"

"He does," I say without hesitation.

"So does it matter when you actually do the wedding thing if you're already happy?"

"Not really. We've been talking about changing the date and planning for August. Early August."

She looks at me, concern lacing her features.

"But I thought you had your heart set on championship weekend?"

"So did I. But this way I'm done with softball for a few weeks. He won't be back to teaching quite yet since he's taking the summer off. We can take a vacation," I say, thinking out loud. "I still want to have our wedding at a ball field, though, and since neither of us are Catholic, we're just going with a Justice of the Peace, but Murph wants to say a blessing before dinner. It's just a lot to think about because I told him what I wanted and now what I want is changing."

I pull my bottom lip in and nibble at the skin.

"It sounds like you have most of it planned already, Wren. You don't have to do anything big, you know? Keep it small. This is about you and Alex and your love for one another. It has nothing to do with anyone else," she says.

"I know. I just don't want to disappoint anyone," I admit.

"Like who?"

Looking at the top of my coffee cup, I pick at the drink opening, trying to figure out who I might disappoint and when no one of great importance pops into my thoughts, I start to laugh.

"That's what I thought. No one. Stop worrying about who you'd disappoint and focus on the people you want to have there. Me, for starters, because I'm going to be the best damn flower girl you've ever seen," she says, bumping her shoulder into mine.

We laugh together and then I take a deep breath, sighing.

"Thank you. When I found out about you last year, I really wondered what I had gotten myself into," I say. Trying to keep myself from tearing up, I stare at my hands as they surround my cup. I look at my ring and how gorgeous it is — and wonder what it looked like on my grandmother's hand — because it symbolizes not only Alex's love for me, but family. And then I say, "I couldn't have asked for a better family to find while also finding the family I didn't know I had. Thank you."

Harper reaches for my hand and I give it to her willingly. We sit quietly in the hall, silently counting the minutes as we wait for Alex to emerge from the conference room in front of us. The doorknob turns and a stately looking woman comes into view. She holds her hand out and shakes his, smiling, and then tells him the committee will need a few minutes.

Alex steps through the doorway and he appears a thousand pounds lighter than when we left the house early this afternoon. All the anxiety is gone, the stress, the fear, and I know he nailed it.

I let go of Harper's hand and stand to greet him as he takes another step in my direction. He pushes his glasses up on his nose and then slides his hands into the pockets of his slacks. Tipping back on his heels and then up on his toes, he gives me the biggest grin I've ever seen on him.

"I think I might have done okay," he says as I reach up and take his face in my hands.

"You are so fucking amazing," I say, lifting up onto my toes and kissing him quickly.

"Now I just have to wait and, um, I might puke," he says, the most sincere look on his face. "This was the scariest thing I've ever done and I hope I did it well enough I don't have to ever do it again. I think I'm going to sleep for the next two days, okay? Because, as much as I love all my research and learned so much, my brain is totally useless after this."

Harper giggles behind me and as I turn to look at her, her face sobers. A throat clearing behind me and Alex catches our attention, and we both turn back to the door where the same woman — his faculty advisor — stands in the open doorway.

"Congratulations, Doctor Makris," she says, beaming with pride. "You have successfully defended your dissertation and the committee recommends that your doctoral degree be awarded. Come back in so we can discuss."

*****

"Was there really any question?" Maverick asks over drinks at the bar when we get back from Rochester. "I mean, the guy's smart. Not to mention, he's kind of a genius with a guitar."

Alex lifts his chocolate stout to his lips and takes a long sip of the dark liquid. I can't stop smiling at him. He lifts an eyebrow at me and I shrug.

"No revisions?" Maggie asks. "I'm so stinking proud of you. How's it feel, Doctor?"

"I'm … exhausted. And I should probably call my parents and tell them."

His parents have been a sticking point in conversations about the wedding. They have played no part in our love story, but I think he should include them. He would prefer not to. I've met them only once and that was at Jayden and Penelope's wedding. They occasionally text or call Alex, but are not actively in our life, which makes me sad since he talks to his cousins and aunt pretty regularly. When he moved out of their house and into what is now our house, their communication with him was quickly reduced to what it is now.

"You should. Worry about it tomorrow," I say, sipping my water. "Sleep is a priority right now."

"Remember the last time we sat here for drinks, just the three of us?" Harper says to Alex and her brother.

Angela looks at her and then covers her face, knowing a story is coming. Like me, early on, Angela has been introduced to Harper's sometimes not acceptable stories about my fiancé. While I can often laugh about certain things now, I know it's taking Angela some time to get used to it. Particularly since there are some very obvious feelings for Harper. Those of us who know Harper well really hope she's not using Angela as a way to relieve stress like the arrangement she had with Alex, because Angela is super sweet and we all like her.

"Jog my memory," Alex says as he exchanges a worried look with Maverick.

"It was the night I texted Wren and got you two talking again," she says, wildly pleased with herself and completely lacking self-awareness. "That feels like forever ago."

I look at Alex and he is suddenly incredibly intrigued by his glass. Then he takes his glasses off and cleans them with the T-shirt he has on beneath his unbuttoned dress shirt. When he places the glasses back on his face, he finally acknowledges me.

"Oh, really?" I say.

"I think it's time to call it a night," he says, standing from his seat. He picks up his cup and drains the last of his beer before reaching for my hand.

"Sir, you have some explaining to do," I say, putting my hand in his.

"I ... she didn't know," Harper says. Alex shakes his head. "Just call me the matchmaker."

"No," Alex and I say simultaneously as we give quick hugs to Maggie and Maverick.

Leaning in close to Angela, I ask her if she's able to take Harper home since her brother is going in the opposite direction. She nods and offers me a sad smile.

"Girl, no. I'm used to Harper. But now I get to go find out the entire story which I'm sure is just as unhinged," I say, leaning in to give her a quick hug. Smiling I add, "Just get her drunk ass home and into bed. Good thing it's Friday."

Alex pulls me away, my hand snugly in his as we maneuver through the bar, until we hit the fresh evening air. Spring feels different in New York and I'm loving the change of each season. Walking along the side of the building, Alex turns and steps into my space. Walking me back until I'm pressed against the brick wall of the building, I glance in either direction to see we're just beyond the lights illuminating the entrance. Putting his hand against the wall beside my head, he leans in, lifting my chin with his forefinger, and kisses me until I'm panting and begging for more.

"Only if you're not mad," he says. "I didn't tell you about the text because it didn't matter. I missed you regardless and she made it so I stopped getting in my own way."

"I'm not mad," I say, smiling up at him. "It happened that way for a reason."

He leans in again and takes my lips as I reach up and touch his face. The light stubble peppering his jaw scratches my skin when he moves to my neck and I moan feeling the pinpricks. Just the right amount of pain to feel pleasurable, and it triggers something in him when he hears me. Moving his hands down my body, Alex touches my thighs, wrapping his hands around the muscles and lifting me off my feet. He presses his pelvis into me, securely pinning me to the wall.

"If you were wearing a skirt this would be easier," he says against my neck.

"Backseat," I say, whimpering as his thickness presses harder against me. "I left it down after taking equipment out of it."

"Good. Because I have some of my own equipment to put in there," he says, and I start giggling uncontrollably as he sets me down.

Taking my hand once again, Alex and I hurry across the dark parking lot to the car. Pressing me against the car, he breathes out my name.

"I love you so much," he says, kissing me again as he opens the rear passenger door. "I'm absolutely not going to last long."

"I love you, too. It's not a competition. I just need you in me," I say and scoot past him to climb into the back of the car.

He follows suit and before he can even get the door closed, I have my shoes off and my pants halfway down my thighs.

"Are you sure it's not a competition?" he laughs, unbuckling his belt and making quick work of his zipper.

"Lock the doors," I say as I kick my pants the rest of the way off.

"I thought I was supposed to be the dominant one?" he says, leaning over the front seat to hit the lock button and drop the key fob in the cupholder.

He's positioned precariously and I take advantage of him being distracted to lean in and tug his pants and boxers down enough to let his cock spring free. He grunts and then sucks in a surprised breath when my mouth encompasses the exposed head of his penis, swirling my tongue around and under as I grip the base in my fist. I pull more of him into my mouth, pumping his cock in rhythm. He always puts me first and this time I want to give him as much pleasure as he's used to giving me.

Alex's hand finds my hair and he twists it around his fingers as I continue my assault on his erection, each groan urging me to do more, suck a little harder, and then as I taste the sweetness of his precum, I gently trail my bottom teeth along the underside of the satiny smooth skin.

"Not. Going to. Last long," he grits out as I drop my jaw and take as much of him into my throat as possible. I hear him say through clenched teeth, "Wren."

Pulling off him, I innocently look up and, in the darkness, he reaches down and touches my cheek.

"Panties. Off," he demands.

"Well now, I see Alexander has come out to play," I say, giggling as I comply and slip the fabric off my legs to leave piled with my discarded pants.

Laying down in the confined space of the car, I drop my knees and watch as he scoots backward and crawls between my legs. A shiver moves through me as he takes his cock in his hand and slowly, methodically, glides his fist up to the tip and then back down to the base. Reaching between my own legs with one hand, I beckon to him with the other. Teasing me with the head of his cock, Alex gently pushes into me, then backs out, repeating the movement until I'm moaning loudly.

"I'm so close," I say.

"Shh. I know," he says as I clench my eyes shut and bite my lip, trying to pull myself back from the precipice.

Before I can open my eyes again, he fills me, pushing in to the hilt and my body ignites as my orgasm hits. I tighten myself around him, grabbing at his shirt to hold him as close as possible, as he pumps his hips into me and I ride the wave of pleasure he's providing. As my body starts to relax, his stills and spasms. He remains deeply seated inside me, placing his hands on either side of my head and dropping his face near to mine.

"That's my good girl," he whispers.

Taking my bottom lip between his teeth and then kissing my mouth like he's starving, Alex slowly pulls out of me, leaving me feeling empty and full at the same time.

"You weren't lying about not lasting," I say, quietly chuckling.

He kisses me again before moving to kneel beside me, pulling his pants up and adjusting himself while I redress.

"Round two will last way longer," he says, adjusting his glasses.

"Oh … I think I'm going to like Doctor Alexander. We've got the dominance thing going on and now good girl and a round two?"

"Are you picking on me Ms. Leary?"

"Only if it means more of this," I say, sitting up and positioning myself to sit back on my heels in front of him.

Alex lifts my chin and angles his mouth above mine.

"I love how direct you've become. Line drive, straight to my heart," he says, consuming me once more.

Epilogue

Wren

AUGUST

Four months ago, Alex defended his research. With no revisions, and minimal extra work to complete, he was awarded his degree during the May commencement ceremony. In the throes of that, I continued with my already hectic schedule working with the softball team, filling in at the physical therapy office, and volunteering with the girls for various organizations. Murph's guys are always top of our list, though we split our time between them and the community center we connected with while setting up softball clinics for the summer.

Despite my insistence the team could go all the way in my first season coaching with Dylan, I was proven wrong.

We did not win our conference championship game. We didn't even come close to playoffs.

What we did, do, though, is have a season filled with growth and learning as a very new team with me as a mostly new coach. After a difficult fall practice schedule where we all attempted to work together and push through barriers of different backgrounds and work ethics, we were in a good position for spring training.

As we played through the season, it was demonstrated to us time and again that we still had room for improvement. When we finished the season with a dismal W-L record, Dylan and I were not met with a dugout full of women who were sad. They met us with an attitude of gratitude and an enthusiasm to push harder ... not because we asked them to, but because they've seen they are capable of more — athletically, academically, and as people. With Bree leading the charge as one of our only incoming seniors, the team has worked to combine their efforts and make sure our incoming freshmen players are on board to be the best they can be and ask for help when they need it.

Now, as I watch out the corner of my eye as my mom and Harper help the girls finish setting up chairs, and my dad shows Alex's music students where we want them located, I'm amazed even more at what we've accomplished in the last year.

"I wasn't expecting them to show up the way they did for each other. I know it's a team and the idea is your team is your family, but they've actually created a family from the team," Dylan says as she's pushing a pearl hairpin into the bundle of curls I've tied at the back of my neck. "That's not something I did."

"What do you mean?" I ask, leaning toward the mirror I hung at the back of the dugout as I apply eyeliner. "You definitely did that."

"What I mean is, no I didn't. You did. You came in and became the heart of the team. Anytime one of them was in my office it was 'Coach Leary said to try this' or 'Coach Leary mentioned doing it this way.' You brought them all together," she says, adjusting one of the bobby pins. "Between your sunshine-y California attitude and your volunteering and general likability, they found something in you that made them a winning team regardless of the number on the scoreboard."

I turn just as Dylan wipes beneath her eyes, and takes a deep breath.

"Listen, I'm not going to tell you I don't want the credit, but it wasn't just me. It literally took all of us, working together, for them to find their way as a team. I just ... thought outside the box all of you were used to," I say. "It wouldn't have worked at all if I didn't have your support, though. Thank you for taking a chance on me."

Dylan, who does not usually do emotions, pulls me into a quick hug.

"You took a chance on me, too," she says. "And I think that's something I wasn't prepared for. Now, while you finish in here, I'm going to go figure out where to sit. It's almost time."

I smile at her as she walks away and then turn back to the mirror. I apply a thin coating of tinted lip gloss and stick it in the pocket of my dress. Yes, a dress — a floor-length satin ball gown that I found on sale and has absolutely no business being on a dirty softball field, paired with blue Chucks my cousin bought for me because fancy, formal shoes with heels are not my thing.

Dad pops in as I'm adjusting the skirt on my dress and takes a deep breath the moment he sees me.

"You're breathtaking, Wren. I wish Tony was here," he says, taking a deep breath while holding my bouquet. "I know he is in a way, but I wish he was walking with us."

"Hey now," I say, reaching for the flowers and rolling my eyes back in an effort to keep the tears from ruining the makeup I just put on.

We talked about this. We've talked about everything. My dad — Will — was so worried about how people might feel about him walking me out to the pitcher's circle that he almost said no when I asked. When I reminded him that I don't care what people think, and that it's my wedding and I needed him there to do this with Mom, he understood.

"I asked the girls to make sure they saved him a seat," I say, smiling sadly. "It goes you, then Mom, and he's on the other side of Mom."

He nods, and holds his arm out for me. The first notes from a violin begin followed by other strings, and I loop my arm through his as I take a step out of the dugout.

"For not really planning a wedding, you've done a phenomenal job, kiddo," he says, placing a quick kiss to the side of my head.

We make our way forward along a curtained walkway set up to hide me until the moment is right and we stand together behind home plate, just out of view, where I watch Harper and Veronica slowly continue down the fabric aisle.

Harper and Maverick are focused on me, both smiling like they're keeping a secret. Then I notice Danny staring at Veronica, a softness in his eyes that says more than I think he realizes.

And finally, I look at him. I memorize this moment and smile as I see Alex for the last time as my fiancé.

There are 43 feet between me and my future.

As the violins switch to Canon in D, my dad gently tugs my arm and we begin our descent, each step reminding me how deeply I have fallen in love with everything and everyone here.

If it wasn't for the community we have built, the family we have found, Alex and I wouldn't be living like we're famous in a small town — one where he continues to write love notes masquerading as sheet music and I teach kids, both young and old, how to hit line drives.

Together, we keep showing up for each other and for others ... and I have never been happier.

Acknowledgments

Did you know Alex and Wren were never supposed to be part of either of the Brockport series? Of course you didn't. How could you? I haven't told anyone that detail. It's true though.

Alex and Wren were originally supposed to be a short story I wanted to write for a summer fling/on vacation type of anthology years ago. Then, Alexander wrote himself into *Foster to Family* as the professor Maggie ended up going on a date with. Then, instead of being some guy she dated before meeting Maverick, Alex pops back up in *The Bakery on Main* because they're besties and he's a guy who wants to be supportive of his friend's new relationship. It couldn't just stop there because, as you know, my characters run away with almost every story I write. Harper became a love interest but not THE love interest.

Previously erased, Wren's name was added back to my whiteboard next to Alex's as I started writing this book. I was still longing for that "met on the beach" whimsy, and these days I could really use some whimsy. Harper wasn't forever for him as more than a friend, so when Wren started really telling me her story, it felt like this was the way it was always supposed to go.

If you're concerned about Harper, don't worry. She finds her penguin in the next book.

I can't say for certain how long until that book comes out, but I can tell you it and more are coming. In fact, this book has threaded the needle for five other books.

If you've been around any length of time, you know I am not a fast writer. I end up writing even slower than I would like because I tend to "pants" my books. I don't have hard outlines, plotting and I are familiar but not friends, and my characters lead the story. So, when I finished the first (if you can call it that) draft of this book and looked at my writing timeline compared to the wordcount, I was slightly astonished. For transparency, this book clocked in at around 104,000 words and from first word to sending to beta readers, it took just about a year to finish between kids on breaks from school and trying to fold the mountains of laundry a household of six people create.

But those laundry creating people are some of my biggest champions when it comes to being an author. It's a point of pride for me that they think their mom and wife being an author is cool enough to talk about with their teachers, friends, and coworkers. I think it's pretty cool, too.

My biggest thanks go to Boy Wonder — not only do you deal with me talking about people I made up in my head, you also always willingly read the book and give me corrections and feedback. I couldn't do this without your support. I love you.

My beta readers — Carrie, Vicci, Laura, and Emma — thank you for the time and attention to detail you gave this project. I am forever amazed at the people in my corner and how you cheer me on while also giving critical feedback. I'm not sure this book would be seeing the light of day without any of you.

Elizabeth — your help with graphic design has been invaluable. I appreciate all the work you've put into this book to help me bring it to life.

Hannah and Shanna — thank you for the Sunday coffee and writing (sometimes) meet-ups. I look forward to every single one even if we do more talking than authoring.

The plethora of ARC readers who signed up — I hope you enjoyed this book as much as I enjoyed writing it!

I know this list is short, but I've spent the better part of a year not really talking to a lot of people. Alex and Wren's story was written while sitting on gym floors during basketball and softball practices, at the ball field during practices, in my car, in the basement office, the kitchen table, in coffee shops, at my parents' kitchen counter, and at the dojo. I was around people, but always with earbuds in and music on to help me focus. Anyone who saw me working and let me do my thing, you didn't go unnoticed. I just had words that needed to get out of my head. Thank you for giving me space ... particularly if you saw me crying in public because trying to explain to anyone that I'm in tears over a scenario I created is awkward.

About the Author

M.L. Pennock is a former journalist turned author. She attended Alfred University, earning a Bachelor of Arts in English and communication studies, before going on to earn a Master of Arts in communications from SUNY College at Brockport. She lives in Central New York with her husband, four children, and two Siberian huskies.

M.L. Pennock is the author of the To Have series and has begun work on a spinoff series, Famous in a Small Town.

Visit facebook.com/mlpennock or mlpennock.com for more information about what she's working on next.

M.L. Pennock

www.ingramcontent.com/pod-product-compliance
Lightning Source LLC
LaVergne TN
LVHW041622060526
838200LV00040B/1388